D0069695

The Morgesons

AND OTHER WRITINGS,
PUBLISHED AND UNPUBLISHED,
BY *Elizabeth Stoddard*

WITHDRAWN

The Morgesons

AND OTHER WRITINGS,

PUBLISHED AND UNPUBLISHED,

BY *Elizabeth Stoddard*

Edited, with a Critical Introduction, by
Lawrence Buell and Sandra A. Zagarell

ʋʃʃ

University of Pennsylvania Press
PHILADELPHIA

Frontispiece: Daguerreotype of Elizabeth Stoddard as a young woman

Copyright © 1984 by the University of Pennsylvania Press
All rights reserved

Library of Congress Cataloging in Publication Data

Stoddard, Elizabeth, 1823–1902.
  The Morgesons and other writings, published and
unpublished.

  Includes bibliographical references.
    1. Buell, Lawrence. II. Zagarell, Sandra.
III. Title.
PS2934.S3A6 1984   813'.4   83–23439
ISBN 0–8122–7924–7 (cloth)
ISBN 0–8122–1170–7 (pbk.)

Printed in the United States of America

3rd paperback printing 1988

Dedicated

to

THE STUDENTS OF AMERICAN ROMANTICISM

at

OBERLIN COLLEGE

1980–83

whose enthusiastic yet discriminating response
to Elizabeth Stoddard's works
reinforced our conviction that she deserves
a secure place in the canon of American writers

Contents

Preface and Acknowledgments

This volume attempts to present in both a scholarly and a readable form the best work of an excellent but little-known New England author, Elizabeth Barstow Stoddard (1823–1902). Our introduction provides an intellectual portrait, a sketch of her life, an overview of her work, and an appraisal of her place in American literary history. We then present a critical edition of her first and best novel, followed by a selection of her shorter fiction, her literary prose, and her correspondence, as well as her one extant journal. Apart from *The Morgesons,* available only in a 1971 reprint edition, all this material either is long out of print or has never before been published.

This project could not have been completed without assistance from a number of sources. Among the few but discerning scholars who have studied Elizabeth Stoddard heretofore, we are especially indebted to James Matlack, author of the one full-length biographical study, and to Sybil Weir and Richard Foster. At a crucial time, Oberlin College supplied us with two grants for research and typing. Our research assistant Andrew Lewis helped us greatly with the identification and analysis of Stoddard's manuscripts. For assistance and for permission to publish Stoddard's manuscripts in their possession, we are indebted to the Special Collections Division of Colby College Library, Waterville, Maine (for Stoddard's letters to Elizabeth Akers Allen); to the Manuscript Department of Duke University Library (for Stoddard's letter of 4 May 1860 to Edmund Clarence Stedman, in the Edmund Clarence Stedman Papers); and to the Rare Book and Manuscript Library of Columbia University (for Stoddard's other letters to Stedman and for her manuscript journal, both in the Edmund Clarence Stedman Papers). For typing of the manuscript we are grateful to April Paramore, Patt Clarkson, Barbara Marshall, and Joey Lindner.

Many fellow scholars helped us track down allusions in Stoddard, who was an omnivorous if desultory reader and a keen observer of current events. We particularly thank Marlene Merrill, Carol Lasser, Nelson De Jesus, Joseph Reichard, Vinio Rossi, Cynthia Comer, John Druesedow, Carolyn Rabson, and Leonard Ellinwood.

We are grateful to our families for their continued patience and support—and for *their* interest in the project itself. And we are grateful to the students to whom this work is dedicated. Elizabeth Stoddard was a demanding, critical person, but we believe that she too would have been impressed and pleased to find at last a sizable audience responding to her work at a level of sophistication commensurate with the level on which she wrote.

Biographical and Critical Introduction

In her lifetime, Elizabeth Barstow Stoddard was compared to Balzac, Tolstoi, George Eliot, Nathaniel Hawthorne, and the Brontë sisters, but her works were not widely read. Most modern scholars have overlooked her. *Notable American Women* omits her; so does Alexander Cowie's *Rise of the American Novel*. The *Literary History of the United States* gives her one paragraph. The closest thing to a definitive bio-critical study is an unpublished dissertation.[1] This situation will surely change, however, because in fact Stoddard was, next to Melville and Hawthorne, the most strikingly original voice in the mid-nineteenth-century American novel, a voice that unquestionably deserves critical recognition and that ought to gain a more sympathetic and perceptive hearing in our time than in her own. The astringent, elliptical style that baffled Stoddard's contemporaries even as it fascinated them is much more understandable to a modern reader familiar with the ironies and indirections of Emily Dickinson and Henry James. Nor is Stoddard's appeal limited to the professional scholar. Our undergraduate students have read her with almost unanimous enthusiasm.

The present volume features Stoddard's most important work, *The Morgesons* (1862), but it also includes a sampling of her short fiction and prose as well as previously unpublished correspondence and journal material. In this introduction we shall supply a context for that work by surveying Stoddard's life, career, and position in American literature.

Elizabeth Drew Barstow (1823–1902) was born in the Massachusetts seacoast town of Mattapoisett, on Buzzard's Bay, the oldest surviving child of a tailor's daughter and a shipbuilder father whose prosperous family had disapproved of the match. Wilson Barstow, whose firm built the whaler on which Herman Melville sailed to the South Seas, was one of the town's leading citizens, although the financial risks of his business (which led to several bankruptcies) left the family in a position of precarious gentility that sharpened his daughter's natural quickness for perceiving fine social distinctions and slights. As a child, Elizabeth was never accepted as a legitimate member of the local aristocracy; as an adult, she took pleasure in satirizing the stuffiness of her native town.

After meeting Emily Dickinson in Amherst, Thomas Wentworth Higginson wrote his wife that she could understand the household if she had read Mrs. Stoddard's novels.[2] There are indeed a number of parallels between them in attitude, upbringing, and milieu. Dickinson and Stoddard both grew up in small but established New England towns as indulgently reared daughters of locally prominent families whose members were temperamentally quite different yet almost morbidly close-knit. Both were briefly subjected to the best formal education then locally available to young women, at nearby female seminaries: Dickinson at Mount Holyoke, Stoddard at Wheaton. There both encountered and resisted pressure to accept evangelical Protestantism. Both professed disregard for public opinion while at the same time being very conscious of it; both concealed a certain tempestuousness under a surface of ironic reserve, especially Stoddard, who sometimes questioned whether any woman could be more passionate than she.

Unlike Dickinson, however, Stoddard was extroverted, venturesome, and aggressive. Throughout her life, for example, she sought close, intense personal friendships with others of both sexes, to the point of inspiring tales about supposed extramarital affairs. The rumors may have been false, yet they are a fair index of her contempt for Victorian canons of proper female conduct. On one occasion, she wrote a woman friend that she would instantly have accepted a male friend's request that she pay him an extended visit, except that she was sure his wife would have got in the way of a meaningful relationship.

Stoddard seems to have relished performing in public as much as in her highly readable letters, which, like Dickinson's, are full of artful self-dramatizations. When she was at her best the performance seems to have been irresistible. "Brilliant and fascinating, she needed," reports one acquaintance, "neither beauty nor youth, her power was so much beyond such aids. On every variety of subject she talked with originality and ready wit; with impassioned speech expressing an individuality and insight most unusual and rare."[3] The same witness records her first meeting with the eminent Shakespearean actor Edwin Booth:

> Every detail of that hour is very distinct. The opening door; on its threshold a woman of angular slimness, perhaps forty-three or forty-four years old. She wore a dull brown dress, with an arabesque of white in minute pattern woven through the warp. The expression of face and figure was withered like a brown leaf left on the tree before the snow comes. No aura of charm whatever. There was a moment of silence; then Mr. Booth with outstretched arms moved quickly toward her, and in his hands her hands were laid. There were but two words spoken, "Edwin," "Elizabeth." Then Mr.

Booth, releasing her hand, slowly untied the strings of the bonnet that shaded her face, took it off, and still holding it in his hand drew her to a chair.[4]

Romanticized? Yes—but perhaps not excessively when one considers that the two people involved were both incorrigible romantics.

Such an individual was not meant to spend a reclusive life in her native village. At the age of twenty-nine, after some hesitation, Elizabeth Barstow married Richard Stoddard, a Connecticut native who had gravitated to New York to become a penniless poet in a puerile Keatsian mold he never outgrew. From an economic viewpoint the result proved disastrous for a young woman who "loved money, had it and spent it."[5] Neither she nor Richard was a good manager. Lizzie, remarked one friend, would dress her son in silks and complain of poverty. Through literary hackwork and a Custom House job Richard secured through Nathaniel Hawthorne, the couple managed to make a start; indeed for some years, beginning in the 1860s, they maintained a literary salon of local note and looked forward to the day when Richard might be ranked among the major American poets and tastemakers and Elizabeth would be a recognized novelist. Unfortunately he had to settle for a reputation as a third-rate versifier, anthologist, and literary jack-of-all-trades, and she for almost total obscurity.

Chronic financial worries, bad health (hers and Richard's both), and the early deaths of two of their three children embittered the already caustic Elizabeth, who throughout her life showed a talent for alienating even close friends with outbursts of venom. (Said one: "If, as Sam Johnson said, there is a merit in being a good hater, Lizzy is entitled to a high place among the virtuous.")[6] Like her fictional characters, she was memorable for abrasive bluntness. She knew her weakness ("My father said once he never saw any human being with such a talent for the disagreeable"), admitting to one friend, "I should both hurt and offend you I know, if I saw you very often."[7] But she repeatedly succumbed, because at heart she considered her outspokenness a virtue. Both Stoddards, indeed, prided themselves on being absolutely candid about their friends' literary and personal faults—though they did not much like to hear about their own. The friends were doubtless right in attributing this syndrome to envy and disappointment. Elizabeth took all too literally a friend's "advice": "If you can't be happy be terrible."[8]

The less promising their lives, the more tightly the ties of suffering bound the Stoddards together. Elizabeth was always ready to castigate Richard as severely as she did others, yet she remained fiercely loyal to him. They seem to have been sustained by a feeling of kinship as true souls arrayed against an ungrateful, stupid world. "Their loves and hates," wrote their closest literary friend, "were, without exception, the same—right or wrong, and often although they were wrong, each espoused the other's cause, and favoritisms. . . . Each could say of the other: 'I do not love Heathcliff; I *am* Heathcliff.' "[9]

Richard was as supportive of Elizabeth's career as she was of his. He provided some of the initial contacts and much of the initial encouragement for launching her as a professional writer shortly after their marriage. He seems never to have shown any professional jealousy, although she complained at times that he misunderstood and underestimated her particular genius. His generosity was never fully tested, because of the two he was always the more prominent literary figure, due at least in part to his greater conventionalism of style and his less formidable personality. (All witnesses, including Elizabeth, agree that he was the milder of the two.) Today he is forgotten except as the man who helped Melville get a job at the Custom House, but he deserves also to be remembered for the unconventionalism of aiding rather than attempting to suppress the gifts of a wife more talented than he.

Elizabeth Stoddard's career falls roughly into three periods: a decade of apprenticeship, during which she wrote short pieces in various styles; another decade or so of great productivity, beginning in the early 1860s, during which her novels *The Morgesons* (1862), *Two Men* (1865), and *Temple House* (1867) appeared, as well as her best stories; and another three decades of intermittently prolific writing, mostly short pieces in prose and verse designed for the mass market and tacitly acknowledging by their ephemeral character and their frequent vein of reminiscence that the author had given up hope of being widely recognized as a major writer.

According to Richard, the young Elizabeth "had a passion for reading but a great disinclination for study."[10] Not until after her marriage did she do any writing that survives, but she read in childhood whatever she could get her hands on, abetted by the local Congregational minister, Thomas Robbins, the Dr. Snell of *The Morgesons*. Robbins, author of a pro-Calvinist history of New England's founders and editor of the standard contemporary edition of Cotton Mather's *Magnalia Christi Americana*, was hardly fitted to be the intellectual mentor of a young woman who was soon to declare herself fully secularized and to satirize all religion; but he did further her education by giving her the run of his library, which included the classics of eighteenth-century literature. Her father, a drama enthusiast in an age when New Englanders tended to frown on the theater as immoral, helped to broaden her taste. By the mid-1850s she had also become acquainted with a wide range of contemporary European and American authors. George Sand, the Brontë sisters, Emerson, Poe, Thoreau, Dickens, Thackeray, and Tennyson, as well as numerous minor writers, were all surveyed in her semi-monthly column of news and reviews in the *Daily Alta California* (1854–58), which proved to be the ideal means for an eclectic, wide-ranging, outspoken individual to sort out and communicate her preferences.

Elizabeth Stoddard had previously begun to write short poems and prose sketches for the Eastern market, but the seventy-five columns of miscellanea she published in the *Alta* (selections from which are included in this volume, pp. 311ff.) are her real literary debut and altogether the most impressive results of her apprenticeship period.[11] Narrative sketches like "A Village on the Sea Shore" (24 October 1855) and "An Account of a Voyage across the Long Island Sound" (18 November 1855) already show a shrewd eye for the significant or absurd detail and a growing mastery over a range of ironic tones from the genial to the acid. ("New Bedford is distinguished for ready-made trowsers; long lines of them swing through the streets, from some kind of fixture in shop doorways, suggesting very unpleasant ideas of hanging, and of drowned sailors.") Stoddard is a keen witness of the contemporary social scene—business, politics, religion; temperance, feminism, and other antebellum reforms all pass before her satiric eye. Her remarks on the status of women— combining sympathy for feminist goals with intolerance of perceived extremism—are especially notable. Her thumbnail reviews of fellow authors can be read as the disguised autobiography of an ambitious but pragmatic young writer in search of the right medium. Partly, no doubt, because she knew her audience, Stoddard professes much interest in the best-selling "woman's fiction" of the day, whose cleverness she grudgingly praises, whose commercial success she envies, even as she herself aspires to surpass its formulas.[12] Her full admiration is reserved for the likes of the Brontës, George Sand, Tennyson, and Emerson, although she shows a refreshingly earthy sense of the sacrifices entailed in modeling a career on theirs. She herself "has no objection to writing bogus book notices for publishers" or "religious lies for Sunday School publishing houses."

Although Stoddard takes the whole world as her subject in the *Alta*, from this and her other published work of the 1850s it becomes increasingly clear that her literary imagination is rooted in the contemplation of the kind of small, ancient, ingrown New England seaport town in which she grew up. In such a place—her Winesburg, her Paterson, her Yoknapatawpha—her three novels and most of her best stories unfold. Stoddard is particularly concerned with dramatizing the idiosyncratic behavior of people and communities where deep, strong, passionate instinct is locked in a perpetual struggle with habit, family allegiances, social taboos, and traditional New England restraint. Critic Richard Foster aptly likens Stoddard to D. H. Lawrence in this regard.[13] It would be more accurate historically, however, to place Stoddard as a transitional figure among New England writers of fiction, combining Hawthornian romance with the regional realism that culminates in the late nineteenth century. The psychological intensity which Hawthorne often neutralized through coyness or urbanity Stoddard accentuates: her picture draws its energy from her characters' mysterious obsessions, which they themselves often do not understand and which Stoddard dramatizes through stylized use of the grotesque in dialogue and description. This gothic intensity, in turn, is partly held in check, partly made still more intense by an emphasis on depiction of manners and daily social interaction that anticipates Sarah Orne Jewett and Mary Wilkins Freeman.

Here, for instance, is a vignette from *The Morgesons* of two children making trouble for each other at a tea party for parish matrons given by their mother (see below, pp. 17–18).

> Veronica . . . walked up and down the room in a blue cambric dress. She was twisting in her fingers a fine gold chain, which hung from her neck. I caught her cunning glance as she flourished some tansy leaves before her face, imitating Mrs. Dexter to the life. I laughed, and she came to me.
>
> "See," she said softly, "I have something from heaven." She lifted her white apron, and I saw under it, pinned to her dress, a splendid black butterfly, spotted with red and gold.
>
> "It is mine," she said, "you shall not touch it. God blew it in through the window; but it has not breathed yet."
>
> "Pooh; I have three mice in the kitchen."
>
> "Where is the mother?"
>
> "In the hayrick, I suppose, I left it there."
>
> "I hate you," she said, in an enraged voice. "I would strike you, if it wasn't for this holy butterfly."
>
> "Cassandra," said Mrs. Dexter, "does look like her pa; the likeness is ex-tri-ordinary. They say my William resembles me; but parients are no judges."
>
> A faint murmur rose from the knitters, which signified agreement with her remark.

The explosion of temper, cut off almost as soon as it arises by the shift back to Mrs. Dexter; the sudden transitions of mood (parody of adults, Veronica's rapturous intensity, her sudden defensiveness, the spat, the surge of hatred, the banal chitchat); the disjunction between different mental worlds ("parients" and children, the two children themselves)— these are vintage Stoddard devices. Later, with equal suddenness, we find that Veronica has pilfered the mice (for which Cassy retaliates by crushing the butterfly), and the chapter ends, also abruptly but appropriately, with a hymn verse on the subject of total depravity. Veronica here and throughout the book has an elusive elfin quality—part angel, part Satan; defiant yet vulnerable—that makes her almost dreamlike, and her oddness is accentuated by the surface realism of the party decor that at the same time fixes it more definitely than Hawthorne's fiction in a recognizable "normal" place and time. Even as they scoff at Mrs. Dexter, the sisters enact on a more elemental level her politer attempts to gain attention by using domestic prattle as verbal counters. The worlds of child and adult do not intersect, but symbolically mirror each other in ways that become more complex the more closely one looks at the passage.

First novels are often the most autobiographical. So too the *The Morgesons*. Cassandra and Veronica are to a considerable extent modeled on Elizabeth Stoddard and a sister who died young; the parents and grandparents also resemble their real-life counterparts; and a number of the events take on additional resonance through comparison with the biographical record. Consider Locke Morgeson's second marriage. In life, the father married his housekeeper; in the novel he marries the widow of Cousin Charles, with whom Cassy has had an unconsummated affair, but the housekeeper Fanny is shown as violently jealous. The latter detail reflects the external life record, while through Cassandra's reaction to the fictional marriage, Stoddard indirectly expresses the shock, disgust, and sense of betrayal she felt at the event.

Stoddard's life, however, is in the long run better seen as a source of raw material than as a skeleton key to her work. Significantly, her later novels are much less autobiographical while at the same time written in a similar style, about similar people, in a similar setting, and marked by similar themes—above all the central situation of the characters' yearning for emotional fulfillment blocked by family structure, town, and the difficulty of translating idiosyncratic, often half-conscious motives into articulated desires. To be sure, a good deal of *The Morgesons'* special power derives from its autobiographical basis, and our anthology as a whole shows that some of Stoddard's most incisive writing was on the subject of herself. Mainly, though, her stories and novels are not embellished personal experience so much as a fictive working out of themes that mattered to her in forms that represent an original recasting of nineteenth-century novelistic genres and conventions.

In much of her best work, including *The Morgesons*, Stoddard was especially concerned with exploring the types of, and impediments to, female power. Her treatment of this theme is one index of her distinctive place in literary history. On the one hand, her concern with woman's self-development links *The Morgesons* with the popular woman's fiction written by Caroline Chesebrough, Ann Stephens, and others shrewdly reviewed in the *Alta*. Like their works, *The Morgesons* centers around a young, maturing protagonist's increasing awareness of the world around her and her relation to that world. In both cases that relation finally includes marriage and home management. On the other hand, Stoddard's exploration of the dynamics of sexual experience and appraisal of society's allocation of power along gender lines differs from that of most woman's fiction. The latter tends to encourage women to cultivate their own strengths within their own sphere, as a counterweight and corrective to what is seen as the corrupt values of a commercial, male world. For Stoddard, separate could never be equal; her temperament committed her to exploring and challenging the systems of power that disadvantaged her as a woman. She rarely invoked—or displayed—the bonds of sister-hood, but she was a farsighted, aggressive combatant for individual rights.

Stoddard here makes an instructive contrast to her distant relative Hawthorne, to whom she sent a complimentary copy of *The Morgesons,* receiving a very complimentary reply.[14] Unlike Hawthorne, Stoddard did not excoriate her more popular rivals as a "damned mob of scribbling women"—though at times she came close. Her critique was more subtle and also more thoroughgoing. Hawthorne, in *The Scarlet Letter,* defied convention by featuring an adulterous rather than an idealized heroine, but he deferred to convention by representing her fallenness as having a moral correlative (in Hester's antinomianism) and as presenting an insu-perable barrier to a fulfilling emotional life. Stoddard, in contrast, being more responsive than Hawthorne to the psychological and social realities underlying woman's fiction, takes her heroine through a plot whose scenario (growing up female in nineteenth-century American middle-class society) and whose stages correspond much more closely to the popular norms; yet in the process she exposes the timidity of those norms more intransigently. Stoddard's Cassandra is more self-confident, more sexually emancipated, less morally self-doubting than Hawthorne's Hes-ter; furthermore Stoddard, more unequivocally than Hawthorne, shows Cassandra's maverick qualities to be an essential means of strength, growth, and survival. Hawthorne, ironically, actually shared the most essential values of the novelists he criticized: for him too the ideal woman was emphatically virtuous and domestic, not a social rebel, fascinated though he was by the latter alternative. Stoddard reacted more sharply against the former model, but she did so by absorbing and then transforming popular generic convention.

Critic Sybil Weir aptly labels the results a feminist *bildungsroman,*[15] one of a mere handful of distinguished nineteenth-century examples of that male-dominated form. In her sympathetic portrayal of Cassandra's quest for sexual fulfillment and social power while also attaining the skills appropriate to a more conventional heroine, Stoddard created a novel that both draws on and critiques the tradition that produced Scott's *Waverley,* Bulwer's *Pelham,* and Dickens' *David Copperfield,* as one quickly sees on inspection of the standard definitions of its norms, which presuppose a male orientation.[16]

Probably Stoddard's closest intellectual affinity, however, was to the novelists whom she most admired at the time, Emily and Charlotte Brontë. The work of all three displays an interfusion of Victorian social realism with romance tradition, in particular that strain of it which present-day feminist critics call "female gothic" (a mode generally avoided by woman's fiction),[17] featuring male and female doubles, intense physical-ity, violence, and melodramatic heightening of sexual relationships in order to suggest far-reaching connections between the heroine's physical and psychic development and her social reality. Stoddard, like the Brontës, depicts that social reality with a keen awareness of how kinship, marriage, property ownership, and inheritance intermesh.

In *The Morgesons,* her concern with what and how a woman inherits, and how much autonomy she has, shapes Stoddard's treatment of family structure and personal development. Stoddard portrays a rebellious, iconoclastic protagonist striving against nineteenth-century social and religious convention toward an autonomy at once sexual, spiritual, and economic. Cassandra is finally able to avoid the usual female fates and become the symbolic heir of the family's original convention-breaker, Great-Grandfather Locke Morgeson, who named her. She attains an equal and complete love with Desmond Somers and eventually becomes possessor of the family's house, a structure whose history and architecture make it the physical embodiment of Morgeson history. Still, her own exceptional experiences are counterpointed by the stultified lives of her aunt, mother, and sister and by the incapacities that shackle most of the novel's men. Her quest for autonomy is muted too by her own final reconciliation to a life of diminished scope. Since there is no sign that she has affected the larger social order with which she has been in conflict, the reader is left with the uneasy sense that the "possession" she has achieved is both very private and ironically circumscribed.

Stoddard's portrait of Cassandra is rare in its insistence on women's need for an extraordinarily wide range of experiences and an extraordinarily strong will. The unconventional definition of true womanhood makes a pragmatic complement to Margaret Fuller's *Woman in the Nineteenth Century,* which draws on some of the same European sources that influenced Stoddard's thinking. For both writers, the incentive to move in a feminist direction seems to have arisen from a strong identification with romantic individualism, to which post-Puritan New Englanders of the early nineteenth century were apparently quite susceptible. This may help account for one of the several traits Fuller and Stoddard shared in common: their aggressiveness and intensity in the cultivation of personal relationships regardless of sex. Fuller's feminism is much more developed, self-conscious, and intellectualized, but Stoddard dramatizes in Cassandra's drive for self-realization the passional, iconoclastic force behind Fuller's critique. Stoddard's resistance to the nineteenth-century ideological division of life into separate spheres for men and women is further reflected in her decision to write her two later novels from a male protagonist's point of view.

The Morgesons was favorably reviewed, but did not sell. Stoddard's late-life explanation was that the Civil War had turned public attention to current events. "The Morgesons was my Bull Run," she said,[18] meaning that the news of the Union's disastrous defeat, ten days after publication, crippled her sales. But the book's difficulty (elliptical dialogue, abrupt juxtaposition of scenes, lack of narrative explanation) and its relatively disillusioned, "pessimistic" tone might have been equally if not more decisive factors. Within five years, Stoddard made two other bids for recognition as a novelist, *Two Men* (1865) and *Temple House* (1867). In addition to having male protagonists, they differ from *The Morgesons* in making greater (though still limited) concessions to lucidity and to popular conventions of plot and character. They show a more secure grasp of overall structure and slightly less power in the execution of individual scenes. Otherwise, they are similar to *The Morgesons* in style, theme, setting, and quality, and they suffered a similar fate: critical praise and popular neglect. Being both discouraged and pragmatic, writing always out of economic as well as artistic necessity, Stoddard then turned almost wholly to the short stories, poems, and sketches with which she had begun her career. For several years she was quite productive. But after 1873, when her husband lost the editorship of *The Aldine,* which had become her main outlet, Stoddard almost ceased publishing until the late 1880s, when the sense of a growing appreciation of her novels and the qualified commercial success of their reissue in 1888–89 prompted another flurry of (inferior) work.

The last significant publication of Stoddard's "major" period was a children's book for adults, *Lolly Dinks's Doings* (1874), a series of curious tales loosely connected by sketches, also whimsical and bizarre, of the author/narrator's family. The text is what one would expect of a grown-up Cassandra: Lolly Dinks, the child-auditor, is a peevish and difficult boy rather than a model child; the mother-narrator intermixes conventional syrupy affection with sardonic humor; the tales themselves are often disconcerting, such as one in which the "hero" is a crocodile presented first as repulsive, then as halfway endearing, only to be killed off abruptly and without tears. In this way, Stoddard preserved some of the starkness of traditional fairy tale amid the usual nineteenth-century overlays.

Such tales illustrate Stoddard's versatility but are not typical of her short fiction. In general, this work falls into two categories: the fictionalized sketch (like "Collected by a Valetudinarian") and the realistic-romantic tale ("Lemorne *Versus* Huell"). Both are strongly regional in flavor, with the same preferred setting as the novels. Both rely on popular literary stereotypes—e.g., the scenario of whirlwind courtship in "Lemorne"—for Stoddard wrote most of her short studies as magazine pieces for ready cash. As with F. Scott Fitzgerald, there is a large quality gap between her run-of-the-mill productions and the pieces reprinted in this volume. The difference consists not so much in whether Stoddard made use of convention as in how she used it: in complexity of tone, for instance, as in the ability to give an open-endedness to the mandatory marriage conclusion of the tales, as when the heroine of "Lemorne" realizes her new husband's baseness in the last line.

Stoddard's private papers are fully as striking as the best of her shorter published work. Her one existing journal (below, pp. 347ff.) and many of her letters are noteworthy examples of their genres because of their frankness and pith. As with other American Victorians, what Stoddard dared to print, although uninhibited by the day's standards, was more restrained than what she dared to think; but to a greater degree than most, she dared to say it in conversation and letters. She was a difficult correspondent—demanding, touchy, erratic, egocentric, imperious, and blunt. But from a century's distance her saltiness looks much more zestful and her self-indulgence less obnoxious, just as Thoreau's prickly manner endears him more quickly to modern readers than Emerson's comparative blandness, although Emerson would surely have been the more palatable acquaintance for most of us. And beyond their interest as a self-portrait, the letters provide a running commentary on the contemporary cultural scene, on what it meant to be a woman and a writer in nineteenth-century New York.

As the letters suggest, the literary world that the Stoddards inhabited was on the whole not so impressive as they liked to think. This may be another clue to the mystery of how so original a writer as Stoddard failed to gain a hearing even though she lived in the nation's largest publishing center and had extensive connections with the publishing establishment. On the one hand, the Stoddards knew about, and in most cases had read, all the contemporary British and American authors now recognized as great. They were personally acquainted with Bryant, Hawthorne, Howells, Lowell, Melville, and Whitman. But their closest literary associates were mediocrities—Edmund Clarence Stedman, Bayard Taylor, George Henry Boker, Elizabeth Akers Allen, Thomas Buchanan Read, Fitz-James O'Brien, Thomas Bailey Aldrich, and the like. Among them, only Boker has any claim to permanent fame, and a marginal one at that. In short, their closest social ties in the literary world were mostly with imitation romantic writers who were eclipsed—and felt themselves to be eclipsed—by the eminent writers of Boston and vicinity. Melville and Whitman, the city's greatest literary geniuses, Stoddard's circle did not recognize as such. Consequently, Elizabeth, the only writer of really first-rate gifts among her artist friends, was always receiving ignorantly sympathetic advice as to how to make her writing "smoother" and being rewarded by compliments like Boker's on reading *Two Men:* " 'The little lady has advanced greatly in 'style' since her first novel.' "[19] This patronizing kind of "approval" undoubtedly had something to do with the fact that she came to doubt her creative powers and produce, after 1875, work that was insipid by comparison with her earlier efforts. She might not have submitted to the verdict of the marketplace had it not been echoed in the verdict of her friends. And the work she produced before this conventionalizing process set in might not have lain in neglect as long as it did had her literary associates not conspired to embalm her for posterity as Richard's talented but eccentric wife. Such a tribute scarcely tempted further inquiries.

What probably made Stoddard vulnerable to internalizing her friends' faint praise as self-criticism, in addition to her poor sales, was an image of herself as inherently undisciplined, lacking in "form," desultory in her training and education, a writer whose forte lay in the somewhat unpredictable if glorious traits of Power, Intensity, Truth. "I have not done my work like an artist," she complained about *Two Men,* "because I *Cant*" (*sic*).[20] And her novelistic craftsmanship *is* better on the level of the vignette or episode than on the level of overall structure, although she chastised herself excessively. Nevertheless, Stoddard retained enough residual self-confidence to interpret the revival of interest in her novels during the late 1880s as more than just fortuitous. Rereading the last (and weakest) of these, she felt it "in comparison with the flood of American novels in the last few years a remarkable original, able study—intellectual in its developement, and true to the human soul," and well crafted ("harmonious, homogeneous") to boot![21] When reviewer Julian Hawthorne ranked her among the great modern novelists, Stoddard was flattered, but with one side of her mind she also considered it her just due.

The brief Stoddard revival came in the wake of the realist movement, whose apostles found in her a precursor. That is the essential meaning of William Dean Howells' glowing tribute to her, the most generous on record from a nineteenth-century writer: "In a time when most of us had to write like Tennyson, or Longfellow, or Browning, she would never write like any one but herself."[22] Howells meant that Stoddard was a realist ahead of her time. Stoddard herself ironically but with some justification resisted this categorization. While she admired realism in the persons of Balzac and Jane Austen and defended the representational accuracy of her own characters against those who criticized them as freakish, Stoddard considered the art of her realist contemporaries Freeman and Howells as rather narrow and insipid and insisted, "I am *not* realistic—I am *romantic,* the very bareness and simplicity of my work is a trap for its romance."[23] The fact is that Stoddard never comprehensively defined her artistry in relation to all the models on which she drew. And here we come to what may have been the final barrier in the way of critical recognition: her transitional position in the history of American fiction. Part of her seeming strangeness for reviewers of the 1860s was that she could not be pigeonholed either as a romantic or as a realist.[24] The realists, by praising her implicitly as an anticipation of themselves, thereby bracketed her as obsolete. The present scholarly practice of dividing nineteenth-century American fiction into two subspecializations—antebellum ("romantic") and postwar ("realistic") fiction—has perhaps contributed to the belatedness of serious attention to her work.

Stoddard's place in American literary history, in any event, is more complicated and noteworthy than has ever been perceived. She must be approached as a writer thoroughly in touch with the literature of her day, a writer who was indeed a pioneer but whose pioneering consisted of a highly original synthesis and transformation of a wide range of fictional traditions previously absorbed: gothic romance, Victorian *bildungsroman,* regional prose, and popular woman's fiction. Apart from her contributions to these and other genres, their characteristic themes, and the social realities to which they refer, Stoddard is historically important also as an experimenter in narrative method. She anticipates modern fiction in using a severely limited mode, with minimal narrative clues (eliminating the "she said"'s as much as possible), minimal transitions, and dramatic, imagistic, and aphoristic impact.

In short, Stoddard belongs among the important American novelists. To make such a discovery after years of supposedly specialized study in nineteenth-century American literary history is both an embarrassment and a delight. The case of Stoddard's discouragement in the face of nonrecognition and the subsequent neglect of her work is not so spectacular as the case of Herman Melville. Yet surely *The Morgesons,* and probably also *Two Men,* deserve a secure place in the American literary canon, as do Stoddard's best short pieces, while her career as a whole, as suggested by the ominous tone of the items from the late 1860s and after anthologized here, deserves to be remembered as another instance of a major American literary talent being stimulated to a remarkable distinctiveness of style and distinction of achievement partly by the same sense of obtuseness in her fellow countrymen which ironically later cut short that achievement and helped drive her into silence and embitterment. We hope that the recognition Stoddard has always deserved will finally come now.

NOTES

1. James Henderson Matlack, "The Literary Career of Elizabeth Barstow Stoddard" (Ph.D. diss., Yale University, 1967), a carefully researched work to which we are much indebted.

2. *The Letters of Emily Dickinson,* ed. Thomas Johnson (Cambridge: Harvard University Press, 1958), 2:473.

3. Mrs. Thomas Bailey Aldrich (Lilian Woodman), *Crowding Memories* (Boston and New York: Houghton, 1920), p. 14. She refers specifically to Elizabeth Stoddard's power over men, but that women felt it too seems clear not only from her account but also from Marie Hansen Taylor, *On Two Continents* (Garden City, N.Y.: Doubleday, Page, & Co., 1905), p. 59; and Eleanor Ruggles, *Prince of Players: Edwin Booth* (New York: W. W. Norton & Co., 1953), p. 132.

4. *Crowding Memories,* p. 13.

5. Elizabeth Stoddard to Elizabeth Akers Allen, 23 April 1874 (Colby College Library).

6. George Boker to Bayard Taylor, 24 March 1866, quoted in Matlack, "Literary Career," p. 399.

7. Elizabeth Stoddard to Allen, 27 [December 1873] and 30 January [1874?] (Colby College Library).

8. Homer Dodge Martin to Elizabeth Stoddard, 8 April 1865, quoted in Matlack, "Literary Career," pp. 279, 333.

9. Edmund Clarence Stedman, quoted in Laura Stedman and George M. Gould, *Life and Letters of Edmund Clarence Stedman* (New York: Moffat, Yard, 1910), 2:533.

10. Richard Henry Stoddard, *Recollections, Personal and Literary,* ed. Ripley Hitchcock (New York: Barnes, 1903), p. 108.

11. Precisely how Stoddard became a correspondent for a paper in faraway San Francisco is not known; probably her favorite brother Wilson Barstow, then in California, played a part. For what is known about her stint as columnist for the *Alta,* see Matlack, "*The Alta California*'s Lady Correspondent," *New-York Historical Society Quarterly* 58 (1974): 280–303.

12. The term "woman's fiction" is used here and below in the sense defined by Nina Baym in *Woman's Fiction* (Ithaca and London: Cornell University Press, 1978), which applies it to a particular genre of American fiction, written by and about women, centering around the maturation of a heroine whose acquisition of the skills and awareness leading to intellectual and practical success within a bourgeois domestic role was designed as a means of instruction in self-reliance for its intended audience. Baym has essentially redefined what earlier scholars called "domestic" or "sentimental fiction," and identified its serious intellectual purpose.

13. "Introduction" to *The Morgesons* (New York and London: Johnson, 1971), p. xi and passim.

14. See Matlack, "Hawthorne and Elizabeth Barstow Stoddard," *New England Quarterly* 50 (1977): 278–302.

15. "*The Morgesons:* A Neglected Feminist *Bildungsroman,*" *New England Quarterly* 49 (1976): 427–39.

16. See, e.g., Jerome Buckley's definition in *Season of Youth: The Bildungsroman from Dickens to Golding* (Cambridge: Harvard University Press, 1974), p. 17, particularly the statement that the *bildungsroman* hero, "sometimes at a quite early age, leaves the repressive atmosphere of home (and also the relative innocence), to make his way independently in the city." Cassandra's visits to Rosville and Belem are rough structural equivalents, but for her, as a young woman, physical departure from the home does not mean more than a very qualified liberation from confinement, while at the end of the novel she in fact achieves independence in the context of the home.

17. Ellen Moers, *Literary Women: The Great Writers* (Garden City, N.Y.: Doubleday & Co., 1976), esp. pp. 90–110. Moers identifies strong elements of childhood eroticism and loathing of adult female physical life in female gothic. There is an undercurrent sense of the adult, aging female body as monstrous in *The Morgesons,* as there is in Elizabeth Stoddard's letters. Cassandra becomes increasingly preoccupied with her possible physical decay, while in the ironically named Belle/vue Somers, the persistence of female sexuality and fertility into middle age seems grotesque. The novel's incest motif can also be seen in the context of female gothic.

18. Elizabeth Stoddard to Stedman, 18 November n.d. (1880s) (Columbia University).

19. Boker to Richard Stoddard, 3 and 26 October 1865, quoted in Matlack, "Literary Career," p. 365.

20. Elizabeth Stoddard to Stedman, n.d. (Columbia University).

21. Ibid. (late 1880s) (Columbia University).

22. William Dean Howells, *Literary Friends and Acquaintance,* ed. David F. Hiatt and Edwin H. Cady (Bloomington and London: Indiana University Press, 1968), p. 77.

23. Elizabeth Stoddard to Stedman, 21 April 1888 (Columbia University).

24. Among early reviews of *The Morgesons,* for instance, Manton Marble in the *New York World* stressed the book's literal realism (4 July 1862, p. 3), while George Ripley, in the *New York Tribune* (19 July 1862, p. 3), stressed its subjective stylization of reality. For excerpts, see Matlack, "Literary Career," pp. 224–27.

A Guide to Writings by and About Elizabeth Stoddard

I. Prior Bibliographies

By far the most complete bibliography of publications by Elizabeth Stoddard is James Matlack, "The Literary Career of Elizabeth Barstow Stoddard" (Ph.D. diss., Yale University, 1967), pp. 625–31. Matlack also includes a helpful annotated list of holdings of manuscripts by and about Stoddard (pp. 632–34). The best bibliography of secondary material on Stoddard is in Richard Foster's edition of *The Morgesons* (New York and London: Johnson, 1971), pp. lii–lv.

II. Writings by Elizabeth Stoddard

Elizabeth Stoddard published five books during her career: *The Morgesons* (New York: Carleton & Co., 1862); *Two Men* (New York: Bunce & Huntington, 1865); *Temple House* (New York: Carleton & Co., 1867): *Lolly Dinks's Doings* (Boston: Gill, 1874); and *Poems* (Boston and New York: Houghton, 1895). The first three, her novels, were brought out in a revised edition, 1888–89 (New York: Cassell), reprinted (with a preface by Elizabeth Stoddard) in 1901 (Philadelphia: Coates; publication transferred to Winston, 1901), and in 1971 edited by Richard Foster (New York and London: Johnson).

Elizabeth Stoddard also published many uncollected short stories, sketches, critical essays, poems, and miscellaneous journalistic pieces. The most significant groups of these are (a) the series of seventy-five semi-monthly newspaper columns she wrote for the *Daily Alta California* (8 October 1854 to 28 February 1858) and (b) a dozen short stories published in *Harper's New Monthly Magazine,* 1862–70. In addition to those included in this volume, the following are of special interest: "A Partie Carée," *Harper's* 25 (1862): 466–79; "Tuberoses," *Harper's* 26 (1863): 191–97; "The Prescription," *Harper's* 28 (1864): 794–800; "The Chimneys," *Harper's* 31 (1865): 726–32; "Lucy Tavish's Journey," *Harper's* 35 (1867): 656–63; "The Visit," *Harper's* 37 (1868): 802–9. Other notable fiction includes "My Own Story," *Atlantic Monthly* 5 (1860): 526–47 (Stoddard's first major story); "The Swanstream Match," *Appleton's Journal,* n.s., 5 (1878): 336–47; "A Study for a Heroine," *Independent* 37 (1885): 1246–48; and "Betty's Downfall," *Independent* 43 (1891): 620–21. Many other items are listed in Matlack's bibliography.

Miscellaneous essays by Elizabeth Stoddard that are revealing of her personality and critical tastes include "A Literary Whim," *Appleton's* 6 (1871): 440–41; "Woman in Art—Rosa Bonheur," *Aldine* 5 (1872): 145 (pseud. Elizabeth B. Leonard); "Characters of Scott," *Lippincott's* 45 (1890): 726–31; "A New England Girl in Old New York," *Saturday Evening Post,* 14 October 1899, pp. 274–75; "My Record of the Stage," *Saturday Evening Post,* 4 November 1899, pp. 354–55; and "Literary Folk as They Came and Went with Ourselves," *Saturday Evening Post,* 2 and 30 June 1900, pp. 1126–27, 1222–23.

By far the largest collection of Elizabeth Stoddard manuscripts is in the Edmund Clarence Stedman Papers, Butler Library, Columbia University. The American Antiquarian Society, Boston Public Library, Colby College Library, Houghton Library (Harvard), Middlebury College Library, New York Public Library, and Pennsylvania State University Library also have significant Stoddard holdings. See also Matlack, "Literary Career," pp. 632–34.

III. Secondary Sources: Early Reminiscences and Assessments

Brief but notable glimpses of Elizabeth Stoddard's life and personality in Victorian-style memoirs include Richard Henry Stoddard, *Recollections, Personal and Literary,* ed. Ripley Hitchcock (New York: Barnes, 1903); Mrs. Thomas Bailey Aldrich (Lilian Woodman), *Crowding Memories* (Boston and New York: Houghton, 1920); Francis Halsey, ed., *American Authors and Their Homes* (New York: James Pott & Co., 1901); William Dean Howells, *Literary Friends and Acquaintance,* ed. David F. Hiatt and Edwin H. Cady (Bloomington and London: Indiana University Press, 1968); Laura Stedman and George M. Gould, *Life and Letters of Edmund Clarence Stedman* (New York: Moffat, Yard, 1910); and Marie Hansen Taylor, *On Two Continents* (Garden City, N.Y.: Doubleday, Page & Co., 1905). Most of these accounts treat Elizabeth Stoddard as Richard's wife rather than as an independent party.

Significant early criticism of Elizabeth Stoddard's works include George Ripley's reviews of *The Morgesons* and *Temple House,* in the *New York Tribune,* 19 July 1862 (p. 3) and ibid., 27 January 1868 (p. 6); W. D. Howells' review of *Two Men,* in *The Nation* 1 (1865): 537–38; Julian Hawthorne, "Novelistic Habits and 'The Morgesons,'" *Lippincott's* 44 (1889): 868–71; H. W. Preston, "Some Recent Novels," *Atlantic Monthly* 88 (1901): 848–50; Mary Moss, "The Novels of Elizabeth Stoddard,"

The Bookman 16 (1902): 260–63; and Edmund Clarence Stedman, *Genius and Other Essays* (New York: Moffat, Yard, 1911), which reprints his 1901 introduction to the Philadelphia edition of Stoddard's novels and his 1895 review of *Poems*. See also Matlack, "Literary Career of Elizabeth Barstow Stoddard," chaps. 6, 8, 9, 10, 11, 12, which summarize many other reviews and notices of her five books and their reprintings.

IV. Modern Scholarship: Biography and Criticism

The principal study of Stoddard's life and career is Matlack's "Literary Career of Elizabeth Barstow Stoddard," which synthesizes a wealth of biographical information from manuscripts as well as printed sources. Matlack also gives detailed synopses and critiques of all major Stoddard works as well as many minor pieces. Portions of Matlack's dissertation appear in revised form in "*The Alta California's* Lady Correspondent," *New-York Historical Society Quarterly* 58 (1974): 280–303, which describes Stoddard's 1854–58 stint as journalist; and "Hawthorne and Elizabeth Barstow Stoddard," *New England Quarterly* 50 (1977): 278–302, which gives an extended analysis of *The Morgesons* in the process of reconstructing the personal and literary links between the two authors. These articles, like the thesis, show a thorough grasp of the details of her career.

The best short overview of Stoddard's life and writing is Richard Foster's "Introduction" to the 1971 Johnson reprint edition of *The Morgesons*, pp. vii–li. Sybil Weir, "*The Morgesons:* A Neglected Feminist *Bildungsroman*," *New England Quarterly* 49 (1976): 427–39, is a perceptive analysis of the protagonist's characterization and development.

Additional glimpses of Stoddard's relations with her contemporaries are provided by Richard Cary, *The Genteel Circle: Bayard Taylor and His New York Friends* (Ithaca: Cornell University Press, 1952), which reprints a number of Taylor letters; and Eleanor Ruggles, *Edwin Booth: Prince of Players* (New York: W. W. Norton & Co., 1953), which recounts (less fully than Matlack) the history of relations between Booth and the Stoddards.

Chronology

1823	Elizabeth Drew Barstow born May 6 in Mattapoisett, Massachusetts, to prominent shipbuilder Wilson Barstow and Betsy Drew Barstow.
1825	Samuel Wilson Barstow, brother, born April 26 (dies July 1826).
1827	Jane Wilson Barstow, Elizabeth's only sister, born January 23.
1829	Samuel Barstow, brother, born April 11 (dies in California, 1865).
1831	Wilson Barstow, Elizabeth's favorite brother, born March 13.
1833	Zaccheus Mead Barstow, brother, born September 1 (dies in Civil War, 1862).
1835	Altol Olmnar Barstow, brother, born October 26.
1837	Summer term: Elizabeth Barstow attends Wheaton Female Seminary in Norton, Massachusetts.
1838	Gideon Barstow, brother, born April 1 (dies in November 1840).
1840–41	Winter term: Elizabeth Barstow again attends Wheaton Seminary.
1848	Jane Wilson Barstow dies of consumption in October.
1849	Betsy Barstow dies in January.
1851	Fall: Elizabeth Barstow meets Margaret Jane Muzzey Sweat in Portland, Maine, and forms her most intimate friendship with another woman; it is broken off in 1854. The pattern of initial amity disrupted or terminated partly because of Elizabeth's acrimony characterizes almost all her later friendships.

On a fall visit to New York City, Elizabeth Barstow attends literary soirees of Anne Lynch, making the acquaintance of poets Richard Henry Stoddard and Bayard Taylor. Along with Edmund Clarence Stedman and George Henry Boker, they would long form the core of her personal and literary circle. Relations with Taylor and Boker become strained as they attain success, but Stedman remains a lifelong friend, adviser, and confidant.

1852   Elizabeth Barstow's first published work, the reverie "Phases," appears in the Duyckinck brothers' *Literary World* in October. A reflection on nature's power, "Phases" is located in Mattapoisett, the model for the setting of most of her later writing.

1852–53   Period of intense conflict between Elizabeth Barstow's feelings for her brother Wilson and her feelings for Richard Henry Stoddard. During much of 1852 she plans to accompany Wilson on a trip to California to search for gold. She marries Richard Stoddard in December, keeping the marriage secret for two months. Settles in New York City with Richard in early February, but is greatly distressed when Wilson sails for California at the end of the month.

1853   Richard Stoddard becomes Inspector of Customs in New York. His annual salary of $1,000 is crucial to the meager family budget, but the appointment is political and he is fired in 1870 for being a Democrat and a critic of the North's role in the Civil War.

Wilson Barstow, Sr., marries Jane Parr, a Barstow family servant, in October; Elizabeth Stoddard is outraged.

1854   In October the first of Elizabeth Stoddard's semi-monthly columns as the "Lady Correspondent" of the San Francisco newspaper the *Daily Alta California* is published; the last appears in February 1858.

In November, Stoddard's "Some Short Poems" are published in *Knickerbocker Magazine*.

1855   Wilson Stoddard (Willy) born in June.

1859   A deformed child is born in late spring and dies unnamed at the end of July.

1860   Elizabeth Stoddard's short story "My Own Story" published by the *Atlantic Monthly* in May, after she makes changes suggested by editor James Russell Lowell to tone down the story's sexual explicitness.

1861   Willy Stoddard dies in December after a brief illness.

1862   *The Morgesons* published in June by George S. Carleton &
            Co. of New York to favorable reviews but modest sales.

            During the 1860s and early 1870s, Elizabeth Stoddard pub-
            lishes many short stories and sketches, mainly in *Harper's*.
            Increasingly written for money, they nevertheless bear the
            Stoddard hallmarks of intensity and unconventionality.

1863   Edwin Lorimer Stoddard (Lorry) born in December.

1865   *Two Men* published by Bunce & Huntington in October. A
            critical success but a popular failure. The firm goes bank-
            rupt in December.

1866   While summering at Mattapoisett with Lorry to work on
            her next novel, Stoddard writes her only extant journal.

1867   *Temple House* is published by George S. Carleton & Co. in
            October. It is not widely reviewed and sales are low.

1869   Wilson Barstow, Jr., dies in March, leaving Stoddard's Mat-
            tapoisett family financially dependent on the Stoddards and
            causing Elizabeth much personal distress.

            Altol Barstow dies in August.

1871   Richard Stoddard becomes editor of the magazine *The Al-
            dine;* he and Elizabeth are frequent contributors. He holds
            the post for only two years.

1872   The Stoddards cease living in boardinghouses and tempo-
            rary quarters and move permanently into the upper floors
            of a small house on East 15th Street.

1873   Elizabeth Stoddard forms friendship with woman of letters
            Elizabeth Akers Allen. It is one in a series of friendships
            with such writers as Louise Chandler Moulton, Lilian
            Whiting, and Julia Dorr, which begins as early as the 1850s.

1874   Publication of the witty, unsentimental children's book *Lolly
            Dinks's Doings* as part of Boston publisher William F. Gill's
            "Little Folks Series." Stoddard writes much less after this.

            Through circa 1880, Stoddard has a close relationship with
            one Edward Smith, a wealthy man some years her junior
            who squires her about and gives her expensive gifts as well
            as advice and support.

1880   Richard Stoddard becomes literary editor of the *New York*

	Evening Mail (later the *Mail and Express*), holding the post until his death.
1888	Interest in Elizabeth Stoddard's novels revives. Edmund Stedman arranges that Cassell publish a revised edition of *Two Men*. It appears in June to excellent reviews, and is followed by *Temple House* (October) and *The Morgesons* (September 1889). The fleeting "revival" spurs Stoddard to write a good number of essays, stories, and poems over the next several years, appearing mainly in the *Independent* and *Harper's*.
1891	Wilson Barstow, Sr., dies in October. The Stoddards' visits to Mattapoisett cease.
1895	Elizabeth Stoddard's selected *Poems* are published in August by Houghton Mifflin, partly because W. D. Howells' praise of her work sparks renewed interest. Reviews are favorable but scattered; sales are poor.
1897	A public dinner given in March honors Richard Stoddard. Congratulatory letters by Arthur Conan Doyle, Edmund Gosse, Howells, Charles Eliot Norton, and others are read; Elizabeth's work also receives frequent praise.
1901	Lorimer Stoddard dies in September of tuberculosis. Beginning in the late 1880s, he had been a successful actor and, increasingly, a successful writer for the stage.
	Henry T. Coates & Company reissues Elizabeth Stoddard's novels in September. The plates from the Cassell edition had been bought at an auction and sent her by an admirer of her work. Little note is taken of this publication.
1902	Elizabeth Stoddard dies of double pneumonia on August 1. She is buried next to Lorry in Sag Harbor, New York. Richard Stoddard dies in May 1903 and is also buried in Sag Harbor.

The Morgesons

Introduction

Elizabeth Stoddard began work on *The Morgesons* in May 1860. On November 7, 1861, Richard Stoddard signed a contract for its publication with George S. Carleton & Co. (New York), which brought it out in late June 1862. The book was no doubt completed in substance by the early winter of 1861, since Stoddard spoke of it as belonging to an era prior to the death of her first son Willy (December 17, 1861).

Stoddard was somewhat unlucky in her choice of publishers, although not quite so unlucky as she believed. All three of her novels were published by minor New York houses, which apparently did little to promote their sales. Carleton & Co., however, might initially have seemed a good choice. Carleton was an up-and-coming firm, actively seeking to "encourage young American writers."[1] Yet ultimately it was more interested in mass-market novels like Augusta Jane Evans' *St. Elmo* (1867), one of the last "classic" best-selling woman's fictions, on which Carleton made large profits. Dissatisfied with what she took to be her publisher's apathy toward the fate of *The Morgesons,* Stoddard gave her second novel, *Two Men,* to Bunce & Huntington, which promptly went bankrupt. She then went back to Carleton with *Temple House,* but with even less commercial success than before.

In the absence of complete information about the motives behind Stoddard's negotiations with publishers, conducted for the most part on her behalf by Richard and (in the 1880s and after) by Edmund Clarence Stedman, one conjectures that the choice of firms resulted from a combination of reluctance of more established publishers to gamble, alluring promises of reward held out by Carleton and Bunce & Huntington, and insecurity on the part of Stoddard and her agents as to the quality or potential appeal of the work. Stoddard's circle was undoubtedly well aware of the relative status of all the New York and Boston publishers, as evinced most poignantly by its delight at the acceptance of her (mediocre) selected *Poems* (1895) by Houghton Mifflin; and its contacts in the publishing industry were certainly far better than those of any minor author

1. John Tebbel, *A History of Book Publishing in the United States* (New York and London: R. R. Bowker Co., 1972), 1:344.

in the hinterlands. In all likelihood, then, Stoddard had as good a chance of gaining a sympathetic hearing for her novels from the publishing industry as could reasonably be expected for a writer without an established reputation.

In any case, Stoddard's spouse and friends seem to have made a concerted if not unequivocally wholehearted effort to stimulate sales of *The Morgesons* and her other novels, as well as the revised editions thereof (1888–89), by word-of-mouth promotion, by cajoling reviews from literary acquaintances, and by writing reviews themselves. The result in each instance, however, was a flurry of critical attention followed by very limited sales.

The present text of *The Morgesons* is based on the revised edition of 1889 (New York: Cassell), the plates from which were used for the 1901 reprint (Philadelphia: Coates, printing transferred to Winston of Philadelphia, 1901). Between the 1862 and 1889 editions, Stoddard made no major structural changes, but she did make extensive minor revisions, mostly for the sake of greater conciseness but sometimes leading to a marked change of effect and occasionally even to a reconception of a scene or chapter. For example, from the novel's conclusion Stoddard eliminated the explicit statement that Ben Somers "died in delirium tremens." She also eliminated some of her other most explicit references to the Somers family curse of alcoholism. The result is to make the ending more mysterious and also to attach more weight to Ben's moral weakness as opposed to the medical symptom of it.

Not all the revisions were improvements. In Chapter XVIII, for instance, the 1862 edition has Alice Morgeson say in response to Cassandra's fascination with Cousin Charles' " 'devilish eyes,' " " 'Cassandra Morgeson, are you possessed?' " The revised edition reads " 'are you mad?' "—thereby effacing the link between this passage and the motif of demonic possession introduced in the very first line of the book. Overall, however, the 1889 revisions made for a more compact, tonally consistent text, one in which Stoddard's provocative traits of laconic innuendo and sudden transition are even more pronounced than in the original. In contrast to the drift in her later short fiction toward the more conventional, Stoddard revised her novels (which she valued much more highly) in such a way as to make even fewer compromises for the sake of the superficial reader.

When *The Morgesons* was reissued in 1901, Stoddard's only change was to add a preface, here printed after the work itself, designed to introduce all three novels.

The Morgesons.

CHAPTER I.

"That child," said my aunt Mercy, looking at me with indigo-colored eyes, "is possessed."

When my aunt said this I was climbing a chest of drawers, by its knobs, in order to reach the book-shelves above it, where my favorite work, "The Northern Regions,"[1] was kept, together with "Baxter's Saints' Rest,"[2] and other volumes of that sort, belonging to my mother; and those my father bought for his own reading, and which I liked, though I only caught a glimpse of their meaning by strenuous study. To this day Sheridan's Comedies, Sterne's Sentimental Journey, and Captain Cook's Voyages are so mixed up in my remembrance that I am still uncertain whether it was Sterne who ate baked dog with Maria, or Sheridan who wept over a dead ass in the Sandwich Islands.[3]

After I had made a dash at and captured my book, I seated myself with difficulty on the edge of the chest of drawers, and was soon lost in an Esquimaux hut. Presently, in crossing my feet, my shoes, which were large, dropped on the painted floor with a loud noise. I looked at my aunt; her regards were still fixed upon me, but they did not interfere with her occupation of knitting; neither did they interrupt her habit of chewing cloves, flagroot, or grains of rice. If these articles were not at hand, she chewed a small chip.

"Aunt Merce, poor Hepburn chewed his shoes, when he was in Davis's Straits."[4]

"Mary, look at that child's stockings."

Mother raised her eyes from the *Boston Recorder*,[5] and the article she had been absorbed in—the proceedings of an Ecclesiastical Council, which had discussed (she read aloud to Aunt Merce) the conduct of Brother Thaddeus Turner, pastor of the Congregational

Church of Hyena. Brother Thaddeus had spoken lightly of the difference between Sprinkling and Immersion, and had even called Hyena's Baptist minister "*Brother*." He was contumacious at first, was Brother Thaddeus, but Brother Boanerges from Andover finally floored him.

"Cassandra," said mother, presently, "come here."

I obeyed with reluctance, making a show of turning down a leaf.

"Child," she continued, and her eyes wandered over me dreamily, till they dropped on my stockings; "why will you waste so much time on unprofitable stories?"

"Mother, I hate good stories, all but the Shepherd of Salisbury Plain;[6] I like that, because it makes me hungry to read about the roasted potatoes the shepherd had for breakfast and supper. Would it make me thankful if you only gave me potatoes without salt?"

"Not unless your heart is right before God."

" '*The Lord my Shepherd is,*' " sang Aunt Merce.

I put my hands over my ears, and looked defiantly round the room. Its walls are no longer standing, and the hands of its builders have crumbled to dust. Some mental accident impressed this picture on the purblind memory of childhood.

We were in mother's winter room. She was in a low, chintz-covered chair; Aunt Merce sat by the window, in a straight-backed chair, that rocked querulously, and likewise covered with chintz, of a red and yellow pattern. Before the lower half of the windows were curtains of red serge, which she rattled apart on their brass rods, whenever she heard a footstep, or the creak of a wheel in the road below. The walls were hung with white paper, through which ran thread-like stripes of green. A square of green and chocolate-colored English carpet covered the middle of the floor, and a row of straw chairs stood around it, on the bare, lead-colored boards. A huge bed, with a chintz top shaped like an elephant's back, was in one corner, and a six-legged mahogany table in another. One side of the room where the fireplace was set was paneled in wood; its fire had burned down in the shining Franklin stove, and broken brands were standing upright. The charred backlog still smoldered, its sap hissed and bubbled at each end.

Aunt Merce rummaged her pocket for flagroot; mother resumed her paper.

"May I put on, for a little while, my new slippers?" I asked, longing to escape the oppressive atmosphere of the room.

"Yes," answered mother, "but come in soon, it will be supper-time."

I bounded away, found my slippers, and was walking down stairs on tiptoe, holding up my linsey-woolsey frock, when I saw the door of my great-grandfather's room ajar. I pushed it open, went in, and saw a very old man, his head bound with a red-silk handkerchief, bolstered in bed. His wife, grandmother-in-law, sat by the fire reading a great Bible.

"Marm Tamor, will you please show me Ruth and Boaz?" I asked.

She complied by turning over the leaves till she came to the picture.

"Did Ruth love Boaz dreadfully much?"[7]

"Oh, oh," groaned the old man, "what is the imp doing here? Drive her away. Scat."

I skipped out by a side door, down an alley paved with blue pebbles, swung the high gate open, and walked up and down the gravel walk which bordered the roadside, admiring my slippers, and wishing that some acquaintance with poor shoes could see me. I thought then I would climb the high gateposts, which had a flat top, and take there the position of the little girl in "The Shawl Dance." I had no sooner taken it than Aunt Merce appeared at the door, and gave a shriek at the sight, which tempted me to jump toward her with extended arms. I was seized and carried into the house, where supper was administered, and I was put to bed.

CHAPTER II.

At this time I was ten years old. We lived in a New England village, Surrey,[8] which was situated on an inlet of a large bay that opened into the Atlantic. From the observatory of our house we could see how the inlet was pinched by the long claws of the land, which nearly enclosed it. Opposite the village, some ten miles across, a range of islands shut out the main waters of the bay. For miles on the outer side of the curving prongs of land stretched a rugged, desolate coast, indented with coves and creeks, lined with bowlders of granite half sunken in the sea, and edged by beaches overgrown with pale sedge, or covered with beds of seaweed. Nothing alive, except the gulls, abode in these solitary shores. No lighthouse stood on any point, to shake its long, warning light

across the mariners' wake. Now and then a drowned man floated
in among the sedge, or a small craft went to pieces on the rocks.
When an easterly wind prevailed, the coast resounded with the
bellowing sea, which brought us tidings from those inaccessible
spots. We heard its roar as it leaped over the rocks on Gloster
Point, and its long, unbroken wail when it rolled in on Whitefoot
Beach. In mild weather, too, when our harbor was quiet, we still
heard its whimper. Behind the village, the ground rose toward the
north, where the horizon was bounded by woods of oak and pine,
intersected by crooked roads, which led to towns and villages near
us. The inland scenery was tame; no hill or dale broke its dull
uniformity. Cornfields and meadows of red grass walled with gray
stone, lay between the village and the border of the woods. Seaward it was enchanting—beautiful under the sun and moon and
clouds.

Our family had lived in Surrey for years. Probably some Puritan
of the name of Morgeson had moved from an earlier settlement,
and, appropriating a few acres in what was now its center, lived
long enough upon them to see his sons and daughters married to
the sons and daughters of similar settlers. So our name was in
perpetuation, though none of our race ever made a mark in his
circle, or attained a place among the great ones of his day. The
family recipes for curing herbs and hams, and making cordials,
were in better preservation than the memory of their makers. It is
certain that they were not a progressive or changeable family. No
tradition of any individuality remains concerning them. There was
a confusion in the minds of the survivors of the various generations
about the degree of their relationship to those who were buried,
and whose names and ages simply were cut in the stones which
headed their graves. The *meum* and *tuum* of blood were inextricably
mixed; so they contented themselves with giving their children the
old Christian names which were carved on the headstones, and
which, in time, added a still more profound darkness to the anti-
heraldic memory of the Morgesons. They had no knowledge of
that treasure which so many of our New England families are
boastful of—the Ancestor who came over in the Mayflower, or by
himself, with a grant of land from Parliament. It was not known
whether two or three brothers sailed together from the Old World
and settled in the New. They had no portrait, nor curious chair,
nor rusty weapon—no old Bible, nor drinking cup, nor remnant
of brocade.

Morgeson—Born—Lived—Died—were all their archives. But there is a dignity in mere perpetuity, a strength in the narrowest affinities. This dignity and strength were theirs. They are still vital in our rural population. Occasionally something fine is their result; an aboriginal reappears to prove the plastic powers of nature.

My great-grandfather, Locke Morgeson, the old man whose head I saw bound in a red handkerchief, was the first noticeable man of the name. He was a scale of enthusiasms, ranging from the melancholy to the sarcastic. When I heard him talked of, it seemed to me that he was born under the influence of the sea, while the rest of the tribe inherited the character of the landscape. Comprehension of life, and comprehension of self, came too late for him to make either of value. The spirit of progress, however, which prompted his schemes benefited others. The most that could be said of him was that he had the rudiments of a Founder.

My father, whose name was Locke Morgeson also, married early. My mother was five years his elder; her maiden name was Mary Warren. She was the daughter of Philip Warren, of Barmouth, near Surrey. He was the best of the Barmouth tailors, though he never changed the cut of his garments; he was a rigidly pious man, of great influence in the church, and was descended from Sir Edward Warren, a gentleman of Devon, who was knighted by Queen Elizabeth. The name of his more immediate ancestor, Richard Warren, was in "New England's Memorial."[9] How father first met mother I know not. She was singularly beautiful—beautiful even to the day of her death; but she was poor, and without connection, for Philip Warren was the last of his name. What the Warrens might have been was nothing to the Morgesons; they themselves had no past, and only realized the present. They never thought of inquiring into that matter, so they opposed, with great promptness, father's wish to marry Mary Warren. All, except old Locke Morgeson, his grandfather, who rode over to Barmouth to see her one day, and when he came back told father to take her, offered him half his house to live in, and promised to push him in the world. His offer quelled the rioters, silencing in particular the opposition of John Morgeson, father's father.

In a month from this time, Locke Morgeson, Jr., took Mary Warren from her father's house as his wife. Grandfather Warren prayed a long, unintelligible prayer over them, helped them into the large, yellow-bottomed chaise which belonged to Grandfather Locke, and the young couple drove to their new home, the old mansion. Grandfather Locke went away in the same yellow-bottomed chaise a week after, and returned in a few days with a tall lady of fifty by his side—"Marm Tamor," a twig of the Morgeson tree, being his third cousin, whom he had married. This marriage was Grandfather Locke's last mistake. He was then near eighty, but lived long enough to fulfill his promises to father. The next year I was born, and four years after, my sister Veronica. Grandfather Locke named us, and charged father not to consult the Morgeson tombstones for names.

CHAPTER III.

"Mrs. Saunders," said mother, "don't let that soap boil over. Cassy, keep away from it."

"Lord," replied Mrs. Saunders, "there's no fat in the bones to bile. Cassy's grown dreadful fast, ain't she? How long has the old man been dead, Mis Morgeson?"

"Three years, Mrs. Saunders."

"How time do fly," remarked Mrs. Saunders, mopping her wrinkled face with a dark-blue handkerchief. "The winter's sass is hardly put in the cellar 'fore we have to cut off the sprouts, and up the taters for planting agin. We shall all foller him soon." And she stirred the bones in the great kettle with the vigor of an ogress.

When I heard her ask the question about Grandfather Locke, the interval that had elapsed since his death swept through my mind. What a little girl I was at the time! How much had since happened! But no thought remained with me long. I was about to settle whether I would go to the beach and wade, or into the woods for snake-flowers, till school-time, when my attention was again arrested by Mrs. Saunders saying, "I spose Marm Tamor went off with a large slice, and Mr. John Morgeson is mad to this day?"

Mother was prevented from answering by the appearance of the said Mr. John Morgeson, who darkened the threshold of the kitchen door, but advanced no further. I looked at him with curiosity; if he were mad, he might be interesting. He was a large, portly man, over sixty, with splendid black hair slightly grizzled, a prominent nose, and fair complexion. I did not like him, and determined not to speak to him.

"Say good-morning, Cassandra," said mother, in a low voice.

"No," I answered loudly, "I am not fond of my grandfather."

Mrs. Saunders mopped her face again, grinning with delight behind her handkerchief.

"Debby, my wife, wants you, Mis Saunders, after you have made Mary's soap," he said.

"Surely," she answered.

"Where is the black horse to-day?" he asked mother.

"Locke has gone to Milford with him."

"I wanted the black horse to-day," he said, turning away.

"He's a mighty grand man, he is," commented Mrs. Saunders. "I am pesky glad, Mis Morgeson, that you have never put foot in his house. I 'plaud your sperit!"

"School-time, Cassy," said mother. "Will you have some gingerbread to carry? Tell me when you come home what you have read in the New Testament."

"My boy does read beautiful," said Mrs. Saunders. "Where's the potash, Mis Morgeson?"

I heard the bell toll as I loitered along the roadside, pulling a dandelion here and there, for it was in the month of May, and throwing it in the rut for the next wheel to crush. When I reached the schoolhouse I saw through the open door that the New Testament exercise was over. The teacher, Mrs. Desire Cushman, a tall, slender woman, in a flounced calico dress, was walking up and down the room; a class of boys and girls stood in a zig-zag line before her, swaying to and fro, and drawling the multiplication table. She was yawning as I entered, which exercise forbade her speaking, and I took my seat without a reprimand. The flies were just coming; I watched their sticky legs as they feebly crawled over my old unpainted notched desk, and crumbled my gingerbread for them; but they seemed to have no appetite. Some of the younger children were drowsy already, lulled by the hum of the whisperers. Feeling very dull, I asked permission to go to the water-pail for a drink; let the tin cup fall into the water so that the floor might be splashed; made faces at the good scholars, and did what I could to make the time pass agreeably. At noon mother sent my dinner, with the request that I should stay till night, on account of my being in the way while the household was in the crisis of soap-making and whitewashing. I was exasperated, but I stayed. In the afternoon the minister came with two strangers to visit the school. I went through my lessons with dignified inaccuracy, and was commended. Going back, I happened to step on a loose board under my seat. I determined to punish Mrs. Desire for the unde-

served praise I had just received, and pushed the board till it clattered and made a dust. When Mrs. Desire detected me she turned
white with anger. I pushed it again, making so much noise that
the visitors turned to see the cause. She shook her head in my
direction, and I knew what was in store, as we had been at enmity
a long time, and she only waited for a decisive piece of mischief
on my part. As soon as the visitors had gone, she said in a loud
voice: "Cassandra Morgeson, take your books and go home. You
shall not come here another day."

I was glad to go, and marched home with the air of a conqueror,
going to the keeping-room where mother sat with a basket of
sewing. I saw Temperance Tinkham, the help,[10] a maiden of thirty,
laying the table for supper.

"Don't wrinkle the tablecloth," she said crossly; "and hang up
your bonnet in the entry, where it belongs," taking it from me as
she gave the order, and going out to hang it up herself.

"I am turned out of school, mother, for pushing a board with
my foot."

"Hi," said father, who was waiting for his supper; "come here,"
and he whistled to me. He took me on his knee, while mother
looked at me with doubt and sorrow.

"She is almost a woman, Mary."

"Locke, do you know that I am thirty-eight?"

"And you are thirty-three, father," I exclaimed. He looked
younger. I thought him handsome; he had a frank, firm face, an
abundance of light, curly hair, and was very robust. I took off his
white beaver hat, and pushed the curls away from his forehead. He
had his riding-whip in his hand. I took that, too, and snapped it
at our little dog, Kip. Father's clothes also pleased me—a lavender-
colored coat, with brass buttons, and trousers of the same color. I
mentally composed for myself a suit to match his, and thought
how well we should look calling at Lady Teazle's house in London,[11] only I was worried because my bonnet seemed to be too
large for me. A loud crash in the kitchen disturbed my dream, and
Temperance rushed in, dragging my sister Veronica, whose hair
was streaming with milk; she had pulled a panful over her from
the buttery shelf, while Temperance was taking up the supper.
Father laughed, but mother said:

"What have I done, to be so tormented by these terrible children?"

Her mild blue eyes blazed, as she stamped her foot and clenched her hands. Father took his hat and left the room. Veronica sat down on the floor, with her eyes fixed upon her, and I leaned against the wall. It was a gust that I knew would soon blow over. Veronica knew it also. At the right moment she cried out: "Help Verry, she is sorry."

"Do eat your supper," Temperance called out in a loud voice. "The hash is burnt to flinders."

She remained in the room to comment on our appetites, and encourage Veronica, who was never hungry, to eat.

Veronica was an elfish creature, nine years old, diminutive and pale. Her long, silky brown hair, which was as straight as an Indian's, like mother's, and which she tore out when angry, usually covered her face, and her wild eyes looked wilder still peeping through it. She was too strange-looking for ordinary people to call her pretty, and so odd in her behavior, so full of tricks, that I did not love her. She was a silent child, and liked to be alone. But whoever had the charge of her must be watchful. She tasted everything, and burnt everything, within her reach. A blazing fire was too strong a temptation to be resisted. The disappearance of all loose articles was ascribed to her; but nothing was said about it, for punishment made her more impish and daring in her pursuits. She had a habit of frightening us by hiding, and appearing from places where no one had thought of looking for her. People shook their heads when they observed her. The Morgesons smiled significantly when she was spoken of, and asked:

"Do you think she is like her mother?"

There was a conflict in mother's mind respecting Veronica. She did not love her as she loved me; but strove the harder to fulfill her duty. When Verry suffered long and mysterious illnesses, which made her helpless for weeks, she watched her day and night, but rarely caressed her. At other times Verry was left pretty much to herself and her ways, which were so separate from mine that I scarcely saw her. We grew up ignorant of each other's character, though Verry knew me better than I knew her; in time I discovered that she had closely observed me, when I was most unaware.

We began to prosper about this time.

"Old Locke Morgeson had a long head," people said, when they talked of our affairs. Father profited by his grandfather's plans, and his means, too; less visionary, he had modified and brought out practically many of his projections. Old Locke had left little to his son John Morgeson, in the belief that father was the man to carry out his ideas. Besides money, he left him a tract of ground running north and south, a few rods beyond the old house, and desired him to build upon it. This he was now doing, and we expected to move into our new house before autumn.

All the Morgesons wished to put money in a company, as soon as father could prove that it would be profitable. They were ready to own shares in the ships which he expected to build, when it was certain that they would make lucky voyages. He declined their offers, but they all "knuckled" to the man who had been bold enough to break the life-long stagnation of Surrey, and approved his plans as they matured. His mind was filled with the hope of creating a great business which should improve Surrey. New streets had been cut through his property and that of grandfather, who, narrow as he was, could not resist the popular spirit; lots had been laid out, and cottages had gone up upon them. To matters of minor importance father gave little heed; his domestic life was fast becoming a habit. The constant enlargement of his schemes was already a necessary stimulant.

I did not go back to Mrs. Desire's school. Mother said that I must be useful at home. She sent me to Temperance, and Temperance sent me to play, or told me to go "a visitin'." I did not care to visit, for in consequence of being turned out of school, which was considered an indelible disgrace and long remembered, my schoolmates regarded me in the light of a Pariah, and put on insufferably superior airs when they saw me. So, like Veronica, I amused myself, and passed days on the sea-shore, or in the fields and woods, mother keeping me in long enough to make a square of patchwork each day and to hear her read a Psalm—a duty which I bore with patience, by guessing when the "Selahs" would come in,[12] and counting them. But wherever I was, or whatever I did, no feeling of beauty ever stole into my mind. I never turned my face up to the sky to watch the passing of a cloud, or mused before the undulating space of sea, or looked down upon the earth with the curiosity of thought, or spiritual aspiration. I was moved and governed by my sensations, which continually changed, and passed away—to come again, and deposit vague ideas which ignorantly haunted me. The literal images of all things which I saw were impressed on my shapeless mind, to be reproduced afterward by faculties then latent. But what satisfaction was that? Doubtless the ideal faculty was active in Veronica from the beginning; in me it was developed by the experience of years. No remembrance of any ideal condition comes with the remembrance of my childish days, and I conclude that my mind, if I had any, existed in so rudimental a state that it had little influence upon my character.

CHAPTER IV.

One afternoon in the following July, tired of walking in the mown fields, and of carrying a nest of mice, which I had discovered under a hay-rick, I concluded I would begin a system of education with them; so arranging them on a grape-leaf, I started homeward. Going in by the kitchen, I saw Temperance wiping the dust from the best china, which elated me, for it was a sign that we were going to have company to tea.

"You evil child," she said, "where have you been? Your mother has wanted you these hours, to dress you in your red French calico with wings to it. Some of the members are coming to tea; Miss Seneth Jellatt, and she that was Clarissa Tripp, Snow now, and Miss Sophrony G. Dexter, and more besides."

I put my mice in a basket, and begged Temperance to allow me to finish wiping the china; she consented, adjuring me not to let it fall. "Mis Morgeson would die if any of it should be broken." I adored it, too. Each piece had a peach, or pear, or a bunch of cherries painted on it, in lustrous brown. The handles were like gold cords, and the covers had knobs of gilt grapes.

"What preserves are you going to put on the table?" I asked.

"Them West Ingy things Capen Curtis's son brought home, and quartered quince, though I expect Mis Dexter will remark that the surup is ropy."

"I wish you wouldn't have cheese."

"We *must* have cheese," she said solemnly. "I expect they'll drink our green tea till they make bladders of themselves, it is so good. Your father is a first-rate man; he is an excellent provider, and any woman ought to be proud of him, for he does buy number one in provisions."

I looked at her with admiration and respect.

"Capen Curtis," she continued, pursuing a train of thought which the preserves had started, "will never come home, I guess. He has been in furen parts forever and a day; his wife has looked for him, a-twirling her thumb and fingers, every day for ten years. I heard your mother had engaged her to go in the new house; she'll take the upper hand of us all. Your grandfather, Mr. John Morgeson, is willing to part with her; tired of her, I spose. She has been housekeeping there, off and on, these thirty years. She's fifty, if she is a day, is Hepsy Curtis."

"Is she as stingy as you are?" I asked.

"You'll find out for yourself, Miss. I rather think you won't be allowed to crumble over the buttery shelves."

I finished the cup, and was watching her while she grated loaf-sugar over a pile of doughnuts, when mother entered, and begged me to come upstairs with her to be dressed.

"Where is Verry, mother?"

"In the parlor, with a lemon in one hand and Robinson Crusoe in the other. She will be good, she says. Cassy, you won't teaze me to-day, will you?"

"No, indeed, mother," and clapping my hands, "I like you too well."

She laughed.

"These Morgesons beat the dogs," I heard Temperance say, as we shut the door and went upstairs.

I skipped over the shiny, lead-colored floor of the chamber in my stockings, while mother was taking from the bureau a clean suit for me, and singing "Bonny Doon,"[13] with the sweetest voice in the world. She soon arrayed me in my red calico dress, spotted with yellow stars. I was proud of its buckram undersleeves, though they scratched my arms, and admired its wings, which extended over the protecting buckram.

"It is three o'clock; the company will come soon. Be careful of your dress. You must stand by me at the table to hand the cups of tea."

She left me standing in a chair, so that I might see my pantalettes in the high-hung glass, and the effect of my balloon-like sleeves. Then I went back to the kitchen to show myself to Temperance, and to enjoy the progress of tea.

The table was laid in the long keeping-room adjoining the kitchen, covered with a striped cloth of crimson and blue, smooth as satin to the touch. Temperance had turned the plates upside-down around the table, and placed in a straight line through the middle a row of edibles. She was going to have waffles, she said, and shortcake; they were all ready to bake, and she wished to the Lord they would come and have it over with. With the silver sugar-tongs I slyly nipped lumps of sugar for my private eating, and surveyed my features in the distorting mirror of the pot-bellied silver teapot, ordinarily laid up in flannel. When the company had arrived, Temperance advised me to go in the parlor.

"Sit down, when you get there, and show less," she said. I went in softly, and stood behind mother's chair, slightly abashed for a moment in the presence of the party—some eight or ten ladies, dressed in black levantine, or cinnamon-colored silks, who were seated in rocking-chairs, all the rocking-chairs in the house having been carried to the parlor for the occasion. They were knitting, and every one had a square velvet workbag. Most of them wore lace caps, trimmed with white satin ribbon. They were larger, more rotund, and older than mother, whose appearance struck me by contrast. Perhaps it was the first time I observed her dress; her face I must have studied before, for I knew all her moods by it. Her long, lusterless, brown hair was twisted around a high-topped tortoise-shell comb; it was so heavy and so carelessly twisted that the comb started backward, threatening to fall out. She had minute rings of filigreed gold in her ears. Her dress was a gray pongee, simply made and short; I could see her round-toed morocco shoes, tied with black ribbon. She usually took out her shoestrings, not liking the trouble of tying them. A ruffle of fine lace fell around her throat, and the sleeves of her short-waisted dress were puffed at the shoulders. Her small white hands were folded in her lap, for she was idle; on the little finger of her left hand twinkled a brilliant garnet ring, set with diamonds. Her face was colorless, the forehead extremely low, the nose and mouth finely cut, the eyes of heavenly blue. Although youth had gone, she was beautiful, with an indescribable air of individuality. She influenced all who were near her; her atmosphere enveloped them. She was not aware of it, being too indifferent to the world to observe what effect she had in it, and only realized that she was to herself a self-tormentor. Whether she attracted or repelled, the power was the same. I make no attempt to analyze her character. I describe her as she appeared, and as my memory now holds her. I never understood her, and for that reason she attracted my attention. I felt puzzled now, she seemed so different from anybody else. My observation was next drawn to Veronica, who, entirely at home, walked up and down the room in a blue cambric dress. She was twisting in her fingers a fine gold chain, which hung from her neck. I caught her cunning glance as she flourished some tansy leaves before her face, imitating Mrs. Dexter to the life. I laughed, and she came to me.

"See," she said softly, "I have something from heaven." She lifed her white apron, and I saw under it, pinned to her dress, a splendid black butterfly, spotted with red and gold.

"It is mine," she said, "you shall not touch it. God blew it in through the window; but it has not breathed yet."

"Pooh; I have three mice in the kitchen."

"Where is the mother?"

"In the hayrick, I suppose, I left it there."

"I hate you," she said, in an enraged voice. "I would strike you, if it wasn't for this holy butterfly."

"Cassandra," said Mrs. Dexter, "does look like her pa; the likeness is ex-tri-ordinary. They say my William resembles me; but parients are no judges."

A faint murmur rose from the knitters, which signified agreement with her remark.

"I do think, " she continued, "that it is high time Dr. Snell had a colleague; he has outlived his usefulness. I never could say that I thought he was the right kind of man for our congregation; his principalls as a man I have nothing to say against; but *why* don't we have revivals?"

When Mrs. Dexter wished to be elegant she stepped out of the vernacular. She was about to speak again when the whole party broke into a loud talk on the subject she had started, not observing Temperance, who appeared at the door, and beckoned to mother. I followed her out.

"The members are goin' it, aint they?" she said. "Do see if things are about right, Mis Morgeson." Mother made a few deviations from the straight lines in which Temperance had ranged the viands, and told her to put the tea on the tray, and the chairs round the table.

"There's no place for Mr. Morgeson," observed Temperance.

"He is in Milford," mother replied.

"The brethren wont come, I spose, till after dark?"

"I suppose not."

"Glad to get rid of their wives' clack, I guess."

From the silence which followed mother's return to the parlor, I concluded they were performing the ancient ceremony of waiting for some one to go through the doorway first. They came at last with an air of indifference, as if the idea of eating had not yet occurred, and delayed taking seats till mother urged it; then they drew up to the table, hastily, turned the plates right-side up, spread

large silk handkerchiefs over their laps, and, with their eyes fixed
on space, preserved a dead silence, which was only broken by
mother's inquiries about their taste in milk or sugar. Temperance
came in with plates of waffles and buttered shortcake, which she
offered with a cut and thrust air, saying, as she did so, "I expect
you can't eat them; I know they are tough."

Everybody, however, accepted both. She then handed round the
preserves, and went out to bake more waffles.

By this time the cups had circled the table, but no one had tasted
a morsel.

"Do help yourselves," mother entreated, whereat they fell upon
the waffles.

"Temperance is as good a cook as ever," said one; "she is a
prize, isn't she, Mis Morgeson?"

"She is faithful and industrious," mother replied.

All began at once on the subject of help, and were as suddenly
quenched by the reappearance of Temperance, with fresh waffles,
and a dish of apple-fritters.

"Do eat these if you can, ladies; the apples are only russets, and
they are kinder dead for flavoring. I see you don't eat a mite; I
expected you could not; it's poor trash." And she passed the cake
along, everybody taking a piece of each kind.

After drinking a good many cups of tea, and praising it, their
asceticism gave way to its social effect, and they began to gossip,
ridiculing their neighbors, and occasionally launching innuendoes
against their absent lords. It is well known that when women meet
together they do not discuss their rights, but take them, in revealing the little weaknesses and peculiarities of their husbands. The
worst wife-driver would be confounded at the air of easy superiority assumed on these occasions by the meekest and most un-
suspicious of her sex. Insinuations of So and So's not being any
better than she should be passed from mouth to mouth, with a
glance at me; and I heard the proverb of "Little pitchers," when
mother rose suddenly from the table, and led the way to the parlor.

"Where is Veronica?" asked Temperance, who was piling the
débris of the feast. "She has been in mischief, I'll warrant; find her,
Cassandra."

She was upstairs putting away her butterfly, in the leaves of her
little Bible. She came down with me, and Temperance coaxed her
to eat her supper, by vowing that she should be sick abed, unless
she liked her fritters and waffles. I thought of my mice, while

making a desultory meal standing, and went to look at them; they were gone. Wondering if Temperance had thrown the creatures away, I remembered that I had been foolish enough to tell Veronica, and rushed back to her. When she saw me, she raised a saucer to her face, pretending to drink from it.

"Verry, where are the mice?"

"Are they gone?"

"Tell me."

"What will you do if I don't?"

"I know," and I flew upstairs, tore the poor butterfly from between the leaves of the Bible, crushed it in my hand, and brought it down to her. She did not cry when she saw it, but choked a little, and turned away her head.

It was now dark, and hearing a bustle in the entry I looked out, and saw several staid men slowly rubbing their feet on the door-mat; the husbands had come to escort their wives home, and by nine o'clock they all went. Veronica and I stayed by the door after they had gone.

"Look at Mrs. Dexter," she said; "I put the mice in her work-bag."

I burst into a laugh, which she joined in presently.

"I am sorry about the butterfly, Verry." And I attemped to take her hand, but she pushed me away, and marched off whistling.

A few days after this, sitting near the window at twilight, intent upon a picture in a book of travels, of a Hindoo swinging from a high pole with hooks in his flesh, and trying to imagine how much it hurt him, my attention was arrested by a mention of my name in a conversation held between mother and Mr. Park, one of the neighbors. He occasionally spent an evening at our house, passing it in polemical discussion, revising the prayers and exhortations which he made at conference meetings. The good man was a little vain of having the formulas of his creed at his tongue's end. She sometimes lost the thread of his discourse, but argued also as if to convince herself that she could rightly distinguish between Truth and Illusion, but never discussed religious topics with father. Like all the Morgesons, he was Orthodox, accepting what had been provided by others for his spiritual accommodation. He thought it well that existing Institutions should not be disturbed. "Something worse might be established instead." His turn of mind, in short, was not Evangelical.

"Are the Hindoos in earnest, mother?" and I thrust the picture before her. She warned me off.

"Do you think, Mr. Park, that Cassandra can understand the law of transgression?"

An acute perception that it was in my power to escape a moral penalty, by willful ignorance, was revealed to me, that I could continue the privilege of sinning with impunity. His answer was complicated, and he quoted several passages from the Scriptures. Presently he began to sing, and I grew lonesome; the life within me seemed a black cave.

> "Our nature's totally depraved—
>   The heart a sink of sin;
>   Without a change we can't be saved,
>   Ye must be born again."[14]

Temperance opened the door. "Is Veronica going to bed to-night?" she asked.

CHAPTER V.

The next September we moved. Our new house was large and handsome. On the south side there was nothing between it and the sea, except a few feet of sand. No tree or shrub intercepted the view. To the eastward a promontory of rocks jutted into the sea, serving as a pier against the wash of the tide, and adding a picturesqueness to the curve of the beach. On the north side flourished an orchard, which was planted by Grandfather Locke. Looking over the tree-tops from the upper north windows, one would have had no suspicion of being in the neighborhood of the sea. From these windows, in winter, we saw the nimbus of the Northern Light. The darkness of our sky, the stillness of the night, mysteriously reflected the perpetual condition of its own solitary world. In summer ragged white clouds rose above the horizon, as if they had been torn from the sky of an underworld, to sail up the blue heaven, languish away, or turn livid with thunder, and roll off seaward. Between the orchard and the house a lawn sloped easterly to the border of a brook, which straggled behind the outhouses into a meadow, and finally lost itself among the rocks on the shore. Up by the lawn a willow hung over it, and its outer bank was fringed by the tangled wild-grape, sweet-briar, and alder bushes. The premises, except on the seaside, were enclosed by a high wall of rough granite. No houses were near us, on either side of the shore; up the north road they were scattered at intervals.

Mother said I must be considered a young lady, and should have my own room. Veronica was to have one opposite, divided from it by a wide passage. This passage extended beyond the angle of the stairway, and was cut off by a glass door. A wall ran across the lower end of the passage; half the house was beyond its other side, so that when the door was fastened, Veronica and myself were in a cul-de-sac.

The establishment was put on a larger footing. Mrs. Hepsey Curtis was installed mistress of the kitchen. Temperance declared that she could not stand it; that she wasn't a nigger; that she must go, but she had no home, and no friends—nothing but a wood lot, which was left her by her father the miller. As the trees thereon grew, promising to make timber, its value increased; at present her income was limited to the profit from the annual sale of a cord or two of wood. So she staid on, in spite of Hepsey. There were also two men for the garden and stable. A boy was always attached to the house; not the same boy, but a Boy dynasty, for as soon as one went another came, who ate a great deal—a crime in Hepsey's eyes—and whose general duty was to carry armfuls of wood, pails of milk, or swill, and to shut doors.

We had many visitors. Though father had no time to devote to guests, he was continually inviting people for us to entertain, and his invitations were taken as a matter of course, and finally for granted. A rich Morgeson was a new feature in the family annals, and distant relations improved the advantage offered them by coming to spend the summer with us, because their own houses were too hot, or the winter, because they were too cold! Infirm old ladies, who were not related to us, but who had nowhere else to visit, came. As his business extended, our visiting list extended. The captains of his ships whose homes were elsewhere brought their wives to be inconsolable with us after their departure on their voyages. We had ministers often, who always quarter at the best houses, and chance visitors to dinner and supper, who made our house a way-station. There was but small opportunity to cultivate family affinities; they were forever disturbed. Somebody was always sitting in the laps of our Lares and Penates.[15] Another class of visitors deserving notice were those who preferred to occupy the kitchen and back chambers, humbly proud and bashfully arrogant people, who kept their hats and bonnets by them, and small bundles, to delude themselves and us with the idea that they "had not come to stay, and had no occasion for any attention." These people criticised us with insinuating severity, and proposed amendments with unrelenting affability. To this class Veronica was most attracted—it repelled me; consequently she was petted, and I was amiably sneered at.

This period of our family life has left small impression of dramatic interest. There was no development of the sentiments, no betrayal of the fluctuations of the passions which must have existed. There was no accident to reveal, no coincidence to surprise us. Hidden among the Powers That Be, which rule New England, lurks the Deity of the Illicit. This Deity never obtained sovereignty in the atmosphere where the Morgesons lived. Instead of the impression which my after-experience suggests to me to seek, I recall arrivals and departures, an eternal smell of cookery, a perpetual changing of beds, and the small talk of vacant minds.

Despite the rigors of Hepsey in the kitchen, and the careful supervision of Temperance, there was little systematic housekeeping. Mother had severe turns of planning, and making rules, falling upon us in whirlwinds of reform, shortly allowing the band of habit to snap back, and we resumed our former condition. She had no assistance from father in her ideas of change. It was enough for him to know that he had built a good house to shelter us, and to order the best that could be bought for us to eat and to wear. He liked, when he went where there were fine shops, to buy and bring home handsome shawls, bonnets, and dresses, wholly unsuited in general to the style and taste of each of us, but much handsomer than were needful for Surrey. They answered, however, as patterns for the plainer materials of our neighbors. He also bought books for us, recommended by their covers, or the opinion of the bookseller. His failing was to buy an immense quantity of everything he fancied.

"I shall never have to buy this thing again," he would say; "let us have enough."

Veronica and I grew up ignorant of practical or economical ways. We never saw money, never went shopping. Mother was indifferent in regard to much of the business of ordinary life which children are taught to understand. Father and mother both stopped at the same point with us, but for a different reason; father, because he saw nothing beyond the material, and mother, because her spiritual insight was confused and perplexing. But whatever a household may be, the Destinies spin the web to their will, out of the threads which drop hither and thither, floating in its atmosphere, white, black, or gray.

From the time we moved, however, we were a stirring, cheerful family, independent of each other, but spite of our desultory tastes, mutual habits were formed. When the want of society was felt, we sought the dining-room, sure of meeting others with the same want. This room was large and central, connecting with the halls, kitchen, and mother's room. It was a caravansary where people dropped in and out on their way to some other place. Our most public moments were during meal-time. It was known that father was at home at breakfast and supper, and could be consulted. As he was away at our noonday dinner, generally we were the least disturbed then, and it was a lawless, irregular, and unceremonious affair. Mother established her arm-chair here, and a stand for her workbasket. Hepsey and Temperance were at hand, the men came for orders, and it was convenient for the boy to transmit the local intelligence it was his vocation to collect. The windows commanded a view of the sea, the best in the house. This prospect served mother for exercise. Her eyes roved over it when she wanted a little out-of-doors life. If she desired more variety, which was seldom, she went to the kitchen. After we moved she grew averse to leaving the house, except to go to church. She never quitted the dining-room after our supper till bedtime, because father rarely came from Milford, where he went on bank days, and indeed almost every other day, till late, and she liked to be by him while he ate his supper and smoked a cigar. All except Veronica frequented this room; but she was not missed or inquired for. She liked the parlor, because the piano was there. As soon as father had bought it she astonished us by a persistent fingering of the keys, which produced a feeble melody. She soon played all the airs she had heard. When I saw what she could do, I refused to take music lessons, for while I was trying to learn "The White Cockade," she pushed me away, played it, and made variations upon it. I pounded the keys with my fist, by way of a farewell, and told her she should have the piano for her own.

CHAPTER VI.

One winter morning before daylight, Veronica came to my room, and asked me if I had heard any walking about the house during the night. She had, and was going to inquire about it. She soon returned with, "You have a brother. Temperance says my nose is broken. He will be like you, I suppose, and have everything he asks for. I don't care for him; but," crying out with passion, "get up. Mother wants to see *you*, I know."

I dressed quickly, and went downstairs with a feeling of indignation that such an event should have happened without my knowledge.

There was an unwonted hush. A bright fire was burning on the dining-room hearth, the lamps were still lighted, and father was by the fire, smoking in a meditative manner. He put out his hand, which I did not take, and said, "Do you like his name—Arthur?"

"Yes," I mumbled, as I passed him, and went to the kitchen, where Hepsey and Temperance were superintending the steeping of certain aromatic herbs, which stood round the fire in silver porringers and earthern pitchers.

"Another Morgeson's come," said Temperance. "There's enough of them, such as they are—not but what they are good enough," correcting herself hastily.

"Go into your mother's room, softly," said Hepsey, rubbing her fingers against her thumb—her habit when she was in a tranquil frame of mind.

"*You* are mighty glad, Hepsey," said Temperance.

"Locke Morgeson ought to have a son," she replied, "to leave his money to."

"I vow," answered Temperance, "girls are thought nothing of in this 'ligous section; they may go to the poor house, as long as the sons have plenty."

An uncommon fit of shyness seized me, mixed with a feeling of dread, as I crept into the room where mother was. My eyes first fell upon an elderly woman, who wore a long, wide, black apron, whose strings girded the middle of her cushion-like form. She was taking snuff. It was the widow Mehitable Allen, a lady whom I had often seen in other houses on similar occasions.

"Shoo," she whispered nasally.

I was arrested, but turned my eyes toward mother; hers were

closed. Presently she murmured, "Thank God," opened them, and saw me. A smile lighted her pale countenance. "Cassy, my darling, kiss me. I am glad it is not a woman." As I returned her kiss her glance dropped on a small bunch by her side, which Mehitable took and deftly unrolled, informing me as she did so that it was a "Rouser."

Aunt Mercy came the next day. She had not paid us a visit in a long time, being confined at home with the care of her father, Grandfather Warren. She took charge of Veronica and me, if taking charge means a series of guerilla skirmishes on both sides. I soon discovered, however, that she was prone to laughter, and that I could provoke it; we got on better after that discovery; but Veronica, disdaining artifice, was very cross with her. Aunt Mercy had a spark of fun in her composition, which was not quite crushed out by her religious education. She frequented the church oftener than mother, sang more hymns, attended all the anniversary celebrations, but she had no dreams, no enthusiasm. Her religion had leveled all needs and all aspirations. What the day brought forth answered her. She inspired me with a secret pity; for I knew she carried in her bosom the knowledge that she was an old maid.

Before mother left her room Veronica was taken ill, and was not convalescent till spring. Delicacy of constitution the doctor called her disorder. She had no strength, no appetite, and looked more elfish than ever. She would not stay in bed, and could not sit up, so father had a chair made for her, in which she could recline comfortably. Aunt Merce put her in it every morning, and took her out every evening. My presence irritated her, so I visited her but seldom. She said I looked so well, it hurt her, and wished me to keep out of her sight, begged me never to talk loud in the vicinity of her room, my voice was so breezy. She amused herself in her own strange way. One of her amusements was to cut off her hair, lock by lock, and cut it short before she was well enough to walk about. She played on a jewsharp, and on a little fife when her breath permitted, and invented grotesque costumes out of bits of silk and lace. Temperance was much engaged, at her dictation, in the composition of elaborate dishes, which she rarely ate, but forced Temperance to. She was more patient with her than any other person; with us she was excessively high-tempered, especially with father. She could not bear to catch a glimpse of the sea, not to hear it; if she heard it echoing in the house, she played on her fife, or jewsharp, or asked Aunt Merce to sing some old song.

But she liked the view from the north windows, even when the boughs were bare and the fields barren. When the grass came, she ordered handfuls to be brought her and put in saucers of water. With the coming of the blossoms she began to mend. As for me, I was as much an animal as ever—robust in health—inattentive, and seeking excitement and exhilaration. I went everywhere, to Bible class, to Sunday school, and to every funeral which took place within our precincts. But I never looked upon the dead; perhaps that sight would have marred the slumbrous security which possessed me—the instinctive faith in the durability of my own powers of life.

But a change was approaching. Aunt Merce considered my present state a hopeless one. She was outside the orbit of the family planet, and saw the tendency of its revolutions, perceiving that father and mother were absorbed in their individual affairs. She called mother's attention to my non-improvement, and proposed that I should return to Barmouth with her for a year, and become a pupil in a young lady's school, which had been recently established there, by a graduate of the Nipswich Female Seminary, a school distinguished for its ethics. Mother looked astonished, when she heard this proposal. "What!" she began with vehemence, "shall I subject"—but checked herself when she caught my eye, and continued more calmly: "We will decide soon."

It was decided that I should go, without my being consulted in the matter. I felt resentful against mother, and could not understand till afterward, why she had consented to the plan. It was because she wished me to comprehend the influences of her early life, and learn some of the lessons she had been taught. At first, father "poohed" at the plan, but finally said it was a good place to tame me. When Veronica heard that I was going, she told me that I would be stifled, if I lived at Grandfather Warren's; but added that the plums in his garden were good, and advised me to sit on the yellow stone doorstep, under which the toads lived. She also informed me that she was glad of it, and hoped I would stay forever.

To Barmouth I went, and in May entered Miss Black's genteel school. Miss Black had a conviction that her vocation was teaching. Necessity did not compel it, for she was connected with one of the richest families in Barmouth. At the end of the week my curiosity regarding my new position was quenched, and I dropped into the depths of my first wretchedness. I frantically demanded of father, who had stopped to see me on his way to Milford, to be taken home. He firmly resisted me. Once a month, I should go home and spend a Sunday, if I chose, and he would come to Barmouth every week.

My agitation and despair clouded his face for a moment, then it cleared, and pinching my chin, he said, "Why don't you look like your mother?"

"But she *is* like her mother," said Aunt Merce.

"Well, Cassy, good-by"; and he gave me a kiss with cruel nonchalance. I knew my year must be stayed out.

CHAPTER VII.

My life at Grandfather Warren's was one kind of penance and my life in Miss Black's school another. Both differed from our home-life. My filaments found no nourishment, creeping between the two; but the fibers of youth are strong, and they do not perish. Grandfather Warren's house reminded me of the casket which imprisoned the Genii. I had let loose a Presence I had no power over—the embodiment of its gloom, its sternness, and its silence.

With feeling comes observation; after that, one reasons. I began to observe. Aunt Mercy was not the Aunt Merce I had known at home. She wore a mask before her father. There was constraint between them; each repressed the other. The result of this relation was a formal, petrifying, unyielding system,—a system which, from the fact of its satisfying neither, was kept up the more rigidly; on the one side from a morbid conscience, which reiterated its monitions against the dictates of the natural heart; on the other, out of respect and timidity.

Grandfather Warren was a little, lean, leather-colored man. His head was habitually bent, his eyes cast down; but when he raised them to peer about, their sharpness and clear intelligence gave his face a wonderful vitality. He chafed his small, well-shaped hands continually; his long polished nails clicked together with a shelly noise, like that which beetles make flying against the ceiling. His features were delicate and handsome; gentle blood ran in his veins, as I have said. All classes in Barmouth treated him with invariable courtesy. He was aboriginal in character, not to be moved by antecedent or changed by innovation—a Puritan, without gentleness or tenderness. He scarcely concealed his contempt for the emollients of life, or for those who needed them. He whined over no misfortune, pined for no pleasure. His two sons, who broke loose from him, went into the world, lived a wild, merry life, and died there, he never named. He found his wife dead by his side one morning. He did not go frantic, but selected a text for the funeral sermon; and when he stood by the uncovered grave, took off his hat and thanked his friends for their kindness with a loud, steady voice. Aunt Mercy told me that after her mother's death his habit of chafing his hands commenced; it was all the difference she saw in him, for he never spoke of his trouble or acknowledged his grief by sign or word.

Though he had been frugal and industrious all his life, he had no more property than the old, rambling house we lived in, and a long, narrow garden attached to it, where there were a few plum and quince trees, a row of currant bushes, Aunt Mercy's beds of chamomile and sage, and a few flowers. At the end of the garden was a peaked-roof pigsty; it was cleanly kept, and its inhabitant had his meals served with the regularity which characterized all that Grandfather Warren did. Beautiful pigeons lived in the roof, and were on friendly terms with the occupant on the lower floor. The house was not unpicturesque. It was built on a corner, facing two streets. One front was a story high, with a slanting roof; the other, which was two-storied, sloped like a giraffe's back, down to a wood-shed. Clean cobwebs hung from its rafters, and neat heaps of fragrant chips were piled on the floor.

The house had many rooms, all more or less dark and irregularly shaped. The construction of the chambers was so involved, I could not get out of one without going into another. Some of the ceilings slanted suddenly, and some so gradually that where I could stand erect, and where I must stoop, I never remembered, until my head was unpleasantly grazed, or my eyes filled with flakes of ancient lime-dust. A long chamber in the middle of the house was the shop, always smelling of woolen shreds. At sunset, summer or winter, Aunt Mercy sprinkled water on the unpainted floor, and swept it. While she swept I made my thumb sore, by snipping the bits of cloth that were scattered on the long counter by the window with Grand'ther's shears, or I scrawled figures with gray chalk, where I thought they might catch his eye. When she had finished sweeping she carefully sorted the scraps, and put them into boxes under the counter; then she neatly rolled up the brown-paper curtains, which had been let down to exclude the afternoon sun; shook the old patchwork cushions in the osier-bottomed chairs;

watered the rose-geranium and the monthly rose, which flourished wonderfully in that fluffy atmosphere; set every pin and needle in its place, and shut the door, which was opened again at sunrise. Of late years, Grand'ther's occupation had declined. No new customers came. A few, who did not change the fashion of their garb, still patronized him. His income was barely three hundred dollars a year—eked out to this amount by some small pay for offices connected with the church, of which he was a prominent member. From this income he paid his pulpit tithe, gave to the poor, and lived independent and respectable. Mother endeavored in an unobtrusive way to add to his comfort; but he would only accept a few herrings from the Surrey Weir every spring, and a basket of apples every fall. He invariably returned her presents by giving her a share of his plums and quinces.

I had only seen Grand'ther Warren at odd intervals. He rarely came to our house; when he did, he rode down on the top of the Barmouth stagecoach, returning in a few hours. As mother never liked to go to Barmouth, she seldom came to see me.

CHAPTER VIII.

It was five o'clock on Saturday afternoon when father left me. Aunt Mercy continued her preparations for tea, and when it was ready, went to the foot of the stairs, and called, "Supper." Grand'ther came down immediately followed by two tall, cadaverous women, Ruth and Sally Aikin, tailoresses, who sewed for him spring and fall. Living several miles from Barmouth, they stayed through the week, going home on Saturday night, to return on Monday morning. We stood behind the heavy oak chairs round the table, one of which Grand'ther tipped backward, and said a long grace, not a word of which was heard; for his teeth were gone, and he prayed in his throat. Aunt Mercy's "Moltee" rubbed against me, with her back and tail erect. I pinched the latter, and she gave a wail. Aunt Mercy passed her hand across her mouth, but the eyes of the two women were stony in their sockets. Grand'ther ended his grace with an upward jerk of his head as we seated ourselves. He looked sharply at me, his gray eyebrows rising hair by hair, and shaking a spoon at me said, "You are playing over your mother's capers."

"The caper-bush grows on the shores of the Mediterranean sea,

Grand'ther. Miss Black had it for a theme, out of the *Penny Maga-zine*;[16] it is full of themes."

"She had better give you a gospel theme."

He was as inarticulate when he quoted Scripture as when he prayed, but I heard something about "thorns"; then he helped us to baked Indian pudding—our invariable Saturday night's repast. Aunt Mercy passed cups of tea; I heard the gulping swallow of it in every throat, the silence was so profound. After the pudding we had dried apple-pie, which we ate from our hands, like bread. Grand'ther ate fast, not troubling himself to ask us if we would have more, but making the necessary motions to that effect by touching the spoon in the pudding or knife on the pie. Ruth and Sally still kept their eyes fixed on some invisible object at a dis-tance. What a disagreeable interest I felt in them! What had they in common with me? What could they enjoy? How unpleasant their dingy, crumbled, needle-pricked fingers were! Sally hiccoughed, and Ruth suffered from internal rumblings. Without waiting for each other when we had finished, we put our chairs against the wall and left the room. I rushed into the garden and trampled the chamomile bed. I had heard that it grew faster for being subjected to that process, and thought of the two women I had just seen while I crushed the spongy plants. Had *they* been trampled upon? A feeling of pity stung me; I ran into the house, and found them on the point of departure, with little bundles in their hands.

"Aunt Mercy will let me carry your bundles a part of the way for you; shall I?"

"No indeed," said Ruth, in a mild voice; "there's no heft in them; they are mites to carry."

"Besides," chimed Sally, "you couldn't be trusted with them."

"Are they worth anything?" I inquired, noticing then that both wore better dresses, and that the bundles contained their shop-gowns.

"What made you pinch the moltee's tail?" asked Sally. "If you pinched my cat's tail, I would give you a sound whipping."

"How could she, Sally," said Ruth, "when our cat's tail is cut short off?"

"For all the world," remarked Sally, "that's the only way she can be managed. If things are cut off, and kept out of sight, or never mentioned before her, she may behave very well; not other-wise."

"Good-by, Miss Ruth, and Sally, good-by," modulating my voice to accents of grief, and making a "cheese."[17]

They retreated with a less staid pace than usual, and I sought Aunt Mercy, who was preparing the Sunday's dinner. Twilight drew near, and the Sunday's clouds began to fall on my spirits. Between sundown and nine o'clock was a tedious interval. I was not allowed to go to bed, nor to read a secular book, or to amuse myself with anything. A dim oil-lamp burned on the high shelf of the middle room, our ordinary gathering-place. Aunt Mercy sat there, rocking in a low chair; the doors were open, and I wandered softly about. The smell of the garden herbs came in faintly, and now and then I heard a noise in the water-butt under the spout, the snapping of an old rafter, or something falling behind the wall. The toads crawled from under the plantain leaves, and hopped across the broad stone before the kitchen door, and the irreverent cat, with whom I sympathized, raced like mad in the grass. Growing duller, I went to the cellar door, which was in the front entry, opened it, and stared down in the black gulf, till I saw a gray rock rise at the foot of the stairs which affected my imagination. The foundation of the house was on the spurs of a great granite bed, which rose from the Surrey shores, dipped and cropped out in the center of Barmouth. It came through the ground again in the woodhouse, smooth and round, like the bald head of some old Titan, and in the border of the garden it burst through in narrow ridges full of seams. As I contemplated the rock, and inhaled a moldy atmosphere whose component parts were charcoal and potatoes, I heard the first stroke of the nine o'clock bell, which hung in the belfry of the church across the street. Although it was so near us that we could hear the bellrope whistle in its grooves, and its last hoarse breath in the belfry, there was no reverberation of its clang in the house; the rock under us struck back its voice. It was an old Spanish bell, Aunt Mercy told me. How it reached Barmouth she did not know. I recognized its complaining voice afterward. It told me it could never forget it had been baptized a Catholic; and it pined for the beggar who rang it in the land of fan-leaved chestnuts! It would growl and strangle as much as possible in the hands of Benjamin Beals, the bell-ringer and coffin-maker of Barmouth. Except in the morning when it called me up, I was glad to hear it. It was the signal of time past; the oftener I heard it, the nearer I was to the end of my year. Before it ceased to ring now Aunt Mercy called me in a low voice. I returned to the middle room, and took a seat in one of the oak chairs, whose back of upright rods was my nightly penance. Aunt Mercy took the lamp from the shelf, and placed it upon a small oak stand, where the Bible lay. Grand'ther entered, and sitting by the stand read a chapter. His voice was like opium. Presently my head rolled across the rods, and I felt conscious of slipping down the glassy seat. After he had read the chapter he prayed. If the chapter had been long, the prayer was short; if the chapter had been short, the prayer was long. When he had ceased praying, he left the room without speaking, and betook himself to bed. Aunt Mercy dragged me up the steep stairs, undressed me, and I crept into bed, drugged with a monotony which served but to deepen the sleep of youth and health. When the bell rang the next morning, Aunt Mercy gave me a preparatory shake before she began to dress, and while she walked up and down the room lacing her stays entreated me to get up.

If the word lively could ever be used in reference to our life, it might be in regard to Sunday. The well was so near the church that the house was used as an inn for the accommodation of the church-goers who lived at any distance, and who did not return home between the morning and afternoon services. A regular set took dinner with us, and there were parties who brought lunch, which they ate off their handkerchiefs, on their knees. It was also a watering-place for the Sunday-school scholars, who filed in troops before the pail in the well-room, and drank from the cocoanut dipper. When the weather was warm our parlor was open, as it was to-day. Aunt Mercy had dusted it and ornamented the hearth with bunches of lilacs in a broken pitcher. Twelve yellow chairs, a mahogany stand, a dark rag-carpet, some speckled Pacific sea-shells on the shelf, among which stood a whale's tooth with a drawing of a cranky ship thereon, and an ostrich's egg that hung by a string from the ceiling, were the adornments of the room. When we were dressed for church, we looked out of the window till the bell tolled, and the chaise of the Baxters and Sawyers had driven to the gate; then we went ourselves. Grand'ther had preceded us, and was already in his seat. Aunt Mercy went up to the head of the pew, a little out of breath, from the tightness of her dress, and the ordeal of the Baxter and Sawyer eyes, for the pew, though off a side aisle, was in the neighborhood of the élite of the church; a clove, however, tranquilized her. I fixed my feet on a cricket, and examined the bonnets. The house filled rapidly, and last of all the minister entered. The singers began an anthem, singing in an advanced style of the art, I observed, for they shouted "*Armen*," while our singers in Surrey bellowed "*Amen.*" When the sermon began I settled myself into a vague speculation concerning my future days of freedom; but my dreams were disturbed by the conduct of the Hickspold boys, who were in a pew in front of us. As in the morning, so in the afternoon and all the Sundays in the year. The variations of the season served but to deepen the uniformity of my heartsickness.

CHAPTER IX.

Aunt Mercy had not introduced me to Miss Black as the daughter of Locke Morgeson, the richest man in Surrey, but simply as her niece. Her pride prevented her from making any exhibition of my antecedents, which was wise, considering that I had none. My grandfather, John Morgeson, was a nobody,—merely a "Co."; and though my great-grandfather, Locke Morgeson, was worthy to be called a Somebody, it was not his destiny to make a stir in the world. Many of the families of my Barmouth schoolmates had the fulcrum of a moneyed grandfather. The knowledge of the girls did not extend to that period in the family history when its patriarchs started in the pursuit of Gain. Elmira Sawyer, one of Miss Black's pupils, never heard that her grandfather "Black Peter," as he was called, had made excursions, in an earlier part of his life, on the River Congo, or that he was familiar with the soundings of Loango Bay. As he returned from his voyages, bringing more and more money, he enlarged his estate, and grew more and more respectable, retiring at last from the sea, to become a worthy landsman; he paid taxes to church and state, and even had a silver communion cup, among the pewter service used on the occasion of the Lord's Supper; but he never was brought to the approval of that project of the Congregational Churches,—the colonization of the Blacks to Liberia.[18] Neither was Hersila Allen aware that the pink calico in which I first saw her was remotely owing to West India Rum. Nor did Charlotte Alden, the proudest girl in school, know that her grandfather's, Squire Alden's, stepping-stone to fortune was the loss of the brig *Capricorn*, which was wrecked in the vicinity of a comfortable port, on her passage out to the whaling-ground. An auger had been added to the meager outfit, and long after the sea had leaked through the hole bored through her bottom, and swallowed her, and the insurance had been paid, the truth leaked out that the captain had received instructions, which had been fulfilled. Whereupon two Insurance Companies went to law with him, and a suit ensued, which ended in their paying costs, in addition to what they had before paid Squire Alden, who winked in a derisive manner at the Board of Directors when he received its check.

There were others who belonged in the category of Decayed Families, as exclusive as they were shabby. There were parvenus, which included myself. When I entered the school it was divided into clans, each with its spites, jealousies, and emulations. Its *esprit de corps*, however, was developed by my arrival; the girls united against me, and though I perceived, when I compared myself with them, that they were partly right in their opinions, their ridicule stupefied and crushed me. They were trained, intelligent, and adroit; I uncouth, ignorant, and without tact. It was impossible for Miss Black not to be affected by the general feeling in regard to me. Her pupils knew sooner than I that she sympathized with them. She embarrassed me, when I should have despised her. At first her regimen surprised, then filled me with a dumb, clouded anger, which made me appear apathetic.

Miss Emily Black was a young woman, and, I thought, a hand-some one. She had crenelated black hair, large black eyes, a Roman nose, and long white teeth. She bit her nails when annoyed, and when her superiority made her perceive the mental darkness of others she often laughed. Being pious, she conducted her school after the theologic pattern of the Nipswich Seminary, at which she had been educated. She opened the school each day with a religious exercise, reading something from the Bible, and commenting upon it, or questioning us regarding our ideas of what she read. She often selected the character of David, and was persistent in her efforts to explain and reconcile the discrepancies in the history of the royal Son of Israel.

"Miss C. Morgeson, we will call you," she said, in our first interview; "the name of Cassandra is too peculiar."

"My Grandfather Locke liked the name; my sister's is Veronica; do you like that better?"

"It is of no consequence in the premises what your sister may be named," she replied, runing her eyes over me. "What will she study, Miss Warren?"

Aunt Mercy's recollections of my studies were dim, and her knowledge of my school days was not calculated to prepossess a teacher in my favor; but after a moment's delay, she said: "What you think best."

"Very well," she answered; "I will endeavor to fulfill my Christian duty toward her. We will return to the schoolroom."

We had held the conversation in the porch, and now Aunt Mercy gave me a nod of encouragement, and bidding Miss Black "Good day," departed, looking behind her as long as possible. I followed my teacher. As she opened the door forty eyes were leveled at me; my hands were in my way suddenly; my feet impeded my progress; how could I pass that wall of eyes? A wisp of my dry, rough hair fell on my neck and tickled it; as I tried to poke it under my comb, I glanced at the faces before me. How spirited and delicate they were! The creatures had their heads dressed as if they were at a party—in curls or braids and ribbons. An open, blank, *noli me tangere*[19] expression met my perturbed glance. I stood still, but my head went round. Miss Black mounted her desk, and surveyed the schoolroom. "Miss Charlotte Alden, the desk next you is vacant; Miss C. Morgeson, the new pupil, may take it."

Miss Charlotte answered, "Yes mim," and ostentatiously swept away an accumulation of pencils, sponges, papers, and books, to make room for me. I took the seat, previously stumbling against her, whereat all the girls, whose regards were fixed upon me, smiled. That was my initiation.

The first day I was left to myself, to make studies. The schoolroom was in the vestry of the church, a building near grand'ther's house. Each girl had a desk before her. Miss Black occupied a high stool in a square box, where she heard single recitations, or lectured a pupil. The vestry yard, where the girls romped, and exercised with skipping ropes, a swing, and a set of tilting-boards, commanded a view of grand'ther's premises; his street windows were exposed to the fire of their eyes and tongues.

After I went home I examined myself in the glass, and drew an unfavorable conclusion from the inspection. My hair was parted zigzag; one shoulder was higher than the other; my dress came up to my chin, and slipped down to my shoulder-blades. I was all waist; no hips were developed; my hands were red, and my nails chipped. I opened the trunk where my wardrobe was packed; what belonged to me was comfortable, in reference to weather and the wash, but not pretty. I found a molasses-colored silk, called Turk satin—one of mother's old dresses, made over for me, or an invidious selection of hers from the purchases of father, who sometimes made a mistake in taste, owing to the misrepresentations of shopkeepers and milliners. While thus engaged Aunt Mercy came for me, and began to scold when she saw that I had tumbled my clothes out of the trunk.

"Aunt Mercy, these things are horrid, all of them. Look at this shawl," and I unrolled a square silk fabric, the color of a sick orange. "Where did this come from?"

"Saints upon earth!" she exclaimed, "your father bought it at the best store in New York. It was costly."

"Now tell me, why do the pantalettes of those girls look so graceful? They do not twirl round the ankle like a rope, as mine do."

"I can't say," she answered, with a sigh. "But you ought to wear long dresses; now yours are tucked, and could be let down."

"And these red prunella boots—they look like boiled crabs." I put them on, and walked round the room crab-fashion, till she laughed hysterically. "Miss Charlotte Alden wears French kid slippers every day, and I must wear mine."

"No," she said, "you must only wear them to church."

"I shall talk to father about that, when he comes here next."

"Cassy, did Charlotte Alden speak to you to-day?"

"No; but she made an acquaintance by stares."

"Well, never mind her if she says anything unpleasant to you; the Aldens are a high set."

"Are they higher than we are in Surrey? Have they heard of my father, who is equal to the President?"

"We are all equal in the sight of God."

"You do not look as if you thought so, Aunt Mercy. Why do you say things in Barmouth you never said in Surrey?"

"Come downstairs, Cassandra, and help me finish the dishes."

Our conversation was ended; but I still had my thoughts on the clothes question, and revolved my plans.

After the morning exercises the next day, Miss Black called me in to her desk. "I think," she said, "you had better study Geology. It is important, for it will lead your mind up from nature to nature's God. My young ladies have finished their studies in that direction; therefore you will recite alone, once a day."

"Yes 'em," I replied; but it was the first time that I had heard of Geology. The compendium she gave me must have been dull and dry. I could not get its lessons perfectly. It never inspired me with any interest for land or sea. I could not associate any of its terms, or descriptions, with the great rock under grand'ther's house. It was not for Miss Black to open the nodules of my understanding, with her hammer of instruction. She proposed Botany also. The young ladies made botanical excursions to the fields and woods outside Barmouth; I might as well join the class at once. It was now in the family of the Legumes. I accompanied the class on one excursion. Not a soul appeared to know that I was present, and I declined going again. Composition I must write once a month. A few more details closed the interview. I mentioned in it that father desired me to study arithmetic. Miss Black placed me in a class; but her interests were in the higher and more elegant branches of education. I made no more advance in the humble walks of learning than in those adorned by the dissection of flowers, the disruption of rocks, or the graces of composition. Though I entered upon my duties under protest, I soon became accustomed to their routine, and the rest of my life seemed more like a dream of the future than a realization of the present. I refused to go home at the end of the month. I preferred waiting, I said, to the end of the year. I was not urged to change my mind; neither was I applauded for my resolution. The day that I could have gone home, I asked father to drive me to Milford, on the opposite side of the river which ran by Barmouth. I shut my eyes tight, when the horse struck the boards of the long wooden bridge between the towns, and opened them when we stopped at an inn by the water side of Milford. Father took me into a parlor, where sat a handsome, fat woman, hemming towels.

"Is that you, Morgeson?" she said. "Is this your daughter?"

"Yes; can I leave her with you, while I go the the bank? She has not been here before."

"Lord ha' mercy on us; you clip her wings, don't you? Come here, child, and let me pull off your pelisse."

I went to her with a haughty air; it did not please me to hear my father called "Morgeson," by a person unknown to me. She understood my expression, and looked up at father; they both smiled, and I was vexed with him for his unwarrantable familiarity. Pinching my cheek with her fat fingers, which were covered with red and green rings, she said, "We shall do very well together. What a pretty silk pelisse, and silver buckles, too."

After father went out, and my bonnet was disposed of, Mrs. Tabor gave me a huge piece of delicious sponge-cake, which softened me somewhat.

"What is your name, dear?"

"Morgeson."

"It is easy to see that."

"Well, Cassandra."

"Oh, what a lovely name," and she drew from her workbasket a paper-covered book; "there is no name in this novel half so pretty; I wish the heroine's name had been Cassandra instead of Aldebrante."[20]

"Let me see it," I begged.

"There is a horrid monk in it"; but she gave it to me, and was presently called out. I devoured its pages, and for the only time in that year of Barmouth life, I forgot my own wants and woes. She saw my interest in the book when she came back, and coaxed it from me, offering me more cake, which I accepted. She told me that she had known father for years, and that he kept his horse at the inn stables, and dined with her. "But I never knew that he had a daughter," she continued. "Are you the only child?"

"I have a sister," and after a moment remembered that I had a brother, too; but did not think it a fact necessary to mention.

"I have no children."

"But you have novels to read."

She laughed, and by the time father returned we were quite chatty. After dinner I asked him to go to some shops with me. He took me to a jeweler's, and without consulting me bought an immense mosaic brooch, with a ruined castle on it, and a pretty ring with a gold stone.

"Is there anything more?" he asked, "you would like?"

"Yes, I want a pink calico dress."

"Why?"

"Because the girls at Miss Black's wear pink calico."

"Why not get a pink silk?"

"I must have a pink French calico, with a three-cornered white cloud on it; it is the fashion."

"The fashion!" he echoed with contempt. But the dress was bought, and we went back to Barmouth.

When I appeared in school with my new brooch and ring the girls crowded round me.

"What does that pin represent, whose estate?" inquired one, with envy in her voice.

"Don't the ring make the blood rush into your hand?" asked another; "it looks so."

"Does it?" I answered; "I'll hold up my hand in the air, as you do, to make it white."

"What is your father's business?" asked Elmira Sawyer, "is he a tailor?"

Her insolence made my head swim; but I did not reply. When recess was over a few minutes afterward, I cried under the lid of my desk. These girls overpowered me, for I could not conciliate them, and had no idea of revenge, believing that their ridicule was deserved. But I thought I should like to prove myself respectable. How could I? Grand'ther *was* a tailor, and I could not demean myself by assuring them that my father was a gentleman.

In the course of a month Aunt Mercy had my pink calico made up by the best dressmaker in Barmouth. When I put it on I thought I looked better than I ever had before, and went into school triumphantly with it. The girls surveyed me in silence; but criticised me. At last Charlotte Alden asked me in a whisper if old Mr. Warren made my dress. She wrote on a piece of paper, in large letters— "Girls, don't let's wear our pink calicoes again," and pushing it over to Elmira Sawyer, made signs that the paper should be passed to all the girls. They read it, and turning to Charlotte Alden nodded. I watched the paper as it made its round, and saw Mary Bennett drop it on the floor with a giggle.

It was a rainy day, and we passed the recess indoors. I remained quiet looking over my lesson. "The first period ends with the carboniferous system; the second includes the saliferous and magnesian systems; the third comprises the oolitic and chalk systems; the fourth—" "How attentive some people are to their lessons," I heard Charlotte Alden say. Looking up, I saw her near me with Elmira Sawyer.

"What is that you say?" I asked sharply.

"I am not speaking to you."

"I am angry," I said in a low tone, and rising, "and have borne enough."

"Who are *you* that you should be angry? We have heard about your mother, when she was in love, poor thing."

I struck her so violent a blow in the face that she staggered backward. "You are a liar," I said, "and you must let me alone." Elmira Sawyer turned white, and moved away. I threw my book at her; it hit her head, and her comb was broken by my geological systems. There was a stir; Miss Black hurried from her desk, saying, "Young ladies, what does this mean? Miss C. Morgeson, your temper equals your vulgarity, I find. Take your seat in my desk."

I obeyed her, and as we passed Mary Bennett's desk, where I saw the paper fall, I picked it up. "See the good manners of your favorite, Miss Black; read it." She bit her lips as she glanced over it, turned back as if to speak to Charlotte Alden, looked at me again, and went on: "Sit down, Miss C. Morgeson, and reflect on the blow you have given. Will you ask pardon?"

"I will not; you know that."

"I have never resorted to severe punishment yet; but I fear I shall be obliged to in your case."

"Let me go from here." I clenched my hands, and tried to get up. She held me down on the seat, and we looked close in each other's eyes. "You are a bad girl." "And you are a bad woman," I replied; "mean and cruel." She made a motion to strike me, but her hand dropped; I felt my nostrils quiver strangely. "For shame," she said, in a tremulous voice, and turned away. I sat on the bench at the back of the desk, heartily tired, till school was dismissed; as Charlotte Alden passed out, courtesying, Miss Black said she hoped she would extend a Christian forgiveness to Miss C. Morgeson, for her unladylike behavior. "Miss C. Morgeson is a peculiar case."

She gave her a meaning look, which was not lost upon me. Charlotte answered, "Certainly," and bowed to me gracefully, whereat I felt a fresh sense of my demerits, and concluded that I was worsted in the fray.

Miss Black asked no explanation of the affair; it was dropped, and none of the girls alluded to it by hint or look afterward. When I told Aunt Mercy of it, she turned pale, and said she knew what Charlotte Alden meant, and that perhaps mother would tell me in good time.

"We had a good many troubles in our young days, Cassy."

CHAPTER X.

The atmosphere of my two lives was so different, that when I passed into one, the other ceased to affect me. I forgot all that I suffered and hated at Miss Black's, as soon as I crossed the threshold, and entered grand'ther's house. The difference kept up a healthy mean; either alone would perhaps have been more than I could then have sustained. All that year my life was narrowed to that house, my school, and the church. Father offered to take me to ride, when he came to Barmouth, or carry me to Milford; but the motion of the carriage, and the conveying power of the horse, created such a fearful and realizing sense of escape, that I gave up riding with him. Aunt Mercy seldom left home; my schoolmates did not invite me to visit them; the seashore was too distant for me to ramble there; the storehouses and wharves by the river-side offered no agreeable saunterings; and the street, in Aunt Mercy's estimation, was not the place for an idle promenade. My exercise, therefore, was confined to the garden—a pleasant spot, now that midsummer had come, and inhabited with winged and crawling creatures, with whom I claimed companionship, especially with the red, furry caterpillars, that have, alas, nearly passed away, and given place to a variegated, fantastic tribe, which gentleman farmers are fond of writing about.

Mother rode over to Barmouth occasionally, but seemed more glad when she went away than when she came. Veronica came with her once, but said she would come no more while I was there. She too would wait till the end of the year, for I spoiled the place. She said this so calmly that I never thought of being offended by it. I told her the episode of the pink calico. "It is a lovely color," she said, when I showed it to her. "If you like, I will take it home and burn it."

As I developed the dramatic part of my story—the blow given Charlotte Alden, Verry rubbed her face shrinkingly, as if she had felt the blow. "Let me see your hand," she asked; "did I ever strike anybody?"

"You threw a pail of salt downstairs, once, upon my head, and put out my sight."

"I wish, when you are home, you would pound Mr. Park; he talks too much about the Resurrection. And," she added mysteriously, "he likes mother."

"Likes mother!" I said aghast.

"He watches her so when she holds Arthur! Why do you stare at me? Why do I talk to you? I am going. Now mind, I shall never leave home to go to any school; I shall know enough without."

While Veronica was holding this placable talk with me, I discovered in her the high-bred air, the absence of which I deplored in myself.

How cool and unimpressionable she looked! She did not attract me then. My mind wandered to what I had heard Mary Bennett say, in recess one day, that her brother had seen me in church, and came home with the opinion that I was the handsomest girl in Miss Black's school.

"Is it possible!" replied the girl to whom she had made the remark. "I never should think of calling her pretty."

"Stop, Veronica," I called; "am I pretty?" She turned back. "Everybody in Surrey says so; and everybody says I am not." And she banged the door against me.

She did not come to Barmouth again. She was ill in the winter, and, father told me, queerer than ever, and more trouble. The summer passed, and I had no particular torment, except Miss Black's reference to composition. I could not do justice to the themes she gave us, not having the books from which she took them at command, and betrayed an ignorance which excited her utmost contempt, on "The Scenery of Singapore," "The Habits of the Hottentots," and "The Relative Merits of Homer and Virgil."

In October Sally and Ruth Aiken came for the fall sewing. They had farmed it all summer, they said, and were tanned so deep a hue that their faces bore no small resemblance to ham. Ruth brought me some apples in an ochre-colored bag, and Sally eyed me with her old severity. As they took their accustomed seats at the table, I thought they had swallowed the interval of time which had gone by since they left, so precisely the same was the moment of their leaving and that of their coming back. I knew grand'ther no better than when I saw him first. He was sociable to those who visited the house, but never with those abiding in his family. Me he never noticed, except when I ate less than usual; then he peered into my face, and said, "What ails you?" We had the benefit of his taciturn presence continually, for he rarely went out; and although he did not interfere with Aunt Mercy's work, he supervised it, weighed and measured every article that was used, and kept the cellar and garden in perfect order.

It was approaching the season of killing the pig, and he con-

ferred often with Aunt Mercy on the subject. The weather was
watched, and the pig poked daily, in the hope that the fat was
thickening on his ribs. When the day of his destiny arrived, there
was almost confusion in the house, and for a week after, of evenings,
grand'ther went about with a lantern, and was not himself till a
new occupant was obtained for the vacant pen, and all his idiosyn-
cracies revealed and understood.

"Grand'ther," I asked, "will the beautiful pigeons that live in
the pig's roof like the horrid new pig?"

"Yes," he answered, briskly rubbing his hands, "but they eat
the pig's corn; and I can't afford that; I shall have to shoot them, I
guess."

"Oh, don't, grand'ther."

"I will this very day. Where's the gun, Mercy?"

In an hour the pigeons were shot, except two which had flown
away.

"Why did you ask him not to shoot the pigeons?" said Aunt
Mercy. "If you had said nothing, he would not have done it."

"He is a disagreeable relation," I answered, "and I am glad he is
a tailor."

Aunt Mercy reproved me; but the loss of the pigeons vexed her.
Perhaps grand'ther thought so, for that night he asked after her
geraniums, and told her that a gardener had promised him some
fine slips for her. She looked pleased, but did not thank him. There
was already a beautiful stand of flowers in the middle room, which
was odorous the year round with their perfume.

The weather was now cold, and we congregated about the fire;
for there was no other comfortable room in the house. One afternoon, when I was digging in Aunt Mercy's geranium pots, and
picking off the dead leaves, two deacons came to visit grand'ther,
and, hovering over the fire with him, complained of the luke-
warmness of the church brethren in regard to the spiritual condition of the Society. A shower of grace was needed; there were
reviving symptoms in some of the neighboring churches, but none
in Barmouth. Something must be done—a fast day appointed, or
especial prayer-meetings held. This was on Saturday; the next day
the ceremony of the Lord's Supper would take place, and grand'ther
recommended that the minister should be asked to suggest something to the church which might remove it from its hardness.

"Are the vessels scoured, Mercy?" he asked, after the deacons
had gone.

"I have no sand."

He presently brought her a biggin of fine white sand, which brought the shore of Surrey to my mind's eye. I followed her as she carried it to the well-room, where I saw, on the meal-chest, two large pewter plates, two flagons of the same metal, and a dozen or more cups, some of silver, and marked with the owner's name. They were soon cleaned. Then she made a fire in the oven, and mixed loaves in a peculiar shape, and launched them into the oven. She watched the bread carefully, and took it out before it had time to brown.

"This work belongs to the deacons' wives," she said; "but it has been done in this house for years. The bread is not like ours—it is unleavened."

Grand'ther carried it into the church after she had cut it with a sharp knife so that at the touch it would fall apart into square bits. When the remains were brought back, I went to the closet, where they were deposited, and took a piece of the bread, eating it reflectively, to test its solemnizing powers. I felt none, and when Aunt Mercy boiled the remnants with milk for a pudding, the sacred ideality of the ceremony I had seen at church was destroyed for me.

Was it a pity that my life was not conducted on Nature's plan, who shows us the beautiful, while she conceals the interior? We do not see the roots of her roses, and she hides from us her skeletons.

November passed, with its Thanksgiving—the sole day of all the year which grand'ther celebrated, by buying a goose for dinner, which goose was stewed with rye dumplings, that slid over my plate like glass balls. Sally and Ruth betook themselves to their farm, and hybernated. December came, and with it a young woman named Caroline, to learn the tailor's trade. Lively and pretty, she changed our atmosphere. She broke the silence of the morning by singing the "Star-spangled Banner," or the "Braes of Balquhither,"[21] and disturbed the monotony of the evenings by making molasses candy, which grand'ther ate, and which seemed to have a mollifying influence. Grand'ther kept his eye on Caroline; but his eye had no disturbing effect. She had no perception of his character; was fearless with him, and went contrary to all his ideas, and he liked her for it. She even reproved him for keeping such a long face. Her sewing, which was very bad, tried his patience so, that if it had not been for her mother, who was a poor widow, he would have given up the task of teaching her the trade. She said she knew she couldn't learn it; what was the use of trying? She meant to go West, and thought she might make a good home-missionary, as she did, for she married a poor young man, who had forsaken the trade of a cooper, to study for the ministry, and was helped off to Ohio by the Society of Home Missions.[22] She came to see me in Surrey ten years afterward, a gaunt, hollow-eyed woman, of forbidding manners, and an implacable faith in no rewards or punishments this side of the grave.

I suffered so from the cold that December that I informed mother of the fact by letter. She wrote back:

"My child, have courage. One of these days you will feel a tender pity, when you think of your mother's girlhood. You are learning how she lived at your age. I trembled at the prosperity of your opening life, and believed it best for you to have a period of contrast. I thought you would, by and by, understand me better than I do myself; for you are not like me, Cassy, you are like your father. You shall never go back to Barmouth, unless you wish it. Dear Cassy, do you pray any? I send you some new petticoats, and a shawl. Does Mercy warm the bed for you?

Your affectionate Mother."

I dressed and undressed in Aunt Mercy's room, which was under the roof, with benumbed fingers. My hair was like the coat of a cow in frosty weather; it was so frowzy, and so divided against itself, that when I tried to comb it, it streamed out like the tail of a comet. Aunt Mercy discovered that I was afflicted with chil-blains, and had a good cry over them, telling me, at the same moment, that my French slippers were the cause. We had but one fire in the house, except the fire in the shop, which was allowed to go down at sunset. Sometimes I found a remaining warmth in the goose,[23] which had been left in the ashes, and borrowed it for my stiffened fingers. I did not get thoroughly warm all day, for the fire in the middle room, made of green wood, was continually in the process of being stifled with a greener stick, as the others kindled. The school-room was warm; but I had a back seat by a window, where my feet were iced by a current, and my head exposed to a draught. In January I had so bad an ague that I was confined at home a week. But I grew fast in spite of all my discom-forts. Aunt Mercy took the tucks out of my skirts, and I burst out where there were no tucks. I assumed a womanly shape. Stiff as my hands were, and purple as were my arms, I could see that they were plump and well shaped. I had lost the meagerness of childhood and began to feel a new and delightful affluence. What an appetite I had, too!

"The creature will eat us out of house and home," said grand'ther one day, looking at me, for him good humoredly.

"Well, don't shoot me, as you shot the pigeons."

"Pah, have pigeons a soul?"

In February the weather softened, and a great revival broke out. It was the dullest time of the year in Barmouth. The ships were at sea still, and the farmers had only to fodder their cattle, so that everybody could attend the protracted meeting. It was the same as Sunday at our house for nine days. Miss Black, in consequence of the awakening, dismissed the school for two weeks, that the pupils might profit in what she told us was The Scheme of Salvation.

Caroline was among the first converts. I observed her from the moment I was told she was under Conviction, till she experienced Religion. She sang no more of mornings, and the making of molasses candy was suspended in the evenings. I thought her less pleasing, and felt shy of holding ordinary conversations with her, for had she not been set apart for a mysterious work? I perceived that when she sewed between meetings her work was worse done than ever; but grand'ther made no mention of it. I went with Aunt Mercy to meetings three times a day, and employed myself in scanning the countenances around me, curious to discover the first symptoms of Conviction.

One night when grand'ther came in to prayers, he told Aunt Mercy that Pardon Hitch was awfully distressed in mind, in view of his sins. She replied that he was always a good man.

"As good as any unregenerate man can be."

"I might as well be a thorough reprobate then," I thought, "like Sal Thompson, who seems remarkably happy, as to try to behave as well as Pardon Hitch, who is a model in Barmouth."

When we went to church the next morning, I saw him in one of the back pews, leaning against the rail, as if he had no strength. His face was full of anguish. He sat there motionless all day. He was prayed for, but did not seem to hear the prayers. At night his wife led him home. By the end of the third day, he interrupted an exhorting brother by rising, and uttering an inarticulate cry. We all looked. The tears were streaming down his pale face, which was lighted up by a smile of joy. He seemed like a man escaped from some great danger, torn, bruised, breathless, but alive. The minister left the pulpit to shake hands with him; the brethren crowded round to congratulate him, and the meeting broke up at once.

Neither grand'ther nor Aunt Mercy had spoken to me concerning my interest in Religion; but on that very evening Mr. Boold, the minister, came in to tea and asked me, while he was taking off his overcoat, if I knew that Christ had died for me? I answered that I was not sure of it.

"Do you read your Bible, child?"

"Every day."

"And what does it teach you?"

"I do not know."

"Miss Mercy, I will thank you for another cup. 'Now is the day, and now is the hour; come unto me all ye that labor and are heavy laden, I will give you rest.' "

"But I do not want rest; I have no burden," I said.

"Cassandra," thundered grand'ther, "have you no respect for God nor man?"

"Have you read," went on the minister, "the memoir of Nathan Dickerman? A mere child, he realized his burden of sin in time, and died sanctified."

I thought it best to say no more. Aunt Mercy looked disturbed, and left the table as soon as she could with decency.

"Cassandra," she said, when we were alone, "what will become of you?"

"What will, indeed? You have always said that I was possessed. Why did you not explain this fact to Mr. Boold?"

She kissed me,—her usual treatment when she was perplexed.

The revival culminated and declined. Sixty new members were admitted into the church, and things settled into the old state. School was resumed; I found that not one of my schoolmates had met with a change, but Miss Black did not touch on the topic. My year was nearly out; March had come and gone, and it was now April. One mild day, in the latter part of the month, the girls went to the yard at recess. Charlotte Alden said pleasantly that the weather was fair enough for out-of-doors play, and asked if I would try the tilt. I gave a cordial assent. We balanced the board so that each could seat herself, and began to tilt slowly. As she was heavy, I was obliged to exert my strength to keep my place, and move her. She asked if I dared to go higher. "Oh yes, if you wish it." Happening to look round, I caught her winking at the girls near us, and felt that she was brewing mischief, but I had no time to dwell on it. She bore the end she was on to the ground with a sudden jerk, and I fell from the other, some eight feet, struck a stone, and fainted.

The next thing that I recollect was Aunt Mercy's carrying me across the street in her arms. She had seen my fall from the window. Reaching the house, she let me slide on the floor in a heap, and began to wring her hands and stamp her feet.

"I am not hurt, Aunt Mercy."

"You are nearly killed, you know you are. This is your last day at that miserable school. I am going for the doctor, as soon as you say you wont faint again."

Thus my education at Miss Black's was finished with a blow.

When Aunt Mercy represented to Miss Black that I was not to return to school, and that she feared I had not made the improvement that was expected, Miss Black asked, with hauteur, what had been expected—what my friends *could* expect. Aunt Mercy was intimidated, and retired as soon as she had paid her the last quarter's bills.

A week after my tournament with Charlotte Alden I went back to Surrey. There was little preparation to make—few friends to bid farewell. Ruth and Sally had emerged from their farm, and were sewing again at grand'ther's. Sally bade me remember that riches took to themselves wings and flew away; she *hoped* they had not been a snare to my mother; but she wasn't what she was, it was a fact.

"No, she isn't," Ruth affirmed. "Do you remember, Sally, when she came out to the farm once, and rode the white colt bare-back round the big meadow, with her hair flying?"

"Hold your tongue, Ruth."

Ruth looked penitent as she gave me a paper of hollyhock seeds, and said the flowers were a beautiful blood-red, and that I must plant them near the sink drain. Caroline had already gone home, so Aunt Mercy had nothing cheery but her plants and her snuff; for she had lately contracted the habit of snuff-taking but very privately.

"Train her well, Locke; she is skittish," said grand'ther as we got into the chaise to go home.

"Grand'ther, if I am ever rich enough to own a peaked-roof pig-sty, will you come and see me?"

"Away with you." And he went nimbly back to the house, chafing his little hands.

CHAPTER XI.

I was going home! When we rode over the brow of the hill within a mile of Surrey, and I saw the crescent-shaped village, and the tall chimneys of our house on its outer edge, instead of my heart leaping for joy, as I had expected, a sudden indifference filled it. I felt averse to the change from the narrow ways of Barmouth, which, for the moment, I regretted. When I entered the house, and saw mother in her old place, her surroundings unaltered, I suffered a disappointment. I had not had the power of transferring the atmosphere of my year's misery to Surrey.

The family gathered round me. I heard the wonted sound of the banging of doors. "The doors at grand'ther's," I mused, "had list nailed round their edges; but then he *had* the list, being a tailor."

"I vum," said Temperance, with her hand on her hip, and not offering to approach me, "your hair is as thick as a mop."

Hepsey, rubbing her fingers against her thumb, remarked that she hoped learning had not taken away my appetite. "I have made an Indian bannock for you, and we are going to have broiled sword-fish, besides, for supper. Is it best to cook more, Mrs. Morgeson, now that Cassandra has come?"

The boy, by name Charles, came to see the new arrival, but smitten with diffidence crept under the table, and examined me from his retreat.

"Don't you wish to see Arthur?" inquired mother; "he is getting his double teeth."

"Oh yes, and where's Veronica?"

"She's up garret writing geography, and told me nothing in the world must disturb her, till she had finished an account of the city of Palmiry," said Temperance.

"Call her when supper is ready," replied mother, who asked me to come into the bedroom where Arthur was sleeping. He was a handsome child, large and fair, and as I lifted his white, lax fingers, a torrent of love swept through me, and I kissed him.

"I am afraid I make an idol of him, Cassy."

"Are you unhappy because you love him so well, mother, and feel that you must make expiation?"

"Cassandra," she spoke with haste, "did you experience any shadow of a change during the revival at Barmouth?"

"No more than the baby here did."

"I shall have faith, though, that it will be well with you, because you have had the blessing of so good a man as your grand'ther."

"But I never heard a word of grand'ther's prayers. Do you remember his voice?"

A smile crept into her blue eye, as she said: "My hearing him, or not, would make no difference, since God could hear and answer."

"Grand'ther does not like me; I never pleased him."

She looked astonished, then reflective. It occurred to her that she, also, had been no favorite of his. She changed the subject. We talked on what had happened in Surrey, and commenced a discussion on my wardrobe, when we were summoned to tea. Temperance brought Arthur to the table half asleep, but he roused when she drummed on his plate with a spoon. Hepsey was stationed by the bannock, knife in hand, to serve it. As we began our meal, Veronica came in from the kitchen, with a plate of toasted crackers. She set the plate down, and gravely shook hands with me, saying she had concluded to live entirely on toast, but supposed I would eat all sorts of food, as usual. She had grown tall; her face was still long and narrow, but prettier, and her large, dark eyes had a slight cast, which gave her face an indescribable expression. Distant, indifferent, and speculative as the eyes were, a ray of fire shot into them occasionally, which made her gaze powerful and concentrated. I was within a month of sixteen, and Veronica was in her thirteenth year; but she looked as old as I did. She carefully prepared her toast with milk and butter, and ate it in silence. The plenty around me, the ease and independence, gave me a delightful sense of comfort. The dishes were odd, some of china, some of delf, and were continually moved out of their places, for we helped ourselves, although Temperance stayed in the room, ostensibly as a waiter. She was too much engaged in conversation to fulfill her duties that way. I looked round the room; nothing had been added to it, expect red damask curtains, which were out of keeping with the old chintz covers. It was a delightful room, however; the blue sea glimmered between the curtains, and, turning my eyes toward it, my heart gave the leap which I had looked for. I grew blithe as I saw it winking under the rays of the afternoon sun, and, clapping my hands, said I was glad to get home. We left Veronica at the table, and mother resumed her conversation with me in a corner of the room. Presently Temperance came in with Charles, bringing fresh plates. As soon as they began their supper, Veronica asked Temperance how the fish tasted.

"Is it salt?"

"Middling."

"How is the bannock?"

"Excellent. I will say it for Hepsey that she hasn't her beat as a cook; been at it long enough," she added, in expiation of her praise.

"Temperance, is that pound cake, or sponge?"

"Pound."

"Charles can eat it," Verry said with a sigh.

"A mighty small piece he'll have—the glutton. But he has not been here long; they are all so when they first come."

She then gave him a large slice of the cake.

Veronica, contrary to her wont, huddled herself on the sofa. Arthur played round the chair of mother, who looked happy and forgetful. After Temperance had rearranged the table for father's supper we were quiet. I meditated how I could best amuse myself, where I should go, and what I should do, when Veronica, whom I had forgotten, interrupted my thoughts.

"Mother," she said, "eating toast does not make me better-tempered; I feel evil still. You know," turning to me, "that my temper is worse than ever; it is like a tiger's."

"Oh, Verry," said mother, "not quite so bad; you are too hard upon yourself."

"Mother, you said so to Hepsey, when I tore her turban from her head, it was so ugly. Can you forget you said such a thing?"

"Verry, you drive me wild. Must I say that I was wrong? Say so to my own child?"

Verry turned her face to the wall and said no more; but she had started a less pleasant train of thought. It was changed again by Temperance coming with lights. Though the tall brass lamps glittered like gold, their circle of light was small; the corners of the room were obscure. Mr. Park, entering, retreated into one, and mother was obliged to forego the pleasure of undressing Arthur; so she sent him off with Temperance and Charles, whose duty it was to rock the cradle as long as his babyship required.

Soon after father came, and Hepsey brought in his hot supper; while he was eating it, Grandfather John Morgeson bustled in. As he shook hands with me, I saw that his hair had whitened; he held a tasseled cane between his knees, and thumped the floor whenever he asked a question. Mr. Park buzzed about the last Sunday's discourse, and mother listened with a vague, respectful attention. Her hand was pressed against her breast, as if she were repressing an inward voice which claimed her attention. Leaning her head against her chair, she had quite pushed out her comb, her hair dropped on her shoulder, and looked like a brown, coiled serpent. Veronica, who had been silently observing her, rose from the sofa, picked up the comb, and fastened her hair, without speaking. As she passed she gave me a dark look.

"Eh, Verry," said father, "are you there? Were you glad to see Cassy home again?"

"Should I be glad? What can *she* do?"

Grandfather pursed up his mouth, and turned toward mother, as if he would like to say: "You understand bringing up children, don't you?"

She comprehended him, and, giving her head a slight toss, told Verry to go and play on the piano.

"I was going," she answered pettishly, and darting out a moment after we heard her.

Grandfather went, and presently Mr. Park got up in a lingering way, said that Verry must learn to play for the Lord, and bade us "Good night." But he came back again, to ask me if I would join Dr. Snell's Bible Class. It would meet the next evening; the boys and girls of my own age went. I promised him to go, wondering whether I should meet an ancient beau, Joe Bacon. Mother retired; Verry still played.

"Her talent is wonderful," said father, taking the cigar from his mouth. "By the way, you must take lessons in Milford; I wish you would learn to sing." I acquiesced, but I had no wish to learn to play. I could never perform mechanically what I heard now from Verry. When she ceased, I woke from a dream, chaotic, but not tumultuous, beautiful, but inharmonious. Though the fire had gone out, the lamps winked brightly, and father, moving his cigar to the other side of his mouth, changed his regards from one lamp to the other, and said he thought I was growing to be an attractive girl. He asked me if I would take pains to make myself an accomplished one also? I must, of course, be left to myself in many things; but he hoped that I would confide in him, if I did not ask his advice. A very strong relation of reserve generally existed between parent and child, instead of a confidential one, and the child was apt to discover that reserve on the part of the parent was not superiority, but cowardice, or indifference. "Let it not be so with us," was his conclusion. He threw away the stump of his cigar, and went to fasten the hall-door. I took one of the brass lamps, proposing to go to bed. As I passed through the upper entry, Veronica opened her door. She was undressed, and had a little book in her hand, which she shook at me, saying, "There is the day of the month put down on which you came home; and now mind," then shut the door. I pondered over what father had said; he had perceived something in me which I was not aware of. I resolved to think seriously over it; in the morning I found I had not thought of it at all.

CHAPTER XII.

The next evening I dressed my hair after the fashion of the Barmouth girls, with the small pride of wishing to make myself look different from the Surrey girls. I expected they would stare at me in the Bible Class. It would be my début as a grown girl, and I must offer myself to their criticism. I went late, so that I might be observed by the assembled class. It met in the upper story of Temperance Hall—a new edifice. As I climbed the steep stairs, Joe Bacon's head came in view; he had stationed himself on a bench at the landing to watch for my arrival, of which he had been apprized by our satellite, Charles. Joe was the first boy who had ever offered his arm as my escort home from a party. After that event I had felt that there was something between us which the world did not understand. I was flattered, therefore, at the first glimpse of him on this occasion. When Dr. Snell made his opening prayer, Joe thrust a Bible before me, open at the lesson of the evening, and then, rubbing his nose with embarrassment, fixed his eyes with timid assurance on the opposite wall. Several of my Morgeson cousins were present, greeting me with sniffs. But I was disappointed in Joe Bacon; how young and shabby he looked! He wore a monkey jacket, probably a remnant of his sea-going father's wardrobe. He had done his best, however, for his hair was greased, and combed to a marble smoothness; its sleekness vexed me, not remembering at that moment the pains I had taken to dress my own hair, for a more ignoble end.

The girls gathered round me, after the class was dismissed; and when Dr. Snell came down from his desk, he said he was glad to see me, and that I must come to his rooms to look over the new books he had received. Dr. Snell was no exception to the rule that a minister must not be a native among his own people. His long residence in Surrey had failed to make him appear like one. A bachelor, with a small private fortune, his style of living differed from the average of Congregational parsons. His library was the only lion in our neighborhood. His taste as a collector made him known abroad, and he had a reputation which was not dreamed of by his parishioners, who thought him queer and simple. He loved old fashions; wore knee-breeches, and silver buckles in his shoes; brewed metheglin in his closet, and drank it from silver-pegged flagons; and kept diet bread on a salver to offer his visitors. He lived near us on the north road, and was very much afraid of his landlady, Mrs. Crossman, who sat in terrible state in her parlor, the year through, wearing a black satin cloak and an awful structure of a cap, which had a potent nod.

I was pleased with Dr. Snell's notice; his smile was courtly and his bow Grandisonian.[24]

Joe Bacon was waiting at the foot of the stairs. He obtruded his arm, and hoarsely muttered, "See you home." I took it, and we marched along silently, till we were beyond the sound of voices. He began, rather inarticulately, to say how glad he was to see me, and that he hoped he was going to have better times now; but I could make no response to his wishes; the suspicion that he had a serious liking for me was disgusting. As he talked on I grew irritable, and replied shortly. When we reached our house, I slipped my hand from his arm, and ran up the steps, turning back with my hand on the door-knob to say, "Good-night." The lamp in the hall shone through the fanlight upon his face; it looked intelligent with pain. I skipped down the steps. "Please open the door, Joe." He brightened, but before he could comply with my request Temperance flung it wide, for the purpose of making a survey of the clouds and guessing at to-morrow's weather. His retreat was precipitate.

"Oh ho," said Temperance, "a feller came home with you. We shall have somebody sitting up a-Thursday nights, I reckon, before long."

"Nonsense with your Thursday nights."

"Everybody is just alike. We shall have rain, see if we don't; rain or no rain, I'll whitewash to-morrow."

Poor Joe! That night ended my first sentiment. He died with the measles in less than a month.

"I wish," said Temperance, who was spelling over a newspaper, "that Dr. Snell would come in before the plumcake is gone, that Hepsey made last. The old dear loves it; he is always hungry. I candidly believe Mis Crossman keeps him short."

I expected that Temperance would break out then about Joe; but she never mentioned him, except to tell me that she had heard of his death. She did not whitewash the next day, for Charles came down with the measles, and was tended by her with a fretful tenderness. Veronica was seized soon after, and then Arthur, and then I had them. Veronica was the worst patient. When her room was darkened she got out of bed, tore down the quilt that was fastened to the window, and broke three panes of glass before she could be captured and taken back. The quilt was not put up again, however. She cried with anger, unless her hands were continually washed with lavender water, and made little pellets of cotton which she stuffed in her ears and nose, so that she might not hear or smell.

I went to Dr. Snell's as soon as I was able. He was in his bedchamber, writing a sermon on fine note-paper, and had disarranged the wide ruffles of his shirt so that he looked like a mildly angry turkey. Thrusting his spectacles up into the roots of his hair, he rose, and led me into a large room adjoining his bedroom, which contained nothing but tall bookcases, threw open the doors of one, pushed up a little ladder before it, for me to mount to a row of volumes bound in calf, whose backs were labeled "British Classics." "There," he said, "you will find 'The Spectator,' " and trotted back to his sermon, with his pen in his mouth. I examined the books, and selected Tom Jones and Goldsmith's Plays to take home. From that time I grazed at pleasure in his oddly assorted library, ranging from "The Gentleman's Magazine" to a file of the "Boston Recorder"; but never a volume of poetry anywhere. I became a devourer of books which I could not digest, and their influence located in my mind curious and inconsistent relations between facts and ideas.[25]

My music lessons in Milford were my only task. I remained inapt, while Veronica played better and better; when I saw her fingers interpreting her feelings, touching the keys of the piano as if they were the chords of her thoughts, practice by note seemed a soulless, mechanical effort, which I would not make. One day mother and I were reading the separate volumes of charming Miss Austen's "Mansfield Park," when a message arrived from Aunt Mercy, with the news of Grand'ther Warren's dangerous illness. Mother dropped her book on the floor, but I turned down the leaf where I was reading. She went to Barmouth immediately, and the next day grand'ther died. He gave all he had to Aunt Mercy, except six silver spoons, which he directed the Barmouth silversmith to make for Caroline, who was now married to her missionary. Mother came home to prepare for the funeral. When the bonnets, veils, and black gloves came home, Veronica declared she would not go. As she had been allowed to stay away from Grand'ther Warren living, why should she be forced to go to him when dead? She was so violent in her opposition that mother ordered Temperance to keep her in her room. Father tried to persuade her, but she grew white, and trembled so that he told her she should stay at home. While we were gone she sent her bonnet to the Widow Smith's daughter, who appeared in the Poor Seats wearing it, on the very Sunday after the funeral, when we all went to church in our mourning to make the discovery, which discomposed us exceedingly.

All the church were present at grand'ther's funeral,—obsequies, as Mr. Boold called it, who exalted his character and behavior so greatly in his discourse that his nearest friends would not have recognized him, although everybody knew that he was a good man. Mr. Boold expatiated on his tenderness and delicate appreciation, and his study of the feelings and wants of others, till he was moved to tears himself by the picture he drew. I thought of the pigeons he had shot, and of the summary treatment he gave me—of his coldness and silence toward Aunt Mercy, and my eyes remained dry; but mother and Aunt Mercy wept bitterly. After it was over, and they had gone back to the empty house, they removed their heavy bonnets, kissed each other, said they knew that he was in heaven, and held a comforting conversation about the future; but my mind was chained to the edge of the yawning grave into which I had seen his coffin lowered.

"Shut up the old shell, Mercy," said father. "Come, and live with us."

She was rejoiced at the prospect, for the life at our house was congenial, and she readily and gratefully consented. She came in a few days, with a multitude of boxes, and her plants. Mother established her in the room next the stairs—a good place for her, Veronica said, for she could be easily locked out of our premises. The plants were placed on a new revolving stand, which stood on the landing-place beneath the stair window. Veronica was so delighted with them that she made amicable overtures to Aunt Mercy, and never quarreled with her afterward, except when she was ill. She entreated her to leave off her bombazine dresses; the touch of them interfered with her feelings for her, she said; in fact, their contact made her crawl all over.

Aunt Mercy took upon herself many of mother's irksome cares; such as remembering where the patches and old linen were—the hammer and nails; watching the sweetmeat pots; keeping the run of the napkins and blankets; packing the winter clothing, and having an eye on mice and ants, moth and mold. Occasionally she read a novel; but was faithful to all the week-day meetings, making the acquaintance thereby of mother's tea-drinking friends, who considered her an accomplished person, because she worked lace so beautifully, and had *such* a faculty for raising plants! Mother left the house in her charge, and made several journeys with father this year. This period was perhaps her happiest. The only annoyance, visible to me, that I can remember, was one between her and father on the subject of charity. He was for giving to all needy persons, while she only desired to bestow it on the deserving, but they had renounced the wish of manufacturing each other's habits and opinions. Whether mother ever desired the expression of that exaltation of feeling which only lasts in a man while he is in love, I cannot say. It was not for me to know her heart. It is not ordained that these beautiful secrets of feeling should be revealed, where they might prove to be the sweetest knowledge we could have.

Though the days flew by, days filled with the busy nothings of prosperity, they bore no meaning. I shifted the hours, as one shifts the kaleidoscope, with an eye only to their movement. Neither the remembrance of yesterday nor the hope of to-morrow stimulated me. The mere fact of breathing had ceased to be a happiness, since the day I entered Miss Black's school. But I was not yet thoughtful. As for my position, I was loved and I was hated, and it pleased me as much to be hated as to be loved. My acquaintances were kind enough to let me know that I was generally thought proud, exacting, ill-natured, and apt to expect the best of everything. But one thing I know of myself then—that I concealed nothing; the desires and emotions which are usually kept as a private fund I displayed and exhausted. My audacity shocked those who possessed this fund. My candor was called anything but truthfulness; they named it sarcasm, cunning, coarseness, or tact, as those were constituted who came in contact with me. Insight into character, frankness, generosity, disinterestedness, were sometimes given me. Veronica alone was uncompromising; she put aside by instinct what baffled or attracted others, and, setting my real value upon me, acted accordingly. I do not accuse her of injustice, but of a fience harshness which kept us apart for long years. As for her, she was the most reticent girl I ever knew, and but for her explosive temper, which betrayed her, she would have been a mystery. The difference in our physical constitutions would have separated us, if there had been no other cause. The weeks that she was confined to her room, preyed upon by some inscrutable disease, were weeks of darkness and solitude. Temperance and Aunt Merce took as much care of her as she would allow; but she preferred being alone most of the time. Thus she acquired the fortitude of an Indian; pain could extort no groan from her. It reacted on her temper, though, for after an attack she was exasperating. Her invention was put to the rack to tease and offend. I kept out of her way; if by chance she caught sight of me, she forced me to hear the bitter truth of myself. Sometimes she examined me to learn if I had improved by the means which father so *generously* provided for me. "Is he not yet tired of his task?" she asked once. And, "Do you carry everything before you, with your wide eyebrows and sharp teeth? Temperance, where's the Buffon Dr. Snell sent me?[26] I want to classify Cass."

"I'll warrant you'll find her a sheep," Temperance replied.

"Sheep are innocent," said Veronica. "You may go," nodding to me, over the book, and Temperance also made energetic signs to me to go, and not bother the poor girl.

Always regarding her from the point of view she presented, I felt little love for her; her peculiarities offended me as they did mother. We did not perceive the process, but Verry was educated by sickness; her mind fed and grew on pain, and at last mastered it. The darkness in her nature broke; by slow degrees she gained health, though never much strength. Upon each recovery a change was visible; a spiritual dawn had risen in her soul; moral activity blending with her ideality made her life beautiful, even in the humblest sense. Veronica! you were endowed with genius; but while its rays penetrated you, we did not see them. How could we profit by what you saw and heard, when we were blind and deaf?

To us, the voices of the deep sang no epic of grief; the speech of the woods was not articulate; the sea-gull's flashing flight, and the dark swallow's circling sweep, were facts only. Sunrise and sunset were not a pæan to day and night, but five o'clock A.M. or P.M. The seasons that came and went were changes from hot to cold; to you, they were the moods of nature, which found response in those of your own life and soul; her storms and calms were pulses which bore a similitude to the emotions of your heart!

Veronica's habits of isolation clung to her; she would never leave home. The teaching she had was obtained in Surrey. But her knowledge was greater than mine. When I went to Rosville she was reading "Paradise Lost," and writing her opinions upon it in a large blank book. She was also devising a plan for raising trees and flowers in the garret, so that she might realize a picture of a tropical wilderness. Her tastes were so contradictory that time never hung heavy with her; though she had as little practical talent as any person I ever knew, she was a help to both sick and well. She remembered people's ill turns, and what was done for them; and for the well she remembered dates and suggested agreeable occupations—gave them happy ideas. Besides being a calendar of domestic traditions, she was weather-wise, and prognosticated gales, meteors, high tides, and rains.

Home, father said, was her sphere. All that she required, he thought he could do; but of me he was doubtful. Where did I belong? he asked.

I was still "possessed," Aunt Merce said, and mother called me "lawless." "What upon earth are you coming to?" asked Temperance. "You are sowing your wild oats with a vengeance."

"Locke Morgeson's daughter can do anything," commented the villagers. In consequence of the unlimited power accorded me I was unpopular. "Do you think she is handsome?" inquired my friends of each other. "In what respect *can* she be called a beauty?" "Though she reads, she has no great wit," said one. "She dresses oddly for effect," another avowed, "and her manners are ridiculous." But they borrowed my dresses for patterns, imitated my bonnets, and adopted my colors. When I learned to manage a sailboat, they had an aquatic mania. When I learned to ride a horse, the ancient and moth-eaten sidesaddles of the town were resuscitated, and old family nags were made back-sore with the wearing of them, and their youthful spirits revived by new beginners sliding about on their rounded sides. My whims were sneered at, and then followed. Of course I was driven from whim to whim, to keep them busy, and to preserve my originality, and at last I became eccentric for eccentricity's sake. All this prepared the way for my Nemesis. But as yet my wild oats were green and flourishing in the field of youth.

CHAPTER XIII.

I was preaching one day to mother and Aunt Merce a sermon after the manner of Mr. Boold, of Barmouth, taking the sofa for a desk, and for my text "Like David's Harp of solemn sound," and had attracted Temperance and Charles into the room by my declamation, when my audience was unexpectedly increased by the entrance of father, with a strange gentleman. Aunt Merce laughed hysterically; I waved my hand to her, *à la* Boold, and descended from my position.

"Take a chair," said Temperance, who was never abashed, thumping one down before the stranger.

"What is all this?" inquired father.

"Only a *Ranz des Vaches,*[27] father, to please Aunt Merce."

The stranger's eyes were fastened upon me, while father introduced us to "Mr. Charles Morgeson, of Rosville."

"Please receive me as a relative," he said, turning to shake hands with mother. "We have an ancestor in common that makes a sufficient cousinship for a claim, Mrs. Morgeson."

"Why not have looked us up before?" I asked.

"Why," said Veronica, who had just come in, "there are six Charles Morgesons buried in our graveyard."

"I supposed," he said, "that the name was extinct. I lately saw your father's in a State Committee List, and feeling curious regarding it, I came here."

He bowed distantly to Veronica when she entered, but she did not return his bow, though she looked at him fixedly. Temperance and Hepsey hurried up a fine supper immediately. A visitor was a creature to be fed. Feeding together removes embarrassment, and before supper was over we were all acquainted with Mr. Morgeson. There were three cheerful old ladies spending the week with us—the widow Desire Carver, and her two maiden sisters, Polly and Serepta Chandler. They filled the part of chorus in the domestic drama, saying, "Aha," whenever there was a pause. Veronica affected these old ladies greatly, and when they were in the house gave them her society. But for their being there at this time, I doubt whether she would have seen Mr. Morgeson again. That evening she played for them. Her wild, pathetic melodies made our visitor's gray eyes flash with pleasure, and light up his cold face with gleams of feeling; but she was not gratified by his interest. "I think it strange that you should like my music," she said crossly.

"Do you" he answered, amused at her tone, "perhaps it is; but why should I not as well as your friends here?" indicating the old ladies.

"Ah, we like it very much," said the three, clicking their snuffboxes.

"You, too, play?" he asked me.

"Miss Cassy don't play," answered the three, looking at me over their spectacles. "Miss Verry's sun puts out her fire."

"Cassandra does other things better than playing," Veronica said to Mr. Morgeson.

"Why, Veronica," I said, surprised, going toward her.

"Go off, go off," she replied, in an undertone, and struck up a loud march. He had heard her, and while she played looked at her earnestly. Then, seeming to forget the presence of the three, he turned and put out his hand to me, with an authority I did not resist. I laid my hand in his; it was not grasped, but upheld. Veronica immediately stopped playing.

He stayed several days at our house. After the first evening we found him taciturn. He played with Arthur, spoke of his children to him, and promised him a pony if he would go to Rosville. With father he discussed business matters, and went out with him to the shipyards and offices. I scarcely remember that he spoke to me, except in a casual way, more than once. He asked me if I knew whether the sea had any influence upon me; I replied that I had not thought of it. "There are so many things you have not thought of," he answered, "that this is not strange."

Veronica observed him closely; he was aware of it, but was not embarrassed; he met her dark gaze with one keener than her own, and neither talked with the other. The morning he went away, while the chaise was waiting, which was to go to Milford to meet the stagecoach, and he was inviting us to visit him, a thought seemed to strike him. "By the way, Morgeson, why not give Miss Cassandra a finish at Rosville? I have told you of our Academy, and of the advantages which Rosville affords in the way of society. What do you say, Mrs. Morgeson, will you let her come to my house for a year?"

"Locke decides for Cassy," she answered; "I never do now," looking at me reproachfully.

Cousin Charles's hawk eyes caught the look, and he heard me too, when I tapped her shoulder till she turned round and smiled. I whispered, "Mother, your eyes are as blue as the sea yonder, and I love you." She glanced toward it; it was murmuring softly, creeping along the shore, licking the rocks and sand as if recognizing a master. And I saw and felt its steady, resistless heaving, insidious and terrible.

"Well," said father, "we will talk of it on the way to Milford."

"I have kinder of a creeping about your Cousin Charles, as you call him," said Temperance, after she had closed the porch door. "He is too much shut up for me. How's Mis Cousin Charles, I wonder?"

"He is fond of flowers," remarked Aunt Merce; "he examined all my plants, and knew all their botanical names."

"That's a balm for every wound with you, isn't it?" Temperance said. "I spose I can clean the parlor, unless Mis Carver and Chandler are sitting in a row there?"

Veronica, who had hovered between the parlor and the hall while Cousin Charles was taking his leave, so that she might avoid the necessity of any direct notice of him, had heard his proposition about Rosville, said, "Cassandra will go there."

"Do you feel it in your bones, Verry?" Temperance asked.

"Cassandra does."

"Do I? I believe I do."

"You are eighteen; you are too old to go to school."

"But I am not too old to have an agreeable time; besides, I am not eighteen, and shall not be till four days from now."

"You think too much of having a good time, Cassandra," said mother. "I foresee the day when the pitcher will come back from the well broken. You are idle and frivolous; eternally chasing after amusement."

"God knows I don't find it."

"I know you are not happy."

"Tell me," I cried, striking the table with my hand, making Veronica wink, "tell me how to feel and act."

"I have no influence with you, nor with Veronica."

"Because," said Verry, "we are all so different; but I like you, mother, and all that you do."

"Different!" she exclaimed, "children talk to parents about a difference between them."

"I never thought about it before." I said, "but *where* is the family likeness?"

Aunt Merce laughed.

"There's the Morgesons," I continued, "I hate 'em all."

"All?" she echoed; "you are like this new one."

"And Grand'ther Warren"—I continued.

"Your talk," interrupted Aunt Merce, jumping up and walking about, "is enough to make him rise out of his grave."

"I believe," said Veronica, "that Grand'ther Warren nearly crushed you and mother, when girls of our age. Did you know that you had any wants then? or dare to dream anything beside that he laid down for you?"

Aunt Merce and mother exchanged glances.

"Say, mother, what shall I do?" I asked again.

"Do," she answered in a mechanical voice; "read the Bible, and sew more."

"Veronica's life is not misspent," she continued, and seeming to forget that Verry was still there. "Why should she find work for her hands when neither you nor I do?"

Veronica slipped out of the room; and I sat on the floor beside mother. I loved her in an unsatisfactory way. What could we be to each other? We kissed tenderly; I saw she was saddened by something regarding me, which she could not explain, because she refused to explain me naturally. I thought she wished me to believe she could have no infirmity in common with me—no temptations, no errors—that she must repress all the doubts and longings of her heart for example's sake.

There was a weight upon me all that day, a dreary sense of imperfection.

When father came home he asked me if I would like to go to Rosville. I answered, "Yes." Mother must travel with me, for he could not leave home. The sooner I went the better. He also thought Veronica should go. She was called and consulted, and, provided Temperance would accompany us to take care of her, she consented. It was all arranged that evening. Temperance said we must wait a week at least, for her corns to be cured, and the plum-colored silk made, which had been shut up in a band-box for three years.

We started on our journey one bright morning in June, to go to Boston in a stagecoach, a hundred miles from Surrey, and thence to Rosville, forty miles further, by railroad. We stopped a night on the way to Boston at a country inn, which stood before an egg-shaped pond. Temperance remade our beds, declaiming the while against the unwholesome situation of the house; the idea of anybody's living in the vicinity of fresh water astonished her; to impose upon travelers' health that way was too much. She went to the kitchen to learn whether the landlady cooked, or hired a cook. She sat up all night with our luggage in sight, to keep off what she called "prowlers"—she did not like to say robbers, for fear of exciting our imaginations—and frightened us by falling out of her chair toward morning. Veronica insisted upon her going to bed, but she refused, till Veronica threatened to sit up herself, when she carried her own carpet-bag to bed with her.

We arrived in Boston the next day and went to the Bromfield House in Bromfield Street, whither father had directed us. We were ushered to the parlor by a waiter, who seemed struck by Temperance, and who was treated by her with respect. "Mr. Shepherd, the landlord, himself, I guess," she whispered.

Three cadaverous children were there eating bread and butter from a black tray on the center-table.

"Good Lord!" exclaimed Temperance, "what bread those children are eating! It is made of sawdust."

"It's good, you old cat," screamed the little girl.

Veronica sat down by her, and offered her some sugar-plums, which the child snatched from her hand.

"We are missionaries," said the oldest boy, "and we are going to Bombay next week in the *Cabot*. I'll make the natives gee, I tell ye."

"Mercy on us!" exclaimed Temperance, "did you ever?"

Presently a sickly, gentle-looking man entered, in a suit of black camlet, and carrying an umbrella; he took a seat by the children, and ran his fingers through his hair, which already stood upright.

"That girl gave Sis some sugar-plums," remarked the boy.

"I hope you thanked her, Clarissa," said the father.

"No; she didn't give me enough," the child answered.

"They have no mother," the poor man said apologetically to

Veronica, looking up at her, and, as he caught her eye, blushing deeply. She bowed, and moved away. Mother rang the bell, and when the waiter came gave him a note for Mr. Shepherd, which father had written, bespeaking his attention. Mr. Shepherd soon appeared, and conveyed us to two pleasant rooms with an unmitigated view of the wall of the next house from the windows.

"This," remarked Temperance, "is worse than the pond."

Mr. Shepherd complimented mother on her fine daughters; hoped Mr. Morgeson would run for Congress soon; told her she should have the best the house afforded, and retired.

I wanted to shop, and mother gave me money. I found Washington Street, and bought six wide, embroidered belts, a gilt buckle, a variety of ribbons, and a dozen yards of lace. I repented the whole before I got back; for I saw other articles I wanted more. I found mother alone; Temperance had gone out with Veronica, she said, and she had given Veronica the same amount of money, curious to know how she would spend it, as she had never been shopping. It was nearly dark when they returned.

"I like Boston," said Verry.

"But what have you bought?"

She displayed a beautiful gold chain, and a little cross for the throat; a bundle of picture-books for the missionary children; a sewing-silk shawl for Hepsey, and some toys for Arthur.

"To-morrow, I shall go shopping," said mother. "What did you buy, Temperance?"

"A mean shawl. In my opinion, Boston is a den of thieves."

She untied a box, from which she took a sky-blue silk shawl, with brown flowers woven in it.

"I gave eighteen dollars for it, if I gave a cent, Mis Morgeson; I know I am cheated. It's sleazy, isn't it?"

The bell for tea rang, and Mr. Shepherd came up to escort us to the table. Temperance delayed us, to tie on a silk apron, to protect the plum-colored silk, for, as she observed to Mr. Shepherd, she was afraid it would show grease badly. I could not help exchanging smiles with Mr. Shepherd, which made Veronica frown. The whole table stared as we seated ourselves, for we derived an importance from the fact that we were under the personal charge of the landlord.

"How they gawk at you," whispered Temperance. I felt my color rise.

"The gentlemen do not guess that we are sisters," said Veronica quietly.

"How do I look?" I asked.

"You know how, and that I do not agree with your opinion. You look cruel."

"I am cruel hungry."

Her eyes sparkled with disdain.

"What do you mean to do for a year?" I continued.

"Forget you, for one thing."

"I hope you wont be ill again, Verry."

"I shall be," she answered with a shudder; "I need all the illnesses that come."

"As for me," I said, biting my bread and butter, "I feel well to my fingers' ends; they tingle with strength. I am elated with health."

I had not spoken the last word before I became conscious of a streak of pain which cut me like a knife and vanished; my surprise at it was so evident that she asked me what ailed me.

"Nothing."

"I never had the feeling you speak of in my finger ends," she said sadly, looking at her slender hand.

"Poor girl!"

"What has come over you, Cass? An attack of compassion? Are you meaning to leave an amiable impression with me?"

After supper Mr. Shepherd asked mother if she would go to the theater. The celebrated tragedian, Forrest, was playing; would the young ladies like to see Hamlet? We all went, and my attention was divided between Hamlet and two young men who lounged in the box door till Mr. Shepherd looked them away. Veronica laughed at Hamlet, and Temperance said it was stuff and nonsense. Veronica laughed at Ophelia, also, who was a superb, black-haired woman, toying with an elegant Spanish fan, which Hamlet in his energy broke. "It is not Shakespeare," she said.

"Has she read Shakespeare?" I asked mother.

"I am sure I do not know."

That night, after mother and Veronica were asleep, I persuaded Temperance to get up, and bore my ears with a coarse needle, which I had bought for the purpose. It hurt me so, when she pierced one, that I could not summon resolution to have the other operated on; so I went to bed with a bit of sewing silk in the hole she had made. But in the morning I roused her, to tell her I thought I could bear to have the other ear bored. When mother appeared I showed her my ears red and sore, insisting that I must have a certain pair of white cornelian ear-rings, set in chased gold, and three inches long, which I had seen in a shop window. She scolded Temperance, and then gave me the money.

The next day mother and I started for Rosville. Veronica decided to remain in Boston with Temperance till mother returned. She said that if she went she might find Mrs. Morgeson as disagreeable as Mr. Morgeson was; that she liked the Bromfield; besides, she wanted to see the missionary children off for Bombay, and intended to go down to the ship on the day they were to sail. She was also going to ask Mr. Shepherd to look up a celebrated author for her. She must see one if possible.

CHAPTER XIV.

It was sunset when we arrived in Rosville, and found Mr. Morgeson waiting for us with his carriage at the station. From its open sides I looked out on a tranquil, agreeable landscape; there was nothing saline in the atmosphere. The western breeze, which blew in our faces, had an earthy scent, with fluctuating streams of odors from trees and flowers. As we passed through the town, Cousin Charles pointed to the Academy, which stood at the head of a green. Pretty houses stood round it, and streets branched from it in all directions. Flower gardens, shrubbery, and trees were scattered everywhere. Rosville was larger and handsomer than Surrey.

"That is my house, on the right," he said.

We looked down the shady street through which we were going, and saw a modern cottage, with a piazza and peaked roof, and on the side toward us a large yard, and stables.

We drove into the yard, and a woman came out on the piazza to receive us. It was Mrs. Morgeson, or "My wife, Cousin Alice," as Mr. Morgeson introduced her. Giving us a cordial welcome, she led us into a parlor where tea was waiting. A servant came in for our bonnets and baskets. Cousin Alice begged us to take tea at once. We were hardly seated when we heard the cry of a young child; she left the table hastily, to come back in a moment with an apology, which she made to Cousin Charles rather than to us. I had never seen a table so well arranged, so fastidiously neat; it glittered with glass and French china. Cousin Charles sent away a glass and a plate, frowning at the girl who waited; there must have been a speck or a flaw in them. The viands were as pretty as the dishes, the lamb chops were fragile; the bread was delicious, but cut in transparent slices, and the butter pat was nearly stamped through with its bouquet of flowers. This was all the feast except sponge cake, which felt like muslin in the fingers; I could have squeezed the whole of it into my mouth. Still hungry, I observed that Cousin Charles and Alice had finished; and though she shook her spoon in the cup, feigning to continue, and he snipped crumbs in his plate, I felt constrained to end my repast. He rose then, and pushing back folding-doors, we entered a large room, leaving Alice at the table. Windows extending to the floor opening on the piazza, but notwithstanding the stream of light over the carpet, I thought it somber, and out of keeping with the cottage exterior. The walls were covered with dark red velvet paper, the furniture was dark, the mantel and table tops were black marble, and the vases and candelabra were bronze. He directed mother's attention to the portraits of his children, explaining them, while I went to a table between the windows to examine the green and white sprays of some delicate flower I had never before seen. Its fragrance was intoxicating. I lifted the heavy vase which contained it; it was taken from me gently by Charles, and replaced.

"It will hardly bear touching," he said. "By to-morrow these little white bells will be dead."

I looked up at him. "What a contrast!" I said.

"Where?"

"Here, in this room, and in you."

"And between you and me?"

His face was serene, dark, and delicate, but to look at it made me shiver. Mother came toward us, pleading fatigue as an excuse for retiring, and Cousin Charles called Cousin Alice, who went with us to our room. In the morning, she said, we should see her three children. She never left them, she was so afraid of their being ill, also telling mother that she would do all in her power to make my stay in Rosville pleasant and profitable. As a mother, she could appreciate her anxiety and sadness in leaving me. Mother thanked her warmly, and was sure that I should be happy; but I had an inward misgiving that I should not have enough to eat.

"I hear Edward," said Alice. "Good-night."

Presently a girl, the same who had taken our bonnets, came in with a pitcher of warm water and a plate of soda biscuit. She directed us where to find the apparel she had nicely smoothed and folded; took off the handsome counterpane, and the pillows trimmed with lace, putting others of a plainer make in their places; shook down the window curtains; asked us if we would have anything more, and quietly disappeared. I offered mother the warm water, and appropriated the biscuits. There were six. I ate every one, undressing meanwhile, and surveying the apartment.

"Cassy, Mrs. Morgeson is an excellent housekeeper."

"Yes," I said huskily, for the dry biscuit choked me.

"What would Temperance and Hepsey say to this?"

"I think they would grumble, and admire. Look at this," showing her the tassels of the inner window curtains done up in little bags. "And the glass is pinned up with nice yellow paper; and here is a damask napkin fastened to the wall behind the washstand. And everything stands on a mat. I wonder if this is to be my room?"

"It is probably the chamber for visitors. Why, these are beautiful pillow-cases, too," she exclaimed, as she put her head on the pillow. "Come to bed; don't read."

I had taken up a red morocco-bound book, which was lying alone on the bureau. It was Byron, and turning over the leaves till I came to Don Juan, I read it through, and began Childe Harold, but the candle expired. I struck out my hands through the palpable darkness, to find the bed without disturbing mother, whose soul was calmly threading the labyrinth of sleep. I finished Childe Harold early in the morning, though, and went down to breakfast, longing to be a wreck![28]

The three children were in the breakfast-room, which was not the one we had taken tea in, but a small apartment, with a door opening into the garden. They were beautifully dressed, and their mother was tending and watching them. The oldest was eight years, the youngest three months. Cousin Alice gave us descriptions of their tastes and habits, dwelling with emphasis on those of the baby. I drew from her conversation the opinion that she had a tendency to the rearing of children. I was glad when Cousin Charles came in, looking at his watch. "Send off the babies, Alice, and ring the bell for breakfast."

She sent out the two youngest, put little Edward in his chair, and breakfast began.

"Mrs. Morgeson," said Charles, "the horses will be ready to

take you round Rosville. We will call on Dr. Price, for you to see
the kind of master Cassandra will have. I have already spoken to
him about receiving a new pupil."

"Oh, I am homesick at the idea of school and a master," I said.

Mother tried in vain to look hard-hearted, and to persuade that
it was good for me, but she lost her appetite, with the thought of
losing me, which the mention of Dr. Price brought home. The
breakfast was as well adapted to a delicate taste as the preceding
supper. The ham was most savory, but cut in such thin slices that
it curled; and the biscuits were as white and feathery as snowflakes.
I think also that the boiled eggs were smaller than any I had seen.
Cousin Alice gave unremitting attention to Edward, who ate as
little as the rest.

"Mother," I said afterward, "I am afraid I am an animal. Did
you notice how little the Morgesons ate?"

"I noticed how elegant their table appointments were, and I shall
buy new china in Boston to-morrow. I wish Hepsey would not
load our table as she does."

"Hepsey is a good woman, mother; do give my love to her.
Now that I think of it, she was always making up some nice dish;
tell her I remember it, will you?"

When Cousin Charles put us into the carriage, and hoisted little
Edward on the front seat, mother noticed that two men held the
horses, and that they were not the same he had driven the night
before. She said she was afraid to go, they looked ungovernable;
but he reassured her, and one of the men averring that Mr. Morgeson could drive anything, she repressed her fears, and we drove
out of the yard behind a pair of horses that stood on their hind
legs as often as that position was compatible with the necessity
they were under of getting on, for they evidently understood that
they were guided by a firm hand. Edward was delighted with their
behavior, and for the first time I saw his father smile on him.

"These are fine brutes," he said, not taking his eyes from them;
"but they are not equal to my mare, Nell. Alice is afraid of her;
but I hope that you, Cassandra, will ride with me sometimes when
I drive her."

"Oh!" exclaimed mother, grasping my arm.

"You would, would you?" he said, taking out the whip, as the
horses recoiled from a man who lay by the roadside, leaping so
high that the harness seemed rattling from their backs. He struck

them, and said, "Go on now, go on, devils." There was no further
trouble. He encouraged mother not to be afraid, looking keenly at
me. I looked back at him.

"How much worse is the mare, cousin Charles?"

"You shall see."

After driving round the town we stopped at the Academy.
Morning prayers were over, and the scholars, some sixty boys and
girls, were coming downstairs from the hall, to go into the rooms,
each side of a great door. Dr. Price was behind them. He stopped
when he saw us, an introduction took place, and he inquired for
Dr. Snell, as an old college friend. Locke Morgeson sounded familiarly, he said; a member of his mother's family named Somers
had married a gentlemen of that name. He remembered it from an
old ivory miniature which his mother had shown him, telling him
it was the likeness of her cousin Rachel's husband. I replied we
knew that grandfather had married a Rachel Somers. Cousin Charles
was surprised and a little vexed that the doctor had never told him,
when he must have known that he had been anxiously looking up
the Morgeson pedigree; but the doctor declared he had not thought
of it before, and that only the name of Locke had recalled it to his
mind. He then proposed our going to Miss Prior, the lady who
had charge of the girls' department, and we followed him to her
school-room.

I was at once interested and impressed by the appearance of my
teacher that was to be. She was a dignified, kind-looking woman,
who asked me a few questions in such a pleasant, direct manner
that I frankly told her I was eighteen years old, very ignorant, and
averse from learning; but I did not speak loud enough for anybody
beside herself to hear.

"Now," said mother, when we came away, "think how much
greater your advantages are than mine have ever been. How miserable was my youth! It is too late for me to make any attempt at
cultivation. I have no wish that way. Yet now I feel sometimes as
if I were leaving the confines of my old life to go I know not
whither, to do I know not what."

But her countenance fell when she heard that Dr. Price had been
a Unitarian minister, and that there was no Congregational church
in Rosville.

She went to Boston that Friday afternoon, anxious to get safely
home with Veronica. We parted with many a kiss and shake of the
hand and last words. I cried when I went up to my room, for I

found a present there—a beautiful workbox, and in it was a small Bible with my name and hers written on the fly-leaf in large print-like, but tremulous letters. I composed my feelings by putting it away carefully and unpacking my trunk.

CHAPTER XV.

Rosville was a county town.[29] The courts were held there, and its society was adorned with several lawyers of note who had law students, which fact was to the lawyers' daughters the most agreeable feature of their fathers' profession. It had a weekly market day and an annual cattle show. I saw a turnout of whips and wagons about the hitching-posts round the green of a Tuesday the year through, and going to and from school met men with a bovine smell. Caucuses were prevalent, and occasionally a State Convention was held, when Rosville paid honor to some political hero of the day with banners and brass bands. It was a favorite spot for the rustication of naughty boys from Harvard or Yale. Dr. Price had one or two at present who boarded in his house so as to be immediately under his purblind eyes, and who took Greek and Latin at the Academy.

Social feuds raged in the Academy coteries between the collegians and the natives on account of the superior success of the former in flirtation. The latter were not consoled by their experience that no flirtation lasted beyond the period of rustication. Dr. Price usually had several young men fitting for college also, which fact added more piquancy to the provincial society. In the summer riding parties were fashionable, and in the winter county balls and cotillion parties; a professor came down from Boston at this season to set up a dancing school, which was always well attended.

The secular concerns of life engaged the greatest share of the interests of its inhabitants; and although there existed social and professional dissensions, there was little sectarian spirit among them and no religious zeal. The rich and fashionable were Unitarians. The society owned a tumble-down church; a mild preacher stood in its pulpit and prayed and preached, sideways and slouchy. This degree of religious vitality accorded with the habits of its generations. Surrey and Barmouth would have howled over the Total Depravity of Rosville. There was no probationary air about it. Human Nature was the infallible theme there. At first I missed the vibration of the moral sword which poised in our atmosphere. When I felt an emotion without seeing the shadow of its edge turning toward me, I discovered my conscience, which hitherto had only been described to me.

There were churches in the town beside the Unitarian. The Universalists had a bran-new one, and there was still another frequented by the sedimentary part of the population—Methodists.

I toned down perfectly within three months. Soon after my arrival at his house I became afraid of Cousin Charles. Not that he ever said anything to justify fear of him—he was more silent at home than elsewhere; but he was imperious, fastidious, and sarcastic with me by a look, a gesture, an inflection of his voice. My perception of any defect in myself was instantaneous with his discovery of it. I fell into the habit of guessing each day whether I was to offend or please him, and then into that of intending to please. An intangible, silent, magnetic feeling existed between us, changing and developing according to its own mysterious law, remaining intact in spite of the contests between us of resistance and defiance. But my feeling died or slumbered when I was beyond the limits of his personal influence. When in his presence I was so pervaded by it that whether I went contrary to the dictates of his will or not I moved as if under a pivot; when away my natural elasticity prevailed, and I held the same relation to others that I should have held if I had not known him. This continued till the secret was divined, and then his influence was better remembered.

I discovered that there was little love between him and Alice. I never heard from either an expression denoting that each felt an interest in the other's individual life; neither was there any of that conjugal freemasonry which bores one so to witness. But Alice was not unhappy. Her ideas of love ended with marriage; what came afterward—children, housekeeping, and the claims of society—sufficed her needs. If she had any surplus of feeling it was expended upon her children, who had much from her already, for she was devoted and indulgent to them. In their management she allowed no interference, on this point only thwarting her husband. In one respect she and Charles harmonized; both were worldly, and in all the material of living there was sympathy. Their relation was no unhappiness to him; he thought, I dare say, if he thought at all, that it was a natural one. The men of his acquaintance called him a lucky man, for Alice was handsome, kind-hearted, intelligent, and popular.

Whether Cousin Alice would have found it difficult to fulfill the promise she made mother regarding me, if I had been a plain, unnoticeable girl, I cannot say, or whether her anxiety that I should make an agreeable impression would have continued beyond a few days. She looked after my dress and my acquaintances. When she found that I was sought by the young people of her set and the Academy, she was gratified, and opened her house for them, giving little parties and large ones, which were pleasant to everybody except Cousin Charles, who detested company—"it made him lie so." But he was very well satisfied that people should like to visit and praise his house and its belongings, if Alice would take the trouble of it upon herself. I made calls with her Wednesday afternoons, and went to church with her Sunday mornings. At home I saw little of her. She was almost exclusively occupied with the children—their ailments or their pleasures—and staid in her own room, or the nursery.

When in the house I never occupied one spot long, but wandered in the garden, which had a row of elms, or haunted the kitchen and stables, to watch black Phœbe, the cook, or the men as they cleaned the horses or carriages. My own room was in a wing of the cottage, with a window overlooking the entrance into the yard and the carriage drive; this was its sole view, except the wall of a house on the other side of a high fence. I heard Charles when he drove home at night, or away in the morning; knew when Nell was in a bad humor by the tone of his voice, which I heard whether my window was open or shut. It was a pretty room, with a set of maple furniture, and amber and white wallpaper, and amber and white chintz curtains and coverings. It suited the color of my hair, Alice declared, and was becoming to my complexion.

"Yes," said Charles, looking at my hair with an expression that made me put my hand up to my head as if to hide it; I knew it was carelessly dressed.

I made a study that day of the girls' heads at school, and from that time improved in my style of wearing it, and I brushed it with zeal every day afterward. Alice had my room kept so neatly for me that it soon came to be a reproach, and I was finally taught by her example how to adjust chairs, books, and mats in straight lines, to fold articles without making odd corners and wrinkles; at last I improved so much that I could find what I was seeking in a drawer, without harrowing it with my fingers, and began to see beauty in order. Alice had a talent for housekeeping, and her talent was fostered by the exacting, systematic taste of her husband. He examined many matters which are usually left to women, and he applied his business talent to the art of living, succeeding in it as he did in everything else.

Alice told me that Charles had been poor; that his father was never on good terms with him. She fancied they were too much alike; so he had turned him off to shift for himself, when quite young. When she met him, he was the agent of a manufacturing company, in the town where her parents lived, and even then, in [his] style of living, he surpassed the young men of her acquaintance. The year before they were married his father died, and as Charles was his only child, he left his farm to him, and ten thousand dollars—all he had. The executors of the will were obliged to advertise for him, not having any clue of his place of residence. He sold the farm as soon as it was put in his hands, took the ten thousand dollars, and came back to be married. A year after, he went to Rosville, and built a cotton factory, three miles from town, and the cottage, and then brought her and Edward, who was a few months old, to live in it. He had since enlarged the works, employed more operatives, and was making a great deal of money. Morgeson's Mills, she believed, were known all over the country. Charles was his own agent, as well as sole owner. There were no mills beside his in the neighborhood; to that fact she ascribed the reason of his having no difficulties in Rosville, and no enmities; for she knew he had no wish to make friends. The Rosville people, having no business in common with him, had no right to meddle, and could find but small excuse for comment. They spent, she said, five or six thousand a year; most of it went in horses, she was convinced, and she believed his flowers cost him a great deal too. "You must know, Cassandra, that his heart is with his horses and his flowers. He is more interested in them than he is in his children."

She looked vexed when she said this; but I took hold of the edge of her finely embroidered cape, and asked her how much it cost. She laughed, and said, "Fifty dollars; but you see how many lapels it has. I have still a handsomer one that was seventy-five."

"Are they a part of the six thousand a year, Alice?"

"Of course; but Charles wishes me to dress, and never stints me in money; and, after all, I like for him to spend his money in his own way. It vexes me sometimes, he buys such wild brutes, and endangers his life with them. He rides miles and miles every year; and it relieves the tedium of his journeys to have horses he must watch, I suppose."

Nobody in Rosville lived at so fast a rate as the Morgesons. The oldest families there were not the richest—the Ryders, in particular. Judge Ryder had four unmarried daughters; they were the only girls in our set who never invited us to visit them. They could not help saying, with a fork of the neck, "Who are the Morgesons?" But all the others welcomed Cousin Alice, and were friendly with me. She was too pretty and kind-hearted not to be liked, if she was rich; and Cousin Charles was respected, because he made no acquaintance beyond bows, and "How-de-do's." It was rather a stirring thing to have such a citizen, especially when he met with an accident, and he broke many carriages in the course of time; and now and then there was a row at the mills, which made talk. His being considered a hard man did not detract from the interest he inspired.

My advent in Rosville might be considered a fortunate one; appearances indicated it; I am sure I thought so, and was very satisfied with my position. I conformed to the ways of the family with ease, even in the matter of small breakfasts and light suppers. I found that I was more elastic than before, and more susceptible to sudden impressions; I was conscious of the ebb and flow of blood through my heart, felt it when it eddied up into my face, and touched my brain with its flame-colored wave. I loved life again. The stuff of which each day was woven was covered with an arabesque which suited my fancy. I missed nothing that the present unrolled for me, but looked neither to the past nor to the future. In truth there was little that was elevated in me. Could I have perceived it if there had been? Whichever way the circumstances of my life vacillated, I was not yet reached to the quick; whether spiritual or material influences made sinuous the current of being, it still flowed toward an undiscovered ocean.

Half the girls at the Academy, like myself, came from distant towns. Some had been there three years. They were all younger than myself. There never had been a boarding-house attached to the school, and it was not considered a derogatory thing for the best families to receive these girls as boarders. We were therefore on the same footing, in a social sense. I was also on good terms with Miss Prior. She was a cold and kindly woman, faithful as a teacher, gifted with an insight into the capacity of a pupil. She gave me a course of History first, and after that Physical Philosophy; but never recommended me to Moral Science. When I had been with her a few months, she proposed that I should study the common branches; my standing in the school was such that I went down into the primary classes without shame, and I must say that I was the dullest scholar in them. We also had a drawing master and a music-teacher. The latter was an amiable woman, with theatrical manners. She was a Mrs. Lane; but no Mr. Lane had ever been seen in Rosville. We girls supposed he had deserted her, which was the fact, as she told me afterward. She cried whenever she sang a sentimental song, but never gave up to her tears, singing on with blinded eyes and quavering voice. I laughed at her dresses which had been handsome, with much frayed trimming about them, the hooks and eyes loosened and the seams strained, but liked her, and although I did not take lessons, saw her every day when she came up to the Academy. She asked me once if I had any voice. I answered her by singing one of our Surrey hymns, *"Once on the raging seas he rode."* She grew pale, and said, "Don't for heaven's sake sing that! I can see my old mother, as she looked when she sang that hymn of a stormy night, when father was out to sea. Both are dead now, and where am I?"

She turned round on the music stool, and banged out the accompaniment of *"O pilot, 'tis a fearful night,"* and sang it with great energy. After her feelings were composed, she begged me to allow her to teach me to sing. "You can at least learn the simple chords of song accompaniments, and I think you have a voice that can be made effective."

I promised to try, and as I had taken lessons before, in three months I could play and sing *"Should those fond hopes e'er forsake thee,"* tolerably well. But Mrs. Lane persisted in affirming that I had a dramatic talent, and as she supposed that I never should be an actress, I must bring it out in singing; so I persevered, and, thanks to her, improved so much that people said, when I was mentioned, "She sings."[30]

The Moral Sciences went to Dr. Price, and he had a class of girls in Latin; but my only opportunity of going before him was at morning prayers and Wednesday afternoons, when we assembled in the hall to hear orations in Latin, or translations, and "pieces" spoken by the boys; and at the quarterly reviews, when he marched us backward and forward through the books we had conned, like the sharp old gentleman he was, notwithstanding his purblind eyes.

CHAPTER XVI.

I heard from home regularly; father, however, was my only correspondent. He stipulated that I should write him every other Saturday, if not more than a line; but I did more than that at first, writing up the events of the fortnight, interspersing my opinions of the actors engaged therein, and dwindling by degrees down to the mere acknowledgment of his letter. He read without comment, but now and then he asked me questions which puzzled me to answer.

"Do you like Mr. Morgeson?" he asked once.

"He is very attentive," I wrote back. "But so is Cousin Alice,— she is fond of me."

"You do not like Morgeson?" again.

"Are there no agreeable young men," he asked another time, "with Dr. Price?"

"Only boys," I wrote—"cubs of my own age."

Among the first letters I received was one with the news of the death of my grandfather, John Morgeson. He had left ten thousand dollars for Arthur, the sum to be withdrawn from the house of Locke Morgeson & Co., and invested elsewhere, for the interest to accumulate, and be added to the principal, till he should be of age. The rest of his property he gave to the Foreign Missionary Society.[31] "Now," wrote father, "it will come your turn next, to stand in the gap, when your mother and I fall back from the forlorn hope—life." This merry and unaccustomed view of things did not suggest to my mind the change he intimated; I could not dwell on such an idea, so steadfast a home-principle were father and mother. It was different with grandfathers and grandmothers, of course; they died, since it was not particularly necessary for them to live after their children were married.

It was early June when I went to Rosville; it was now October. There was nothing more for me to discover there. My relations at home and at school were established, and it was probable that the next year's plans were all settled.

"It is the twentieth," said my friend, Helen Perkins, as we

lingered in the Academy yard, after school hours. "The trees have thinned so we can see up and down the streets. Isn't that Mr. Morgeson who is tearing round the corner of Gold Street? Do you think he is strange-looking? I do. His hair, and eyes, and complexion are exactly the same hue; what color is it? A pale brown, or a greenish gray?"

"Is he driving this way?"

"Yes; the fore-legs of his horse have nearly arrived."

I moved on in advance of Helen, toward the gate; he beckoned when he saw me, and presently reined Nell close to us. "You can decide now what color he is," I whispered to her.

"Will you ride home?" he asked. "And shall I take you down to Bancroft's, Miss Helen?"

She would have declined, but I took her arm, pushed her into the chaise, and then sprang in after her; she seized the hand-loop, in view of an upset.

"You are afraid of my horse, Miss Helen," he said, without having looked at her.

"I am afraid of your driving," she answered, leaning back and looking behind him at me. She shook her head and put her finger on her eyelid to make me understand that she did not like the color of his eyes.

"Cassandra is afraid of neither," he said.

"Why should I be?" I replied coldly.

We were soon at the Bancrofts', where Helen lived, which was a mile from the Academy, and half a mile from our house. When we were going home, he asked:

"Is she your intimate friend?"

"The most in school."

"Is there the usual nonsense about her?"

"What do you mean by nonsense?"

"When a girl talks about her lover or proposes one to her friend."

"I think she is not gifted that way."

"Then I like her."

"Why should she not talk about lovers, though? The next time I see her I will bring up the subject."

"You shall think and talk of your lessons, and nothing more, I charge you. Go on, Nell," he said, in a loud voice, turning into the yard and grazing one of the gate-posts, so that we struck together. I was vexed, thinking it was done purposely, and brushed my shoulder where he came in contact, as if dust had fallen on me, and jumped out without looking at him, and ran into the house.

"Are you losing your skill in driving, Charles?" Alice asked, when we were at tea, "or is Nell too much for you? I saw you crash against the gate-post."

"Did you? My hand was not steady, and we made a lurch."

"Was there a fight at the mills last night? Jesse said so."

"Jesse must mind his business."

"He told Phœbe about it."

"I knocked one of the clerks over and sprained my wrist."

I met his eye then. "It was your right hand?" I asked.

"It was my right hand," in a deferential tone, and with a slight bow in my direction.

"Was it Parker?" she asked.

"Yes, he is a puppy; but don't talk about it."

Nothing more was said, even by Edward, who observed his father with childish gravity, I meditated on the injustice I had done him about the gate-post. After tea he busied himself in the garden among the flowers which were still remaining. I lingered in the parlor or walked the piazza with an undefined desire of speaking to him before I should go to my room. After he had finished his garden work he went to the stable; I heard the horses stepping about the floor as they were taken out for his inspection. The lamps were lighted before he came in again; Alice was upstairs as usual. When I heard him coming, I opened my book, and seated myself in a corner of a sofa; he walked to the window without noticing me, and drummed on the piano.

"Does your wrist pain you, Charles?" still reading.

"A trifle," adjusting his wristband.

"Do you often knock men down in your employ?"

"When they deserve it."

"It is a generous and manly sort of pastime."

"I am a generous man and very strong; do you know that, you little fool? Here, will you take this flower? There will be no more this year." I took it from his hand; it was a pink, faintly odorous blossom.

"I love these fragile flowers best," he continued—"where I have to protect them from my own touch, even." He relapsed into forgetfulness for a moment, and then began to study his memorandum book.

"A note from the mills, sir," said Jesse, "by one of the hands."

"Tell him to wait."

He read it, and threw it over to me. It was from Parker, who informed Mr. Morgeson that he was going by the morning's train to Boston, thinking it was time for him to leave his employ; that, though the fault was his own in the difficulty of the day before, a Yankee could not stand a knock-down. It was too damned aristocratic for an employer to have that privilege; our institutions did not permit it. He thanked Mr. Morgeson for his liberality; he couldn't thank him for being a good fellow. "And would he oblige him by sending per bearer the arrears of salary?"

"Parker is in love with a factory girl. He quarreled with one of the hands because he was jealous of him, and would have been whipped by the man and his friends; to spare him that, I knocked him down. Do you feel better now, Cassy?"

"Better? How does it concern me?"

He laughed.

"Put Black Jake in the wagon." he called to Jesse.

Alice heard him and came downstairs; we went out on the piazza to see him off. "Why do you go?" she asked, in an uneasy tone.

"I must. Wont you go too?"

She refused; but whispered to me, asking if I were afraid?

"Of what?"

"Men quarreling?"

"Cassandra, will you go?" he asked. "If not, I am off. Jump in behind, Sam, will you?"

"Go," said Alice; and she ran in for a shawl, which she wrapped round me.

"Alice," said Charles, "you are a silly woman."

"As you have always said," she answered, laughing. "Ward the blows from him, Cassandra."

"It's a pretty dark night for a ride," remarked Sam.

"I have rode in darker ones."

"I dessay," replied Sam.

"Cover your hand with my handkerchief," I said; "the wind is cutting."

"Do you wish it?"

"No, I do not wish it; it was a humanitary idea merely."

He refused to have it covered.

The air had a moldy taint, and the wind blew the dead leaves

around us. As we rode through the darkness I counted the glim-
mering lights which flashed across our way till we got out on the
high-road where they grew scarce, and the wind whistled loud
about our faces. He laid his hand on my shawl. "It is too light;
you will take cold."

"No."

We reached the mills, and pulled up the corner of a building,
where a light shone through a window.

"This is my office. You must go in—it is too chilly for you to
wait in the wagon. Hold Jake, Sam, till I come back."

I followed him. In the farthest corner of the room where we
had seen the light, behind the desk, sat Mr. Parker, with his light
hair rumpled, and a pen behind his ear.

I stopped by the door, while Charles went to the desk and stood
before him to intercept my view, but he could not help my hearing
what was said, though he spoke low.

"Did you give something to Sam, Parker, for bringing me your
note at such a late hour?"

"Certainly," in a loud voice.

"He must be fifty, at least."

"I should say so," rather lower.

"Well, here is your money; you had better stay. I shall be devilish sorry for your father, who is my friend; you know he will be
disappointed if you leave; depend upon it he will guess at the girl.
Of course you would like to have me say I was in fault about
giving you a blow—as I was. Stay. You will get over the affair. We
all do. Is she handsome?"

"Beautiful," in a meek but enthusiastic tone.

"That goes, like the flowers; but they come every year again."

"Yes?"

"Yes, I say."

"No; I'll stay and see."

Charles turned away.

"Good-evening, Mr. Parker," I said, stepping forward. I had
met him at several parties at Rosville, but never at our house.

"Excuse me, Miss Morgeson; I did not know you. I hope you
are well."

"Come," said Charles, with his hand on the latch.

"Are you going to Mrs. Bancroft's whist party on Wednesday
night, Mr. Parker?"

"Yes; Miss Perkins was kind enough to invite me."

"Cassandra, come." And Charles opened the door. I fumbled for the flower at my belt. "It's nice to have flowers so late; don't you think so?" inhaling the fragrance of my crushed specimens; "if they would but last. Will you have it?" stretching it toward him. He was about to take it with a blush, when Charles struck it out of my hand and stepped on it.

"Are you ready now?" he said, in a quick voice.

I declared it was nothing, when I found I was too ill to rise the next morning. At the end of three days, as I still felt a disinclination to get up, Alice sent for her physician. I told him I was sleepy and felt dull pains. He requested me to sit up in bed, and rapped my shoulders and chest with his knuckles, in a forgetful way.

"Nothing serious," he said; "but, like many women, you will continue to do something to keep in continual pain. If Nature does not endow your constitution with suffering, you will make up the loss by some fatal trifling, which will bring it. I dare say, now, that after this, you never will be quite well."

"I will take care of my health."

He looked into my face attentively.

"You wont—you can't. Did you ever notice your temperament?"[32]

"No, never; what is it?"

"How old are you?"

"Eighteen, and four months."

"Is it possible? How backward you are! You are quite interesting."

"When may I get up?"

"Next week; don't drink coffee. Remember to live in the day. Avoid stirring about in the night, as you would avoid Satan. Sleep, sleep then, and you'll make that beauty of yours last longer."

"Am I a beauty? No living creature ever said so before."

"Adipose beauty."

"Fat?"

"No; not that exactly. Good-day."

He came again, and asked me questions concerning my father and mother; what my grandparents died of; and whether any of my family were strumous. He struck me as being very odd.

My school friends were attentive, but I only admitted Helen Perkins to see me. Her liking for me opened my heart still more toward her. She was my first intimate friend—and my last. Though younger than I, she was more experienced, and had already passed through scenes I knew nothing of, which had sobered her judgment, and given her feelings a practical tinge. She was noted for having the highest spirits of any girl in school—another result of her experiences. She never allowed them to appear fluctuating; she was, therefore, an aid to me, whose moods varied.

After my illness came a sense of change. I had lost that careless security in my strength which I had always possessed, and was troubled with vague doubts, that made me feel I needed help from without.

I did not see Charles while I was ill, for he was absent most of the time. I knew when he was at home by the silence which pervaded the premises. When he was not there, Alice spread the children in all directions, and the servants gave tongue.

He was not at home the day I went downstairs, and I missed him, continually asking myself, "Why do I?" As I sat with Alice in the garden-room, I said, "Alice." She looked up from her sewing. "I am thinking of Charles."

"Yes. He will be glad to see you again."

"Is he really related to me?"

"He told you so, did he not? And his name certainly is Morgeson."

"But we are wholly unlike, are we not?"

"Wholly; but why do you ask?"

"He influences me so strongly."

"Influences you?" she echoed.

"Yes"; and, with an effort, "I believe I influence him."

"You are very handsome," she said, with a little sharpness. "So are flowers," I said to myself.

"It is not that, Alice," I answered peevishly; "you know better."

"You are peculiar, then; it may be he likes you for being so. He is odd, you know; but his oddity never troubles me." And she resumed her sewing with a placid face.

"Veronica is odd, also," was my thought; "but oddity there runs in a different direction." Her image appeared to me, pale, delicate, unyielding. I seemed to wash like a weed at her base.

"You should see my sister, Alice."

"Charles spoke of her; he says she plays beautifully. If you feel strong next week, we will go to Boston, and make our winter purchases. By the way, I hope you are not nervous. To go back to

Charles, I have noticed how little you say to him. You know he never talks. The influence you speak of—it does not make you dislike him?"

"No; I meant to say—my choice of words must be poor—that it was possible I might be thinking too much of him; he is your husband, you know, though I do not think he is particularly interesting, or pleasing."

She laughed, as if highly amused, and said; "Well, about our dresses. You need a ball dress, so do I; for we shall have balls this winter, and if the children are well, we will go. I think, too, that you had better get a gray cloth pelisse, with a fur trimming. We dress so much at church."

"Perhaps," I said. "And how will a gray hat with feathers look? I must first write father, and ask for more money."

"Of course; but he allows you all you want."

"He is not so very rich; we do not live as handsomely as you do."

It was tea-time when we had finished our confab, and Alice sent me to bed soon after. I was comfortably drowsy when I heard Charles driving into the stable. "There he is," I thought, with a light heart, for I felt better since I had spoken to Alice of him. Her matter-of-fact air had blown away the cobwebs that had gathered across my fancy.

I saw him at the breakfast-table the next morning. He was noting something in his memorandum book, which excused him from offering me his hand; but he spoke kindly, said he was glad to see me, hoped I was well, and could find a breakfast that I liked.

"For some reason or other, I do not eat so much as I did in Surrey."

Alice laughed, and I blushed.

"What do you think, Charles?" she said, "Cassandra seems worried by the influence, as she calls it, you have upon each other."

"Does she?"

He raised his strange, intense eyes to mine; a blinding, intelligent light flowed from them which I could not defy nor resist, a light which filled my veins with a torrent of fire.

"You think Cassandra is not like you," he continued with a curious intonation.

"I told her that your oddities never troubled me."

"That is right."

"To-day," I muttered, "Alice, I shall go back to school."

"You must ride," she answered.

"Jesse will drive you up," said Charles, rising. Alice called him back, to tell him her plan of the Boston visit.

"Certainly; go by all means," he said, and went on his way.

I made my application to father, telling him I had nothing to wear. He answered with haste, begging me to clothe myself at once.

CHAPTER XVII.

It was November when we returned from Boston. One morning when the frost sparkled on the dead leaves, which still dropped on the walks, Helen Perkins and I were taking a stroll down Silver Street, behind the Academy, when we saw Dr. White coming down the street in his sulky, rocking from side to side like a cradle. He stopped when he came up to us.

"Do ye sit up late of evenings, Miss Morgeson?"

"No, Doctor; only once a week or so."

"You are a case." And he meditatively pulled his shaggy whiskers with a loose buckskin glove. "There's a ripple coming under your eyes already; what did I tell you? Let me see, did you say you were like father or mother?"

"I look like my father. By the way, Doctor, I am studying my temperament. You will make an infidel of me by your inquiries."

Helen laughed, and staring at him, called him a bear, and told him he ought to live in a hospital, where he would have plenty of sick women to tease.

"I should find few like you there."

He chirruped to his horse, but checked it again, put out his head and called, "Keep your feet warm, wont you? And read Shakespeare."

Helen said that Dr. White had been crossed in love, and long after had married a deformed woman—for science's sake, perhaps. His talent was well known out of Rosville; but he was unambitious and eccentric.

"He is interested in you, Cass, that I see. Are you quite well? What about the change you spoke of?"

"Dr. White has theories; he has attached one to me. Nature has adjusted us nicely, he thinks, with fine strings; if we laugh too much, or cry too long, a knot slips somewhere, which 'all the

king's men' can't take up again. Perhaps he judges women by his
deformed wife. Men do judge that way, I suppose, and then pride
themselves on their experience, commencing their speeches about
us, with 'you women.' I'll answer your question, though,—there's
a blight creeping over me, or a mildew."

"Is there a worm i' the bud?"

"There may be one at the root; my top is green and flourishing,
isn't it?"

"You expect to be in a state of beatitude always. What is a mote
of dust in another's eye, in yours is a cataract. You are mad at your
blindness, and fight the air because you can't see."

"I feel that I see very little, especially when I understand the
clearness of your vision. Your good sense is monstrous."

"It will come right somehow, with you; when twenty years are
wasted, maybe," she answered sadly. "There's the first bell! I
haven't a word yet of my rhetoric lesson," opening her book and
chanting, " 'Man, thou pendulum betwixt a smile and tear.' Are
you going to Professor Simpson's class?" shutting it again. "I
know the new dance"; and she began to execute it on the walk.
The door of a house opposite us opened, and a tall youth came
out, hat in hand. Without evincing surprise, he advanced toward
Helen, gravely dancing the same step; they finished the figure with
unmoved countenances. "Come now," I said, taking her arm. He
then made a series of bows to us, retreating to the house, with his
face toward us, till he reached the door and closed it. He was tall
and stout, with red hair, and piercing black eyes, and looked about
twenty-three. "Who can that be, Helen?"

"A stranger; probably some young man come to Dr. Price, or a
law student. He is new here, at all events. His is not an obscure
face; if it had been seen, we should have known it."

"We shall meet him, then."

And we did, the very next day, which was Wednesday, in the
hall, where we went to hear the boys declaim. I saw him, sitting
by himself in a chair, instead of being with the classes. He was in
a brown study, unaware that he was observed; both hands were in
his pockets, and his legs were stretched out till his pantaloons had
receded up his boots, whose soles he knocked together, oblivious
of the noise they made. In spite of his red hair, I thought him
handsome, with his Roman nose and firm, clefted chin. Helen and
I were opposite him at the lower part of the hall, but he did not
see us, till the first boy mounted the platform, and began to spout

one of Cicero's orations; then he looked up, and a smile spread over his face. He withdrew his hands from his pockets, updrew his legs, and surveyed the long row of girls opposite, beginning at the head of the hall. As his eyes reached us, a flash of recognition shot across; he raised his hand as if to salute us, and I noticed that it was remarkably handsome, small and white, and ornamented with an old-fashioned ring. It was our habit, after the exercises were over, to gather round Dr. Price, to exchange a few words with him. And this occasion was no exception, for Dr. Price, with his double spectacles, and his silk handkerchief in his hand, was answering our questions, when feeling a touch, he stopped, turned hastily, and saw the stranger.

"Will you be so good as to introduce me to the two young ladies near you? We have met before, but I do not know their names."

"Ah," said the Doctor, taking off his spectacles and wiping them leisurely; then raising his voice, said, "Miss Cassandra Morgeson and Miss Helen Perkins, Mr. Ben Somers, of Belem, requests me to present him to you. I add the information that he is, although a senior, suspended from Harvard College, for participating in a disgraceful fight. It is at your option to notice him."

"If he would be kind enough," said Mr. Somers, moving toward us, "to say that I won it."

"With such hands?" I asked.

"Oh, Somers," interposed the Doctor, "have you much knowledge of the Bellevue Pickersgills' pedigree?"

"Certainly; my grandpa, Desmond Pickersgill, although he came to this country as a cabin boy, was brother to an English earl. This is our coat of arms," showing the ring he wore.

"That is a great fact," answered the Doctor.

"This lad," addressing me, "belongs to the family I spoke of to you, a member of which married one of your name."

"Is it possible? I never heard much of my father's family."

"No," said the Doctor dryly; "Somers has no coat of arms. I expected, when I asked you, to hear that the Pickersgills' history was at your fingers' ends."

"Only above the second joint of the third finger of my left hand."

I thought Dr. Price was embarrassing.

"Is your family from Troy?" Mr. Somers asked me, in a low tone.

"Do you dislike my name? Is that of Veronica a better one? It is my sister's, and we were named by our great-grandfather, who married a Somers, a hundred years ago."

Miss Black, my Barmouth teacher, came into my mind, for I had said the same thing to her in my first interview; but I was recalled from my wandering by Mr. Somers asking, "Are you looking for your sister? Far be it from me to disparage any act of your great-grandfather's, but I prefer the name of Veronica, and fancy that the person to whom the name belongs has a narrow face, with eyes near together, and a quantity of light hair, which falls straight; that she has long hands; is fond of Gothic architecture, and has a will of her own."

"But never dances," said Helen.

There was a whist party at somebody's house every Wednesday evening. Alice had selected the present for one, and had invited more than the usual number. I asked Mr. Somers to come.

"Dress coat?" he inquired.

"Oh, no."

"Is Rosville highly starched?"

"Oh, no."

"I'll be sure to go into society, then, as long as I can go limp."

He bowed, and, retiring with Dr. Price, walked through the green with him, perusing the ground.

I wore a dark blue silk for the party, with a cinnamon-colored satin stripe through it; a dress that Alice supervised. She fastened a pair of pearl ear-rings in my ears, and told me that I never looked better. It was the first time since grandfather's death that I had worn any dress except a black one. My short sleeves were puffed velvet, and a lace tucker was drawn with a blue ribbon across the corsage. As I adjusted my dress, a triumphant sense of beauty possessed me; Cleopatra could not have been more convinced of her charms than I was of mine. "It is a pleasant thing," I thought, "that a woman's mind may come and go by the gate Beautiful."

I went down before Alice, who stayed with the children till she heard the first ring at the door.

"Where is Charles?" I asked, after we had greeted the Bancrofts.

"He will come in time to play, for he likes whist; do you?"

"No."

We did not speak again, but I noticed how gay and agreeable she was through the evening.

Ben Somers came early, suffering from a fit of nonchalance, to the disgust of several young men, standard beaux, who regarded him with an impertinence which delighted him.

"Here comes," he said, " 'a daughter of the gods, divinely tall, and most divinely fair.' " Meaning me, which deepened their disgust.[33]

"Come to the piano," I begged. Helen was there, but his eyes did not rest upon her, but upon Charles, whom I saw for the first time that evening. I introduced them.

"Cassandra," said Charles, "let us make up a game in the East Room. Miss Helen, will you join? Mr. Somers, will you take a hand?"

"Certainly. Miss Morgeson, will you be my partner?"

"Will you play with me then, Miss Helen?" asked Charles.

"If you desire it," she answered, rather ungraciously.

We took our seats in the East Room, which opened from the parlor, at a little table by the chimney. The astral lamp from the center table in the parlor shone into our room, intercepting any view toward us. I sat by the window, the curtain of which was drawn apart, and the shutters unclosed. A few yellow leaves stuck against the panes, unstirred by the melancholy wind, which sighed through the crevices. Charles was at my right hand, by the mantel; the light from a candelabra illuminated him and Mr. Somers, while Helen and I were in shadow. Mr. Somers dealt the cards, and we began the game.

"We shall beat you," he said to Charles.

"Not unless Cassandra has improved," he replied.

I promised to do my best, but soon grew weary, and we were beaten. To my surprise Mr. Somers was vexed. His imperturbable manner vanished; he sat erect, his eyes sparkled, and he told me I must play better. We began another game, which he was confident of winning. I kept my eyes on the cards, and there was silence till Mr. Somers exclaimed, "Don't trump now, Mr. Morgeson."

I watched the table for his card to fall, but as it did not, looked at him for the reason. He had forgotten us, and was lost in contemplation, with his eyes fixed upon me. The recognition of some impulse had mastered him. I must prevent Helen and Mr. Somers perceiving this! I shuffled the cards noisily, rustled my dress, looked right and left for my handkerchief to break the spell.

"How the wind moans!" said Helen. I understood her tone; she understood him, as I did.

"I *like* Rosville, Miss Perkins," cried Mr. Somers.

"Do you?" said Charles, clicking down his card, as though his turn had just come. "I must trump this in spite of you."

"I am tired of playing," I said.

"We are beaten, Miss Perkins," said Mr. Somers, rising. "Bring it here," to a servant going by with a tray and glasses. He drank a goblet of wine, before he offered us any. "Now give us music!" offering his arm to Helen, and taking her away. Charles and I remained at the table. "By the way," he said abruptly, "I have forgotten to give you a letter from your father—here it is." I stretched my hand across the table, he retained it. I rose from my chair and stood beside him.

"Cassandra," he said at last, growing ashy pale, "is there any other world than this we are in now?"

I raised my eyes, and saw my own pale face in the glass over the mantel above his head.

"What do you see?" he asked, starting up.

I pointed to the glass.

"I begin to think," I said, "there is another world, one peopled with creatures like those we see there. What are they—base, false, cowardly?"

"Cowardly," he muttered, "will you make me crush you? Can we lie to each other? Look!"

He turned me from the glass.

At that moment Helen struck a crashing blow on the piano keys.

"Charles, give me—give me the letter."

He looked vaguely round the floor, it was crumpled in his hand. A side door shut, and I stood alone. Pinching my cheeks and wiping my lips to force the color back, I returned to the parlor. Mr. Somers came to me with a glass of wine. It was full, and some spilled on my dress; he made no offer to wipe it off. After that, he devoted himself to Alice; talked lightly with her, observing her closely. I made the tour of the party, overlooked the whist players, chatted with the talkers, finally taking a seat, where Helen joined me.

"Now I am going," she said.

"Why don't they all go?"

"Look at Mr. Somers playing the agreeable to Mrs. Morgeson. What kind of a woman is she, Cass?"

"Go and learn for yourself."

"I fear I have not the gift for divining people that you have."

"Do you hear the wind moan now, Helen?"

She turned crimson, and said: "Let us go to the window; I think
it rains."

We stood within the curtains, and listened to its pattering on
the floor of the piazza, and trickling down the glass like tears.

"Helen, if one could weep as quietly as this rain falls, and keep
the face as unwrinkled as the glass, it would be pretty to weep."

"Is it hard for you to cry?"

"I can't remember; it is so long since."

My ear caught the sound of a step on the piazza.

"Who is that?" she asked.

"It is a man."

"Morgeson?"

"Morgeson."

"Cassandra?"

"Cassandra."

"I can cry," and Helen covered her face.

"Cry away, then. Give me a fierce shower of tears, with thunder
and lightning between, if you like. Don't sop, and soak, and driz-
zle."

The step came close to the window; it was not in harmony with
the rain and darkness, but with the hot beating of my heart.

"We are breaking up," called Mr. Somers. "Mr. Bancroft's carriage is ready, I am bid to say. It is inky outside."

"Yes," said Helen, "I am quite ready."

"There are a dozen chaises in the yard; Mr. Morgeson is there,
and lanterns. He is at home among horses, I believe."

"Do you like horses?" I asked.

"Not in the least."

Somebody called Helen.

"Good-night, Cass."

"Good-night; keep out of the rain."

"Good-night, Miss Morgeson," said Mr. Somers, when she had
gone. "Good-night and good-morning. My acquaintance with you
has begun; it will never end. You thought me a boy; I am just your
age."

" 'Never,' is a long word, Boy Somers."

"It is."

It rained all night; I wearied of its monotonous fall; if I slept it
turned into a voice which was pent up in a letter which I could not
open.

CHAPTER XVIII.

Alice was unusually gay the next morning. She praised Mr. Somers, and could not imagine what had been the cause of his being
expelled from the college.

"Don't you like him, Cassandra? His family are unexceptionable."

"So is he, I believe, except in his fists. But how did you learn
that his family were unexceptionable?"

"Charles inquired in Boston, and heard that his mother was one
of the greatest heiresses in Belem."

"Did you enjoy last night, Alice?"

"Yes, I am fond of whist parties. You noticed that Charles has
not a remarkable talent that way. Did he speak to Mr. Somers at
all, while you played? I was too busy to come in. By the by, I
must go now, and see if the parlor is in order."

I followed her with my bonnet in hand, for it was school time.
She looked about, then went up to the mantel, and taking out the
candle-ends from the candelabra, looked in the glass, and said, "I
am a fright this morning."

"Am I?" I asked over her shoulder, for I was nearly a head taller.

"No; you are too young to look jaded in the morning. Your
eyes are as clear as a child's; and how blue they are."

"Mild and babyish-like, are they not? almost green with innocence. But Charles has devilish eyes, don't you think so?"

She turned with her mouth open in astonishment, and her hand
full of candle-ends. "Cassandra Morgeson, are you mad?"

"Good-by, Alice."

I only saw Mr. Somers at prayers during the following fortnight. But in that short time he made many acquaintances. Helen
told me that he had decided to study law with Judge Ryder, and
that he had asked her how long I expected to stay in Rosville.
Nothing eccentric had been discovered in his behavior; but she
was convinced that he would astonish us before long. The first
Wednesday after our party, I was absent from the elocutionary
exercise; but the second came round, and I took my place as usual
beside Helen.

"This will be Mr. Somers's first and last appearance on our
stage," she whispered; "some whim prompts him to come to-
day."

He delighted Dr. Price by translating from the Agamemnon of Æschylus.[34]

"Re-enter Clytemnestra.

"Men! Citizens! ye Elders of Argos present here."

"Who was Agamemnon?" I whispered.

"He gave Cassandra her last ride."

"Did he upset her?"

"Study Greek and you will know," she replied, frowning at him as he stepped from the platform.

We went to walk in Silver Street after school, and he joined us.

"Do you read Greek?" he asked her.

"My father is a Greek Professor, and he made me study it when I was a little girl."

"The name of Cassandra inspired me to rub up my knowledge of the tragedies."

Helen and he had a Homeric talk, while I silently walked by them, thinking that Cassandra would have suited Veronica, and that no name suited me. From some reason I did not discover, Helen began to loiter, pretending that she wanted to have a look at the clouds. But when I looked back her head was bent to the ground. Mr. Somers offered to carry my books.

"Carry Helen's; she is smaller than I am."

"Confound Helen!"

"And the books, too, if you like. Helen," I called, "why do you loiter? It is time for dinner. We must go home."

"I am quite ready for my dinner," she replied. "Wont you come to our house this afternoon and take tea with me?"

"Oh, Miss Perkins, do invite me also," he begged. "I want to bring Tennyson to you."

"Is he related to Agamemnon?" I asked.

"I'll ask Mrs. Bancroft if I may invite you," said Helen, "if you are sure that you would like a stupid, family tea."

"I am positive that I should. Tennyson, though an eminent Grecian, is not related to the person you spoke of."

We parted at the foot of Silver Street, with the expectation of meeting before night. Helen sent me word not to fail, as she had sent for Mr. Somers, and that Mrs. Bancroft was already preparing tea. Alice drove down there with me, to call on Mrs. Bancroft.

The two ladies compared children, and by the time Alice was ready to go, Mr. Somers arrived. She staid a few moments more to chat with him, and when she went at last, told me Charles would come for me on his way from the mills.

My eyes wandered in the direction of Mr. Somers. His said: "No; go home with *me*."

"Very well, Alice, whatever is convenient," I answered quietly.

Mrs. Bancroft was a motherly woman, and Mr. Bancroft was a fatherly man. Five children sat round the tea-table, distinguished by the Bancroft nose. Helen and I were seated each side of Mr. Somers. The table reminded me of our table at Surrey, it was so covered with vast viands; but the dishes were alike, and handsome. I wondered whether mother had bought the new china in Boston, and, buttering my second hot biscuit, I thought of Veronica; then, of the sea. How did it look? Hark! Its voice was in my ear! Could I climb the housetop? Might I not see the mist which hung over our low-lying sea by Surrey?

"Will you take quince or apple jelly, Miss Morgeson?" asked Mrs. Bancroft.

"Apple, if you please."

"Do you write that sister of yours often?" asked Mr. Somers, as he passed me the apple jelly.

"I never write her."

"Will you tell me something of Surrey?"

"Mr. Somers, shall I give you a cup-custard?"

"No, thank you, mam."

"Surrey is lonely, evangelical, primitive."

"Belem is dreary too; most of it goes to Boston, or to India."

"Does it smell of sandal wood? And has everybody tea-caddies? *Vide* Indian stories."

"We have a crate of queer things from Calcutta."

"Are you going to study law with Judge Ryder?" Mr. Bancroft inquired.

"I think so."

Then Helen pushed back her chair; and Mrs. Bancroft stood in her place long enough for us to reach the parlor door.

"And I must go to the office," Mr. Bancroft said, so we had the parlor to ourselves; but Mr. Somers did not read from Tennyson— for he had forgotten to bring the book.

"Now for a compact," he said. "I must be called Ben Somers by you; and may I call you Cassandra, and Helen?"

"Yes," we answered.

"Let us be confidential."

And we were. I was drawn into speaking of my life at home; my remarks, made without premeditation, proved that I possessed ideas and feelings hitherto unknown. I felt no shyness before him, and, although I saw his interest in me, no agitation. Helen was also moved to tell us that she was engaged. She rolled up her sleeve to show us a bracelet, printed in ink on her arm, with the initials, "L.N." Those of her cousin, she said; he was a sailor, and some time, she supposed, they would marry.

"How could you consent to have your arm so defaced?" I asked.

Her eyes flashed as she replied that she had not looked upon the mark in that light before.

"We may all be tattooed," said Mr. Somers.

"I am," I thought.

He told us in his turn that he should be rich. "There are five of us. My mother's fortune cuts up rather; but it wont be divided till the youngest is twenty-one. I assure you we are impatient."

"Some one of your family happened to marry a Morgeson," I here remarked.

"I wrote father about that; he must know the circumstance, though he never has a chance to expatiate on *his* side of the house. Poor man! he has the gout, and passes his time in experiments with temperature and diet. Will you ever visit Belem? I shall certainly go to Surrey."

Mrs. Bancroft interrupted us, and soon after Mr. Bancroft arrived, redolent of smoke. Ten o'clock came, and nobody for me. At half-past ten I put on my shawl to walk home, when Charles drove up to the gate.

"Say," said Ben Somers, in a low voice, "that you will walk with me."

"I am not too late, Cassandra?" called Charles, coming up the steps, bowing to all. "I am glad you are ready; Nell is impatient."

"My dear," asked Mrs. Bancroft, "how dare you trust to the mercy of such vicious beasts as Mr. Morgeson loves to drive?"

"Come," he said, touching my arm.

"Wont you walk?" said Mr. Somers aloud.

"Walk?" echoed Charles. "No."

I followed him. Nell had already bitten off a paling; and as he untied her he boxed her ears. She did not jump, for she knew the hand that struck her. We rushed swiftly away through the long shadows of the moonlight.

"Charles, what did Ben Somers do at Harvard?"

"He was in a night-fight, and he sometimes got drunk; it is a family habit."

"Pray, why did you inquire about him?"

"From the interest I feel in him."

"You like him, then?"

"I detest him; do you too?"

"I like him."

He bent down and looked into my face.

"You are telling me a lie."

I made no reply.

"I should beg your pardon, but I will not. I am going away to-morrow. Give me your hand, and say farewell."

"Farewell then. Is Alice up? I see a light moving in her chamber."

"If you do, she is not waiting for me."

"I have been making coffee for you," she said, as soon as we entered, "in my French biggin. I have packed your valise too, Charles, and have ordered your breakfast. Cassy, we will breakfast after he has gone."

"I have to sit up to write, Alice. See that the horses are exercised. Ask Parker to drive them. The men will be here to-morrow to enlarge the conservatory."

"Yes."

"I shall get a better stock while I am away."

I sipped my coffee; Alice yawned fearfully, with her hand on the coffee-pot, ready to pour again. "Why, Charles," she exclaimed, "there is no cream in your coffee."

"No, there isn't" looking into his cup; "nor sugar."

She threw a lump at him, which he caught, laughing one of his abrupt laughs.

"How extraordinarily affectionate," I thought, but somehow it pleased me.

"Why do you tempt me, Alice?" I said. "Doctor White says I must not drink coffee."

"Tempted!" Charles exclaimed. "Cassandra is never tempted. What she does, she does because she will. Don't worry yourself, Alice, about her."

"Because I will," I repeated.

A nervous foreboding possessed me, the moment I entered my room. Was it the coffee? Twice in the night I lighted my candle, looked at the little French clock on the mantel, and under the bed. At last I fell asleep, but starting violently from its oblivious dark, to become aware that the darkness of the room was sentient. A breath passed over my face; but I caught no sound, though I held my breath to listen for one. I moved my hands before me then, but they came in contact with nothing. My forebodings passed away, and I slept till Alice sent for me. I sat up in bed philosophizing, and examining the position of the chairs, the tops of the tables and the door. No change had taken place. But my eyes happened to fall on my handkerchief, which had dropped by the bedside. I picked it up; there was a dusty footprint upon it. The bell rang, and, throwing it under the bed, I dressed and ran down. Alice was taking breakfast, tired of waiting. She said the baby had cried till after midnight, and that Charles never came to bed at all.

"Do eat this hot toast; it has just come in."

"I shall stay at home to-day, Alice, I feel chilly; is it cold?"

"You must have a fire in your room."

"Let me have one to day; I should like to sit there."

She gave orders for the fire, and went herself to see that it burned. Soon I was sitting before it, my feet on a stool, and a poker in my hand with which I smashed the smoky lumps of coal which smoldered in the grate.

I stayed there all day, looking out of the window when I heard the horses tramp in the stable or a step on the piazza. It was a dull November day; the atmosphere was glutinous with a pale mist, which made the leaves stick together in bunches, helplessly cumbering the ground. The boughs dropped silent tears over them, under the gray, pitiless sky. I read Byron, which was the only book in the house, I believe; for neither Charles nor Alice read anything except the newspapers. I looked over my small stores also, and my papers, which consisted of father's letters. As I was sorting them the thought struck me of writing to Veronica, and I arranged my portfolio, pulled the table nearer the fire, and began, "Dear Veronica." After writing this a few times I gave it up, cut off the "Dear Veronicas," and made lamplighters of the paper.

Ben Somers called at noon, to inquire the reason of my absence from school, and left a book for me. It was the poems he had spoken of. I lighted on "Fatima,"[35] read it and copied it. In the afternoon Alice came up with the baby.

"Let me braid your hair," she said, "in a different fashion."

I assented; the baby was bestowed on a rug, and a chair was put before the glass, that I might witness the operation.

"What magnificent hair!" she said, as she unrolled it. "It is a yard long."

"It is a regular mane, isn't it?"

She began combing it; the baby crawled under the bed, and coming out with the handkerchief in its hand, crept up to her, trying to make her take it. She had combed my hair over my face, but I saw it.

"Do I hurt you, Cass?"

"No, do I ever hurt you, Alice?" And I divided the long bands over my eyes, and looked up at her.

"Were any of your family ever cracked? I have long suspected you of a disposition that way."

"The child is choking itself with that handkerchief."

She took it, and, tossing it on the bed, gave Byron to the child to play with, and went on with the hair-dressing.

"There, now," she said, "is not this a masterpiece of barber's craft? Look at the back of your head, and then come down."

"Yes, I will, for I feel better."

When I returned to my room again it was like meeting a confidential friend.

A few days after, father came to Rosville. I invited Ben Somers and Helen to spend with us the only evening he stayed. After they were gone, we sat in my room and talked over many matters. His spirits were not as buoyant as usual, and I felt an undefinable anxiety which I did not mention. When he said that mother was more abstracted than ever, he sighed. I asked him how many years he thought I must waste; eighteen had already gone for nothing.

"You must go in the way ordained, waste or no waste. I have tried to make your life differ from mine at the same age, for you are like me, and I wanted to see the result."

"We shall see."

"Veronica has been let alone—is master of herself, except when in a rage. She is an extraordinary girl; independent of kith and kin, and everything else. I assure you, Miss Cassy, she is very good."

"Does she ever ask for me?"

"I never heard her mention your name but once. She asked one day what your teachers were. You do not love each other, I suppose. What hatred there is between near relations! Bitter, bitter," he said calmly, as if he thought of some object incapable of the hatred he spoke of.

"That's Grandfather John Morgeson you think of. I do not hate Veronica. I think I love her; at least she interests me."

"The same creeping in the blood of us all, Cassy. I did not like my father; but thank God I behaved decently toward him. It must be late."

As he kissed me, and we stood face to face, I recognized my likeness to him. "He has had experiences that I shall never know," I thought. "Why should I tell him mine?" But an overpowering impulse seized me to speak to him of Charles. "Father," and I put my hands on his shoulders. He set his candle back on the table.

"You look hungry-eyed, eager. What is it? Are you well?"

"No."

"You are faded a little. Your face has lost its firmness."

My impulse died a sudden death. I buried it with a swallow.

"Do you think so?"

"You are all alike. Let me tell you something; don't get sick. If you are, hide it as much as possible. Men do not like sick women."

"I'll end this fading business as soon as possible. It *is* late. Good-night, dad."

I examined my face as soon as he closed the door. There *was* a change. Not the change from health to disease, but an expression lurking there—a reflection of some unrevealed secret.

The next morning was passed with Alice and the children. He was pleased with her prettiness and sprightliness, and his gentle manner and disposition pleased her. She asked him to let me spend another year in Rosville; but he said that I must return to Surrey, and that he never would allow me to leave home again.

"She will marry."

"Not early."

"Never, I believe," I said.

"It will be as well."

"Yes," she replied; "if you leave her a fortune, or teach her some trade, that will give her some importance in the world."

Her wisdom astonished me.

He was sorry, he said, that Morgeson was not at home. When he mentioned him I looked out of the window, and saw Ben Somers coming into the yard. As he entered, Alice gave him a meaning look, which was not lost upon me, and which induced him to observe Ben closely.

"The train is nearly due, Mr. Morgeson; shall I walk to the station with you?"

"Certainly; come, Cassy."

On the way he touched me, making a sign toward Ben. I shook my head, which appeared satisfactory. The rest of the time was consumed in the discussion of the relationship, which ended in an invitation, as I expected, to Surrey.

"The governor is not worried, is he?" asked Ben, on our way back.

"No more than I am."

"What a pity Morgeson was not at home!"

"Why a pity?"

"I should like to see them together, they are such antipodal men. Does your father know him well?"

"Does any one know him well?"

"Yes, I know him. I do not like him. He is a savage, living by his instincts, with one element of civilization—he loves Beauty— beauty like yours." He turned pale when he said this, but went on. "He has never seen a woman like you; who has? Forgive me, but I watch you both."

"I have perceived it."

"I suppose so, and it makes you more willful."

"You said you were but a boy."

"Yes, but I have had one or two manly wickednesses. I have done with them, I hope."

"So that you have leisure to pry into those of others."

"You do not forgive me."

"I like you; but what can I do?"

"Keep up your sophistry to the last."

CHAPTER XIX.

Alice and I were preparing for the first ball, when Charles came home, having been absent several weeks. The conservatory was finished, and looked well, jutting from the garden-room, which we used often, since the weather had been cold. The flowers and plants it was filled with were more fragrant and beautiful than rare. I never saw him look so genial as when he inspected it with us. Alice was in good-humor, also, for he had brought her a set of jewels.

"Is it not her birthday," he said, when he gave her the jewel case, "or something, that I can give Cassandra this?" taking a little box from his pocket.

"Oh yes," said Alice; "show it to us."

"Will you have it?" he asked me.

I held out my hand, and he put on my third finger a diamond ring, which was like a star.

"How well it looks on your long hand!" said Alice.

"What unsuspected tastes I find I have!" I answered. "I am passionately fond of rings; this delights me."

His swarthy face flushed with pleasure at my words; but, according to his wont, he said nothing.

A few days after his return, a man came into the yard, leading a powerful horse chafing in his halter, which he took to the stable. Charles asked me to look at a new purchase he had made in Pennsylvania. The strange man was lounging about the stalls when we went in, inspecting the horses with a knowing air.

"I declare, sir," said Jesse, "I am afeared to tackle this ere animal; he's a reglar brute, and no mistake."

"He'll be tame enough; he is but four years old."

"He's never been in a carriage," said the man.

"Lead him out, will you?"

The man obeyed. The horse was a fine creature, black, and thick-maned; but the whites of his eyes were not clear; they were streaked with red, and he attempted continually to turn his nostrils inside out. Altogether, I thought him diabolical.

"What's the matter with his eyes?" Charles asked.

"I think, sir," the man replied, "as how they got inflamed like, in the boat coming from New York. It's nothing perticalar, I believe."

Alice declared it was too bad, when she heard there was another horse in the stable. She would not look at him, and said she would never ride with Charles when he drove him.

I had been taking lessons of Professor Simpson, and was ready for the ball. All the girls from the Academy were going in white, except Helen, who was to wear pink silk. It was to be a military ball, and strangers were expected. Ben Somers, and our Rosville beaux, were of course to be there, all in uniform, except Ben, who preferred the dress of a gentleman, he said,—silk stockings, pumps, and a white cravat.

We were dressed by nine o'clock, Alice in black velvet, with a wreath of flowers in her black hair—I in a light blue velvet bodice, and white silk skirt. We were waiting for the ball hack to come for us, as that was the custom, for no one owned a close coach in Rosville, when Charles brought in some splendid scarlet flowers which he gave to Alice.

"Where are Cassandra's?"

"She does not care for flowers; besides, she would throw them away on her first partner."

He put us in the coach, and went back. I was glad he did not come with us, and gave myself up to the excitement of my first ball. Alice was surrounded by her acquaintances at once, and I was asked to dance a quadrille by Mr. Parker, whose gloves were much too large, and whose white trowsers were much too long.

"I kept the flowers you gave me," he said in a breathless way.

"Oh yes, I remember; mustn't we forward now?"

"Mr. Morgeson's very fond of flowers."

"So he is. How de do, Miss Ryder."

Miss Ryder, my vis-à-vis, bowed, looking scornfully at my partner, who was only a clerk, while hers was a law student. I immediately turned to Mr. Parker with affable smiles, and went into a kind of dumb-show of conversation, which made him warm and uncomfortable. Mrs. Judge Ryder sailed by on Ben Somers's arm.

"Put your shoulders down," she whispered to her daughter, who had poked one very much out of her dress. "My love," she spoke aloud, "you mustn't dance *every* set."

"No, ma," and she passed on, Ben giving a faint cough, for my benefit. We could not find Alice after the dance was over. A brass band alternated with the quadrille band, and it played so loudly that we had to talk at the top of our voices to be heard. Mine soon gave out, and I begged Mr. Parker to bring Helen, for I had not yet seen her. She was with Dr. White, who had dropped in to see the miserable spectacle. The air, he said, shaking his finger at me, was already miasmal; it would be infernal by midnight. Christians ought not to be there. "Go home early, Miss. Your mother never went to a ball, I'll warrant."

"We are wiser than our mothers."

"And wickeder; you will send for me to-morrow."

"Your Valenciennes lace excruciates the Ryders," said Helen. "I was standing near Mrs. Judge Ryder and the girls just now. 'Did you ever see such an upstart?' And, 'What an extravagant dress she has on—it is ridiculous,' Josephine Ryder said. When Ben Somers heard this attack on you, he told them that your lace was an heirloom. Here he is." Mr. Parker took her away, and Ben Somers went in pursuit of a seat. The quadrille was over, I was engaged for the next, and he had not come back. I saw nothing of him till the country dance before supper. He was at the foot of the long line, opposite a pretty girl in blue, looking very solemn and stately. I took off the glove from my hand which wore the new diamond, and held it up, expecting him to look my way soon. Its flash caught his eyes, as they roamed up and down, and, as I expected, he left his place and came up behind me.

"Where did you get that ring?" wiping his face with his handkerchief.

"Ask Alice."

"You are politic."

"Handsome, isn't it?"

"And valuable; it cost as much as the new horse."

"Have you made a memorandum of it?"

"Destiny has brilliant spokes in her wheel, hasn't she?"

"Is that from the Greek tragedies?"

"To your places, gentlemen," the floor-manager called, and the band struck up the Fisher's Hornpipe. At supper, I saw Ben Somers, still with the pretty girl in blue; but he came to my chair and asked me if I did not think she was a pretty toy for a man to play with.

"How much wine have you drunk? Enough to do justice to the family annals?"

"Really, you have been well informed. No, I have *not* drunk enough for that; but Mrs. Ryder has sent her virgins home with me. I am afraid their lamps are upset again. I drink nothing after to-night. You shall not ask again, 'How much?' "

My fire was out when I reached home. My head was burning and aching. I was too tired to untwist my hair, and I pulled and dragged at my dress, which seemed to have a hundred fastenings. Creeping into bed, I perceived the odor of flowers, and looking at my table discovered a bunch of white roses.

"Roses are nonsense, and life is nonsense," I thought.

When I opened my eyes, Alice was standing by the bed, with a glass of roses in her hand.

"Charles put these roses here, hey?"

"I suppose so; throw them out of the window, and me too; my head is splitting."

"To make amends for not giving you any last night," she went on; "he is quite childish."

"Can't you unbraid my hair, it hurts my head so?"

She felt my hands. I was in a fever, she said, and ran down for Charles. "Cass is sick, in spite of your white roses."

"The devil take the roses. Can't you get up, Cassandra?"

"Not now. Go away, will you?"

He left the room abruptly. Alice loosened my hair, bound my head, and poured cologne-water over me, lamenting all the while that she had not brought me home; and then went down for some tea, presently returning to say that Charles had been for Dr. White, who said he would not come. But he was there shortly afterward. By night I was well again.

Dr. Price gave us a lecture on late hours that week, requesting us, if we had any interest in our education, or expected him to have any, to abstain from balls.

Ben Somers disappeared; no one knew where he had gone. The Ryders were in consternation, for he was an intimate of the family, since he had gone into Judge Ryder's office, six weeks before. He returned, however, with a new overcoat trimmed with fur, the same as that with which my new cloak was trimmed. A great snowstorm began the day of his return, and blocked us indoors for several days, and we had permanent sleighing afterward.

In January it was proposed that we should go to the Swan Tavern, ten miles out of Rosville.

I had made good resolutions since the ball, and declined going to the second, which came off three weeks afterward. The truth was, I did not enjoy the first; but I preferred to give my decision a virtuous tinge. I also determined to leave the Academy when the spring came, for I felt no longer a schoolgirl. But for Helen, I could not have remained as I did. She stayed for pastime now, she confessed, it was so dull at home; her father was wrapped in his studies, and she had a stepmother. I resolved again that I would study more, and was translating, in view of this resolve, "Corinne,"[36] with Miss Prior, and singing sedulously with Mrs. Lane, and had begun a course of reading with Dr. Price.

I refused two invitations to join the sleighing party, and on the night it was to be had prepared to pass the evening in my own room with Oswald and Corinne. Before the fire, with lighted candles, I heard a ringing of bells in the yard and a stamping of feet on the piazza. Alice sent up for me. I found Ben Somers with her, who begged me to take a seat in his sleigh. Helen was there, and Amelia Bancroft. Alice applauded me for refusing him; but when he whispered in my ear that he had been to Surrey I changed my mind. She assisted me with cheerful alacrity to put on a merino dress, its color was purple;—a color I hate now, and never wear—and wrapped me warmly. Charles appeared before we started. "Are you really going?" he asked, in a tone of displeasure.

"She is really going," Ben answered for me. "Mr. and Mrs. Bancroft are going," Helen said. "Why not drive out with Mrs. Morgeson?"

"The night is splendid," Ben remarked.

"Wont you come?" I asked.

"If Alice wishes it. Will you go?" he asked her.

"Would you?" she inquired of all, and all replied, "Yes."

We started in advance. Helen and Amelia were packed on the back seat, in a buffalo robe, while Ben and I sat in the shelter of the driver's box, wrapped in another. It was moonlight, and as we passed the sleighs of the rest of the party, exchanging greetings, we grew very merry. Ben, voluble and airy, enlivened us by his high spirits.

We were drinking mulled wine round the long pine dinner-table of the Swan, when Charles and Alice arrived. There were about thirty in the room, which was lighted by tallow candles. When he entered, it seemed as if the candles suddenly required snuffing, and we ceased to laugh. All spoke to him with respect, but with an inflection of the voice which denoted that he was not one of us. As he carelessly passed round the table all made a movement as he approached, scraping their chairs on the bare floor, moving their glass of mulled wine, or altering the position of their arms or legs. An indescribable appreciation of the impression which he made upon others filled my heart. His isolation from the sympathy of every person there gave me a pain and a pity, and for the first time I felt a pang of tenderness, and a throe of pride for him. But Alice, upon whom he never made any impression, saw nothing of this; her gayety soon removed the stiffness and silence he created. The party grew noisy again, except Ben, who had not broken the silence into which he fell as soon as he saw Charles. The mulled wine stood before him untouched. I moved to the corner of the table to allow room for the chair which Charles was turning toward me. Ben ordered more wine, and sent a glass full to him. Taking it from the boy who brought it, I gave it to him. "Drink," I said. My voice sounded strangely. Barely tasting it, he set the glass down, and leaning his arm on the table, turned his face to me, shielding it with his hand from the gaze of those about us. I pushed away a candle that flared in our faces.

"You never drink wine?"

"No, Cassandra."

"How was the ride down?"

"Delightful."

"What about the new horse?"

"He is an awful brute."

"When shall we have a ride with him?"

"When you please."

The boy came in to say would we please go to the parlor; our room was wanted for supper. An immediate rush, with loud laughing, took place, for the parlor fire; but Charles and I did not move. I was busy remaking the bow of my purple silk cravat.

" 'I drink the cup of a costly death,' " Ben hummed, as he sauntered along by us, hands in his pockets—the last in the room, except us two.

"Indeed, Somers; perhaps you would like this too." And Charles offered him his glass of wine.

Ben took it, and with his thumb and finger snapped it off at the stem, tipping the wine over Charles's hand.

I saw it staining his wristband, like blood. He did not stir, but a slight smile traveled swiftly over his face.

"I know Veronica," said Ben, looking at me. "Has this man seen *her?*"

His voice crushed me. What a barrier his expression of contempt made between her and me!

Withal, I felt a humiliating sense of defeat.

Charles read me.

As he folded his wristband under his sleeve, carefully and slowly, his slender fingers did not tremble with the desire that possessed him, which I saw in his terrible eyes as plainly as if he had spoken, "I would kill him."

They looked at my hands, for I was wringing them, and a groan burst from me.

"Somers," said Charles, rising and touching his shoulder, "behave like a man, and let us alone; I love this girl."

His pale face changed, his eyes softened, and mine filled with tears.

"Cassandra," urged Ben, in a gentle voice, "come with me; come away."

"Fool," I answered; "leave *me* alone, and go."

He hesitated, moved toward the door, and again urged me to come.

"Go! go!" stamping my foot, and the door closed without a sound.

For a moment we stood, transfixed in an isolation which separated us from all the world beside.

"Now Charles, we"—a convulsive sob choked me, a strange taste filled my mouth, I put my handkerchief to my lips and wiped away streaks of blood. I showed it to him.

"It is nothing, by God!" snatching the handkerchief. "Take mine— oh, my dear—"

I tried to laugh, and muttered the imperative fact of joining the rest.

"Be quiet, Cassandra."

He opened the window, took a handful of snow from the sill and put it to my mouth. It revived me.

"Do you hear, Charles? Never say those frightful words again. Never, never."

"Never, if it must be so."

He touched my hand; I opened it; his closed over mine.

"Go, now," he said, and springing to the window, threw it up, and jumped out. The boy came in with a tablecloth on his arm, and behind him Ben.

"Glass broken, sir."

"Put it in the bill."

He offered me his arm, which I was glad to take.

"Where is Charles?" Alice asked, when we went in.

"He has just left us," Ben answered; "looking after his horses, probably."

"Of course," she replied. "You look blue, Cass. Here, take my chair by the fire; we are going to dance a Virginia reel."

I acccepted her offer, and was thankful that the dance would take them away. I wanted to be alone forever. Helen glided behind my chair, and laid her hand on my shoulder; I shook it off.

"What is the matter, Cass?"

"I am going away from Char—school."

"We are all going; but not to-night."

"I am going to-night."

"So you shall, dear; but wait till after supper."

"Do you think, Helen, that I shall ever have consumption?" fumbling for my handkerchief, forgetting in whose possession it was. Charles came in at that instant, and I remembered that he had it.

"What on earth has happened to you? Oh!" she exclaimed, as I looked at her. "You were out there with Morgeson and Ben Somers," she whispered; "something has occurred; what is it?"

"You shall never know; never—never—never."

"Cassandra, that man is a devil."

"I like devils."

"The same blood rages in both of you."

"It's mulled wine,—thick and stupid."

"Nonsense."

"Will there be tea, at supper?"

"You shall have some."

"Ask Ben to order it."

"Heaven forgive us all, Cassandra!"

"Remember the tea."

Charles stood near his wife; wherever she moved afterwards he moved. I saw it, and felt that it was the shadow of something which would follow.

At last the time came for us to return. Helen had plied me with tea, and was otherwise watchful, but scarcely spoke.

"It is an age," I said, "since I left Rosville."

She raised her eyebrows merely, and asked me if I would have more tea.

"In my room," I thought, "I shall find myself again." And as I opened my door, it welcomed me with so friendly and silent an aspect, that I betrayed my grief, and it covered my misery as with a cloak.

CHAPTER XX.

Helen was called home by the illness of her father and did not return to Rosville. She would write me, she said; but it was many weeks before I received a letter. Ben Somers about this time took a fit of industry, and made a plan for what he called a well-regulated life, averring that he should always abide by it. Every hour had its duty, which must be fulfilled. He weighed his bread and meat, ate so many ounces a day, and slept watch and watch, as he nautically termed it. I guessed that the meaning of his plan was to withdraw from the self-chosen post of censor. His only alienation was an occasional disappearance for a few days. I never asked him where he went, and had never spoken to him concerning his mysterious remark about having been in Surrey. Neither had I heard anything of his being there from father. Once he told me that his father had explained the marriage of old Locke Morgeson; but that it was not clear to him that we were at all related.

In consequence of his rigorous life, I saw little of him. Though urged by Alice, he did not come to our house, and we rarely met him elsewhere. People called him eccentric, but as he was of a rich family he could afford to be, and they felt no slight by his neglect.

There was a change everywhere. The greatest change of all was in Charles. From the night of the sleigh-ride his manner toward me was totally altered. As far as I could discern, the change was a confirmed one. The days grew monotonous, but my mind avenged itself by night in dreams, which renewed our old relation in all its mysterious vitality. So strong were their impressions that each morning I expected to receive some token from him which would prove that they were not lies. As my expectations grew cold and faint, the sense of a double hallucination tormented me—the past and the present.

The winter was over. I passed it like the rest of Rosville, going out when Alice went, staying at home when she stayed. It was all one what I did, for my aspect was one of content.

Alice alone was unchanged; her spirits and pursuits were always the same. Judging by herself, if she judged at all, she perceived no change in us. Her theory regarding Charles was too firm to be shaken, and all his oddity was a matter of course. As long as I ate, and drank, and slept as usual, I too must be the same. He was not at home much. Business kept him at the mills, where he often slept, or out of town. But the home machinery was still under his controlling hand. Not a leaf dropped in the conservatory that he did not see; not a meal was served whose slightest detail was not according to his desire. The horses were exercised, the servants managed, the children kept within bounds; nothing in the formula of our daily life was ever dropped, and yet I scarcely ever saw him! When we met, I shared his attentions. He gave me flowers; noticed my dress; spoke of the affairs of the day; but all in so public and matter-of-fact a way that I thought I must be the victim of a vicious sentimentality, or that he had amused himself with me. Either way, the sooner I cured myself of my vice the better. But my dreams continued.

"I miss something in your letters," father complained. "What is it? Would you like to come home? Your mother is failing in health— she may need you, though she says not."

I wrote him that I should come home.

"Are you prepared," he asked in return, "to remain at home for the future? Have you laid the foundation of anything by which you can abide contented, and employed? Veronica has been spending two months in New York, with the family of one of my business friends. All that she brings back serves to embellish her quiet life, not to change it. Will it be so with you?"

I wrote back, "No; but I am coming."

He wrote again of changes in Surrey. Dr. Snell had gone, library and all, and a new minister, red hot from Andover, had taken his place. An ugly new church was building. His best ship, the *Locke Morgeson,* was at the bottom of the Indian Ocean, he had just heard. Her loss bothered him, but his letters were kinder than ever.

I consulted with Alice about leaving the Academy. She approved my plan, but begged me not to leave her. I said nothing of my determination to that effect, feeling a strange disinclination toward owning it, though I persisted in repeating it to myself. I applied diligently to my reading, emulating Ben Somers in the regularity of my habits, and took long walks daily—a mode of exercise I had adopted since I had ceased my rides with Charles. The pale blue sky of spring over me, and the pale green grass under me, were charming perhaps; but there was the same monotony in them, as in other things. I did not frequent our old promenade, Silver Street, but pushed my walks into the outskirts of Rosville, by farms bordered with woods. My schoolmates, who were familiar with all the pleasant spots of the neighborhood, met me in groups. "Are you really taking walks like the rest of us?" they asked. "Only alone," I answered.

I bade farewell at last to Miss Prior. We parted with all friendliness and respect; from the fact, possibly, that we parted ignorant of each other. It was the most rational relation that I had ever held with any one. We parted without emotion or regret, and I started on my usual walk.

As I was returning I met Ben Somers. When he saw me he threw his cap into the air, with the information that he had done with his plans, and had ordered an indigestible supper, in honor of his resolve. As people had truly remarked, he could afford to be eccentric. He was tired of it; he had money enough to do without law. "Not as much as your cousin Morgeson, who can do without the Gospel, too."

This was the first time that he had referred to Charles since that memorable night. Trifling as his words were, they broke into the foundations of my stagnant will, and set the tide flowing once more.

"You went to Surrey."

"I was there a few hours. Your father was not at home. He asked me there, you remember. I introduced myself, therefore, and was politely received by your mother, who sent for Veronica. She came in with an occupied air, her hands full of what I thought were herbs; but they were grasses, which she had been re-arranging, she said.

" 'You know my sister?' she asked, coming close, and looking at me with the most singular eyes that were ever on earth." He stopped a moment. "Not like yours, in the least," he continued. " 'Cassandra is very handsome now, is she?'

" 'Why, Veronica,' said your mother, 'you astonish Mr. Somers.'

" 'You are not astonished,' she said with vehemence, 'you are embarrassed.'

" 'Upon my soul I am,' I replied, feeling at ease as soon as I had said so.

" 'Tell me, what has Cassandra been taught? Is Rosville suited to her? We are not.'

" 'Veronica!' said your mother again.

" 'Mother,' and she shook the grasses, and made a little snow fall round her; 'what shall I say then? I am sure he knows Cassandra. What did you come here for?' turning to me again.

" 'To see you,' I answered foolishly.

" 'And has Cassandra spoken of me?' Her pale face grew paler, and an indescribable expression passed over it. 'I do not often speak of her.'

" 'She does not of you,' I was obliged to answer. And then I said I must go. But your mother made me dine with them. When I came away Veronica offered me her hand, but she sent no message to you. She has never been out of my mind a moment since."

"You remember the particulars of the interview very well."

"Why not?"

"Would she bear your supervision?"

"Forgive me, Cassandra. Have I not been making a hermit of myself, eating bread and meat by the ounce, for an expiation?"

"How did it look there? Oh, tell me!"

"You strange girl, have you a soul then? It is a grand place, where it has not been meddled with. I hired a man to drive me as far as any paths went, into those curving horns of land, on each side of Surrey to the south. The country is crazy with barrenness, and the sea mocks it with its terrible beauty."

"You will visit us, won't you?"

"Certainly; I intend to go there."

"Do you know that I left school to-day?"

"It is time."

I hurried into the house, for I did not wish to hear any questions from him concerning my future. Charlotte, who was rolling up an umbrella in the hall, said it was tea-time, adding that Mr. Morgeson had come, and that he was in the dining-room. I went upstairs to leave my bonnet. As I pulled off my glove the ring on my finger twisted round. I took it off, for the first time since Charles had given it to me. A sense of haste came upon me; my hands trembled. I brushed my hair with the back of the brush, shook it out, and wound it into a loose mass, thrust in my comb and went down. Charlotte was putting candles on the tea table. Edward was on his father's knee; Alice was waiting by the tray.

"Here—is—Cassandra," said Charles, mentioning the fact as if he merely wished to attract the child's attention.

"Here—is—Cassandra," I repeated, imitating his tone. He started. Some devil broke loose in him, and looking through his eyes an instant, disappeared, like a maniac who looks through the bars of his cell, and dodges from the eye of his keeper. Jesse brought me a

letter while we were at the table. It was from Helen. I broke its
seal to see how long it was, and put it aside.

"I am free, Alice. I have left the Academy, and am going to set
up for an independent woman."

"What?" said Charles; "you did not tell me. Did you know it,
Alice?"

"Yes; we can't expect her to be at school all her days."

"Cassandra," he said suddenly, "will you give me the salt?"

He looked for the ring on the hand which I stretched toward
him.

He not only missed that, but he observed the disregard of his
wishes in the way I had arranged my hair. I shook it looser from
the comb and pushed it from my face. An expression of unspeak-
able passion, pride, and anguish came into his eyes; his mouth
trembled; he caught up a glass of water to hide his face, and drank
slowly from it.

"Are you going away again soon?" Alice asked him presently.

"No."

"To keep Cassandra, I intend to ask Mrs. Morgeson to come
again. Will you write Mr. Morgeson to urge it?"

"Yes."

"I shall ask them to give up Cass altogether to us."

"You like her so much, do you, Alice?"

His voice sounded far off and faint.

Again I refrained from speaking my resolution of going home.
I would give up thinking of it even! I felt again the tension of the
chain between us. That night I ceased to dream of him.

"My letter is from Helen, Alice," I said.

"When did you see Somers?" Charles asked.

"To-day. I have an idea he will not remain here long."

"He is an amusing young man," Alice remarked.

"Very," said Charles.

Helen's letter was long and full of questions. What had I done?
How had I been? She gave an account of her life at home. She was
her father's nurse, and seldom left him. It was a dreary sort of
business, but she was not melancholy. In truth, she felt better
pleased with herself than she had been in Rosville. She could not
help thinking that a chronic invalid would be a good thing for me.
How was Ben Somers? How much longer should I stay in Rosville? It would know us no more forever when we left, and both

of us would leave it at the same time. Would I visit her ever? They lived in a big house with a red front door. On the left was a lane with tall poplars dying on each side of it, up which the cows passed every night. At the back of it was a huge barn round which martins and pigeons flew the year through. It was dull but respectable and refined, and no one knew that she was tattooed on the arm.

I treasured this letter and all she wrote me. It was my first school-girl correspondence and my last.

Relations of Alice came from a distance to pay her a visit. There was a father, a mother, a son about twenty-one, and two girls who were younger. Alice wished that they had stayed at home; but she was polite and endeavored to make their visit agreeable. The son, called by his family "Bill," informed Charles that he was a judge of horseflesh, and would like to give his nags a try, having a high-flyer himself at home that the old gentleman would not hear of his bringing along. His actions denoted an admiration of me. He looked over the book I was reading or rummaged my workbox, trying on my thimble with an air of tenderness, and peeping into my needlebook. He told Alice that he thought I was a whole team and a horse to let, but he felt rather balky when he came near me, I had such a smartish eye.

"What am I to do, marm?" asked Jesse one morning when Charles was away. "That ere young man wants to ride the new horse, and it is jist the one he mus'n't ride."

"I will speak to Cousin Bill myself," she said.

"He seems a sperrited young feller, and if he wants to break his neck it's most a pity he shouldn't."

"I think," she said when Jesse had retired, "that Charles must be saving up that beast to kill himself with. He will not pull a chaise yet."

"Has Charles tried him?"

"In the lane in an open wagon. He has a whim of having him broken to drive without blinders, bare of harness; he has been away so of late that he has not accomplished it."

Bill entered while we were talking, and Alice told him he must not attempt to use the horse, but proposed he should take her pair and drive out with me. I shook my head in vain; she was bent on mischief. He was mollified by the proposal, and I was obliged to get ready. On starting he placed his cap on one side, held his whip upright, telling me that it was not up to the mark in length, and doubled his knuckles over the reins. He was a good Jehu,[37] but I could not induce him to observe anything along the road.

"Where's Mr. Morgeson's mills?"

We turned in their direction.

"He is a man of property, aint he?"

"I think so."

"He has prime horses anyhow. That stallion of his would bring a first-rate price if he wanted to sell. Do you play the piano?"

"A little."

"And sing?"

"Yes."

"I have not heard you. Will you sing 'A place in thy memory, dearest,' some time for me?"

"Certainly."

"Are you fond of flowers and the like?"

"Very fond of them."

"So am I; our tastes agree. Here we are, hey?"

Charles came out when he saw us coming over the bridge, and Bill pulled up the horses scientifically, giving him a coachman's salute. "You see I am quite a whip."

"You are," said Charles.

"What a cub!" he whispered me. "I think I'll give up my horses and take to walking as you have."

On the way home Bill held the reins in one hand and attempted to take mine with the other, a proceeding which I checked, whereupon he was exceedingly confused. The whip fell from his clutch over the dasher, and in recovering it his hat fell off; shame kept him silent for the rest of the ride.

I begged Alice to propose no more rides with Cousin Bill. That night he composed a letter which he sent me by Charlotte early the next morning.

"Why, Charlotte, what nonsense is this?"

"I expect," she answered sympathizingly, "that it is an offer of his hand and heart."

"Don't mention it, Charlotte."

"Never while I have breath."

In an hour she told Phœbe, who told Alice, who told Charles, and there it ended. It was an offer, as Charlotte predicted. My first! I was crestfallen! I wrote a reply, waited till everybody had gone to breakfast, and slipping into his room, pinned it to the pincushion. In the evening he asked if I ever sang *"Should these fond hopes e'er forsake thee."* I gave him the *"Pirate's Serenade"* instead, which his mother declared beautiful. I saw Alice and Charles laughing, and could hardly help joining them, when I looked at Bill, in whose countenance relief and grief were mingled.

It was a satisfaction to us when they went away. Their visit was shortened, I suspected, by the representations Bill made to his mother. She said, "Good-by," with coldness; but he shook hands with me, and said it was all right he supposed.

The day they went I had a letter from father which informed me that mother would not come to Rosville. He reminded me that I had been in Rosville over a year. "I am going home soon," I said to myself, putting away the letter. It was a summer day, bright and hot. Alice, busy all day, complained of fatigue and went to bed soon after tea. The windows were open and the house was perfumed with odors from the garden. At twilight I went out and walked under the elms, whose pendant boughs were motionless. I watched the stars as they came out one by one above the pale green ring of the horizon and glittered in the evening sky, which darkened slowly. I was coming up the gravel walk when I heard a step at the upper end of it which arrested me. I recognized it, and slipped behind a tree to wait till it should pass by me; but it ceased, and I saw Charles pulling off a twig of the tree, which brushed against his face. Presently he sprang round the tree, caught me, and held me fast.

"I am glad you are here, my darling. Do you smell the roses?"

"Yes; let me go."

"Not till you tell me one thing. Why do you stay in Rosville?"

The baby gave a loud cry in Alice's chamber which resounded through the garden.

"Go and take care of your baby," I said roughly, "and not busy yourself with me."

"Cassandra," he said, with a menacing voice, "how dare you defy me? How dare you tempt me?"

I put my hand on his arm. "Charles, is love a matter of temperament?"

"Are you mad? It is life—it is heaven—it is hell."

"There is something in this soft, beautiful, odorous night that makes one mad. Still I shall not say to you what you once said to me."

"Ah! you do not forget those words—*'I love you.'* "

Some one came down the lane which ran behind the garden whistling an opera air.

"There is your Providence," he said quietly, resting his hand against the tree.

I ran round to the front piazza, just as Ben Somers turned out of the lane, and called him.

"I have wandered all over Rosville since sunset," he said "and at last struck upon that lane. To whom does it belong?"

"It is ours, and the horses are exercised there."

> " 'In such a night,
> Troilus, methinks, mounted the Trojan walls,
> And sighed his soul towards the Grecian tents,
> Where Cressid lay that night.' "

> " 'In such a night,
> Stood Dido with a willow in her hand,
> Upon the wild sea banks, and waved her love
> To come again to Carthage.' "[38]

"Talk to me about Surrey, Cassandra."

"Not a word."

"Why did you call me?"

"To see what mood you were in."

"How disagreeable you are! What is the use of venturing one's mood with you?"

CHAPTER XXI.

Alice called me to her chamber window one morning. "Look into the lane. Charles and Jesse are there with that brute. He goes very well, now that they have thrown the top of the chaise back; he quivered like a jelly at first."

"I must have a ride, Alice."

"Charles," she called. "Breakfast is waiting."

"What shall be his name, girls?" he asked.

"Aspen," I suggested.

"That will do," said Alice.

"Shall we ride soon?" I asked.

"Will you?" he spoke quickly. "In a day or two, then."

"Know what you undertake, Cass," said Alice.

"She always does," he answered.

"Let me go, papa," begged Edward.

"By and by, my boy."

"What a compliment, Cass! He does not object to venture you."

He proposed Fairtown, six miles from Rosville, as he had business there. The morning we were to go proved cloudy, and we waited till afternoon, when Charles, declaring that it would not rain, ordered Aspen to be harnessed. I went into Alice's room tying my bonnet; he was there, leaning over the baby's crib, who lay in it crowing and laughing at the snapping of his fingers. Alice was hemming white muslin.

"Take a shawl with you, Cass; I think it will rain, the air is so heavy."

"I guess not," said Charles, going to the window. "What a nuisance that lane is, so near the garden! I'll have it plowed soon, and enclosed."

"For all those wild primroses you value so?" she asked.

"I'll spare those."

Charlotte came to tell us that the chaise was ready.

"Good-bye, Alice," he said, passing her, and giving her work a toss up to the ceiling.

"Be careful."

"Take care, sir," said Penn, after we were in the chaise, "and don't give way to him; if you do, he'll punish you. May be he feels the thunder in the air."

We reached Fairtown without any indication of mischief from Aspen, although he trotted along as if under protest. Charles was delighted, and thought he would be very fast, by the time he was trained. It grew murky and hot every moment, and when we reached Fairtown the air was black and sultry with the coming storm. Charles left me at the little hotel, and returned so late in the afternoon that we decided not to wait for the shower. Two men led Aspen to the door. He pulled at his bridle, and attempted to run backward, playing his old trick of trying to turn his nostrils inside out, and drawing back his upper lip.

"Something irritates him, Charles."

"If you are afraid, you must not come with me. I can have you sent home in a carriage from the tavern."

"I shall go back with you."

But I felt a vague alarm, and begged him to watch Aspen, and not talk. Aspen went faster and faster, seeming to have lost his shyness, and my fears subsided. We were within a couple of miles of Rosville, when a splashing rain fell.

"You must not be wet," said Charles. "I will put up the top. Aspen is so steady now, it may not scare him."

"No, no," I said; but he had it up already, and asked me to snap the spring on my side. I had scarcely taken my arm inside the chaise when Aspen stopped, turned his head, and looked at us with glazed eyes; flakes of foam flew from his mouth over his mane. The flesh on his back contracted and quivered. I thought he was frightened by the chaise-top, and looked at Charles in terror.

"He has some disorder," he cried. "Oh, Cassandra! My God!"

He tried to spring at his head, but was too late, for the horse was leaping madly. He fell back on his seat.

"If he will keep the road," he muttered.

I could not move my eyes from him. How pale he was! But he did not speak again. The horse ran a few rods, leaped across a ditch, clambered up a stone wall with his fore-feet, and fell backward!

Dr. White was in my room, washing my face. There was a smell of camphor about the bed. "You crawled out of a small hole, my child," he said, as I opened my eyes. It was quite dark, but I saw people at the door, and two or three at the foot of my bed, and I heard low, constrained talking everywhere.

"His iron feet made a dreadful noise on the stones, Doctor!"

I shut my eyes again and dozed. Suddenly a great tumult came to my heart.

"Was he killed?" I cried, and tried to rise from the bed. "Let me go, will you?"

"He is dead," whispered Dr. White.

I laughed loudly.

"Be a good girl—be a good girl. Get out, all of you. Here, Miss Prior."

"You are crying, Doctor; my eyes feel dry."

"Pooh, pooh, little one. Now I am going to set your arm; simple fracture, that's all. The blow was tempered, but you are paralyzed by the shock."

"Miss Prior, is my face cut?"

"Not badly, my dear."

My arm was set, my face bandaged, some opium administered, and then I was left alone with Miss Prior. I grew drowsy, but suffered so from the illusion that I was falling out of bed that I could not sleep.

It was near morning when I shook off my drowsiness and looked about; Miss Prior was nodding in an arm-chair. I asked for drink, and when she gave it to me, begged her to lie down on the sofa; she did not need urging, and was soon asleep.

"What room is he in?" I thought. "I must know where he is."

I sat up in the bed, and pushed myself out by degrees, keeping my eyes on Miss Prior; but she did not stir. I staggered when I got into the passage, but the cool air from some open window revived me, and I crept on, stopping at Alice's door to listen. I heard a child murmur in its sleep. He could not be there. The doors of all the chambers were locked, and I must go downstairs. I went into the garden-room—the door was open, the scent of roses came in and made me deadly sick; into the dining-room, and into the parlor—he was there, lying on a table covered with a sheet. Alice sat on the floor, her face hid in her hands, crying softly. I touched her. She started on seeing me. "Go away, Cassy, for God's sake! How came you out of bed?"

"Hush! Tell me!" And I went down on the floor beside her. "Was he dead when they found us?"

She nodded.

"What was said? Did you hear?"

"They said he must have made a violent effort to save you. The side of the chaise was torn. The horse kicked him after you were thrust out over the wheel. Or did you creep out?"

I groaned. "Why did he thrust me out?"

"What?"

"Where is Aspen?"

She pointed to the stable. "He had a fit. Penn says he has had one before; but he thought him cured. He stood quiet in the ditch after he had broken from the chaise."

"Alice, did you love him?"

"My husband!"

A door near us opened, and Ben Somers and young Parker looked in. They were the watchers. Parker went back when he saw me; but Ben came in. He knelt down by me, put his arm around me, and said, "Poor girl!" Alice raised her tear-stained face, looking at me curiously, when he said this. She took hold of my streaming hair and pulled my head round. "Did *you* love him?" Ben rose quickly and went to the window.

"Alice!" I whispered, "you may or you may not forgive me, but I was strangely bound to him. And I must tell you that I hunger now for the kiss he never gave me."

"I see. Enough. Go back to your room. I must stay by him till all is over."

"I can't go back. Ben!"

"What is it?"

"Take me upstairs."

Raising me in his arms, he whispered: "Leave him forever, body and soul. I am not sorry he is dead." He called Charlotte on the way, and with her he put me to back to bed. I asked him to let me see the dress they had taken off.

"That is enough," I said, "Charles broke my arm."

It was torn through the shoulder, and the skirt had been twisted like a rope. Ben made no reply, but bent over me and kissed me tenderly. All this time Miss Prior had slept the sleep of the just; but he had barely gone when she started up and said, "Did you call, my dear?"

"No, it is day."

"So it is; but you must sleep more."

I could not obey, and kept awake so long that Dr. White said he himself should go crazy unless I slept.

"Presently, presently," I reiterated; "and am I going home?"

At last my mind went astray; it journeyed into a dismal world, and came back without an account of its adventures. While it was gone, my friends were summoned to witness a contest, where the odds were in favor of death. But I recovered. Whether it was youth, a good constitution, or the skill of Dr. White, no one could decide. It was a faint, feeble, fluttering return at first. The faces round me, mobile with life, wearied me. I was indifferent to existence, and was more than once in danger of lapsing into the void I had escaped.

When I first tottered downstairs, he had been buried more than three weeks. It was a bright morning; the windows of the parlor, where Charlotte led me, were open. Little Edward was playing round the table upon which I had seen his father stretched, dead. I measured it with my eye, remembering how tall he looked. I would have retreated, when I saw that Alice had visitors, but it was too late. They rose, and offered congratulations. I was angry that there was no change in the house. The rooms should have been dismantled, reflecting disorder and death, by their perpetual darkness and disorder. It was not so. No dust had been allowed to gather on the furniture, no wrinkles or stains. No mist on the mirrors, no dimness anywhere. Alice was elegantly dressed, in the deepest mourning. I examined her with a cynical eye; her bombazine was trimmed with crape, and the edge of her collar was beautifully crimped. A mourning brooch fastened it, and she wore jet ear-rings. She looked handsome, composed, and contented, holding a black-edged handkerchief. Charlotte had placed my chair opposite a glass; I caught sight of my elongated visage in it. How dull I looked! My hair was faded and rough; my eyes were a pale, lusterless blue. The visitors departed, while I still contemplated my rueful aspect, and Alice and I were alone.

"I want some broth, Alice. I am hungry."

"How many bowls have you had this morning?"

"Only two."

"You must wait an hour for the third; it is not twelve o'clock."

We were silent. The flies buzzed in and out of the windows; a great bee flew in, tumbled against the panes, loudly hummed, and after a while got out again. Alice yawned, and I pulled the threads out of the border of my handkerchief.

"The hour is up; I will get your broth."

"Bring me a great deal."

She came back with a thin, impoverished liquid.

"There is no chicken in it," I said tearfully.

"I took it out."

"How could you?" And I wept.

She smiled. "You are very weak, but shall have a bit." She went for it, returning with an infinitesimal portion of chicken.

"What a young creature it must have been, Alice!"

She laughed, promising me more, by and by.

"Now you must lie down. Take my arm and come to the sofa."

"Not here; let us go into another room."

"Come, then."

"Don't leave me," I begged, after she had arranged me comfortably. She sat down by me with a fan.

"What happened while I was ill?"

She fanned rapidly for an instant, taking thought what to say.

"I shot Aspen, a few days after."

"With your own hand?"

"Yes."

"Good."

"Penn protested, said I interfered with Providence. Jesse added, also, that what had happened was ordained, and no mistake, and then I sent them both away."

"And I am going at last, Alice; father will be here again in a few days."

"You did not recognize Veronica, when they came."

"Was she here?"

"Yes, and went the same day. What great tears rolled down her unmovable face, when she stood by your bed! She would not stay; the atmosphere distressed her so, she went back to Boston to wait for your father. I could neither prevail on her to eat, drink, or rest."

"What will you do, Alice?"

"Take care of the children, and manage the mills."

"Manage the mills?"

"I can. No wonder you look astonished," she said, with a sigh. "I am changed. When perhaps I should feel that I have done with life, I am eager to begin it. I have lamented over myself lately."

"How is Ben?"

"He has been here often. How strange it was that to him alone Veronica gave her hand when they met! Indeed, she gave him both her hands."

"And he?"

"Took them, bowing over them, till I thought he wasn't coming up again. I do not call people eccentric any more," she said, faintly blushing. "I look for a reason in every action. Tell me fairly, have you had a contempt for me—for my want of perception? I understand you now, to the bone and marrow, I assure you."

"Then you understand more than I do. But you will remember that once or twice I attempted to express my doubts to you?"

"Yes, yes, with a candor which misled me. But you are talking too much."

"Give me more broth, then."

CHAPTER XXII.

I was soon well enough to go home. Father came for me, bringing Aunt Merce. There was no alteration in her, except that she had taken to wearing a false front, which had a claret tinge when the light struck it, and a black lace cap. She walked the room in speechless distress when she saw me, and could not refrain from taking an immense pinch of snuff in my presence.

"Didn't you bring any flag-root, Aunt Merce?"

"Oh Lord, Cassandra, won't anything upon earth change you?"

And then we both laughed, and felt comfortable together. Her knitting mania had given way to one she called transferring. She brought a little basket filled with rags, worn-out embroideries, collars, cuffs, and edges of handkerchiefs, from which she cut the needle-work, to sew again on new muslin. She looked at embroidery with an eye merely to its capacity for being transferred. Alice proved a treasure to her, by giving her heaps of fine work. She and Aunt Merce were pleased with each other, and when we were ready to come away, Alice begged her to visit her every year. I made no farewell visits—my ill health was sufficient excuse; but my schoolmates came to bid me good-bye, and brought presents of needlebooks, and pincushions, which I returned by giving away yards of ribbon, silver fruit-knives, and Mrs. Hemans's poems, which poetess had lately given my imagination an apostrophizing direction. Miss Prior came also, with a copy of "Young's Night Thoughts," bound in speckled leather.[39] This hilarious and refreshing poem remained at the bottom of my trunk, till Temperance fished it out, to read on Sundays, in her own room, where she usually passed her hours of solitude in hemming dish-towels, or making articles called "Takers." Dr. Price came, too, and even the haughty four Ryders. Alice was gratified with my popularity. But I felt cold at heart, doubtful of myself, drifting to nothingness in thought and purpose. None saw my doubts or felt my coldness.

I shook hands with all, exchanged hopes and wishes, and repeated the last words which people say on departure. Alice and I neither kissed nor shook hands. There was that between us which kept us apart. A hard, stern face was still in our recollection. We remembered a certain figure, whose steps had ceased about the house, whose voice was hushed, but who was potent yet.

"We shall not forget each other," she said.

And so I took my way out of Rosville. Ben Somers went with us to Boston, and stayed at the Bromfield. In the morning he disappeared, and when he returned had an emerald ring, which he begged me to wear, and tried to put it on my finger, where he had seen the diamond. I put it back in its box, thanking him, and saying it must be stored with the farewell needlebooks and pincushions.

"Shall we have some last words now?"

Aunt Merce slipped out, with an affectation of not having heard him. We laughed, and Ben was glad that I could laugh.

"How do you feel?"

"Rather weak still."

"I do not mean so, but in your mind; how are you?"

"I have no mind."

"Must I give up trying to understand you, Cassandra?"

"Yes, do. You'll visit Alice? You can divine her intentions. She is a good woman."

"She will be, when she knows how."

"What o'clock is it?"

"Incorrigible! Near ten."

"Here is father, and we must start."

The carriage was ready; where was Aunt Merce?

"Locke," she said, when she came in, "I have got a bottle of port for Cassandra, some essence of peppermint, and sandwiches; do you think that will do?"

"We can purchase supplies along the road, if yours give out. Come, we are ready. Mr. Somers, we shall see you at Surrey? Take care, Cassy. Now we are off."

"I shall leave Rosville," were Ben's last words.

"What a fine, handsome young man he is! He is a gentleman," said Aunt Merce.

"Of course, Aunt Merce."

"Why of course? I should think from the way you speak that you had only seen young gentlemen of his stamp. Have you forgotten Surrey?"

Father and she laughed. They could laugh very easily, for they were overjoyed to have me going home with them. Mother would be glad, they said. I felt it, though I did not say so.

How soundly I slept that night at the inn on the road! A little after sunset, on the third day, for we traveled slowly, we reached the woods which bordered Surrey, and soon came in sight of the sea encircling it like a crescent moon. It was as if I saw the sea for the first time. A vague sense of its power surprised me; it seemed to express my melancholy. As we approached the house, the orchard, and I saw Veronica's window, other feelings moved me. Not because I saw familiar objects, nor because I was going home— it was the relation in which *I* stood to them, that I felt. We drove through the gate, and saw a handsome little boy astride a windowsill, with two pipes in his mouth. "Papa!" he shrieked, threw his pipes down, and dropped on the ground, to run after us.

"Hasn't Arthur grown?" Aunt Merce asked. "He is almost seven."

"Almost seven? Where have the years gone?"

I looked about. I had been away so long, the house looked diminished. Mother was in the door, crying when she put her arms round me; she could not speak. I know now there should have been no higher beatitude than to live in the presence of an unselfish, unasking, vital love. I only said, "Oh, mother, how gray your hair is! Are you glad to see me? I have grown old too!"

We went in by the kitchen, where the men were, and a young girl with a bulging forehead. Hepsey looked out from the buttery door, and put her apron to her eyes, without making any further demonstration of welcome. Temperance was mixing dough. She made an effort to giggle, but failed; and as she could not cover her face with her doughy hands, was obliged to let the tears run their natural course. Recovering herself in a moment, she exclaimed:

"Heavenly Powers, how you're altered! I shouldn't have known you. Your hair and skin are as dry as chips; they didn't wash you with Castile soap, I'll bet."

"How you do talk, Temperance," Hepsey quavered.

The girl with the bulging forehead laughed a shrill laugh.

"Why, Fanny!" said mother.

The hall door opened. "Here *she* is," muttered this Fanny.

"Veronica!"

"Cassandra!"

We grasped hands, and stared mutely at each other. I felt a contraction in the region of my heart, as if a cord of steel were binding it. She, at least, was glad that I was alive!

"They look something alike now," Hepsey remarked.

"Not at all," said Veronica, dropping my hand, and retreating.

"Why, Arthur dear, come here!"

He clambered into my lap.

"Were you killed, my dear sister?"

"Not quite, little boy."

"Well; do you know that I am a veteran officer, and smoke my pipe, lots?"

"You must rest, Cassy," said mother. "Don't go upstairs, though, till you have had your supper. Hurry it up, Temperance."

"It will be on the table in less than no time, Miss Morgeson," she answered, "provided Miss Fanny is agreeable about taking in the teapot."

I had a comfortable sense of property, when I took possession of my own room. It was better, after all, to live with a father and mother, who would adopt my ideas. Even the sea might be mine. I asked father the next morning, at breakfast, how far out at sea his property extended.

"I trust, Cassandra, you will now stay at home," said mother; "I am tired of table duty; you must pour the coffee and tea, for I wish to sit beside your father."

"You and Aunt Merce have settled down into a venerable condition. You wear caps, too! What a stage forward!"

"The cap is not ugly, like Aunt Merce's; I made it," Veronica called, sipping from a great glass.

"Gothic pattern, isn't it?" father asked, "with a tower, and a bridge at the back of the neck?"

"This hash is Fanny's work, mother," said Verry.

"So I perceive."

"Hepsey is not at the table," I said.

"It is her idea not to come, since I have taken Fanny. Did you notice her? She prefers to have her wait."

"Who is Fanny?"

"Her father is old Ichabod Bowles, who lives on the Neck. Last winter her mother sent for me, and begged me to take her. I could not refuse, for she was dying of consumption; so I promised. The poor woman died, in the bitterest weather, and a few days after Ichabod brought Fanny here, and told me he had done with womankind forever. Fanny was sulky and silent for a long time. I thought she never would get warm. If obliged to leave the fire, she sat against the wall, with her face hid in her arms. Veronica has made some impression on her; but she is not a good girl."

"She will be, mother. I am better than I was."

"Never; her disposition is hateful. She is angry with those who are better off than herself. I have not seen a spark of gratitude in her."

"I never thought of gratitude," said Verry, "it is true; but why must people be grateful?"

"We might expect little from Fanny, perhaps; she saw her mother die in want, her father stern, almost cruel to them, and soured by poverty. Fanny never had what she liked to eat or wear, till she came here, or even saw anything that pleased her; and the contrast makes her bitter."

"She is proud, too," said Aunt Merce. "I hear her boasting of what she would have had if she had stayed at home."

"She is a child, you know," said Verry.

"A year younger than you are."

"Where is the universal boy?"

"Abolished," father answered. "Arthur is growing into that estate."

"Papa, don't forget that I am a veteran officer."

"Here, you rascal, come and get this nice egg."

He slipped down, went to his father, who took him on his knee.

"What shall I do first? the garden, orchard, village, or what?" I asked.

"Gardens?" said Verry. "Have they been a part of your education?"

"I like flowers."

"Have you seen my plants?" Aunt Merce inquired.

"I will look at them. How different this is from Rosville."

Then a pang cut me to the soul. The past whirled up, to disappear, leaving me stunned and helpless. Veronica's eye was upon me. I forced myself to observe her. The difference between us was plainer than ever. I was in my twentieth year, she was barely sixteen; handsome, and as peculiar-looking as when a child. Her straight hair was a vivid chestnut color. Her large eyes were near together; and, as Ben Somers said, the most singular eyes that were ever upon earth. They tormented me. There was nothing willful in them; on the contrary, when she was willful, she had no power over them; the strange cast was then perceptible. Neither were they imperious nor magnetic; they were *baffling*. She pushed her chair from the table, and stood by me quiet. Tall and slender, she stooped slightly, as if she were not strong enough to stand upright. Her dress was a buff-colored cambric, trimmed with knots of ribbon of the same color, dotted with green crosses. It harmonized with her colorless, fixedly pale complexion. I counted the bows of ribbon on her dress, and would have counted the crosses, if she had not interrupted me with, "What do you think of me?"

"Do you ever blush, Verry?"

"I grow paler, you know, when I blush."

"What do you think of me?"

"As wide-eyed as ever, and your eyebrows as black. Who ever saw light, ripply hair with such eyebrows? I see wrinkles, too."

"Where?"

"Round your eyes, like an opening umbrella."

We dispersed as our talk ended, in the old fashion. I followed Aunt Merce to the flower-stand, which stood in its old place on the landing.

"I have a poor lot of roses," she said, "but some splendid cactuses."

"I do not love roses."

"Is it possible? But Verry does not care so much for them, either. Lilies are her favorites; she has a variety. Look at this Arab lily; it is like a tongue of fire."

"Where does she keep her flowers?"

"In wire baskets, in her room. But I must go to make Arthur some gingerbread. He likes mine the best, and I like to please him."

"I dare say you spoil him."

"Just as you were spoiled."

"Not in Barmouth, Aunt Merce."

"No, not in Barmouth, Cassy."

I went from room to room, seeing little to interest me. My zeal oozed away for exploration, and when I entered my chamber I could have said, "This spot is the summary of my wants, for it contains me." I must be my own society, and as my society was not agreeable, the more circumscribed it was, the better I could endure it. What a dreary prospect! The past was vital, the present dead! Life in Surrey must be dull. How could I forget or enjoy? I put the curtains down, and told Temperance, who was wandering about, not to call me to dinner. I determined, if possible, to surpass my dullness by indulgence. But underneath it all I could not deny that there was a specter, whose aimless movements kept me from stagnating. I determined to drag it up and face it.

"Come," I called, "and stand before me; we will reason together."

It uncovered, and asked:

"Do you feel remorse and repentance?"

"Neither!"

"Why suffer then?"

"I do not know why."

"You confess ignorance. Can you confess that you are selfish, self-seeking—devilish?"

"Are you my devil?"

No answer.

"Am I cowardly, or a liar?"

It laughed, a faint, sarcastic laugh.

"At all events," I continued, "are not my actions better than my thoughts?"

"Which makes the sinner, and which the saint?"

"Can I decide?"

"Why not?"

"My teachers and myself are so far apart! I have found a counterpart; but, specter, you were born of the union."

My head was buried in my arms; but I heard a voice at my elbow—a shrill, scornful voice it was. "Are you coming down to tea, then?"

Looking up, I saw Fanny. "Tea-time so soon?"

"Yes, it is. You think nothing of time; have nothing to do, I suppose."

And she clasped her hands over her apron—hands so small and thin that they looked like those of an old woman. Her hair was light and scanty, her complexion sallow, and her eyes a palish gray; but her features were delicate and pretty. She seemed to understand my thoughts.

"You think I am stunted, don't you?"

"You are not large to my eye."

"Suppose you had been fed mostly on Indian meal, with a herring or a piece of salted pork for a relish, and clams or tautog for a luxury, as I have been, would you be as tall and as grand-looking as you are now? And would you be covering up your face, making believe worry?"

"May be not. You may tell mother that I am coming."

"I shall not say 'Miss Morgeson,' but 'Cassandra.' 'Cassandra Morgeson,' if I like."

"Call me what you please, only tone down that voice of yours; it is sharper than the east wind."

I heard her beating a tattoo on Veronica's door next. She had been taught to be ceremonious with her, at least. No reply was made, and she came to my door again. "I expect Miss Veronica has gone to see poor folks; it is a way *she* has," and spitefully closed it.

After tea mother came up to inquire the reason of my seclusion. My excuse of fatigue she readily accepted, for she thought I still looked ill. I had changed so much, she said, it made her heart ache to look at me. When I could speak of the accident at Rosville, would I tell her all? And would I describe my life there; what friends I had made; would they visit me? She hoped so. And Mr. Somers, who made them so hurried a visit, would he come? She liked him. While she talked, she kept a pitying but resolute eye upon me.

"Dear mother, I never can tell you all, as you wish. It is hard enough for me to bear my thoughts, without the additional one that my feelings are understood and speculated upon. If I should tell you, the barrier between me and self-control would give way. You will see Alice Morgeson, and if she chooses she can tell you what my life was in her house. She knows it well."

"Cassandra, what does your bitter face and voice mean?"

"I mean, mother, all your woman's heart might guess, if you were not so pure, so single-hearted."

"No, no, no."

"Yes."

"Then I understand the riddle you have been, one to bring a curse."

"There is nothing to curse, mother; our experiences are not foretold by law. We may be righteous by rule, we do not sin that way. There was no beginning, no end, to mine."

"Should women curse themselves, then, for giving birth to daughters?"

"Wait, mother; what is bad this year may be good the next. You blame yourself, because you believe your ignorance has brought me into danger. Wait, mother."

"You are beyond me; everything is beyond."

"I will be a good girl. Kiss me, mother. I have been unworthy of you. When have I ever done anything for you? If you hadn't been my mother, I dare say we might have helped each other, my friendship and sympathy have sustained you. As it is, I have behaved as all young animals behave to their mothers. One thing you may be sure of. The doubt you feel is needless. You must neither pray nor weep over me. Have I agitated you?"

"My heart *will* flutter too much, anyway. Oh, Cassy, Cassy, why are you such a girl? Why will you be so awfully headstrong?" But she hugged and kissed me. As I felt the irregular beating of her heart, a pain smote me. What if she should not live long? Was I not a wicked fool to lacerate myself with an intangible trouble— the reflex of selfish emotions?

CHAPTER XXIII.

Veronica's room was like no other place. I was in a new atmosphere there. A green carpet covered the floor, and the windows had light blue silk curtains.

"Green and blue together, Veronica?"

"Why not? The sky is blue, and the carpet of the earth is green."

"If you intend to represent the heavens and the earth here, it is very well."

The paper on the wall was ash-colored, with penciled lines. She had cloudy days probably. A large-eyed Saint Cecilia, with white roses in her hair, was pasted on the wall. This frameless picture had a curious effect. Veronica, in some mysterious way, had contrived to dispose of the white margin of the picture, and the saint looked out from the soft ashy tint of the wallpaper. Opposite was an exquisite engraving, which was framed with dark red velvet. At the end of an avenue of old trees, gnarled and twisted into each other, a man stood. One hand grasped the stalk of a ragged vine, which ran over the tree near him; the other hung helpless by his side, as if the wrist was broken. His eyes were fixed on some object behind the trees, where nothing was visible but a portion of the wall of a house. His expression of concentrated fury—his attitude of waiting—testified that he would surely accomplish his intention.

"What a picture!"

"The foliage attracted me, and I bought it; but when I unpacked it, the man seemed to come out for the first time. Will you take it?"

"No; I mean to give my room a somnolent aspect. The man is too terribly sleepless."

A table stood near the window, methodically covered with labelled blank-books, a morocco portfolio, and a Wedgewood inkstand and vase. In an arch, which she had manufactured from the space under the garret stairs, stood her bed. At its foot, against the wall, a bunch of crimson autumn leaves was fastened, and a bough, black and bare, with an empty nest on it.

"Where is the feminine portion of your furnishing?"

"Look in the closet."

I opened a door. What had formerly been appropriated by mother to blankets and comfortables, she had turned into a magazine of toilet articles. There were drawers and boxes for everything which pertained to a wardrobe, arranged with beautiful skill and neatness. She directed my attention to her books, on hanging shelves, within reach of the bed. Beneath them was a small stand, with a wax candle in a silver candlestick.

"You read o' nights?"

"Yes; and the wax candle is my pet weakness."

"Have you put away Gray, and Pope, and Thomson?"[40]

"The Arabian Nights and the Bible are still there. Mother thought you would like to refurnish your room. It is the same as when we moved, you know."

"Did she? I will have it done. Good-by."

"Good-by."

She was at the window now, and had opened a pane.

"What's that you are doing?"

"Looking through my wicket."

I went back again to understand the wicket. It had been made, she said, so that she might have fresh air in all weathers, without raising the windows. In the night she could look out without danger of taking cold. We looked over the autumn fields; the crows were flying seaward over the stubble, or settling in the branches of an old fir, standing alone, midway between the woods and the orchard. The ground before us, rising so gradually, and shortening the horizon, reminded me of my childish notion that we were near the North Pole, and that if we could get behind the low rim of sky we should be in the Arctic Zone.

"The Northern Lights have not deserted us, Veronica?"

"No; they beckon me over there, in winter."

"Do you never tire of this limited, monotonous view—of a few uneven fields, squared by grim stone walls?"

"That is not all. See those eternal travelers, the clouds, that hurry up from some mysterious region to go over your way, where I never look. If the landscape were wider, I could never learn it. And the orchard—have you noticed that? There are bird and butterfly lives in it, every year. Why, morning and night are wonderful from these windows. But I must say the charm vanishes if I go from them. Surrey is not lovely." She closed the wicket, and sat down by the table. My dullness vanished with her. There might be something to interest me beneath the calm surface of our family life after all.

"Veronica, do you think mother is changed? I think so."

"She is always the same to me. But I have had fears respecting her health."

Outside the door I met Temperance, with a clothes-basket.

"Oh ho!" she said, "you are going the rounds. Verry's room beats all possessed, don't it? It is cleaned spick and span every three months. She calls it inaugurating the seasons. She is as queer as Dick's hatband. Have you any fine things to do up?"

Her question put me in mind of my trunks, and I hastened to them, with the determination of putting my room to rights. The call to dinner interrupted me before I had begun, and the call to supper came before anything in the way of improvement had been accomplished. My mind was chaotic by bed-time. The picture of Veronica, reading by her wax candle, or looking through the wicket, collected and happy in her orderly perfection, came into my mind, and with it an admiration which never ceased, though I had no sympathy with her. We seemed as far apart as when we were children.

I was eager for employment, promising to perform many tasks, but the attempt killed my purpose and interest. My will was nerveless, when I contemplated Time, which stretched before me—a vague, limitless sea; and I only kept Endeavor in view, near enough to be tormented.

One day father asked me to go to Milford, and I then asked him for money to spend for the adornment of my room.

"Be prudent," he replied. "I am not so rich as people think me. Although the *Locke Morgeson* was insured, she was a loss. But you need not speak of this to your mother. I never worry her with my business cares. As for Veronica, she has not the least idea of the value of money, or care for what it represents."

When we went into the shops, I found him disposed to be more extravagant than I was. I bought a blue and white carpet; a piece of blue and white flowered chintz; two stuffed chairs, covered with hair-cloth (father remonstrated against these), and a long mirror to go between the windows, astonishing him with my vanity. What I wanted besides I could construct myself, with the help of the cabinet maker in Surrey.

In one of the shops I heard a familiar voice, which gave me a thrill of anger. I turned and saw Charlotte Alden, of Barmouth, the girl who had given me the fall on the tilt. She could not control an expression of surprise at the sight of the well-dressed woman before her. It was my dress that astonished her. Where could *I* have obtained style?

"Miss Alden, how do you do? Pray tell me whether you have collected any correct legends respecting my mother's early history. And do you tilt off little girls nowadays?"

She made no reply, and I left her standing where she was when I began speaking. When we got out of town, my anger cooled, and I grew ashamed of my spitefulness, and by way of penance I related the affair to father. He laughed at what I said to her, and told me that he had long known her family. Charlotte's uncle had paid his addresses to mother. There might have been an engagement; whether there was or not, the influence of his family had broken the acquaintance. This explained what Charlotte said to me in Miss Black's school about mother's being in love.

"You might have been angry with the girl, but you should not have felt hurt at the fact implied. Are you so young still as to believe that only those who love marry? or that those who marry have never loved, except each other?"

"I have thought of these things; but I am afraid that Love, like Theology, if examined, makes one skeptical."

We jogged along in silence for a mile or two.

"Whether every men's children overpower him, I wonder? I am positively afraid of you and Veronica."

"What do you mean?"

"I am always unprepared for the demonstrations of character you and she make. My traditional estimate, which comes from thoughtfulness, or the putting off of responsibility, or God knows what, I find will not answer. I have been on my guard against that which everyday life might present—a lie, a theft, or a meanness; but of the undercurrent, which really bears you on, I have known nothing."

"If you happen to dive below the surface, and find the roots of our actions which are fixed beneath its tide—what then? Must you lament over us?"

"No, no; but this is vague talk."

Was he dissatisfied with me? What could he expect? We all went our separate ways, it is true; was it that? Perhaps he felt alone. I studied his face; it was not so cheerful as I remembered it once, but still open, honest, and wholesome. I promised myself to observe his tastes and consult them. It might be that his self-love had never been encouraged. But I failed in that design, as in all others.

"Much of my time is consumed in passing between Milford and Surrey, you perceive."

"I will go with you often."

According to habit, on arriving, I went into the kitchen. It was dusk there, and still. Temperance was by the fire, attending to something which was cooking.

"What is there for supper, Temperance? I am hungry."

"I spose you are," she answered crossly. "You'll see when it's on the table."

She took a coal of fire with the tongs, and blew it fiercely, to light a lamp by. When it was alight, she set it on the chimneyshelf, revealing thereby a man at the back of the room, balancing his chair on two legs against the wall; his feet were on its highest round, and he twirled his thumbs.

"Hum," he said, when he saw me observing him; "this is the oldest darter, is it?"

"Yes," Temperance bawled.

"She is a good solid gal; but I can't recollect her christened name."

"It is Cassandra."

"Why, 'taint Scriptur'."

"Why don't you go and take off your things?" Temperance asked, abruptly.

"I'll leave them here; the fire is agreeable."

"There is a better fire in the keeping-room."

"How are you, Mr. Handy?" father inquired, coming in.

"I should be well, if my grinders didn't trouble me; they play the mischief o'nights. Have you heard from the *Adamant,* Mr. Morgeson? I should like to get my poor boy's chist. The Lord ha' mercy on him, whose bones are in the caverns of the deep."

"Now, Abram, do shut up. Tea is ready, Mr. Morgeson. I'll bring in the ham directly," said Temperance.

There was no news from the *Adamant.* I lingered in the hope of discovering why Mr. Handy irritated Temperance. He was a man of sixty, with a round head, and a large, tender wart on one cheek; the two tusks under his upper lip suggested a walrus. Though he was no beauty, he looked thoroughly respectable, in garments whose primal colors had disappeared, and blue woolen stockings gartered to a miracle of tightness.

"Temperance," he said, "my quinces have done fust rate this year. I haint pulled 'em yet; but I've counted them over and over agin. But my pig wont weigh nothin' like what I calkerlated on. Sarved me right. I needn't have bought him out of a drove; if Charity had been alive, I shouldn't ha' done it. A man can't—I say, Tempy—a man *can't* git along while here below, without a woman."

She gave my arm a severe pinch as she passed with the ham, and I thought it best to follow her. Mother looked at her with a smile, and said: "Deal gently with Brother Abram, Temperance."

"Brother be fiddlesticked!" she said tartly. "Miss Morgeson, *do* you want some quinces?"

"Certainly."

"We'll make hard marmalade this year, then. You shall have the quinces to-morrow." And she retired with a softened face. I was told that Abram Handy was a widower anxious to take Temperance for a second helpmeet, and that she could not decide whether to accept or refuse him. She had confessed to mother that she was on the fence, and didn't know which way to jump. He was a poor, witless thing, she knew; but he was as good a man as ever breathed, and stood as good a chance of being saved as the wisest church-member that ever lived! Mother thought her inclined to be mistress of an establishment over which she might have sole control. Abram owned a house, a garden, and kept pigs, hens, and a cow; these were his themes of conversation. Mother could not help thinking he was influenced by Temperance's fortune. She was worth two thousand dollars, at least. The care of her wood-lot, the cutting, selling, or burning the wood on it, would be a supreme happiness to Abram, who loved property next to the kingdom of heaven. The tragedy of the old man's life was the loss of his only son, who had been killed by a whale a year since. The *Adamant*, the ship he sailed in, had not returned, and it was a consoling hope with Abram that his boy's chist might come back.

"We heard of poor Charming Handy's death the tenth of September, about three months after Abram began his visits to Temperance," Veronica said.

"Was his name Charming?" I asked.

"His mother named him," Abram said, "with a name that she

had picked out of Novel's works, which she was forever and 'tarnally reading."

"What day of the month is it, Verry?"

"Third of October."

"What happened a year ago to-day?"

"Arthur fell off the roof of the wood-house."

"Verry," he cried, "you needn't tell my sister of that; now she knows about my scar. You tell everything; she does not. You have scars," he whispered to me; "they look red sometimes. May I put my finger on your cheek?"

I took his hand, and rubbed his fingers over the cuts; they were not deep, but they would never go away.

"I wish mine were as nice; it is only a little hole under my hair. Soldiers ought to have long scars, made with great big swords, and I am a soldier, aint I, Cassy?"

"Have I heard you sing, Cassy?" asked father. "Come, let us have some music."

" 'And the cares which infest the day,' " added Verry.

I had scarcely been in the parlor since my return, though the fact had not been noticed. Our tacit compact was that we should be ignorant of each other's movements. I ran up to my room for some music, and, not having a lamp, stumbled over my shawl and bonnet and various bundles which somebody had deposited on the floor. I went down by the back way, to the kitchen; Fanny was there alone, standing before the fire, and whistling a sharp air.

"Did you carry my bonnet and shawl upstairs?"

"I did."

"Will you be good enough to take this music to the parlor for me?"

She turned and put her hands behind her. "Who was your waiter last year?"

"I had one," putting the leaves under her arm; they fluttered to the floor, one by one.

"You must pick them up, or we shall spend the night here, and father is waiting for me."

"Is he?" and she began to take them up.

"I am quite sure, Fanny, that I could punish you awfully. I am sick to try."

She moved toward the door slowly. "Don't tell him," she said, stopping before it.

"I'll tell nobody, but I am angry. Let us arrive."

She marched to the piano, laid the music on it, and marched out.

"By the way, Fanny," I whispered, "the bonnet and shawl are yours, if you need them."

"I guess I do," she whispered back.

When I returned to my room, I found it in order and the bundles removed.

One day some Surrey friends called. They told me I had changed very much, and I inferred from their tone they did not consider the change one for the better.

"How much Veronica has improved," they continued, "do not you think so?"

"You know," she interrupted, "that Cassandra has been dangerously ill, and has barely recovered."

Yes, they had heard of the accident, everybody had; Mr. Morgeson must be a loss to his family, a man in the prime of life, too.

"The prime of life," Veronica repeated.

She was asked to play, and immediately went to the piano. Strange girl; her music was so filled with a wild lament that I again fathomed my desires and my despair. Her eyes wandered toward me, burning with the fires of her creative power, not with the feelings which stung me to the quick. Her face was calm, white, and fixed. She stopped and touched her eyelids, as if she were weeping, but there were no tears in her eyes. They were in mine, welling painfully beneath the lids. I turned over the music books to hide them.

"That is a singular piece," said one. "Now, Cassandra, will you favor us? We expect to find you highly accomplished."

"I sang myself out before you came in."

In the bustle of their going, Veronica stooped over my hand and kissed it, unseen. It was more like a sigh upon it than a kiss, but it swept through me, tingling the scars on my face, as if the flesh had become alive again.

"Take tea with us soon, do. We do not see you in the street or at church. It must be dull for you after coming from a boarding-school. Still, Surrey has its advantages." And the doors closed on them.

"Still, Surrey has its advantages," Veronica repeated.

"Yes, the air is sleepy; I am going to bed."

I made resolutions before I slept that night, which I kept, for I said, "Let the dead bury its dead."

CHAPTER XXIV.

Helen's letters followed me. She had heard from Rosville all that had happened, but did not expatiate on it. Her letters were full of minute details respecting her affairs. It was her way of diverting me from the thoughts which she believed troubled me. "L. N." was expected soon. Since his last letter, she had caught herself more than once making inventories of what she would like to have in the way of a wardrobe for a particular occasion, which he had hinted at.

I heard nothing from Alice, and was content that it should be so. Our acquaintance would be resumed in good time, I had no doubt. Neither did I hear from Ben Somers. He very likely was investing in another plan. Of its result I should also hear.

My chief occupation was to drive with father. The wharves of Milford, the doors of its banks and shipping offices, became familiar. I witnessed bargains and contracts, and listened to talk of shipwrecks, mutinies, insurance cases, perjuries, failures, ruin, and rascalities. His private opinions, and those who sought him, were kept in the background; the sole relation between them was— Traffic. Personality was forgotten in the absorbed attention which was given to business. They appeared to me, though, as if pursuing something beyond Gain, which should narcotize or stimulate them to forget that man's life was a vain going to and fro.

Mother reproached father for allowing me to adopt the habits of a man. He thought it a wholesome change; besides, it would not last. While I was his companion there were moments when he left his ledger for another book.

"You never call yourself a gambler, do you, Locke?" mother asked. "Strange, too, that you think of Cassy in your business life instead of me."

"Mary, could I break your settled habits? Cassy is afloat yet. I can guide her hither and yon. Moreover, with her, I dream of youth."

"Is youth so happy?" we both asked.

"We think so, when we see it in others."

"Not all of us," she said. "You think Cassandra has no ways of her own! She can make us change ours; do you know that?"

"May be."

A habit grew upon me of consulting the sea as soon as I rose in the morning. Its aspect decided how my day would be spent. I watched it, studying its changes, seeking to understand its effect, ever attracted by an awful materiality and its easy power to drown me. By the shore at night the vague tumultuous sphere, swayed by an influence mightier than itself, gave voice, which drew my soul to utter speech for speech. I went there by day unobserved, except by our people, for I never walked toward the village. Mother descried me, as she would a distant sail, or Aunt Merce, who had a vacant habit of looking from all the windows a moment at a time, as if she were forever expecting the arrival of somebody who never came. Arthur, too, saw me, as he played among the rocks, waded, caught crabs and little fish, like all boys whose hereditary associations are amphibious. But Veronica never came to the windows on that side of the house, unless a ship was arriving from a long voyage. Then her interest was in the ship alone, to see whether her colors were half-mast, or if she were battered and torn, recalling to mind those who had died or married since the ship sailed from port; for she knew the names of all who ever left Surrey, and their family relations.

Weeks passed before I had completed the furnishing of my room; I had been to Helen's wedding, and had returned, and it was still in progress. The ground was covered with snow. The sea was dark and rough under the frequent north wind, sometimes gray and silent in an icy atmosphere; sometimes blue and shining beneath the pale winter sun. The day when the room was ready, Fanny made a wood fire, which burned merrily, and encouraged the new chairs, tables, carpet, and curtains into a friendly assimilation; they met and danced on the round tops of the brass dogs. It already seemed to me that I was like the room. Unlike Veronica, I had nothing odd, nothing suggestive. My curtains were blue chintz, and the sofa and chairs were covered with the same; the ascetic aspect of my two hair-cloth arm-chairs was entirely concealed. The walls were painted amber color, and varnished. There were no pictures but the shining shadows. A row of shelves covered with blue damask was on one side, and my tall mirror on the other. The doors were likewise covered with blue damask, nailed round with brass nails. When I had nothing else to do I counted the nails. The wooden mantel shelf, originally painted in imitation of black marble, I covered with damask, and fringed it. I sent Fanny down for mother and Aunt Merce. They declared, at once, they were stifled; too many things in the room; too warm; too dark; the fringe on the mantel would catch fire and burn me up;

too much trouble to take care of it. What was under the carpet that made it so soft and the steps so noiseless: How nice it was! Temperance, who had been my aid, arrived at this juncture and croaked.

"Did you ever see such a stived-up hole, Mis Morgeson?"

"I like it now," she answered, "it is so comfortable. How lovely this blue is!"

"It's a pity she wont keep the blinds shut. The curtains will fade to rags in no time; the sun pours on 'em."

"How could I watch the sea then?" I asked.

"Good Lord! it's a mystery to me how you can bother over that salt water."

"And the smell of the sea-weed," added Aunt Merce.

"And its thousand dreary cries," said mother.

"Do you like my covered doors?" I inquired.

"I vow," Temperance exclaimed, "the nails are put in crooked! And I stood over Dexter the whole time. He said it was damned nonsense, and that you must be awfully spoiled to want such a thing. 'You get your pay, Dexter,' says I, 'for what you do, don't you?' 'I guess I do,' says he, and then he winked. 'None of your gab,' says I. I do believe that man is a cheat and a rascal, I vow I do. But they are all so."

"In my young days," Aunt Merce remarked, "young girls were not allowed to have fires in their chambers."

"In our young days, Mercy," mother replied, "*we* were not allowed to have much of anything."

"Fires are not wholesome to sleep by," Temperance added.

"Miss Veronica never has a fire," piped Fanny, who had remained, occasionally making a stir with the tongs.

"But she ought to have!" Temperance exclaimed vehemently. "I do wonder, Mis Morgeson, that you do not insist upon it, though it's none of my business."

Father was conducted upstairs, after supper. The fire was freshly made; the shaded lamp on the table before the sofa and the easy-chair pleased him. He came often afterward, and stayed so long, sometimes, that I fell asleep, and found him there, when I woke, still smoking and watching the fire.

Veronica looked in at bed-time. "I recognize you here," she said as she passed. But she came back in a few moments in a wrapper, with a comb in her hand, and stood on the hearth combing her hair, which was longer than a mermaid's. The fire was grateful to her, and I believe that she was surprised at the fact.

"Why not have a fire in your room, Verry?"

"A fire would put me out. One belongs in this room, though. It is the only reality here."

"What if I should say you provoke me, perverse girl?"

"What if you should?"

She gathered up her hair and shook it round her face, with the same elfish look she wore when she pulled it over her eyes as a child. It made me feel how much older I was.

"I do not say so, and I will not."

"I wish you would; I should like to hear something natural from you."

Fanny, coming in with an armful of wood, heard her. Instead of putting it on the fire, she laid it on the hearth, and, sitting upon it with an expression of enjoyment, looked at both of us with an expectant air.

"You love mischief, Fanny," I said.

"Is it mischief for me to look at sisters that don't love each other?" and, laughing shrilly, she pulled a stick from under her, and threw it on the fire.

Veronica's eyes shot more sparks than the disturbed coals, for Fanny's speech enraged her. Giving her head a toss, which swept her hair behind her shoulders, she darted at Fanny, and picked her up from the wood, with as much ease as if it had been her hand-kerchief, instead of a girl nearly as heavy as herself. I started up.

"Sit still," she said to me, in her low, inflexible voice, holding Fanny against the wall. "I must attend to this little demon. Do you dare to think," addressing Fanny with a gentle vehemence, "that what you have just said, is true of *me?* Are you, with your small, starved spirit, equal to any judgment against *her?* I admire her; you do, too. I *love* her, and I love you, you pitiful, ignorant brat."

Her strength gave way, and she let her go.

"All declarations in my behalf are made to third persons," I thought.

"I do believe, Miss Veronica," said Fanny, who did not express any astonishment or resentment at the treatment she had received, "that you are going to be sick; I feel so in my bones."

"Never mind your bones. Twist up my hair, and think, while you do it, how to get rid of your diabolical curiosity."

"I have had nothing to do all my life," she answered, carefully knotting Verry's hair, "but to be curious. I never found out much, though, till lately"; and she cast her eyes in my direction.

"Put her out, Cassandra," said Verry, "if you like to touch her."

"I'll sweep the hearth, if you please, first," Fanny answered. "I am a good drudge, you know. Good-night, ladies."

I followed Veronica, wishing to know if her room was uncomfortable. She had made slight changes since my visit to her. The flowers had been moved, the stand where the candle stood was covered with crimson cloth. The dead bough and the autumn leaves were gone; but instead there was a branch of waving grasses, green and fresh, and on the table was a white flower, in a vase.

"It is freezing here, but it looks like summer. Is it design?"

"Yes; I can't sit here much; still, I can read in bed, and write, especially under my new quilt, which you have not seen."

It was composed of red, black, and blue bits of silk, and beautifully quilted. Hepsey and Temperance had made it for her.

"How about the wicket, these winter nights?"

"I drag the quilt off, and wrap it round me when I want to look out."

We heard a bump on the floor, and Temperance appeared with warm bricks wrapped in flannel.

"You know that I will not have those things," Verry said.

"Dear me, how contrary you are! And you have not eaten a thing to-day."

"Carry them out."

Her voice was so unyielding, but always so gentle! Temperance was obliged to deposit the bricks outside the door, which she did with a bang.

"I should think you might sleep in Cassandra's room; her bed is big enough for three."

No answer was made to this proposition, but Verry said,

"You may undress me, if you like, and stay till you are convinced I shall not freeze."

"I've stayed till I am in an ager. I might as well finish the night here, I spose."

She called me after midnight, for she had not left Verry, who had been attacked with one of her mysterious disorders.

"You can do nothing for her; but I am scared out, when she faints so dreadful; I don't like to be alone."

Veronica could not speak, but she shook her head at me to go away. Her will seemed to be concentrated against losing consciousness; it slipped from her occasionally, and she made a rotary motion with her arms, which I attempted to stop, but her features contracted so terribly, I let her alone.

"Mustn't touch her," said Temperance, whose efforts to relieve her were confined to replacing the coverings of the bed, and drawing her nightgown over her bosom, which she often threw off again. Her breath scarcely stirred her breast. I thought more than once she did not breathe at all. Its delicate, virgin beauty touched me with a holy pity. We sat by her bed in silence a long time, and although it was freezing cold, did not suffer. Suddenly she turned her head and closed her eyes. Temperance softly pulled up the clothes over her and whispered: "It is over for this time; but Lord, how awful it is! I hoped she was cured of these spells."

In a few minutes she asked, "What time is it?"

"It must be about eleven," Temperance replied; but it was nearly four. She dozed again, but, opening her eyes presently, made a motion toward the window.

"There's no help for it," muttered Temperance, "she must go."

I understood her, and put my arm under Verry's neck to raise her. Temperance wrapped the quilt round her, and we carried her to the window. Temperance pushed open the pane; an icy wind blew against us.

"It is the winter that kills little Verry," she said, in a childlike voice. "God's breath is cold over the world, and my life goes. But the spring is coming; it will come back."

I looked at Temperance, whose face was so corrugated with the desire for crying and the effort to keep from it, that for the life of me, I could not help smiling. As soon as I smiled I laughed, and then Temperance gave way to crying and laughing together. Veronica stared, and realized the circumstances in a second. She walked back to the bed, laughing faintly, too. "Go to bed, do. You have been here a long time, have you?"

I left Temperance tucking the clothes about her, kissing her, and calling her "deary and her best child."

I could not go to bed at once, for Fanny was on my hearth before the fire, which she had rekindled, watching the boiling of something.

"She has come to, hasn't she?" stirring the contents of the kettle. "I knew it was going to be so with her, she was so mad with me. She is like the Old Harry before she has a turn, and like an angel after. I am fond of people who have their ups and downs. I have seen her so before. She asked me to keep the doors locked once; they are locked now. But I couldn't keep *you* out. The doctor said she must have warm drinks as soon as she was better. This is gruel."

"If it is done, away with you. Calamity improves you, don't it? You seem in excellent spirits."

"First-rate; I can be somebody then."

CHAPTER XXV.

Before spring there were three public events in Surrey. A light-house was built on Gloster Point, below our house. At night there was a bridge of red, tremulous light between my window and its tower, which seemed to shorten the distance. A town-clock had been placed in the belfry of the new church in the western part of the village. Veronica could see the tips of its gilded hands from the top of her window, and hear it strike through the night, whether the wind was fair to bring the sound or not. She liked to hear the hours cry that they had gone. Soon after the clock was up, she recollected that Mrs. Crossman's dog had ceased to bark at night, as was his wont, and sent her a note inquiring about it, for she thought there was something poetical in connection with noctur-nal noises, which she hoped Mrs. Crossman felt also. Fanny con-veyed the note, and read it likewise, as Mrs. Crossman declared her inability to read writing with her new spectacles, which a peddler had cheated her with lately. She laughed at it, and sent word to Veronica that she was the curiousest young woman for her age that she had ever heard of; that the dog slept in the house of nights, for he was blind and deaf now; but that Crossman should get a new dog with a loud bark, if the dear child wanted it.

A new dog soon came, so fierce that Abram told Temperance that people were afraid to pass Crossman's. She guessed it wasn't the dog the people were afraid of, but of their evil consciences, which pricked them when they remembered Dr. Snell.

The third event was Mr. Thrasher's revival. It began in Febru-ary, and before it was over, I heard the April frogs croaking in the marshy field behind the church. We went to all the meetings, except Veronica, who continued her custom of going only on Sunday afternoons. Mr. Thrasher endeavored to proselyte me, but he never conversed with her. His manner changed when he was at our house; if she appeared, the man tore away the mask of the minister. She called him a Bible-banger, that he made the dust fly from the pulpit cushions too much to suit her; besides, he denounced sinners with vituperation, larding his piety with a grim wit which was distasteful. He was resentful toward me, especially after he had seen her. It was needful, he said, from my influence in Surrey, that I should become an example, and asked me if I did not think my escape from sudden death in Rosville was an indication from Providence that I was reserved for some especial work?

Surrey was never so evangelical as under his ministration, and it remained so until he was called to a larger field of usefulness, and offered a higher salary to till it. We settled into a milder theocracy after he left us. Mr. Park renewed his zeal, about this time, resuming his discussions; but mother paid little attention to what he said. There were days now when she was confined to her room. Sometimes I found her softly praying. Once when I went there she was crying aloud, in a bitter voice, with her hands over her head. She was her old self when she recovered, except that she was indifferent to practical details. She sought amusement, indeed, liked to have me with her to make her laugh, and Aunt Merce was always near to pet her as of old, and so we forgot those attacks.

Abram Handy, inspired with religious fervor during the revival, was also inspired with the twin passion—love—to visit Temperance, and begged her, with so much eloquence, to marry him before his cow should calve, that she consented, and he was happy. He spent the Sunday evenings with her, coming after conference meeting, hymn-book in hand. She was angry and ashamed, if I happened to see them sitting in the same chair, and singing, in a quavering voice, "Greenland's Icy Mountains," and continued morose for a week, in consequence.

"What will Veronica do without me?" she said. "I vow I wish Abram Handy would keep himself out of my way; who wants him?"

"She will visit you, and so shall I."

"Certain true, will you, really?"

"If you will promise to return our visits, and leave Abram at home, for a week now and then."

"Done. I can mend your things and look after Mis Morgeson. Your mother is not the woman she was, and you and Veronica haven't a mite of faculty. What you are all coming to is more than I can fathom."

"Who will fill your place?"

"I don't want to brag, but you wont find a soul in Surrey to come here and live as I have lived. You will have to take a Paddy; the Paddies are spreading, the old housekeeping race is going. Hepsey and I are the last of the Mohicans, and Hepsey is failing."

She was right, we never found her equal, and when she went, in May, a Celtic dynasty came in. We missed her sadly. Verry refused to be comforted. Symptoms of disorganization appeared everywhere.

In the summer Helen visited Surrey. Her enlivening gayety was the means of our uniting about her. She was never tired of Veronica's playing, nor of our society; so we must stay where she and the piano were. We trimmed the parlor with flowers every day. Veronica transferred some of her favorite books to the round table, and privately sent for a set of flower vases. When they came, she said we must have a new carpet to match them, and although mother protested against it, she was loud in her admiration when she saw the handsome white Brussels, thickly covered with crimson roses. Helen's introduction proved an astonishing incentive; we set a new value on ourselves. I never saw so much of Veronica as at that time; her health improved with her temper. She threw us into fits of laughter with her whimsical talk, never laughing herself, but enjoying the effect she produced. To please her, Helen changed her style of dress, and bought a dress at Milford, which Veronica selected and made. The trying on of this dress was the means of her discovering the letters on Helen's arm, which never ceased to be a source of interest. She asked to see them every day afterward, and touched them with her fingers, as if they had some occult power.

"You think her strange, do you not?" I asked Helen.

"She has genius, but will be a child always."

"You are mistaken; she was always mature."

"She stopped in the process of maturity long ago. It is her genius which takes her on. You advance by experience."

"I shall learn nothing more."

"Of course you have suffered immensely, and endured that which isolates you from the rest of us."

"You are as wise as ever."

"Well, I am married, you know, and shall grow no wiser. Marriage puts an end to the wisdom of women; they need it no longer."

"You are nineteen years old?"

"What is the use of talking to you? Besides, if we keep on we may tell secrets that had better not be revealed. We might not like each other so well; friendship is apt to dull if there is no ground for speculation left. Let us keep the bloom on the fruit, even if we know there is a worm at the core."

I owed it to her that I never had any confidante. My proclivities were for speaking what I felt; but her strong common-sense influenced me greatly against it; her teaching was the more easy to me, as she never invaded my sentiments.

Her visit was the occasion of our exchanging civilities with our acquaintances, which we neglected when alone. Tea parties were always fashionable in Surrey. Veronica went with us to one, given by our cousin, Susan Morgeson. She had taken tea out but twice, since she was grown, she told us, and then it was with her friend Lois Randall, a seamstress. To this girl she read the contents of her blank books, and Lois in her turn confided to Veronica her own compositions. Essays were her forte. We met her at Susan Morgeson's, and, as I never saw her without her having on some article given her by Veronica, this occasion was no exception. She wore an exquisitely embroidered purple silk apron, over a dull blue dress. I saw Verry's grimace when her eyes fell on it, and could not help saying, "I hope Lois's essays are better than her taste in dress."

"She is an idiot in colors; but she admires what I wear so much that she fancies the same must become her."

"As they become you?"

"I make a study of dress—an anomaly must. It may be wicked, but what can I do? I love to look well."

The dress she wore then was an India stuff, of linen, with a cream-colored ground, and a vivid yellow silk thread woven in stripes through it; each stripe had a cinnamon-colored edge. There were no ornaments about her, except a band of violet-colored ribbon round her head. When tea was brought in, she asked me in a whisper whether it was tea or coffee in the cup which was given her.

"Why, Cass," said Helen, "are you making a wonderment because she does not know? It is strange that you have not known that she drinks neither."

"What does she drink?"

"Is it eccentric to drink milk?" Verry asked, swallowing the tea with an accustomed air. "I think this must be coffee, it stings my mouth so."

"It is green tea," said Helen; "don't drink it, Verry."

"Green tea," she said, in a dreamy voice. "We drank green tea ten years ago, in our old house; and I did not know it! Cassandra, do you remember that I drank four cups once, when mother had company? I laughed all night, and Temperance cried."

She contributed her share toward entertaining, and invariably received the most attention. My indifference was called pride, and her reserve was called dignity, and dignity was more popular than pride.

Before Helen went, Ben wrote me that he was going to India. It was a favorite journey with the Belemites. By the time the letter reached me he should be gone. Would I bear him in remembrance? He would not forget me, and promised me an Indian idol. In eighteen months he expected to be at home again; sooner, perhaps. P.S. Would I give his true regards to my sister? N.B. The property might be divided according to his grandfather's will, before his return, and he wanted to be out of the way for sundry reasons, which he hoped to tell me some day. I read the letter to Helen and Veronica. Helen laughed, and said "Unstable as water"; but Veronica looked displeased; she closed her eyes as if to recall him to mind, and asked Helen abruptly if she did not like him.

"Yes; but I doubt him. With all his strength of character he has a capacity for failure."

"I consider him a relation," I said.

"*I* do not own him," said Veronica.

"At all events, he is not an affectionate one," Helen remarked. "You have not heard from him in a year."

"But I knew that I should hear," I said.

"We shall *see* him," said Veronica, "again."

I was dull after I received his letter. My youth grew dim; somehow I felt a self-pity. I found no chance to embalm those phases of sensation which belonged to my period, and I grew careless; Helen's influence went with her. The observances so vital to Veronica, so charming in her, I became utterly neglectful of. For all this a mad longing sometimes seized me to depart into a new world, which should contain no element of the old, least of all a reminiscence of what my experience had made me.

CHAPTER XXVI.

Alice Morgeson sent for Aunt Merce, asking her to fulfill the promise she had made when she was in Rosville. With misgivings she went, stayed a month, and returned with Alice. I felt a throe of pain when we met, which she must have seen, for she turned pale, and the hand she had extended toward me fell by her side; overcoming the impulse, she offered it again, but I did not take it. I had no evidence to prove that she came to Surrey on my account; but I was sure that such was the fact, as I was sure that there was a bond between us, which she did not choose to break, nor to acknowledge. She appeared as if expecting some explanation or revelation from me; but I gave her none, though I liked her better than ever. She was business-like and observant. Her tendencies, never romantic, were less selfish; it was no longer society, dress, housekeeping, which absorbed her, but a larger interest in the world which gave her a desire to associate with men and women, independent of caste. None of her children were with her; had it been three years earlier, she would not have left home without them. Her hair was a little gray, and a wrinkle or two had gathered about her mouth; but there was no other change. I was not sorry to have her go, for she paid me a close and quiet observation. At the moment of departure, she said in an undertone: "What has become of that candor of which you were so proud?"

"I am more candid than ever," I answered, "for I am silent."

"I understand you better, now that I have seen you en famille."

"What do you think now?"

"I don't think I know; the Puritans have much to answer for in your mother—" Turning to her she said, "My children, too, are so different."

Mother gave her a sad smile, as Fanny announced the carriage, and they drove away.

"No more visitors this year," said Veronica, yawning.

"No agreeable ones, I fancy," I answered.

"All the relations have had their turn for this year," remarked Aunt Merce. But she was mistaken; an old lady came soon after this to spend the winter. She lived but four miles from Surrey, but brought with her all her clothes, and a large green parrot, which her son had brought from foreign parts. Her name was Joy Morgeson; the fact of her being cousin to father's grandmother entitled her to a raid upon us at any season, and to call us "cousins." She felt, she said, that she must come and attend the meetings regular, for her time upon earth was short. But Joy was a hearty woman still, and, pious as she was, delighted in rough and scandalous stories, the telling of which gave her severe fits of repentance. She quilted elaborate petticoats for us, knit stockings for Arthur, and was useful. Mr. and Mrs. Elisha Peckham surprised us next. They arrived from "up country" and stayed two weeks. I did not clearly understand why they came before they went; but as they enjoyed their visit, it was of little consequence whether I did or not.

Midwinter passed, and we still had company. There was much to do, but it was done without system. Mother or Aunt Merce detailed from their ordinary duties as keeper of the visitors, Fanny was for the first time able to make herself of importance in the family tableaux, and assumed cares no one had thought of giving her. She left the town-school, telling mother that learning would be of no use to her. The rights of a human being merely was what she wanted; she should fight for them; that was what paupers must do. Mother allowed her to do as she pleased. Her duties commenced with calling us up to breakfast *en masse,* and for once the experiment was successful, for we all met at the table. The dining-room was in complete order, a thing that had never happened early before; the rest of us missed the straggling breakfast which consumed so much time.

"Whose doing is this?" asked father, looking round the table.

"It is Fanny's," I answered, rattling the cups. "All the coffee to be poured out at once, don't agitate me."

Fanny, bearing buckwheat cakes, looked proud and modest, as people do who appreciate their own virtues.

"Why, Fanny," said the father, "you have done wonders; you are more original than Cassy or Verry."

Her green eyes glowed; her aspect was so feline that I expected her hair to rise.

"Father's praise pleases you more than ours," Verry said.

"You never gave me any," she answered, marching out.

Father looked up at Verry, annoyed, but said nothing. We paid no attention to Fanny's call afterward; but she continued her labors, which proved acceptable to him. Temperance told me, when she was with us for a week, that his overcoats, hats, umbrellas, and whips never had such care as Fanny gave them. He omitted from this time to ask us if we knew where his belongings were, but went to Fanny; and I noticed that he required much attendance.

Temperance, who had arrived in the thick of the company, as she termed it, was sorry to go back to Abram. He *was* a good man, she said; but it was a dreadful thing for a woman to lose her liberty, especially when liberty brought so much idle time. "Why, girls, I have quilted and darned up every rag in the house. He *will* do half the housework himself; he is an everlasting Betty." She was cheerful, however, and helped Hepsey, as well as the rest of us.

The guests did not encroach on my time, but it was a relief to have them gone and the house our own once more.

I went to Milford again, almost daily, to feast my eyes on the bleak, flat, gray landscape. The desolation of winter sustains our frail hopes. Nature is kindest then; she does not taunt us with fruition. It is the luxury of summer which tantalizes—her long, brilliant, blossoming days, her dewy, radiant nights.

Entering the house one March evening, when it was unusually still, I had reached the front hall, when masculine tones struck my ears. I opened the parlor door softly, and saw Ben Somers in an easy-chair, basking before a glowing fire, his luminous face set toward Veronica, who was near him, holding a small screen between her and the fire. "She is always ready," I thought, contemplating her as I would a picture. Her ruby-colored merino dress absorbed the light, she was a mass of deep red, except her face and hair, above which her silver crescent comb shone. Her slender feet were tapping the rug. She wore boots the color of her dress; Ben was looking at them. Mother was there, and in the background Aunt Merce and Fanny figured. I pushed the door wide; as the stream of cold air reached them, they looked toward it, and cried— "Cassandra!" Ben started up with extended hands.

"I went as far as Cape Horn only, but I bought you the idol and lots of things I promised from a passing ship. I have been home a week, and I am *here*. Are you glad? Can I stay?"

"Yes, yes," chorused the company, and I was too busy trying to get off my gloves to speak. Father came in, and welcomed him with warmth. Fanny ran out for a lamp; when she brought it, Veronica changed the position of her screen, and held it close to her face.

"Did you have a cold ride, Locke?" asked mother, gazing into the fire with that expression of satisfaction we have when some-body beside ourselves has been exposed to hardships. It is the same principle entertained by those who depend upon and enjoy seeing criminals hung.

Meanwhile my bonnet-strings got in a knot, which Fanny saw, and was about to apply scissors, when Aunt Merce, unable to bear the sacrifice, interfered and untied them, all present so interested in the operation that conversation was suspended. Presently Aunt Merce was called out, and was shortly followed by mother and Fanny. Ben stood before me; his eyes, darting sharp rays, pierced me through; they rested on the thread-like scars which marked my cheek, and which were more visible from the effect of cold.

"Tattooed still," I said in a low voice, pointing to them.

"I see"—a sorrowful look crossed his face; he took my hand and kissed it. Veronica, who had dropped the screen, met my glance toward her with one perfectly impassive. As they watched me, I saw myself as they did. A tall girl in gray, whose deep, controlled voice vibrated in their ears, like the far-off sounds we hear at night from woods or the sea, whose face was ineffaceably marked, whose air impressed with a sense of mystery. I think both would have annihilated my personality if possible, for the sake of comprehending me, for both loved me in their way.

"What are you reading, father?" asked Veronica suddenly.

"To-day's letters, and I must be off for Boston; would you like to go?"

"My sister Adelaide has sent for you, Cassandra, to visit us," said Ben, "and will you go too, Veronica?"

"Thanks, I must decline. If Cass should go—and she will—I may go to Boston."

He looked at her curiously. "It would not be pleasant for you to attempt Belem. I hate it, but I feel a fate-impelling power in regard to Cassandra; I want her there."

"May I go then?" I asked.

"Certainly," father replied.

"Please come out to supper," called Fanny. "We have something particular for you, Mr. Morgeson."

We saw mother at the table, a book in hand. She was finishing a chapter in "The Hour and the Man."[41] Aunt Merce stood eyeing the dishes with the aspect of a judge. As father took his seat, near Veronica, Fanny, according to habit, stood behind it. With the most *degagé* air, Ben suffered nothing to escape him, and I never forgot the picture of that moment.

We talked of Helen's visit—a subject that could be commented on freely. Veronica told Ben Helen's opinion of him; he reddened slightly, and said that such a sage could not be contradicted. When father remarked that the opinions of women were whimsical, Fanny gave an audible sniff, which made Ben smile.

Soon after tea I met Veronica in the hall, with a note in her hand. She stopped and hesitatingly said that she was going to send for Temperance; she wanted her while Mr. Somers stayed.

"Your forethought astonishes me."

"She is a comfort always to me."

"Do you stand in especial need of a comforter?"

She looked puzzled, laughed, and left me.

Temperance arrived that evening, in time to administer a scolding to Fanny.

"That girl needs looking after," she said. "She is as sharp as a needle. She met me in the yard and told me that a man fit for a nobleman had come on a visit. 'It may be for Cass,' says she, 'and it may not be. I have my doubts.' Did you ever?" concluded Temperance, counting the knives. "There's one missing. By jingo! it has been thrown to the pigs, I'll bet."

When Ben made a show of going, we asked him to stay longer. He said "Yes," so cordially, that we laughed. But it hurt me to see that he had forgotten all about my going to Belem. "I like Surrey so much," he said, "and you all, I have a fancy that I am in the Hebrides, in Magnus Troil's dwelling;[42] it is so wild here, so *naïve*. The unadulterated taste of sea-spray is most beautiful."

"We will have Cass for Norna," said Verry; "but, by the way, it is you that must be of the fitful head; have you forgotten that she is going to Belem soon?"

"I shall remember Belem in good time; no fear of my forgetting that acc—ancient spot. At least I may wait till your father goes to Boston, and we can make a party. You will be ready, Cassandra? I wrote Adelaide yesterday that you were coming, and mother will expect you."

It often stormed during his visit. We had driving rains, and a gale from the southeast, oceanward, which made our sea dark and miry, even after the storm had ceased and patches of blue sky were visible.

Our rendezvous was in the parlor, which, from the way in which Ben knocked about the furniture, cushions, and books, assumed an air which somehow subdued Veronica's love for order; she played for him, or they read together, and sometimes talked; he taught her chess, and then they quarreled. One day—a long one to me,—they were so much absorbed in each other, I did not seek them till dusk.

"Come and sing to me," called Ben.

"So you remember that I do sing?"

"Sing; there is a spell in this weird twilight; sing, or I go out on the rocks to break it."

He dropped the window curtains and sat by me at the piano, and I sang:

> "I feel the breath of the summer night,
>   Aromatic fire;
> The trees, the vines, the flowers are astir
>   With tender desire.
>
> If I were alone, I could not sing,
>   Praises to thee;
> O night! unveil the beautiful soul
>   That awaiteth me!"[43]

"A foolish song," said Veronica, pulling her hair across her face. No reply. She glided to the flower-basket, broke a rosebud from its stalk, and mutely offered it to him. Whether he took it, I know not; but he rose up from beside me, like a dark cloud, and my eyes followed him.

"Come Veronica," he whispered, "give me yourself. I love you, Veronica."

He sank down before her; she clasped her hands round his head, and kissed his hair.

"I know it," she said, in a clear voice.

I shut the door softly, thinking of the Wandering Jew,[44] went upstairs, humming a little air between my teeth, and came down again into the dining-room, which was in a blaze of light.

"What preserves are these, Temperance?" I asked, going to the table. "Some of Abram's quinces?"

"Best you ever tasted, since you were born."

"Call Mr. Somers, Fanny," said mother. "Is Verry in the parlor, too?"

"I'll call them," I said; "I have left my handkerchief there."

"Is anything else of yours there?" said Fanny, close to my ear.

Ben had pushed back the curtain, and was staring into the darkness; Veronica was walking to and fro on the rug.

"Haven't I a great musical talent?" I inquired.

"Am I happy?" she asked, coming toward me.

Ben turned to speak, but Veronica put her hand over his mouth, and said:

"Why should I be 'hushed,' my darling?"

"Come to supper, and be sensible," I urged.

The light revealed a new expression in Verry's face—an unsettled, dispossessed look; her brows were knitted, yet she smiled over and over again, while she seemed hardly aware that she was eating like an ordinary mortal. The imp Fanny tried experiments with her, by offering the same dishes repeatedly, till her plate was piled high with food she did not taste.

The next day was clear, and mild with spring. Ben and I started for a walk on the shore. We were half-way to the lighthouse before he asked why it was that Veronica would not come with us.

"She never walks by the shore; she detests the sea."

"Is it so? I did not know that."

"Do you mind that you know few of her tastes or habits? I speak of this as a general truth."

"I am a spectacle to you, I suppose. But this sea charms me; I shall live by it, and build a house with all the windows and doors toward it."

"Not if you mean to have Verry in it."

"I do mean to have her in it. She shall like it. Are you willing to have me for a brother? Will you go to Belem, and help break the ice? *She* could never go," and he began to skip pebbles in the water.

"I will take you for a brother gladly. You are a fool—not for loving her, but all men are fools when in love, they are so besotted with themselves. But I am afraid of *one* fault in you."

"Yes," he answered hurriedly, "don't I know? On my honor, I have tried; why not leave me to God? Didn't you leave yourself that way once?"

"Oh, you are cruel."

"Pardon me, dear Cass. I *must* do well now, surely. Will you believe in me? Oh, do you not know the strength, the power, that comes to us in the stress of passion and duty?"

"This from *you,* Ben."

"Never mind; I knew I wanted to marry her, when I saw her. I love her passionately," and he threw a pebble in the water farther than he had yet; "but she is so pure, so delicate, that when I approach her, in spite of my besottedness, my love grows lambent. That's not like me, you know," with great vehemence. "Will she never understand me?"

His face darkened, and he looked so strangely intent into my eyes that I was obliged to turn away; he disturbed me.

"Veronica probably will not understand you, but you must manage for yourself. As you have discerned, she and I are far apart. She is pure, noble, beautiful, and peculiar. I will have no voice between you."

"You must, you do. We shall hear it if you do not speak. You have a great power, tall enchantress."

"Certainly. What a powerful life is mine!"

"You come to these shores often. Are you not different beside them? This colorless picture before us—these vague spaces of sea and land—the motion of the one—the stillness of the other—have you no sense that you have a powerful spirit?"

"Is it power? It is pain."

"Your gold has not been refined then."

"Yes, I confess I have a sense of power; but it is not a spiritual sense."

"Let us go back," he said abruptly.

We mused by our footprints in the wet sand, as we passed them. We were told when we reached home that Veronica had gone on some expedition with Fanny. She did not return till time for supper, looking elfish, and behaving whimsically, as if she had received instructions accordingly. I fancied that the expression Ben regarded her with might be the Bellevue Pickersgill expression, it was so different from any I had seen. There was a haughty curiosity in his face; as she passed near him, he looked into her eyes, and saw the strange cast which made their sight so far off.

"Veronica, where are you?" he asked.

The tone of his voice attracted mother's regards; an intelligent glance was exchanged, and then her eyes sought mine. "It is not as you thought, mamma," I telegraphed. But Verry, not bringing her eyes back into the world, merely said, "I am here, am I not?" and went to shut herself up in her room. I found her there, looking through the wicket.

"The buds are beginning to swell," she said. "I should hear

small voices breaking out from the earth. I grow happy every day now."

"Because the earth will be green again?" I asked, in a coaxing voice.

She shut the wicket, and, looking in my face, said, "I will go down immediately." For some reason the tears came into my eyes, which she, taking up the candle, saw. "I am going to play," she said hurriedly, "come." She ran down before me, but turning, by the foot of the stairs, she pointed to the parlor door, and said, "Is he my husband?"

"Answer for yourself. Go in, in God's name."

Ben was chatting with father over the fire; he stretched out his hand to her, with so firm and assured an air, and looked so noble, that I felt a pang of admiration for him. She laid her hand in his a moment, passed on to the piano, and began to play divinely, drawing him to her side. Father peeled and twisted his cigar, as he contemplated them with a thoughtful countenance.

CHAPTER XXVII.

When we went to Boston we went to a new hotel, as Ben had advised, deserting the old Bromfield for the Tremont. It was dusk when we arrived, and tea was served immediately, in a large room full of somber mahogany furniture. Its atmosphere oppressed Veronica, who ate her supper in silence.

"Charles Dickens is here, sir," said the waiter, who knew Ben. "Two models of the Curiosity Shop have just gone upstairs, sir. His room is right over here, sir."

Veronica looked adoringly at the ceiling.

"Then," said Ben, "our hunters are up from Belem. Anybody in from Belem, John?"

"Oh yes, sir, every day."

"I'll look them up," he said to us; but he returned soon, and begged us not to look at Dickens, if we had a chance.

Veronica, with a sigh, gave him up, and lost a chance of being immortalized with that perpetual and imperturbable beefsteak, covered with "the blackest of all possible pepper," which was daily served to him.[45]

Father being out in pursuit of a cigar, Ben asked Veronica what she would do while he was in Belem.

"Walk round this lion–clawed table."

"I shall be gone from you."

"Alas!"

"Are we to part this way?"

"Father," she cried, as he entered with a theater bill, "had I better marry this friend of Cassy's?"

"Have you the courage? Do you know each other?"

"Having known Cassandra so long, sir," began Ben, but was interrupted by Veronica's exclaiming, "We do not know each other at all. What is the use of making *that* futile attempt? I am over eighteen, and do you know me, father?"

"If I do not, it is because you have no shadow."

"Shall I, then?" giving Ben a delicious smile. "I promise."

"I promise, too, Veronica," heaven dawning in his eyes.

"We will see about it," said father. "Now who will go to the theater?"

We declined, but Ben signified his willingness to accompany him.

We took the first morning train, so that father could return before evening, and ran through in the course of an hour the wooden suburbs of Belem, bordered by an ancient marsh, from which the sea had long retired.[46] Taking a cab, we turned into Norfolk Street, at the head of which, Ben said, a mile distant, was his father's house. It was not a cheerful street, and when we stopped before an immense, square, three-storied house, it looked still more gloomy. There was a gate on one side, with white wooden urns on the posts, that shut off a paved courtway. On each side of the street were houses of the same pattern, with the same gates. Down the paved court of the opposite house a coach pulled by two fat horses clattered, and as the coach turned we saw two old ladies inside, highly dressed, bowing and smiling at Ben.

"The Miss Hiticutts—hundred thousand apiece."

"Hundred thousand apiece," I echoed in an anguish of admiration, which made my father laugh and Ben scowl. A servant in a linen jacket opened the door. "Is it yourself, Mr. Ben?"

"Open the parlor door, Murph. Where's my mother and my sister?"

"Miss Somers is taking her exercise, sir, and Mrs. Somers is with the owld gentleman"; opening the door, with the performance of taking father's hat.

"Sit down, Cassandra. I'll look up somebody."

It was a bewildering matter where to go; the room, vast and dark, was a complete litter of tables and sofas. The tables were loaded with lamps, books, and knick-knacks of every description; the sofas were strewn with English and French magazines, novels, and papers. I went to the window, while father perched on the music stool.

My attention was diverted to a large dog in the court, chained to a post near a pump, where a man was giving water to a handsome bay horse, at the same time keeping his eye on an individual who stood on a stone block, dressed in a loose velvet coat, a white felt hat, and slippers down at the heel. He had a coach whip in his hand—the handsomest hand I ever saw, which he snapped at the dog, who growled with rage. I heard Ben's voice in remonstrance; then a lazy laugh from velvet coat, who gave the dog a cut which made him bound. Ben, untying him, was overwhelmed with caresses. "Down, you fool! Off, Rash!" he said. "Look there," pointing to the window where I stood. The gentleman with the coach whip looked at me also. The likeness to Ben turned my suspicion into certainty that they were brothers. His disposition, I thought, must be lovely, judging from the episode with "Rash." I turned away, almost running against a lady, who extended her fingers toward me with a quick little laugh, and said:

"How de do? Where's Ben, to introduce us properly?"

"Here, mother," he said behind her, followed by the dog. "You were expecting Cassandra, my old chum; and Mr. Morgeson has come to leave her with us."

"Certainly. Rash, go out, dear. Mr. Morgeson, I am sorry to say," she spoke with more politeness, "that Mr. Somers is confined to his room with gout. May I take you up?"

"I have a short time to stay," looking at his watch and rising. "Do you consider the old school friendship between your son and Cassandra a sufficient reason for leaving her with you? To say nothing of the faint relationship which, we suppose, exists."

"Of course, very happy; Adelaide expects her," she said vaguely. I saw at once that she had never heard a word of our being relations. Ben had managed nicely in the affair of my invitation to Belem. But I desired to remain, in spite of Mrs. Somers's reception.

Mr. Somers was bolstered up in bed, in a flowered dressing gown, with a bottle of colchicum and a pile of Congressional reports on a stand beside him. His urbanity was extreme; it was

evident that the gout was not allowed to interfere with his deportment, though the joints of his hands were twisted and knotty. He
expatiated upon Ben's long ungratified wish for a visit from me,
and thanked father for complying with it. He mentioned the me-
mento of the miniature, and gave every particular of Locke Morgeson's early marriage, explaining the exact shade of consanguin-
ity—a faint one. I glanced at Mrs. Somers, who sat remote, in the
act of inspecting me, with an eye askance, which I afterward found
was her mode of looking at those whom she doubted or disliked;
it changed its expression, as it met mine, into one of haughty
wonder, that said there could be no tie of blood between us. She
irritated and embarrassed me. I tried to think of something to say,
and uttered a few words, which were uncommonly trivial and
awkward. Mr. Somers touched on politics. The door opened, and
Ben's brother entered, with downcast eyes. Advancing to the footboard of the bed, he leaned his chin on its edge, looked at his
father, and in a remarkably clear, ringing voice, said:

"The check."

Mr. Somers coughed behind his hand. "To-morrow will do,
Desmond."

"To-day will do."

"Desmond," said Ben in a low voice, "you do not see Mr.
Morgeson and Miss Morgeson. My brother, Cassandra."

"Beg pardon, good-morning"; and he pulled off his hat with an
air of grace which became him, though it was very indifferent.
Mrs. Somers is a soft voice said: "Ring, Des, dear, will you?" He
warned her with a satirical smile, and gave such a pull at the bell-
rope that it came down. Her florid face flushed a deeper red, but
he had gone. Father looked at his watch, and got up with alacrity.

"You are to dine with us, at least, Mr. Morgeson."

"I must return to Boston on account of my daughter, who is
there alone."

"Have you been remiss, Ben," said his father affectionately, "in
not bringing her also?"

"She would not come, of course, father."

A tall, black-haired girl of twenty-five rushed in.

"Why, Ben," she said, "you were not expected. And this is
Miss Morgeson," shaking hands with me. "You will spend a month,
wont you?" She put her chin in her hand, and scanned me with a
cool deliberateness. "Pa, do you think she is like Caroline Bingham?"

"Yes, so she is; but fairer. She is a great belle," nodding to me.

"Do you *really* think she looks like her, Somers?" said Mrs. Somers, in a tone of denial.

"Certainly, but handsomer," Adelaide replied for him, without looking at her mother.

"Would you like to go to your room?" she asked. "What a pretty dress this is!" taking hold of the sleeve, her chin in her hand still. "We will have some walks; Belem is nice for walking. Pa, how do you feel now?"

She allowed me to go downstairs with father, without following, and sent Murphy in with wine and biscuit. I put my arms round his neck and kissed him, for I had a lonesome feeling, which I could not define at the last moment.

"You will not stay long," he said; "there is something oppressive in this atmosphere."

"Something artificial, is it? It must be the blood of the Bellevue Pickersgills that thickens the air."

"Now," said Ben, with father's hat in his hand, "the time is up."

Adelaide was at the door to take courteous leave of him, and Mrs. Somers bowed from the top of the stairs, revealing a pair of large ankles, whose base rested in a pair of shabby, pudgy slippers. Adelaide then took me to my room, telling me not to change my dress, but to come down soon, for dinner was ready. Hearing a bell, I hurried down to the parlor which we were in before, and waited for directions respecting the dinner. Adelaide came presently. "We are dining; come and sit next me," offering her arm. Mrs. Somers, Desmond, and a girl of fifteen were at the table. The latter had just come from school, I concluded, as a satchel of books hung at her chair. Murphy was removing the soup, and I derived the impression that I had been forgotten. While taking mine, they vaguely stared about till Murphy brought in the roast mutton, except Adelaide, who rubbed her teeth with a dry crust, making a feint of eating it. Desmond kept the decanter, occasionally swallowing a glassful.

"What wine is that, Murphy?" Mrs. Somers asked. He hesitatingly answered, "I think it is the Juno, mum."

"You stole the key from pa's room, Des," said the girl. He shook the carving-knife at her, at which gesture she said "Pooh!" and applied herself to the roast mutton with avidity. They all ate largely, especially the girl, whose wide mouth was filled with splendid teeth. Mrs. Somers made a motion with her glass for

Murphy to bring her the wine, and pouring a teaspoonful, held it
to her mouth, as if she were practicing drinking healths. Her hands
were beautiful, too; they all had handsome hands, whose movements were graceful and expressive. When Ben arrived, Murphy
set the dishes before him, and Adelaide began to talk in a lively,
brilliant way. He did not ask for wine, but I saw him look toward
it and Desmond. The decanter was empty. After the dessert, Mrs.
Somers arose and we followed; but she soon left us, and we went
to the parlor. The girl, taking a seat beside me, said: "My name is
Ann Somers. I am never introduced; Adder, my sister, is in the
way, you know. I dare say Ben never spoke of me to you. I am
never spoken of, am never noticed. I have never had new dresses;
yet pa is my friend, the dear soul."

Adelaide looked upon her with the same superb indifference
with which she regarded her mother and Desmond. "Would you
like to go to your room?" she asked again. "You are too tired to
take a walk, perhaps?"

"Lord!" said Ann, "do let her do as she likes. Adder, don't be
too disagreeable."

I picked up my bonnet, which she took from me, and put on
the top of her head as we went upstairs.

"Murph must bring up your trunk," said Ann, opening the
closet. "But there is no space to hang anything; the great Mogul's
wardrobe stops the way."

My chamber was stately in size and appointments. The afternoon sun shone in, where a shutter was open, behind the dull red
curtains, and illuminated the portrait of a nimble old lady in a
scarlet cloak, which hung near the gigantic curtained bed, over a
vast chair, covered with faded green damask.

"Grandmother Pickersgill," said Ann, who saw me observing
the picture. Adelaide contemplated it also. "It was painted by
Copley," she said, "Lord Lyndhurst afterwards. Grandfather entertained him, and he went to one of grandmother's parties; he
complimented her on her beauty. But you see that she has not a
handsome hand. Ours is the Pickersgill hand," and she spread her
fingers like a fan. "She was a regular old screw," continued Ann,
"and used to have mother's underclothes tucked to last for ever;
she was a beast to servants, too."

My trunk was brought in, which I unlocked and unpacked,
while Adelaide opened a drawer in a great bureau.

"Oh, you know it is full of Marm's fineries," said Ann, in a confidential tone; "I'll ring for Hannah." Adelaide busied herself in throwing the contents of the drawers on the floor. "There's her ball dresses," commented Ann, as a pink satin, trimmed with magnificent lace, tumbled out. "Old Carew brought the lace over for her."

"Bring a basket, Hannah, and take these away somewhere, to some other closet of Mrs. Somers's."

"That gold fringe, do you remember, Adder? She looked like an elephant with his howdah on when she wore it."

Her impertinence inspired Adelaide, who joined her in a flow of vituperative wit at the expense of their mother and other relatives, incidentally brought in. Instead of being aghast, I enjoyed it, and was feverish with a desire to be as brilliant, for my vocabulary was deficient and my sense of inferiority was active during the whole of my visit in Belem. I blushed often, smiled foolishly, and was afflicted with a general apprehension in regard to *gaucherie*.

I changed my traveling dress, as they were not inclined to leave me, with anxiety, for I was weak enough to wish to make an impression with my elegant bearing and appointments. Being so anatomized, I was oppressed with an indefinite discouragement. Their stealthy, sharp, selfish scrutiny brought out my failures. My dress seemed ill-made; my hair unbecomingly dressed; my best collar and ribbon, which I put on, were nothing to the lace I had just seen falling on the floor. When we descended it was twilight. Ann said she must study, and left us by the parlor fire. Adelaide lighted a candle, and took a novel, which she read reclining on a sofa. Reclining on sofas, I discovered, was a family trait, though they were all in a state of the most robust health, with the exception of Mr. Somers. I walked up and down the rooms. "They were fine once," said Ben, who appeared from a dark corner, "but faded now. Mother never changes anything if she can help it. She is a terrible aristocrat," he continued, in a low voice, "fixed in the ideas imbedded in the Belem institutions, which only move backward. We laugh, though, at everybody's claims but our own. You despised me for mentioning the Hiticutts' income; it was the atmosphere."

"It amuses me to be here."

"Of course; but stir up Adelaide, she is genuine; has fine sense, and half despises her life; but she knows no other, and is proud."

"Let's go and find tea," she said, yawning, dropping her book. "Why don't that lazy Murph light the lamp? I wish pa was down to regulate affairs." No one was at the tea-table but Mrs. Somers.

"Ben is very polite, don't you think so?" she said with her peculiar laugh, which made my flesh creep, as he pulled up a chair for me. Her voice made me dizzy, but I smiled. Ben was not the same in Belem, I saw at once, and no longer wondered at its influence, or at the vacillating nature of his plans and pursuits. Mrs. Somers gave me some tea from a spider-shaped silver tea-pot, which was related to a spider-shaped cream-jug and a spider-shaped sugar-dish. The polished surface of the mahogany table reflected a pair of tall silver candlesticks, and the plates, being of warped blue and white Chinese ware, joggled and clattered when we touched them. The tea was delicious; I said so, but Mrs. Somers deigned no answer. We were regaled with spread bread and butter and baked apples. Adelaide ate six.

"We do not have your Surrey suppers," Ben remarked.

"How should you know?" his mother asked. Ben's eyes looked violent and he bit his lips. Adelaide commenced speaking before her mother had finished her question, as if she only needed the spur of her voice to be lively and agreeable, *per contra*.

"Hepburn must ask us to tea. Her jam and her gossip are wonderful. Aunt Tucker might ask us too, with housekeeper Beck's permission. I like tea fights with the old Hindoos. They like us too, Ben; we are the children of Hindoos also—superior to the rest of the world. There will be a party or two for this young person."

"Parties be hanged!" he said. "Then we must have a rout here, and I hate 'em."

"But we owe an entertainment," said Mrs. Somers. "I have been thinking of giving one as soon as Mr. Somers gets out."

"I have no such idea," said Adelaide, with her back toward her mother. "We shall have no party until some one has been given to our young friend, Ben."

Ben and I visited his father, who asked questions relative to the temperature, the water, and the dietetic qualities of Surrey. He was affable, but there was no nearness in his affability. He skated on the ice of appearances, and that was his vocation in his family. He fulfilled it well, but it was a strain sometimes. His family broke the ice now and then, which must have made him plunge into the depths of reality. I learned to respect his courage, bad as his cause was. Marrying Bellevue Pickersgill for her money, he married his master, and was endowed only with the privilege of settling her taxes. Simon Pickersgill, her father, tied up the main part of his money for his grandchildren. It was to be divided among them when the youngest son should arrive at the age of twenty-one—an event which took place, I supposed, while Ben was on his way to India. Desmond and an older son, who resided anywhere except at home, made havoc with the income. As the principal prospectively was theirs, or nearly the whole of it, why should they not dispose of that?

At last Mr. Somers looked at his watch, a gentle reminder that it was time for us to withdraw. Adelaide was still in the parlor, lying on her favorite sofa contemplating the ceiling. I asked permission to retire, which she granted without removing her regards. In spite of my sound sleep that night, I was started from it by the wail of a young child. The strangeness of the chamber, and the continued crying, which I could not locate, kept me awake at intervals till dawn peeped through the curtains.

CHAPTER XXVIII.

A few days after my arrival, some friends dined with Mrs. Somers. The daughters of a senator, as Ann informed me, and an ex-governor, or I should not have known this fact, for I was not introduced. The dinner was elaborate, and Desmond did the honors. With the walnuts one of the ladies asked for the baby.

Mrs. Somers made a sign to Desmond, who pulled the bell-rope—mildly this time. An elderly woman instantly appeared with a child a few months old, puny and anxious-looking. Mrs. Somers took it from her, and placed it on the table; it tottered and nodded to the chirrups of the guests. Ben, from the opposite side of the table, addressed me by a look, which enlightened me. His voyage to India was useless, as the property would stand for twenty-one years more, lacking some months, unless Providence interposed. Adelaide was oblivious of the child, but Desmond thumped his glass on the mahogany to attract it, for its energies were absorbed in swallowing its fists and fretfully crying. When Murphy announced coffee in the parlor, the nurse took it away; and after coffee and sponge cake were served the visitors drove off. That afternoon some friends of Adelaide called, to whom she introduced me as "cousin." She gave graphic descriptions of them, after their departure. One had achieved greatness by spending her winters in Washington, and contracting a friendship with John C. Calhoun. Another was an artist who had painted an ideal head of her ancestor, Sir Roger de Roger, not he who had arrived some years ago as a weaver from Glasgow, but the one who had remained on the family estate. A third reviewed books and collected autographs.

The next afternoon one of the Miss Hiticutts from across the way came, in a splendid camel's-hair shawl and a shabby dress. "How *is* Mr. Somers?" she asked. "He is such a martyr."

Here Mrs. Somers entered. "My dear Bellevue, you are worn out with your devotion to him; when have you taken the air?" She did not wait for a reply, but addressed Adelaide with, "This is your young friend, and where is my favorite, Mr. Ben, and little Miss Ann? Have you anything new? I went down to Harris yesterday to tell her she must sweep away her old trash of a circulating library, and begin with the New Regime of Novels, which threatens to overwhelm us."[47]

Adelaide talked slowly at first, and then soared into a region where I had never seen a woman—an intellectual one. Miss Hiticutt followed her, and I experienced a new pleasure. Mrs. Somers was silent, but listened with respect to Miss Hiticutt, for she was of the real Belem azure in blood as well as in brain; besides, she was rich, and would never marry. It was a Pickersgill hallucination to be attentive to people who had legacies in their power. Mrs. Somers had a bequested fortune already in hair rings and silver ware. While appearing to listen to Adelaide, her eyes wandered over me with speculation askant in them. Adelaide was so full of *esprit* that I was again smitten with my inferiority, and from this time I felt respect for her, which never declined, although she married an Englishman, who, too choleric to live in America, took her to Florence, where they settled with their own towels and silver, and are likely to remain, for her heart is too narrow to comprise any further interest in Belem.

Miss Hiticutt chatted herself out, giving us an invitation to tea, for any day, including Ben and Miss Ann, who had not been visible since breakfast.

April rains kept us indoors for several days. Ann refused to go
to school. She must have a holiday; besides, pa needed her; she
alone could take care of him, after all. Her mother said that she
must go.

"Who can make me, mum?"

Desmond ordered the coach for her. When it was ready he put
her in it, seated himself beside her, with provoking nonchalance,
and carried her to school. Murphy, with his velvet-banded hat, left
her satchel at the door, with a ceremonious air, which made Ann
slap his cheek and call him an old grimalkin. But she was obliged
to walk home in the rain, after waiting an hour for him to come
back.

Mr. Somers hobbled about his room, with the help of his cane,
and said that he sould be out soon, and requested Adelaide to put
in order some book-shelves that were in the third story, for he
wanted to read without confusion. We went there together, and
sorted some odd volumes; piles of Unitarian sermons, bound
magazines, political works, and a heap of histories. Ben found a
seat on a bunch of books, pleased to see us together.

"This is a horrid hole," he said. "I have not been up in this floor
for ages. How do the shelves look?"

A hiccough near us caused us to look toward the door.

"It is only Des, in his usual afternoon trim," said Ben.

She nodded, as he pushed open the door, thrusting in his head.
"What the hell are you doing here? This region is sacred to Chaos
and old Night," striking the panels, first one and then the other,
with the tassels of his dressing-gown. No one answered him.
Adelaide counted a row of books, and Ben whistled.

"Damn you, Ben," he said, in a languid voice: "you never seem
bored. Curse you all. I hate ye, especially that she-Calmuck yonder—that Siberian-steppe-natured, malachite-hearted girl, our sister."

"Oh come away, Mr. Desmond. What are the poor things doing
that you should harry them?" and the woman who had brought in
the baby the day of the dinner laid her hands on him and pulled
him away.

"Sarah will never give him up," said Ben.

"She swears there is good in him. I think he is a wretch,"
turning over the leaves of a book with her beautiful hand, such a
hand as I had just seen beating the door—such a hand as clasped

its fellow in Ben's hair. Adelaide was not embarrassed at my presence. She neither sought nor avoided my look. But Ben said, "You are thinking."

"Is she?" And Adelaide raised her eyes.

"You are all so much alike," I said.

"You are right," she answered seriously. "Our grandfather—"

"Confound him!" broke in Ben. "I wish he had never been born. Are you proud, Addie, of being like the Pickersgills? But I know you are. Remember that the part of us which is Pickersgill hates its like. I am off; I am going to walk."

Adelaide coolly said, after he had gone, that he was very visionary, predicting changes that could not be, and determined to bring them about.

"Why did he bring me here?" I asked, as if I were asking in a dream.

"Ben's hospitality is genuine. He is like pa. Besides, you are related to us—on the Somers side, and are the first visitor we ever saw, outside of mother's connection. Do you not know, too, that Ben's friendship is very sincere—very strong?"

"I begin to comprehend the Pickersgills," I remarked as if in a dream. "How words with any meaning glance off, when addressed to them. How impossible it is to return the impression they give. How incapable they are of appreciating what they cannot appropriate to the use of their idiosyncrasies."

She gazed at me, as if she heard an abstract subject discussed, with a slight interest in her black eyes.

"Are they vicious to the death?" I went on with this dream. "It is not fair—their overpowering personality—it is not fair to others. It overpowers me, though I know it is *all* fallacious."

"I am ignorant of Ethical Philosophy."

"Miss Somers," said Murphy, knocking, "if Major Millard is below?"

"I am coming."

She smiled when she looked at me again. I stared at her with a singular feeling. Had I touched her, or had I made a fool of myself?

"There is some nice gingerbread in the closet. Sha'n't I get you a piece?"

I fell out of my dream.

"Major Millard is an old beau. Come down and captivate him. He likes fair women."

Declining the gingerbread, I accepted the Major. He was an old gentleman, in a good deal of highly starched linen, amusing himself by teazing Ann, who liked it, and paid him in impertinence. Adelaide played chess with him. Desmond sauntered in about nine, threw himself into a chair behind the sofa where I sat, and swung his arm over the back. The chessboard was put aside, and a gossipy conversation was started, which included Mrs. Somers, who was on a sofa across the room, but he did not join in it. I watched Mrs. Somers, as her fingers moved with her Berlin knitting, feeling more composed and settled as to my identity, in spite of my late outburst, than I had felt at any moment since my arrival in Belem. They were laughing at a funny description, which Ann was giving of a meeting she had witnessed between Miss Hiticutt and Mr. Pearsall, a gentleman lately arrived from China, after a twenty years' residence, with several lacs of rupees. Her delineation of Miss Hiticutt, who attempted to appear as she had twenty years before, was excellent. Ben, who was rolling and unrolling his mother's yarn, laughed till the tears ran, but Major Millard looked uneasy, as if he expected to be served à-la-Hiticutt by the satirical Ann after his departure. Before the laughter subsided, I heard a low voice at my ear, and felt a slight touch from the tip of a finger on my cheek.

"How came those scars?"

I brushed my cheek with my handkerchief, and answered, "I got them in battle."

He left his chair, and walked slowly through the room into the dark front parlor. Major Millard took leave, and was followed by Mrs. Somers and Ann, neither of whom returned. As Ben stretched himself on his sofa with an air of relief, Desmond emerged from the dark and stood behind him, leaning against a column, with his hands in his coat pockets and his eyes searchingly fixed upon me. Ben, turning his head in my direction, sprang up so suddenly that I started; but Desmond's eyes did not move till Ben confronted him; then he gave him a haughty smile, and begged him to take his repose again.

I went to the piano and ran my fingers over the keys.

"Do you play? Can you sing?" asked Adelaide, rousing herself.

"Yes."

"Do sing. I never talk music; but I like it."

"Some old song," said Ben.

Singing

> "Drink to me only with thine eyes,
>   And I will pledge with mine,"

I became conscious that Desmond was near me. With a perfectly
pure voice he joined in the song:

> "The thirst that from the soul doth rise,
>   Doth ask a drink divine."[48]

As the tones of his voice floated through the room, I was where
I saw the white sea-birds flashing between the blue deeps of our
summer sea and sky, and the dark rocks that rose and dipped in
the murmuring waves.

CHAPTER XXIX.

One pleasant afternoon Adelaide and I started on a walk. We must
go through the crooked length of Norfolk Street, till we reached
the outskirts of Belem, and its low fields not yet green; that was
the fashionable promenade, she said. After the two o'clock dinner,
Belem walked. All her acquaintances seemed to be in the street, so
many bows were given and returned with ceremony. Nothing
familiar was attempted, nothing beyond the courtliness of an artificial smile.

Returning, we met Desmond with a lady, and a series of bows
took place. Desmond held his hat in his hand till we had passed;
his expression varied so much from what it was when I saw him
last, at the breakfast table, he being in a desperate humor then, that
it served me for mental comment for some minutes.

"That is Miss Brewster," said Adelaide. "She is an heiress, and
fancies Desmond's attentions: she will not marry him, though."

"Is every women in Belem an heiress?"

"Those we talk about are, and every man is a fortune-hunter.
Money marries money; those who have none do not marry. Those
who wait hope. But the great fortunes of Belem are divided; the
race of millionaires is decaying."

"Is that Ann yonder?"

"I think so, from that bent bonnet."

It proved to be Ann, who went by us with the universal bow
and grimace, sacrificing to the public spirit with her fine manners.

She turned soon, however, and overtook us, proposing to make a detour to Drummond Street, where an intimate family friend, "Old Hepburn," lived, so that the prospect of our going to tea with her might be made probable by her catching a passing glimpse of us; at this time she must be at the window with her Voltaire, or her Rousseau. The proposition was accepted, and we soon came near the house, which stood behind a row of large trees, and looked very dismal, with three-fourths of its windows barred with board shutters.

"Walk slow," Ann entreated. "I see her blinking at us. She has not shed her satin pelisse yet."

Before we got beyond it a dirty little girl came out of the gate, in a pair of huge shoes and a canvas apron, which covered her, to call us back. Mrs. Hepburn had seen us, and wished us to come in, wanting to know who Miss Adelaide had with her, and to talk with her. She ran back, reappearing again at the door, out of breath, and minus a shoe. As we entered a small parlor, an old lady in a black dress, with a deep cape, held out her withered hand, without rising from her straight-backed arm-chair, smiling at us, but shaking her head furiously at the small girl, who lingered in the door.

"Mari, Mari," she called, but no Mari came, and the small girl took our shawls, for Mrs. Hepburn said we must stay, now that she had inveigled us inside her doors. Ann mimicked her at her back, but to her face behaved servilely. The name of Morgeson belonged to the early historical time of New England, Mrs. Hepburn informed me. I never knew it; but bowed, as if not ignorant. Old Mari must be consulted respecting the sweetmeats, and she went after her.

"What an old mouser it is!" said Ann. "What unexpected ways she has! She scours Belem in her velvet shoes, to find out everybody's history. Don't you smell buttered toast?"

"Your father is getting the best of the gout," said Mrs. Hepburn, returning. "How is Desmond? He may be the wickedest of you all, but I like him the best. I shall not throw away praise of him on you, Adelaide." And she looked at me.

"He bows well," I said.

"He resembles his mother, who was a great beauty. Mr. Somers was handsome, too. I was at a ball at Governor Flam's thirty years ago. Your mother was barely fifteen, then, Adelaide; she was just married, and opened the ball."

She examined me all the while, with a pair of small, round eyes, from which the color had faded, but which were capable of reading me.

Tea was served by candlelight, on a small table. Mrs. Hepburn kept her eyes on everything, talking volubly, and pulled the small girl's ears, or pushed her by the shoulder, with faith that we were not observing her. The toast was well buttered, the sweetmeats were delicious, and the cake was heavenly, as Ann said. Mrs. Hepburn ate little, but told us a great deal about marriages in prospect and incomes which waxed or waned in consequence. When tea was over, she said to the small girl who removed the tea things, "On your life taste not of the cake or the sweetmeats; and bring me two sticks of wood, you huzzy." She arranged the sticks on a decaying fire, inside a high brass fender, pulled up a stand near the hearth, lighted two candles, and placed on it a pack of cards.

"Some one may come, so that we can play."

Meantime she dozed upright, walking, talking, and dozing again, like a crafty old parrot.

"She has a great deal of money saved," Ann whispered behind a book. "She is over seventy. Oh, she is opening her puss eyes!"

Adelaide mused, after her fashion, on the slippery hair-cloth sofa, looking at the dim fire, and I surveyed the room. Its aspect attracted me, though it was precise and stiff. An ugly Turkey carpet covered the floor; a sideboard was against the wall, with a pair of silver pitchers on it, and two tall vases, filled with artificial flowers, under glass shades. Old portraits hung over it. Upon one I fixed my attention.

"That is the portrait of Count Rumford," Mrs. Hepburn said.

"Can't we see the letters?" begged Ann. "And wont you show us your trinkets? It is three or four years since we looked them over."

"Yes," she answered, good-humoredly; "ring the bell."

An old woman answered it, to whom Mrs. Hepburn said, in a friendly voice, "The box in my desk." Adelaide and Ann said, "How do you do, Mari?" When she brought the box, Mrs. Hepburn unlocked it, and produced some yellow letters, which we looked over, picking out here and there bits of Parisian gossip, many, many years old. They were directed to Cavendish Hepburn, by his friend, the original of the portrait. But the letters were soon laid aside, and we examined the contents of the box. Old brooches, miniatures painted on ivory, silhouettes, hair rings, necklaces, ear-rings, chains, and finger-rings.

"Did you wear this?" asked Ann with a longing voice, slipping an immense sapphire ring on her forefinger.

"In Mr. Hepburn's day," she answered, taking up a small case, which she unfastened and gave me. It contained a peculiar pair of ear-rings, and a brooch of aqua-marina stones, in a setting perfo-rated like a net.

"They suit you. Will you accept such an old-fashioned orna-ment? Put the rings in; here Ann, fasten them."

Ann glared at her in astonishment, and then at me, for the reason which had prompted so unexpected a gift.

"Is it possible that I am to have them? Why do you give them to me? They are beautiful," I replied.

"They came from Europe long ago," she said. "And they hap-pen to suit you."

> " 'Sabrina fair,
> Under the glassy, cool, translucent wave,
> In twisted braids of lilies knitting
> The loose train of thy amber-dropping hair.' "[49]

"Those lines make me forgive Paradise Lost," said Adelaide.

"They are very long, these ear-rings," Ann remarked.

I put the brooch in the knot of ribbon I wore; Mrs. Hepburn joggled the white satin bows of her cap in approbation.

The knocker resounded. "There is our partner," she cried.

"It must be late, ma'am," said Adelaide; "and I suspect it is some one for us. You know we never venture on impromptu visits, except to you, and our people know where to send."

"Late or not, you shall stay for a game," she said, as Ben came in, hat in hand, declaring that he had been scouting for us since dark. Mrs. Hepburn snuffed the candles, and rang the bell. The small girl, with a perturbed air, like one hurried out of a nap, brought in a waiter, which she placed on the sideboard.

"Get to bed," Mrs. Hepburn loudly whispered, looking over the waiter, and taking from it a silver porringer, she put it inside the fender, and then shuffled the cards.

"Now, Ann, you may sit beside me and learn."

"If it is whist, mum, I know it. I played every afternoon at Hampton last summer, and we spoiled a nice polished table, we scratched it so with our nails, picking up the cards."

"Young people do too much, nowadays."

I was in the shadow of the sideboard; Ben stood against it.

"When have you played whist, Cassandra?" he asked in a low voice. "Do you remember?"

"Is my name Cassandra?"

"Have you forgotten that, too?"

"I remember the rain."

"It is not October, yet."

"And the yellow leaves do not stick to the panes. Would you like to see Helen?"

"Come, play with me, Ben," called Mrs. Hepburn.

"Ann, try your skill," I entreated, "and let me off."

"She can try," Mrs. Hepburn said sharply. "Don't you like games? I should have said you were by nature a bold gamester." She dealt the cards rapidly, and was soon absorbed in the game, though she quarreled with Ann occasionally, and knocked over the candlestick once. Adelaide played heroically, and was praised, though I knew she hated play.

Two hours passed before we were released. The fire went out, the candles burnt low, and whatever the contents of the silver porringer, they had long been cold. When Mrs. Hepburn saw us determined to go, she sent us to the sideboard for some refreshment. "My caudle is cold," taking off the cover of the porringer. "Why, Mari, what is this?" she said, as the woman made a noiseless entrance with a bowl of hot caudle.

"I knew how it would be," she answered, putting it into the hands of her mistress.

"I am a desperate old rake, you mean, Mari. There, take your virtue off, you appall me."

She poured the caudle into small silver tumblers, and gave them to us. "The Bequest of a Friend" was engraved on them. Her fingers were like ice, and her head shook with fatigue; but her voice was sprightly and her smile bright. Ann ate a good deal of sponge cake, and omitted the caudle, but I drank mine to the memory of the donor of the cup.

"You know that sherry, Ben," and Mrs. Hepburn nodded him toward a decanter. He put his hand on it, and took it away. "None to-night," he said. Mari came with our shawls, and we hastened away, hearing her shoot the bolt of the door behind us. Ben drew my arm in his, and the girls walked rapidly before us. It was a white, hazy night, and the moon was wallowing in clouds.

"Let us walk off the flavor of Hep's cards," said Adelaide, "and go to Wolf's Point."

"Do you wish to go?" he asked me.

"Yes."

Ann skipped. A nocturnal excursion suited her exactly.

"You are not to have the toothache to-morrow, or pretend to be lame," said Adelaide.

"Not another hiss, Adder. *En avant!*"

We passed down Norfolk Street, now dark and silent, and reached our house. A light was burning in a room in the third story, and a window was open. Desmond sat by it, his arms folded across his chest, smoking, and contemplating some object beyond our view. Ann derisively apostrophized him, under her breath, while Ben unlocked the court gate and went in after Rash, who came out quietly, and we proceeded. In looking behind me, I stumbled.

"What's the matter?" he asked. "Are you afraid?"

"Yes."

"Of what?"

"The Prince of Darkness."

"The devil lives a little behind us."

"In you, too, then?"

"In Rash. Look at him; he is bigger than Faust's dog, jumps higher, and is blacker. You can't hear the least sound from him as he gambols with his familiar."

We left the last regular street on that side of the city, and entered a road, bordered by trees and bushes, which hid the country from us. We crept through a gap in it, crossed two or three spongy fields, and ascended a hill, reaching an abrupt edge of the rocks, over whose earthy crest we walked. Below it I saw a strip of the sea, hemmed in on all sides, for the light was too vague for me to see its narrow outlet. It looked milky, misty, and uncertain; the predominant shores stifled its voice, if it ever had one. Adelaide and Ann crouched over the edge of the rock, reciting, in a chanting tone, from a poem beginning:

> "The river of thy thoughts must keep
> Its solemn course too still and deep
> For idle eyes to see."

Their false intonation of voice and the wordy spirit of the poem convinced me that poetry with them was an artificial taste. I turned away. The dark earth and the rolling sky were better. Ben followed.

"I hope Veronica's letter will come to-morrow," he said with a groan.

"Veronica! Why Veronica?"

"Don't torment me."

"She writes letters seldom."

"I have written her."

"She has never written me."

"It might be the means of revealing you to each other to do so."

"Ben, your native air is deleterious."

"You laugh. I feel what you say. I do not attempt to play the missionary at home, for my field is not here."

"You were wise not to bring Veronica, I see already."

"She would see what I hate myself for."

"One may venture farther with a friend than a lover."

"I thought that *you* might understand the results of my associations. Curse them all! Come, girls, we must go back."

CHAPTER XXX.

I took a cold that night. Belem was damp always, but its midnight damp was worse than any other. Mrs. Somers sent me medicine. Adelaide asked me, with an air of contemplation, what made me sick, and felt her own pulse. Ann criticised my nightgown ruffles, and accused me of wearing imitation lace; but nursing was her forte, and she stayed by me, annoying me by a frequent beating up of my pillow, and the bringing in of bowls of strange mixtures for me to swallow, which she persuaded the cook to make and her father to taste.

Before I left my room, Mrs. Somers came to see me.

"You are about well, I hear," she said, in a cold voice.

I felt as if I had been shamming sickness.

"I thought you were in remarkable health, your frame is so large."

Adelaide was there, and answered for me. "You *are* delicate. It must be because you do not take care of yourself."

"Wolf's Point to be avoided, perhaps!"

"I have walked to Wolf's Point for fifteen years, night and day, many times."

"Mr. Munster's man left this note for you," her mother said, handing it to her.

She read an invitation from Miss Munster, a cousin, to a small party.

"You will not be able to go," Mrs. Somers remarked to me.

"You will go," Adelaide said; "it is an attention to you altogether."

She never replied to her mother, never asked her any questions, so that talking between them was a one-sided affair.

"Let us go out shopping, Adelaide; I want some lace to wear," I begged.

Mrs. Somers looked into her drawers, out of which Adelaide had thrust her finery, and found mine, but said nothing.

"We are going to a party, Ann. Thanks to your messes and your nursing," as I passed her in the hall.

"Where is your evening dress?"

"Pinned in a napkin—like my talent."

"Old Cousin Munster, the pirate, who made his money in the opium trade, has good things in his house. I suppose," with a coquettish air, "that you will see Ned Munster; he *would* walk to the door with me to-day. He wishes me out, I know."

We consumed that evening in talking of dress. Adelaide showed me her camel's-hair scarfs which Desmond had brought, and her dresses. Ann tried them all on, walking up and down, and standing tiptoe before the glass, while I trimmed a handkerchief with the lace I had purchased. I unfolded my dress after they were gone, with a dubious mind. It was a heavy white silk, with a blue satin stripe. It might be too old-fashioned, for it belonged to mother, who would never wear it. The sleeves were puffed with bands of blue velvet, and the waist was covered with a berthé of the same. It must do, however, for I had no other.

We were to go at nine. Adelaide came to my room dressed, and with her hair arranged exactly like mine. She looked well, in spite of her Mongolic face.

"Pa wants to see us in his room; he has gone to bed."

"Wait a moment," I begged. I took my hair down, unbraided it, brushed it out of curl as much as I could, twisted it into a loose mass, through which I stuck pins enough to hold it, bound a narrow fillet of red velvet round my head, and ran after her.

"That is much better," she said; "you are entirely changed."

Desmond was there, in his usual careless dress, hanging over the footboard of the bed, and Ann was huddled on the outside. Mrs. Somers was reading.

"Pa," said Ann, "just think of Old Hepburn's giving her a pair of lovely ear-rings."

"Did she? Where are they?" asked Mrs. Somers.

"I am not surprised," said Mr. Somers. "Mrs. Hepburn knows where to bestow. Why not wear them?"

"I'll get them," said Ann.

Mr. Somers continued his compliments. He thought there was a pleasing contrast between Adelaide and myself, referred to Diana, mentioned that my hair was remarkably thick, and proceeded with a dissertation on the growth and decay of the hair, when she returned with the ear-rings.

"It is too dark here," she said.

Desmond, who had remained silent, took the candle, which Mrs. Somers was reading by, and held it for Ann, close to my face. The operation was over, but the candle was not taken away till Mrs. Somers asked for it sharply.

"I dare say," murmured Mr. Somers, who was growing drowsy, "that Mrs. Hepburn wore them some night, when she went to John Munster's, forty years ago, and now you wear them to the son's. How things come round!"

The Munsters' man opened the door for us.

The rooms were full. "Very glad," said Mr., Mrs., and Miss Munster, and amid a loud buzz we fell back into obscurity. Adelaide joined a group, who were talking at the top of their voices, with most hilarious countenances.

"They pretend to have a Murillo here, let us go and find it," said Ben.

It was in a small room. While we looked at a dark-haired, handsome woman, standing on brown clouds, with hands so fat that every finger stood apart, Miss Munster brought up a young gentleman with the Munster cast of countenance.

"My brother begs an introduction, Miss Morgeson."

Ben retired, and Mr. Munster began to talk volubly, with wandering eyes, repeating words he was in danger of forgetting. No remarks were required from me. At the proper moment he asked me to make the tour of the rooms, and offered his arm. As we were crossing the hall, I saw Desmond, hat in hand, and in faultless evening dress, bowing to Miss Munster.

"Your Cousin Desmond, and mine, is a fine-looking man, is he not? Let us speak to him."

I drew back. "I'll not interrupt his *devoir*."

He bowed submissively.

"My cousin Desmond," I thought; "let me examine this beauty." He was handsomer than Ben, his complexion darker, and his hair black. There was a flush across his cheek-bones, as if he had once blushed, and the blush had settled. The color of his eyes I could not determine. As if to resolve my doubt, he came toward us; they were a deep violet, and the lids were fringed with long black lashes. I speculated on something animal in those eyes. He stood beside me, and twisted his heavy mustache.

"What a pretty boudoir this is," I said, backing into a little room behind us.

"Ned," he said abruptly, "you must resign Miss Morgeson; I am here to see her."

"Of course," Ned answered; "I relinquish."

Before a word was spoken between us, Mrs. Munster touched Desmond on the shoulder, and told him that he must come with her, to be introduced to Count Montholon.

"Bring him here, please."

"Tyrant," she answered playfully, "the Count shall come."

He brought a chair. "Take this; you are pale. You have been ill." Bringing another, he seated himself before me and fanned himself with his hat.

Mrs. Munster came back with the Count, an elderly man, and Desmond rose to meet him, keeping his hand on the back of his chair. They spoke French. The freedom of their conversation precluded the idea of my understanding it. The Count made a remark about me. Desmond replied, glancing at me, and both pulled their mustaches. The Count was called away soon, and Desmond resumed his chair.

"I understood you," I said.

"The deuce you did."

He placed his hat over a vase of flowers, which tipping over, he leisurely righted, and bending toward me, said:

"It was in battle."

"Yes."

"And women like you, pure, with no vice of blood, sometimes are tempted, struggle, and suffer."

His words, still more his voice, made me wince.

"Even drawn battles bring their scars," I replied.

"Convince me beyond all doubt that a woman can reason with her impulses, or even fathom them, and I will be in your debt."

"Maybe—but Ben is coming."

He looked at me strangely.

"You must find this very dull, Cassandra," said Ben, joining us.

"*Cassandra,*" said Desmond, "are you bored?"

The accent with which he spoke my name set my pulses striking like a clock. I got up mechanically, as Ben directed.

"They are going to supper. There's game. Des. Munster told me to take the northeast corner of the table."

"I shall take the southwest, then," he replied, nodding to a tall gentleman who passed with Adelaide. When we left him, he was observing a carved oak chair, in occult sympathy probably with the grain of the wood. Nature strikes us with *her* phenomena at times when other resources are not at hand.

We were compelled to wait at the door of the supper-room, the jam was so great.

"What fairy story do you like best?" asked Ben.

"I know which you like."

"Well?"

"Bluebeard. You have an affinity with Sister Ann in the tower."

"Do you think I see nothing 'but the sun which makes a dust and the grass which looks green'? I believe you like Bluebeard, too."

That was a great joke, at which we both laughed.

When I saw Desmond again, he was surrounded by men, the French Count among them, drinking champagne. He held a bottle, and was talking fast. The others were laughing. His listless, morose expression had disappeared; in the place of a brutal-tempered, selfish, bored man, I saw a brilliant, jovial gentleman. Which was the real man?

"Finish your jelly," said Ben.

"I prefer looking at your brother."

"Leave my brother alone."

"You see nothing but 'the sun which makes a dust, and the grass which looks green.' "

Miss Munster hoped I was cared for. How gay Desmond was! she had not seen such a look in his face in a long time. And how strongly he was marked with the family traits.

"How am I marked, May?" asked Ben.

"Oh, we know worse eccentrics than you are. What are you up to now? You are not as frank as Desmond."

He laughed as he looked at me, and then Adelaide called to us that it was time to leave.

We were among the last; the carriage was waiting. We made our bows to Mrs. Munster, who complained of not having seen more of us. "You are a favorite of Mrs. Hepburn's, Miss Morgeson, I am told. She is a remarkable woman, has great powers." I mentioned my one interview with her. Guests were going upstairs with smiles, and coming down without, released from their company manners. We rode home in silence, except that Adelaide yawned fearfully, and then we toiled up the long stairs, separating with a tired, "good-night."

I extinguished my candle by dropping my shawl upon it, and groped in vain for matches over the tops of table and shelf.

"To bed in the dark, then," I said, pulling off my gloves and the band, from my head, for I felt a tightness in it, and pulled out the hairpins. But a desire to look in the glass overcame me. I felt unacquainted with myself, and must see what my aspect indicated just then.

I crept downstairs, to the dining-room, passed my hands over the sideboard, the mantel shelf, and took the round of the dinner-table, but found nothing to light my candle with.

"The fire may not be out in the parlor," I thought; "it can be lighted there." I ran against the hatstand in the hall, knocking a cane down, which fell with a loud noise. The parlor door was ajar; the fire was not out, and Desmond was before it, watching its decay.

"What is it?" he asked.

"The candle," I stammered, confused with the necessity of staying to have it lighted, and the propriety of retreating in the dark.

"Shall I light it?"

I stepped a little further inside the door and gave it to him. He grew warm with thrusting it between the bars of the grate, and I grew chilly. Shivering, and with chattering teeth, I made out to say, "A piece of paper would do it." Raising his head hastily, it came crash against the edge of the marble shelf. Involuntarily I shut the door, and leaned against it, to wait for the effect of the blow; but feeling a pressure against the outside, I yielded to it, and moved aside. Mrs. Somers entered, with a candle flaring in one hand, and holding with the other her dressing-gown across her bosom.

"What are you doing here?" she asked harshly, but in a whisper, her eyes blazing like a panther's.

"Doing?" I replied; "stay and see."

She swept along, and I followed, bringing up close to Desmond, who had his hand round his head, and was very pale, either from the effect of the blow or some other cause. Even the flush across his cheeks had faded. She looked at him sharply; he moved his hands from his head, and met her eyes. "I am not drunk, you see," he said in a low voice. She made an insulting gesture toward me, which meant, "Is this an adventure of yours?"

The blaze in her eyes kindled a more furious one in his; he stepped forward with a threatening motion.

Anger raged through me—like a fierce rain that strikes flat a violent sea. I laid my hand on her arm, which she snapped at like a wolf, but I spoke calmly:

"You tender, true-hearted creature, full of womanly impulses, allow me to light my candle by yours!"

I picked it from the hearth, lighted it, and held it close to her face, laughing, though I never felt less merry. But I had restrained him.

He took the candle away gently.

"Leave the room," he said to her.

She beckoned me to go.

"No, you shall go."

They made a simultaneous movement with their hands, he to insist, she to deprecate, and I again observed how exactly alike they were.

"*Desmond,*" I implored, "pray allow me to go."

A deep flush suffused his face. He bowed, threw wide the door, and followed me to the foot of the stairs. I reached my hand for the candle, for he retained both.

"You, pardon first."

"For what?"

"For much? oh—for much."

What story my face told, I could not have told him. He kissed my hand and turned away.

At the top of the stairs I looked down. He was there with upturned face, watching me. Whether he went back to confer with his mother, I never knew; if he did, the expression which he wore then must have troubled her. I went to bed, wondering over the mischief that a candle could do. After I had extinguished it, its wick glowed in the dark like a one-eyed demon.

CHAPTER XXXI.

Another week passed. Ben had received a letter from Veronica, informing him that letter-writing was a kind of composition she was not fond of. He must come to her, and then there would be no need for writing. Her letter exasperated him. His tenacious mind, lying in wait to close upon hers, was irritated by her simple, candid behavior. I could give him no consolation, nor did I care to. It suited me that his feelings for her weakened his penetration in regard to me.

When he roused at the expression which he saw Desmond fix upon me the night that Major Millard was there, I expected a rehearsal from him of watchfulness and suspicion; but no symptom appeared. I was glad, for I was in love with Desmond. I had known it from the night of Miss Munster's party. The morning after I woke to know my soul had built itself a lordly pleasure-house;[50] its dome and towers were firm and finished, glowing in the light that "never was on land or sea." How elate I grew in this atmosphere! The face of Nemesis was veiled even. No eye saw the pure, pale nimbus ringed above it. I did not see *him,* except as an apparition, for suddenly he had become the most unobtrusive member of the family, silent and absent. Immunity from espionage was the immutable family rule. Mrs. Somers, under the direction of that spirit which isolated me from all exterior influences, for a little time had shut down the lid of her evil feelings, and was quiet; watching me, perhaps, but not annoying. Mr. Somers was engaged with the subject of ventilation. Ann, to convince herself that she had a musical talent, practiced of afternoons till she was turned out by Adelaide, who had a fit of reading abstruse works, sometimes seeking me with fingers thrust between their leaves to hold abstract conversations, which, though I took small part in them, were of service.

That portion of the world of emotions which I was mapping out she was profoundly indifferent to. My experiences to her would have been debasing. As she would not come to me, I went to her, and gained something.

Ben, always a favorite with his father, pursued him, rode with him, and made visits of pleasure or business, with a latent object which kept him on the alert.

I had been in Belem three weeks; in a week more I decided to return home. My indignation against Mrs. Somers, from our midnight interview, had not suggested that I should shorten my visit. On the contrary, it had freed me from any regard or fear of her opinion. I had discovered her limits.

It was Saturday afternoon. Reflecting that I had but a few days more for Belem, and summing up the events of my visit and the people I had met, their fashions and differences, I unrolled a tolerable panorama, with patches in it of vivid color, and laid it away in my memory, to be unrolled again at some future time. Then a faint shadow dropped across my mind like a curtain, the first that clouded my royal palace, my mental paradise!

I sighed. Joyless, vacant, barren hours prefigured themselves to me, drifting through my brain, till their vacant shapes crowded it into darkness. I must do something! I would go out; a walk would be good for me. Moreover, wishing to purchase a parting gift for Adelaide and Ann, I would go alone. Wandering from shop to shop in Norfolk Street, without finding the articles I desired, I turned into a street which crossed it, and found the right shop. Seeing Drummond Street on an old gable-end house, a desire to exchange with some one a language which differed from my thoughts prompted me to look up Mrs. Hepburn. I soon came to her house, and knocked at the door, which Mari opened. The current was already changed, as I followed her into a room different from the one where I had seen Mrs. Hepburn. It was dull of aspect, long and narrow, with one large window opening on the old-fashioned garden, and from which I saw a discolored marble Flora. Mrs. Hepburn was by the window, in her high chair. She held out her hand and thanked me for coming to see an old woman. Motioning her head toward a dark corner, she said, "There is a young man who likes occasionally to visit an old woman also."

The young man, twenty-nine years old, was Desmond. He crossed the room and offered me his hand. We had not spoken since we parted at the stairs that memorable night. He hastily brought chairs, and placed them near Mrs. Hepburn, who seized her spectacles, which were on a silk workbag beside her, scanned us through them, and exclaimed, "Ah ha! what is this?"

"Is it something in me, ma'am?" said Desmond, putting his head before my face so that it was hid from her.

"Something in both of you; thief! thief!"

She rubbed her frail hand against my sleeve, muttering, "See now, so!—the same characteristics."

I spoke of the difference of the rooms; the one we were in reminded me of a lizard! The walls were faint gray, and every piece of furniture was covered with plain yellow chintz, while the carpet was a pale green. She replied that she always moved from her winter parlor to this summer room on the twenty-second day of April, which had fallen the day before, for she liked to watch the coming out of the shrubs in the garden, which were as old as herself. The chestnut had leaved seventy times and more; and the crippled plum, whose fruit was so wormy to eat, was dying with age. As for the elms at the bottom of the garden, for all she knew they were a thousand years old.

"The elms are a thousand years old," I repeated and repeated to myself, while she glided from topic to topic with Desmond, whose conservation indicated that he was as cultivated as any ordinary gentleman, when the Pickersgill element was not apparent. The form of the garden-goddess faded, the sun had gone below the garden wall. The garden grew dusk, and the elms began to nod their tops at me. I became silent, listening to the fall of the plummet, which dropped again and again from the topmost height of that lordly domain, over which shadows had come. Were they sounding its foundations?

My eyes roved the garden, seeking the nucleus of an emotion which beset me now—not they, but my senses, formed it—in a garden miles away, where nodded a row of elms, under which *Charles Morgeson* stood.

"I am glad you're here, my darling, do you smell the roses?"

"Are you going?" I heard Mrs. Hepburn say in a far-off voice. I was standing by the door.

"Yes, madam; the summer parlor does not delay the sunset."

"Come again. When do you leave Belem?"

"In few days."

Desmond made a grimace, and went to the window.

"Who returns with you," she continued, "Ben? He likes piloting."

"I hope he will; I came here to please him."

"Pooh! You came here because Mr. Somers had a crotchet."

"Well; I was permitted somehow to come."

"It was perfectly right. A woman like you need not question whether a thing is convenable."

Desmond turned from the window, and bestowed upon her a benign smile, which she returned with a satisfied nod.

This implied flattery tinkled pleasantly on my ears, allaying a doubt which I suffered from. Did I realize how much the prestige of those Belem saints influenced me, or how proud I was with the conviction of affiliation with those who were plainly marked with Caste?

"Walk with me," he demanded, as we were going down the steps.

We passed out of Drummond Street into a wide open common. Rosy clouds floated across the zenith, and a warm, balmy wind was blowing. I thought of Veronica, calm and happy, as the spring always made her, and the thought was a finishing blow to the variety of moods I had passed through. The helm of my will was broken.

"There is a good view from Moss Hill yonder," he said. "Shall we go up?"

I bowed, declining his arm, and trudged beside him. From its summit Belem was only half in sight. Its old, crooked streets sloped and disappeared from view; Wolf's Point was at the right of us, and its thread of sea. I began talking of our walk, and was giving an extended description of it, when he abruptly asked why I came to Belem.

"I know," he said, "that you would not have come, had there been any sentiment between you and Ben."

"Thanks for your implication. But I must have made the visit, you know, or how could I learn that I should not have made it?"

"You regret coming?"

"Veronica will give me no thanks."

"Who is she?"

"My sister, whom Ben loves."

"Ben love a sister of yours? My God—how? when first? where? And how came you to meet him?"

"That chapter of accidents need not be recounted. Can you help him?"

"What can I do?" he said roughly. "There is little love between us. You know what a devil's household ours is; but he is one of us—he is afraid."

"Of what?"

"Of mother—of our antecedents—of himself."

"I could not expect you to speak well of him."

"Of course not. Your sister has no fortune?"

"She has not. Men whose merchandise is ships are apt to die bankrupt."

"Your father is a merchant?"

"Even at that, the greatest of the name."

"We are all tied up, you know. Ben's allowance is smaller than mine. He is easy about money; therefore he is pa's favorite."

"Why do you not help yourselves?"

"Do you think so? You have not known us long. Have you influenced Ben to help himself?"

I marched down the hill without reply. Repassing Mrs. Hepburn's, he said, "My grandfather was an earl's son."

"Mrs. Hepburn likes you for that. My grandfather was a tailor; I should have told her so, when she gave me the aqua marina jewels."

"Had you the courage?"

"I forgot both the fact and the courage."

I hurried along, for it grew dark, and presently saw Ben on the steps of the house.

"Have you been walking?" he asked.

"It looks so. Yes, with me," answered Desmond. "Wont you give me thanks for attention to your friend?"

"It must have been a whim of Cassandra's."

"Break her of whims, if you can—"

"I *will*."

We went into the parlor together.

"Where do you think I have been?" Ben asked.

"Where?"

"For the doctor. The *baby* is sick"; and he looked hard at Desmond.

"I hope it will live for years and years," I said.

"I know what you are at, Ben," said Desmond. "I have wished the brat dead; but upon my soul, I have a stronger wish than that— I have *forgotten* it."

There was no falseness in his voice; he spoke the truth.

"Forgive me, Des."

"No matter about that," he answered, sauntering off.

I felt happier; that spark of humanity warmed me. I might not have another. "I would," I said, "that the last day, the last moments of my visit had come. You will see me henceforth in Surrey. I will live and die there.

"To-night," Ben said. "I am going to tell pa."

"That is best."

"Horrible atmosphere!"

"It would kill Verry."

"You thrive in it," he said, with a spice of irritation in his voice. "Thrive!"

Adelaide and Ann proved gracious over my gift. They were talking of the doctor's visit. Ann said the child was teething, for she had felt its gums; nothing else was the matter. There need be no *apprehension*. She should say so to Desmond and Ben, and would post a letter to her brother in unknown parts.

"Miss Hiticutt has sent for us to come over to tea," Adelaide informed me. The black silk I wore would do, for we must go at once.

The quiet, formal evening was a pleasant relief, although I was troubled with a desire to inform Mrs. Somers of Ben's engagement, for the sake of exasperating her. We came home too early for bed, Adelaide said; beside, she had music-hunger. I must sing. Mrs. Somers was by the fire, darning fine napkins, winking over her task, maintaining in her aspect the determination to avert any danger of a midnight interview with Desmond. That gentleman was at present sleeping on a sofa. I seated myself before the piano, wondering whether he slept from wine, ennui, or to while away the time till I should come. I touched the keys softly, waiting for an interpreting voice, and half unconsciously sang the lines of Schiller:

> "I hear the sound of music, and the halls
>   Are full of light. Who are the revelers?"[51]

Desmond made an inarticulate noise and sprang up, as if in answer to a call. A moment after he stepped quietly over the back of the sofa and stood bending over me. I looked up. His eyes were clear, his face alive with intuition. Though Adelaide was close by, she was oblivious; her eyes were cast upward and her fingers lay languid in her lap. Ann, more lively, introduced a note here and there into my song to her own satisfaction. Mrs. Somers I could not see; but I stopped and, giving the music stool a turn, faced her. She met me with her pale, opaque stare, and began to swing her foot over her knee; her slipper, already down at her heel, fell off. I picked it up in spite of her negative movement and hung it on the foot again.

"I shall speak with you presently," she whispered, glancing at Desmond.

He heard her and his face flashed with the instinct of sport, which made me ashamed of any desire for a struggle with her.

"Good-night," I said abruptly, turning away.

"We are all sleepy except this exemplary housewife with her napkins," cried Ann. "We will leave her."

"Cassandra," said Adelaide, when we were on the stairs, "how well you look!"

Ann, elevating her candle, remarked my eyes shone like a cat's.

"Hiticutt's tea was too strong," added Adelaide; "it dilates the pupils. I am sorry you are going away," and she kissed me; this favor would have moved me at any other time, but now I rejoiced to see her depart and leave me alone. I sat down by the toilet table and was arranging some bottles, when Mrs. Somers rustled in. Out of breath, she began haughtily:

"What do you mean?"

A lethargic feeling crept over me; my thoughts wandered; I never spoke nor stirred till she pulled my sleeve violently.

"If you touch me it will rouse me. Did a child of yours ever inflict a blow upon you?"

She turned purple with rage, looming up before my vision like a peony.

"When are you going home?"

I counted aloud, "Sunday—Monday," and stopped at Wednesday. "Ben is going back with me."

"*He* may go."

"And not Desmond?"

"Do you know Desmond?"

"Not entirely."

"He has played with such toys as you are, and broken them."

"Alas, he is hereditarily cruel! Could *I* expect not to be broken?"

She caught up a glass goblet as if to throw it, but only grasped it so tight that it shivered. "There goes one of the Pickersgill treasures, I am sure," I thought.

"I am already scarred, you see. I have been 'nurtured in convulsions.' "

The action seemed to loosen her speech; but she had to nerve herself to say what she intended; for some reason or other, she could not remain as angry as she wished. What she said I will not repeat.

"Madam, I have no plans. If I have a Purpose, it is formless yet. If God saves us what can you do?"

She made a gesture of contempt.

"You have no soul to thank me for what may be my work," and I opened the door.

Ben stood on the threshhold.

"In God's name, what is this?"

I pointed to his mother. She looked uneasy, and stepping forward put her hand on his arm; but he shook her off.

"You may call me a fool, Cassandra, for bringing you here," he said in a bitter voice, "besides calling me cruel for subjecting you to these ordeals. I knew how it would be with mother. What is it, madam?" he asked imperiously, looking so much like her that I shuddered.

"It is not you she is after," she hotly exclaimed.

"No, I should think not." And he led her out swiftly.

I heard Mrs. Somers say at breakfast, as I went in, "We are to lose Miss Cassandra on Wednesday." I looked at Desmond, who was munching toast abstractedly. He made a motion for me to take the chair beside him, which I obeyed. Ben saw this movement, and an expression of pain passed over his face. At that instant I remembered that Desmond's being seen in the evening and in the morning was a rare occurrence. Mr. Somers took up the remark of Mrs. Somers where she had left it, and expatiated on it till breakfast was over, so courteously and so ramblingly that I was convinced the affair Ben had at heart had been revealed. He invited me to go to church, and he spent the whole of the evening in the parlor; and although Desmond hovered near me all day and all the evening, we had no opportunity of speaking to each other.

CHAPTER XXXII.

On Tuesday morning Adelaide sent out invitations to a farewell entertainment, as she called it, for Tuesday evening. Mrs. Somers, affecting great interest in it, engaged my services in wiping the dust from glass and china; "too valuable," she said, "for servants to handle." We spent a part of the morning in the dining-room and pantry. Ann was with us. If she went out, Mrs. Somers was silent; when present she chatted. While we were busy Desmond came in, in riding trousers and whip in hand.

"What nonsense!" he said, touching my hand with the whip-lash. "Will you ride with me after dinner?"

"I must have the horses at three o'clock," said his mother, "to go to Mrs. Flint's funeral. She was a family friend, you know." The funeral could not be postponed, even for Desmond; but he grew ill-humored at once, swore at Murphy, who was packing a waiter at the sideboard, for rattling the plates; called Ann a minx, because she laughed at him; and bit a cigar to pieces because he could not light it. Rash had followed him, his nose against his velveteens, in entreaty to go with him; I was pleased at this sign of amity between them. At a harder push than common he looked down and kicked him away.

"Noble creature," I said, "try your whip on him. Rash, go to your master," and I opened the door. Two smaller dogs, Desmond's property, made a rush to come in; but I shut them out, whereat they whined so loudly that Mrs. Somers was provoked to attack him for bringing his dogs in the house. An altercation took place, and was ended by Desmond declaring that he was on his way after a bitch terrier, to bring it home. He went out, giving me a look from the door, which I answered with a smile that made him stamp all the way through the hall. Mrs. Somers's feelings as she heard him peeped out at me. Groaning in spirit, I finished my last saucer and betook myself to my room and read, till summoned by Mrs. Somers to a consultation respecting the furniture coverings. Desmond came home, but spoke to no one, hovering in my vicinity as on the day before.

In the afternoon Adelaide and I went in the carriage to make calls upon those we did not expect to see in the evening. She wrote P.P.C.[52] on my cards and laughed at the idea of paying farewell visits to strangers. The last one was made to Mrs. Hepburn. A soft melancholy crept over me when I entered the room where I had met Desmond last. We should probably not see each other alone again. Mrs. Somers's policy to that effect would be a success, for I should make no opposition to it. Not a word of my feelings could I speak to Mrs. Hepburn—Adelaide was there—provided I had the impulse; and Mrs. Hepburn would be the last to forgive me should I make the conventional mistake of a scene or an aside. This old lady had taught me something. I went to the window, curious to know whether any nerve of association would vibrate again. Nothing stirred me; the machinery which had agitated and controlled me was effete.

Mrs. Hepburn said, as we were taking leave:

"If you come to Belem next year, and I am above the sod, I invite you to pass a month with me. But let it be in the summer. I ride then, and should like you for a companion."

She might have seen irresolution in me, for she added quickly, "You need not promise—let time decide," and shook my hands kindly.

"Hep. is smitten with you, in her selfish way," Adelaide remarked, as we rode from the door. She ordered the coachman to drive home by the "Leslie House," which she wanted me to see. A great aunt had lived and died there, leaving the house—one of the oldest in Belem—to her brother Ned.

"Who is he like?"

"Desmond; but worse. There's only a year's difference in their ages. They were educated together, kept in the nursery till they were great boys and tyrants, and then sent abroad. They were in Amiens three years."

"There are Desmond and Ben; they are walking in the street we are passing."

She looked out.

"They are quarreling, I dare say. Ben is a prig, and preaches to Des."

While we were in the house, and Adelaide talked with the old servant of her aunt, my thoughts were occupied with Desmond. What had they quarreled on? Desmond was pale, and laughed; but Ben was red, and looked angry.

"Why do you look at me so fixedly?" Adelaide asked, when we were in the carriage again.

It was on my tongue to say, "Because I am beset." I did not, however; instead I asked her if she never noticed what a rigid look people wore in their best bonnets, and holding a card-case? She said, "Yes," and shook out her handkerchief, as if to correct her own rigidity.

After an early tea she compelled me to sing, and we delayed dressing till Mrs. Somers bloomed in, with purple satin and feather head-dress.

"Now we must go," she said, "and get ready."

"What shall you wear?" Mrs. Somers asked, advising a certain ugly, claret-colored silk.

"Be sure not," said Adelaide on the stairs. "That dress makes your hair too yellow."

I heard loud laughing in the third story, and heavy steps, while I was in my room; and when I went down, I saw two gentlemen in evening dress, standing by Desmond, at the piano, and singing, *"Fill, fill the sparkling brimmer."* They were, as Ann informed me, college friends of Des, who had arrived for a few days' visit, she supposed; disagreeable persons, of course. They were often in Belem to ride, fish, or play billiards. "Pa hates them," she said in conclusion. Mr. Somers entering at this moment, in his *diplomatique* style, his gouty white hands shaded with wristbands, and his throat tied with a white cravat, appeared to contradict her assertion, he was so affable in his salutations to the young men. Desmond turned from the piano when he heard his father's voice, and caught sight of me. He started toward me; but his attention was claimed by one of the gentlemen, who had been giving me a prolonged stare, and he dropped back on his seat, with an indifferent air, answering some question relating to myself. He looked as when I first saw him—flushed, haughty, and bored. His hair and dress were disordered, his boots splashed with mud; and it was evident that he did not intend to appear at the party.

Adelaide called me to remain by her; but I slipped away when I thought no more would arrive, and sought a retired corner, to which Mr. Somers brought Desmond's friends, introducing them as the sons of his college chums, and leaving them, one lolling against the mantel, the other over the back of a chair. They were muzzy with drink, and seemed to grow warm, as I looked from one to the other, with an attentive air.

"You are visiting in Belem," said one.

"That is true," I replied.

"It is too confoundedly aristocratic for me; it knocks Beacon Street into nothingness."

"Where is Beacon Street?"

"Don't you know *that?* Nor the Mall?"

"No."

Our conversation was interrupted by Ben, whom I had not seen since the day before. He had been out of town, transacting some business for his father. We looked at each other without speaking, but divined each other's thoughts. "You *are* as true and noble as I think you are, Cassy. I must have it so. You *shall not* thwart me." "Faithful and good Ben,—do you pass a sufficiently strict examination upon yourself? Are you not disposed to carry through your own ideas without considering *me?*" Whatever our internal comments were, we smiled upon each other with the sincerity of friendship, and I detected Mr. Digby in the act of elevating his eyebrows at Mr. Devereaux, who signified his opinion by telegraphing back: "It is all over with them."

"Hey, Somers," said the first; "what are you doing nowadays?"

"Pretty much the same work that I always have on hand."

"Do you mean to stick to Belem?"

"No."

"I thought so. But what has come over Des. lately? He is spoony."

"He is going backward, may be, to some course he omitted in his career with you fellows. We must run the same round somehow, you know."

"He'll not find much reason for it, when he arrives," Mr. Devereaux said.

Miss Munster joined us, with the intention of breaking up our conclave, and soon moved away, with Mr. Digby and Devereaux in her train.

"I have changed my mind," said Ben, "about going home with you."

"Are your plans growing complicated again?"

"Can you go to Surrey alone?"

"Why not, pray?"

"I have an idea of going to Switzerland to spend the summer. Will Veronica be ready in the autumn?"

"How can I answer? Shall you not take leave of her?"

"Perhaps. Yes,—I must," he said excitedly; "but tomorrow we will talk more about it. I shall go to Boston with you; pa is going too. How well you look to-night, Cassy! What sort of dress is this?" taking up a fold of it. "Is it cotton-silk, or silk-cotton? It is soft and light. How delicate you are, with your gold hair and morning-glory eyes!"

"How poetical! My dress is new, and was made by Adelaide's dressmaker."

"Mother beckons me. What a headdress that is of hers!"

"What beckons you to go to Switzerland?" I mused.

I listened for Desmond's voice, which would have sounded like a silver bell, in the loud, coarse buzz which pervaded the rooms. All the women were talking shrill, and the men answering in falsetto. He was not among them, and I moved to and fro unnoticed, for the tide of entertainment had set in, and I could withdraw, if I chose. I took a chair near an open door, commanded a view into a small room, on the other side of the hall, opened only on occasions like these; there was no one in it. Perceiving that my shoelace was untied, I stooped to refasten it, and when I looked in the room again saw Desmond standing under the chandelier, his hands in his pockets, his eyes on the floor, his hair disordered and falling over his forehead; its blackness was intense against the relief of the crimson wall-paper. Was it that which had unaccountably changed his appearance?

He raised his head, looked across the hall, and saw me.

"Come here," he signaled. I rose like an automaton, and cast an involuntary glance about me; the guests were filing through the drawing-room, into the room where refreshments were laid. When the last had gone, I left the friendly protection of the niche by the fire-place, and stood so near him that I saw his nostrils quiver! Then there came into his face an expression of pain, which softened it. I had wished him to please me; *now* I wished to please him. It seemed that he had no intention of speaking, and that he had called me to him to witness a struggle which I must find a key to hereafter, in the depths of my own heart. I watched him in silence, and it passed. As he pushed the door to with his foot, the movement caused something to swing and glitter against his breast— a ring on his watch-ribbon smaller than I could wear, a woman's ruby ring. The small, feminine imp, who abides with those who have beams in their eyes, and helps them to extract motes from the eyes of others, inspired me. I pointed to the ring. Dropping his eyes, he said: "I loved her shamefully, and she loved me shamefully. When shall I take it off—cursed sign?" And he snapped it with his thumb and finger.

I grew rigid with virtue.

"You may not conjure up any tragic ideas on the subject. She is no outcast. She is here to-night; if there was ruin, it was mutual."

"And your other faults?"

"Ah!" he said, with a terrible accent, "we shall see."

There was a tap on the door; it was Ben's. I fell back a step, and he came in. "Will you bring Cassandra to the supper-room?" he said, turning pale.

"No."

"Come with me, then; you must." And he put my arm in his.

"Hail, and farewell, Cassandra!" said Desmond, standing before the door. "Give me your hand."

I gave him both my hands. He kissed one, and then the other, and moved to let us pass out. But Ben did not go; he fumbled for his handkerchief to wipe his forehead, on which stood beads of sweat.

"*Allons,* Ben," I said.

"Go on, go on," said Desmond, holding the door wide open.

A painful curiosity made me anxious to discover the owner of the ruby ring! The friendly but narrow-minded imp I have spoken of composed speeches, with which I might assail her, should she be found. I looked in vain at every women present; there was not a sorrowful or guilty face among them. Another feeling took the place of my curiosity. I forgot the woman I was seeking, to remember the love I bore Desmond. I was mad for the sight of him—mad to touch his hand once more. I could have put the asp on my breast to suck me to sleep, as Cleopatra did; but *Caesar* was in the way.[53] He stayed by me till the lights were turned down.

Digby and Devereaux were commenting on Desmond's disappearance, and Mrs. Somers was politely yawning, waiting their call for candles.

"If you are to accompany me, Ben," I said, "now is the time." And he slipped out. He preserved a determined silence. I shook him, and said—"*Veronica.*" He put his hand over my mouth with an indignant look, which was lost upon me, for I whispered in his ear: "Do you know now that I *love* Desmond?"

"Will you bring him into our Paradise?"

"Where?"

"Our home, in Surrey."

"Wont an angel with a flaming sword make it piquant?"

"If you marry Desmond Somers," he said austerely, "you will contradict three lives,—yours, mine, and Veronica's. What beast was it that suggested this horrible discord? Have you so much passion that you cannot discern the future you offer yourself?"

"Imperator, you have an agreeable way of putting things. But they are coming through the hall. Good-night."

CHAPTER XXXIII.

At eleven o'clock the next day I was ready for departure. All stood by the open hall door, criticising Murphy's strapping of my trunks on a hack. Messrs. Digby and Devereaux, in black satin scarfs, hung over the step railings; Mrs. Somers, Adelaide, and Ann were within the door. Mr. Somers and Ben were already on the walk, waiting for me; so I went through the ceremony of bidding good-by—a ceremony performed with so much cheerfulness on all sides that it was an occasion for well-bred merriment, and I made my exit as I should have made it in a genteel comedy, but with a bitter feeling of mortification, because of their artificial, willful imperturbability I was forced to oppose them with manners copied after their own.

I looked from the carriage window for a last view of my room. The chambermaid was already there, and had thrown open the shutters, to let in daylight upon the scene of the most royal dreams I had ever had. The ghost of my individuality would lurk there no longer than the chairs I had placed, the books I had left, the shreds of paper or flowers I had scattered, could be moved or swept away.

All the way to Boston the transition to my old condition oppressed me. I felt a dreary disgust at the necessity of resuming relations which had no connection with the sentiment that bound me to Belem. After we were settled at the Tremont, while watching a sad waiter engaged in the ceremonial of folding napkins like fans, I discovered an intermediate tone of mind, which gave my thoughts a picturesque tinge. My romance, its regrets, and its pleasures, should be set in the frame of the wild sea and shores of Surrey. I invested our isolated house with the dignity of a stage, where the drama, which my thoughts must continually represent, could go on without interruption, and remain a secret I should have no temptation to reveal. Until after the tedious dinner, a complete rainbow of dreams spanned the arc of my brain. Mr. Somers dispersed it by asking Ben to go out on some errand. That it was a pretext, I knew by Ben's expression; therefore, when we had gone I turned to Mr. Somers an attentive face. First, he circumlocuted; second, he skirmished. I still waited for what he wished to say, without giving him any aid. He was sure, he said at last, that my visit in his family had convinced me that his children could not vary the destiny imposed upon them by their antecedents, without bringing upon *others* lamentable consequences. "Cunning pa," I commented internally. Had I not seen the misery of unequal marriages?

"As in a glass, darkly."

Doubtless, he went on, I had comprehended the erratic tendency in *Ben's* character, good and honorable as he was, but impressive and visionary. Did I think so?

Quite the contrary. Have you never perceived the method of his visions in an unvarying opposition to those antecedents you boast of?"

"Well, *well,* well?"

"Money, Family, Influence,—are a ding-dong bell which you must weary of, Mr. Somers—sometimes."

"Ben has disappointed me; I must confess that."

"My sister is eccentric. Provided she marries him, the family programme will be changed. You must lop him from the family tree."

He took up a paper, bowed to me with an unvexed air, and read a column or so.

"It may be absurd," and he looked over his spectacle tops, as if he had found the remark in his paper, "for parents to oppose the marriages their children choose to make, and I beg you to understand that I may *oppose,* not *resist* Ben. You know very well," and he dropped the paper in a burst of irritation and candor, "that the devil will be to pay with Mrs. Somers, who has a right of dictation in the affair. She does not suspect it. I must say that Ben is mistaking himself again. I mean, I think so."

I looked upon him with a more friendly countenance. The one rude word he had spoken had a wonderful effect, after the surprise of it was over. Real eyes appeared in his face, and a truthful accent pervaded his voice. I think he was beginning to think that he might confide his perplexities to me on other subjects, when Ben returned. As it was, a friendly feeling had been established between us. He said in a confidential tone to Ben, as if we were partners in some guilty secret, "You must mention it to your mother; indeed you must."

"You have been speaking with Cassandra, in reference to her

sister," he answered indifferently. Mr. Somers was chilled in his attempt at a mutual confidence.

"Can you raise money, if Desmond should marry?" asked Ben. "Enough for both of us?"

"Desmond? he will never marry."

"It is certainly possible."

"You know how I am clogged."

I rang for some ice-water, and when the waiter brought it, said that it was time to retire.

"Now," said Mr. Somers, "I shall give you just such a breakfast as will enable you to travel well—a beefsteak, and old bread made into toast. Don't drink that ice-water; take some wine."

I set the glass of ice-water down, and declined the wine. Ben elevated his eyebrows, and asked:

"What time shall I get up, sir?"

"I will call you; so you may sleep untroubled."

He opened the door, and bade me an affectionate goodnight.

"The coach is ready," a waiter announced, as we finished our breakfast. "We are ready," said Mr. Somers. "I have ordered a packet of sandwiches for you—*beef,* not ham sandwiches—and here is a flask of wine mixed with water."

I thanked him, and tied my bonnet.

"Here is a note, also," opening his pocketbook and extracting it, "for your father. It contains our apologies for not accompanying you, and one or two allusions," making an attempt to wink at Ben, which failed, his eyes being unused to such an undignified style of humor.

He excused himself from going to the station on account of the morning air, and Ben and I proceeded. In the passage, the waiter met us with a paper box. "For you, Miss. A florist's boy just left it." I opened it in the coach, and seeing flowers, was about to take them out to show Ben, when I caught sight of the ribbon which tied them—a piece of one of my collar knots I had not missed. Of course the flowers came from Desmond, and half the ribbon was in his possession; the ends were jagged, as if it had been divided with a knife. Instead of taking out the flowers, I showed him the box.

"What a curious bouquet," he said.

In the cars he put into my hand a jewel box, and a thick letter for Verry, kissed me, and was out of sight.

"No vestige but these flowers," uncovering them again. "In my room at Surrey I will take you out," and I shut the box. The clanking of the car wheels revolved through my head in rhythm, excluding thought for miles. Then I looked out at the flying sky— it was almost May. The day was mild and fair; in the hollows, the young grass spread over the earth like a smooth cloth; over the hills and unsheltered fields, the old grass lay like coarse mats. A few birds roved the air in anxiety, for the time of love was at hand, and their nests were not finished. By twelve I arrived at the town where the railroad branched in a direction opposite the road to Surrey, and where a stage was waiting for its complement of passengers from the cars. I was the only lady "aboard," as one of the passengers intelligently remarked, when we started. They were desirable companions, for they were gruff to each other and silent to me. We rode several miles in a state of unadjustment, and then yielded to the sedative qualities of a stagecoach. I lunched on my sandwiches, thanking Mr. Somers for his forethought, though I should have preferred them of ham, instead of beef. When I took a sip from my flask, two men looked surprised, and spat vehemently out of the windows. I offered it to them. They refused it, saying they had had what was needful at the Depot Saloon, conducted on the strictest temperance principles.

"Those principles are cruel, provided travelers ever have colic, or an aversion to Depot tea and coffee," I said.

There was silence for the space of fifteen minutes, then one of them turned and said: "You have a good head, marm."

"Too good?"

"Forgetful, may be."

I bowed, not wishing to prolong the conversation.

"Your circulation is too rapid," he continued.

The man on the seat with him now turned round, and, examining me, informed me that electricity would be first-rate for me.[54]

"Shoo!" he replied, "it's a humbug."

I was forgotten in the discussion which followed, and which lasted till our arrival at a village, where one of them resided. He left, telling us he was a "natral bone-setter." One by one the passengers left the stage, and for the last five miles I was alone. I beguiled the time by elaborating a multitude of trivial opinions, suggested by objects I saw along the roadside, till the old and new church spires of Surrey came in sight, and the curving lines at either end of the ascending shores. We reached the point in the north road, where the ground began its descent to the sea, and I hung from the window, to see all the village roofs humble before it. The streets and dwellings looked as insignificant as those of a toy village. I perceived no movement in it, heard no hum of life. At a cross-road, which would take the stage into the village without its passing our house, a whim possessed me. I would surprise them at home, and go in at the back door, while they were expecting to hear the stage. The driver let me out, and I stood in the road till he was out of sight.

A breeze blew round me, penetrating, but silent; the fields, and the distant houses which dotted them, were asleep in the pale sunshine, undisturbed by it. The crows cawed, and flew over the eastern woods. I walked slowly. The road was deserted. Mrs. Crossman's house was the only one I must pass; its shutters were closed, and the yard was empty. As I drew near home a violent haste grew upon me, yet my feet seemed to impede my progress. They were like lead; I impelled myself along, as in a dream. Under the protection of our orchard wall I turned my merino mantle, which was lined with an indefinite color, spread my veil over my bonnet, and bent my shoulders, and passed down the carriage-drive, by the dining-room windows, into the stable-yard. The rays of sunset struck the lantern-panes in the light-house, and gave the atmosphere a yellow stain. The pigeons were skimming up and down the roof of the wood-house, and cooing round the horses that were in the yard. A boy was driving cows into the shed, whistling a lively air; he suspended it when he saw me, but I shook my finger at him, and ran in. Slipping into the side hall, I dropped my bonnet and shawl, and listened at the door for the familiar voices. Mother must be there, as was her wont, and Aunt Merce. All of them, perhaps, for I had seen nobody on my way. There was no talking within. The last sunset ray struck on my hand its yellow shade, through the fan-light, and faded before I opened the door. I was arrested on the threshold by a silence which rushed upon me, clutching me in a suffocating embrace. Mother was in her chair by the fire, which was out, for the brands were black, and one had fallen close to her feet. A white flannel shawl covered her shoulders; her chin rested on her breast. "She is ill, and has dropped asleep," I thought, thrusting my hands out, through this terrible silence, to break her slumber, and looked at the clock; it was near seven. A door slammed, somewhere upstairs, so loud it made me jump; but she did not wake. I went toward her, confused, and stumbling against the table, which was between us, but reached her at last. Oh, I knew it! She was dead! People must die, even in their chairs, alone! What difference did it make, how? An empty cup was in her lap, bottom up; I set it carefully on the mantel shelf above her head. Her handkerchief was crumpled in her nerveless hand; I drew it away and thrust it into my bosom. My gloves tightened my hands as I tried to pull them off, and was tugging at them, when a door opened, and Veronica came in.

"She is dead," I said. "I can't get them off."

"It is false"; and she staggered backward, with her hand on her heart, till she fell against the wall. I do not know how long we remained so, but I became aware of a great confusion—cries, and exclamations; people were running in and out. Fanny rolled on the floor in hysterics.

"Get up," I said. "I can't move; help me. Where did Verry go?"

She got up, and pulled me along. I saw father raise mother in his arms. The dreadful sight of her swaying arms and drooping head made me lose my breath; but Veronica forced me to endurance by clinging to me, and dragging me out of the room and upstairs. She turned the key of the glass-door at the head of the passage, not letting go of me. I took her by the arms, placed her in a chair, and closing my window curtains, sat down beside her in the dark.

"Where will they carry her?" she asked, shuddering, and putting her fingers in her ears. "How the water splashes on the beach! Is the tide coming in?"

She was appalled by the physical horror of death, and asked me incessant questions.

"Let us keep her away from the grave," she said.

I could not answer, or hear her at last, for sleep overpowered me. I struggled against it in vain. It seemed the greatest good; let death and judgment come, I must sleep. I threw myself on my bed, and the touch of the pillow sealed my eyes. I started from a dream about something that happened when I was a little child. "Veronica, are you here?"

"Mother is dead," she answered.

A mighty anguish filled my breast. Mother!—her goodness and beauty, her pure heart, her simplicity—I felt them all. I pitied her dead, because she would never know how I valued her. Veronica shed no tears, but sighed heavily. *Duty* sounded through her sighs.

"Verry, shall *I* take care of you? I think I can." She shook her head; but presently she stretched her hands in search of my face, kissed it, and answered, "Perhaps."

"You must go to your own room and rest."

"Can you keep everybody from me?"

"I will try."

Opening her window, she looked out over the earth wistfully, and at the sky, thickly strewn with stars, which revealed her face. We heard somebody coming up the back stairs.

"Temperance," said Verry.

"Are you in the dark, girls?" she asked, wringing her hands, when she had put down her lamp. "What an awful Providence!" She looked with a painful anxiety at Veronica.

"It is all Providence, Temperance, whether we are alive or dead," I said. "Let us let Providence alone."

"What did I ever leave her for? She wasn't fit to take care of herself. Why, Cassandra Morgeson, you haven't got off all your things yet. And what's this sticking out of your bosom?"

"It is her handkerchief." I kissed it, and now Verry began to weep over it, begging me for it. I gave it up to her.

"It will kill your father."

I had not thought of him.

"It's most nine o'clock. Sofrony Beals is here; she lays out beautifully."

"No, no; don't let anybody touch her!" shrieked Verry.

"No, they shan't. Come into the kitchen; you must have something to eat."

I was faint from the want of food, and when Temperance prepared us something I ate heartily. Veronica drank a little milk, but would taste nothing. Aunt Merce, who had been out to tea, Temperance said, came into the kitchen.

"My poor girl, I have not seen you," embracing me, half blind with crying, "How pale you are! How sunken! Keep up as well as you can. I little thought that the worthless one of us two would be left to suffer. Go to your father, as soon as possible."

"Drink this tea right down, Mercy," said Temperance, holding a cup before her. "There isn't much to eat in the house. Of all times in the world to be without good victuals! What could Hepsey have meant?"

"Poor old soul," Aunt Merce replied, "she is quite broken. Fanny had to help her upstairs."

The kitchen door opened, and Temperance's husband, Abram, came in.

"Good Lord!" she said in an irate voice, "have you come, too? Did you think I couldn't get home to get your breakfast?"

She hung the kettle on the fire again, muttering too low for him to hear: "Some folks could be spared better than other folks."

Abram shoved back his hat. " 'The Lord gives and the Lord takes away,' but she is a dreadful loss to the poor. There's my poor boy, whose clothes—"

"Aint he the beatum of all the men that ever you see?" broke in Temperance, taking to him a large piece of pie, which he took with a short laugh, and sat down to eat. I could not help exchanging a look with Aunt Merce; we both laughed. Veronica, lost in revery, paid no attention to anything about her. I saw that Temperance suffered; she was perplexed and irritated.

"Let Abram stay, if he likes," I whispered to her; "and be sure to stay yourself, for you are needed."

She brightened with an expression of gratitude. "He is a nuisance," she whispered back; "but as I made a fool of myself, I must be punished according to my folly. I'll stay, you may depend. I'll do *everything* for you. I vow I am mad, that I ever went away."

"Have the neighbors gone?" I asked.

"There's a couple or so round, and will be, you know. I'll take Verry to bed, and sleep on the floor by her. You go to your father."

He was in their bedroom, on the bed. She was lying on a frame of wood, covered with canvas, a kind of bed which went from house to house in Surrey, on occasions of sickness or death.

"Our last night together has passed," he said in a tremulous voice, while scanty tears fell from his seared eyes. "The space between then and now—when her arm was round me, when she slept beside me, when I woke from a bad dream, and she talked gently close to my face, till I slept again—is so narrow that I recall it with a sense of reality which agonizes me; it is so immeasurable when I see her there—*there,* that I am crushed."

If I had had any thought of speaking to him, it was gone.. And I must go too. Were the hands folded across her breast, where I, also, had slept? Were the blue eyes closed that had watched me there? I should never see. A shroud covered her from all eyes but his now. Till I closed the door upon him, I looked my last farewell. An elderly woman met me as I was going upstairs, and offered me a small packet; it was her hair. "It was very long," she said. I tried in vain to thank her. "I will place it in a drawer for you," she said kindly.

CHAPTER XXXIV.

The house was thronged till after the funeral. We sat in state, to be condoled with and waited upon. Not a jot of the customary rites was abated, though I am sure the performers thereof had small encouragement. Veronica alone would see no one; her room was the only one not invaded; for the neighbors took the house into their hands, assisted by that part of the Morgesons who were too distantly related to consider themselves as mourners to be shut up with us. It was put under rigorous funeral law, and inspected from garret to cellar. They supervised all the arrangements, if there were any that they did not make, received the guests who came from a distance, and aided their departure. Every child in Surrey was allowed to come in, to look at the dead, with the idle curiosity of childhood. Veronica knew nothing of this. Her course was taken for granted; mine was imposed upon me. I remonstrated with Temperance, but she replied that it was all well meant, and always done. I endured the same annoyances over and over again, from relays of people. Bed-time especially was their occasion. I was not allowed to undress alone. I must have drinks, either to compose or stimulate; I must have something read to me; I must be watched when I slept, or I must be kept awake to give advice or be told items of news. All the while, like a chorus, they reiterated the character, the peculiarities, the virtues of the mother I had lost, who could never be replaced—who was in a better world. However, I was, in a measure, kept from myself during this interval. The matter is often subservient to the manner. Arthur's feelings were played upon also. He wept often, confiding to me his grief and his plans for the future. "If people would die at the age of seventy-five, things would go well," he said, "for everybody must expect to die then; the Bible says so." He informed me also that he expected to be an architect, and that mother liked it. He had an idea, which he had imparted to her, of an arch; it must be made of black marble, with gold veins, and ought to stand in Egypt, with the word "*Pandemonium*" on it. The kitchen was the focus of interest to him, for meals were prepared at all hours for comers and goers. Temperance told me that the mild and indifferent mourners were fond of good victuals, and she thought their hearts were lighter than their stomachs when they went away. She presided there and wrangled with Fanny, who seemed to have lost her capacity for doing anything steadily, except, as Temperance said, where father was concerned. "It's a pity she isn't his dog; she might keep at his feet then. I found her crying awfully yesterday, because he looked so grief-struck."

Aunt Merce was engaged with a dressmaker, and with the orders for bonnets and veils. She discussed the subject of the mourning with the Morgesons. I acquiesced in all her arrangements, for she derived a simple comfort from these external tokens. Veronica refused to wear the bonnet and veil and the required bombazine. Bombazine made her flesh crawl. Why should she wear it? Mother hated it, too, for she had never worn out the garments made for Grand'ther Warren.

"She's a bigger child than ever," Temperance remarked, "and must have her way."

"Do you think the border on my cap is too deep?" asked Aunt Merce, coming into my room dressed for the funeral.

"No."

"The cap came from Miss Nye in Milford; she says they wear them so. I could have made it myself for half the price. Shall you be ready soon? I am going to put on my bonnet. The yard is full of carriages already."

Somebody handed me gloves; my bonnet was tied, a handkerchief given to me, and the door opened. In the passage I heard a knocking from Veronica's room, and crossed to learn what she wanted.

"Is this like her?" she asked, showing me a drawing.

"How could you have done this?"

"Because I have tried. *Is* it like?"

"Yes, the idea."

But what a picture she had attempted to make! Mother's shadowy face serenely looked from a high, small window, set in clouds, like those which gather over the sun when it "draws water." It was closely pressed to the glass, and she was regarding dark, indefinite creatures below it, which Veronica either could not or would not shape.

"Keep it; but don't work on it any more." And I put it away. She was wan and languid, but collected.

"I see you are ready. Somebody must bury the dead. Go. Will the house be empty?"

"Yes."

"Good; I can walk through it once more."

"The dead must be buried, that is certain; but why should it be certain that *I* must be the one to do it?"

"You think I can go through with it, then?"

"I have set your behavior down to your will."

"You may be right. Perhaps mother was always right about me too; she was against me."

She looked at me with a timidity and apprehension that made my heart bleed. "I think we might kiss each other *now*," she said.

I opened my arms, holding her against my breast so tightly that she drew back, but kissed my cheek gently, and took from her pocket a flaçon of salts, which she fastened to my belt by its little chain, and said again, "Go," but recalling me, said, "One thing more; I will never lose temper with you again."

The landing-stair was full of people. I locked the door, and took out the key; the stairs were crowded. All made way for me with a silent respect. Aunt Merce, when she saw me, put her hand on an empty chair, beside father, who sat by the coffin. Those passages in the Bible which contain the beautifully poetic images relating to the going of man to his long home were read, and to my ear they seemed to fall on the coffin in dull strife with its inmate, who mutely contradicted them. A discourse followed, which was calculated to harrow the feelings to the utmost. Arthur began to cry so nervously, that some considerate friend took him out, and Aunt Merce wept so violently that she grew faint, and caught hold of me. I gave her the flaçon of salts, which revived her; but I felt as father looked—stern, and anxious to escape the unprofitable trial.

As the coffin was taken out to the hearse, my heart twisted and palpitated, as if a command had been laid upon it to follow, and not leave her. But I was imprisoned in the cage of Life—the Keeper would not let me go; her he had let loose.

We were still obliged to sit an intolerable while, till all present had passed before her for the last time. When the hearse moved down the street, father, Arthur, and I were called, and assisted in our own chaise, as if we were helpless; the reins were put in father's hands, and the horse was led behind the hearse. At last the word was given, and the long procession began to move through the street, which was deserted. A cat ran out of a house, and scampered across the way; Arthur laughed, and father jumped nervously at the sound of his laugh.

The graveyard was a mile outside the village—a sandy plain where a few stunted pines transplanted from the woods near it struggled to keep alive. As we turned from the street into the lane which led to it, and rode up a little hill where the sand was so deep that it muffled the wheels and feet of the horses, the whole round of the gray sky was visible. It hung low over us. I wished it to drop and blot out the vague nothings under it. We left the carriage at the palings and walked up the narrow path, among the mounds, where every stone was marked "Morgeson." Some so old that they were stained with blotches of yellow moss, slanting backward and forward, in protest against the folly of indicating what was no longer beneath them. The mounds were covered with mats of scanty, tangled grass, with here and there a rank spot of green. I was tracing the shape of one of those green patches when I felt father's arm tremble. I shut my eyes, but could not close my ears to the sound of the spadeful of sand which fell on the coffin.

It was over. We must leave her to the creatures Veronica had seen. I looked upward, to discern the shadowy reflection behind the gray haze of cloud, where she might have paused a moment on her eternal journey to the eternal world of souls.

It was the custom, and father took his hat off to thank his friends for their sympathy and attention. His lips moved, but no words were audible.

The procession moved down the path again. Arthur's hand was in mine; he stamped his feet firmly on the sand, as if to break the oppressive silence which no one seemed disposed to disturb. The same ceremonies were performed in starting us homeward, by the same person, who let go the reins, and lifted his hat as we passed, as the final token of attention and respect.

The windows were open; a wind was blowing through the house, the furniture was set in order, the doors were thrown back, but not a soul was there when we went in. The duties of friendship and tradition had been fulfilled; the neighbors had gone home to their avocations. For the public, the tragedy was over; all speculation on the degree of our grief, or our indifference, was settled. We could take off our mourning garments and our mourning countenance, now that we were alone; or we could give way to that anguish we are afraid and ashamed to show, except before the One above human emotion.

CHAPTER XXXV.

Temperance stayed to the house-cleaning. It was lucky, she could not help saying, as house-cleaning must always be after a funeral, that it should have happened at the regular cleaning-time. She went back to her own house as soon as it was over. Father drove to Milford as usual; Arthur resumed his school, and Aunt Merce, who had at first busied herself in looking over her wardrobe, and selecting from it what she thought could be dyed, folded it away. She passed hours in mother's room, from which father had fled, crying over her Bible, looking in her boxes and drawers to feed her sorrow with the sight of the familiar things, alternating those periods with her old occupation of looking out of the windows. In regard to myself, and Veronica, she evinced a distress at the responsibility which, she feared, must rest upon her. Veronica, dark and silent, played such heart-piercing strains that father could not bear to hear her; so when she played, for he dared not ask her to desist, he went away. To me she had scarcely spoken since the funeral. She wore the same dress each day—one of black silk— and a small black mantle, pinned across her bosom. Soon the doors began to open and shut after their old fashion, and people came and went as of old on errands of begging or borrowing.

At the table we felt a sense of haste; instead of lingering, as was our wont, we separated soon, with an indifferent air, as if we were called by business, not sent away by sorrow. But if our eyes fell on a certain chair, empty against the wall, a cutting pang was felt, which was not at all concealed; for there were sudden breaks in our commonplace talk, which diverged into wandering channels, betraying the tension of feeling.

Many weeks passed, through which I endured an aching, aimless melancholy. My thoughts continually drifted through the vacuum in our atmosphere, and returned to impress me with a disbelief in the enjoyment, or necessity of keeping myself employed with the keys of an instrument, which, let me strike ever so cunningly, it was certain I could never obtain mastery over.

One day I went to walk by the shore, for the first time since my return. When I set my foot on the ground, the intolerable light of the brilliant day blazed through me; I was luminously dark, for it blinded me. Picking my way over the beach, left bare by the tide, with my eyes fixed downward till I could see, I reached the point between our house and the lighthouse and turned toward the sea, inhaling its cool freshness. I climbed out to a flat, low rock, on the point; it was dry in the sun, and the weeds hanging from its sides were black and crisp; I put my woolen shawl on it, and stretched myself along its edge. Little pools meshed from the sea by the numberless rocks round me engrossed my attention. How white and pellucid was the shallow near me—no shadow but the shadow of my face bending over it—nothing to ripple its surface, but my imperceptible breath! By and by a bunch of knotted wrack floated in from the outside and lodged in a crevice; a minute creature with fringed feet darted from it and swam across it. After the knotted wrack came the fragment of a green and silky substance, delicate enough to have been the remnant of a web, woven in the palace of Circe. "There must be a current," I thought, "which sends them here." And I watched the inlet for other waifs; but nothing more came. Eye-like bubbles rose from among the fronds of the knotted wrack, and, sailing on uncertain voyages, broke one by one and were wrecked to nothingness. The last vanished; the pool showed me the motionless shadow of my face again, on which I pondered, till I suddenly became aware of a slow, internal oscillation, which increased till I felt in a strange tumult. I put my hand in the pool and troubled its surface.

"Hail, Cassandra! Hail!"

I sprang up the highest rock on the point, and looked seaward, to catch a glimpse of the flying Spirit who had touched me. My soul was brought in poise and quickened with the beauty before me! The wide, shimmering plain of sea—its aerial blue, stretching beyond the limits of my vision in one direction, upbearing transverse, cloud-like islands in another, varied and shadowed by shore and sky—mingled its essence with mine.

The wind was coming; under the far horizon the mass of waters begun to undulate. Dark, spear-like clouds rose above it and menaced the east. The speedy wind tossed and teased the sea nearer and nearer, till I was surrounded by a gulf of milky green foam. As the tide rolled in I retreated, stepping back from rock to rock, round which the waves curled and hissed, baffled in their attempt to climb over me. I stopped on the verge of the tide-mark; the sea was seeking me and I must wait. It gave tongue as its lips touched my feet, roaring in the caves, falling on the level beaches with a mad, boundless joy!

"Have then at life!" my senses cried. "We will possess its longing silence, rifle its waiting beauty. We will rise up in its light and warmth, and cry, 'Come, for we wait.' Its roar, its beauty, its madness—we will have—*all*." I turned and walked swiftly homeward, treading the ridges of white sand, the black drifts of seaweed, as if they had been a smooth floor.

Aunt Merce was at the door.

"Now," she said, "we are going to have the long May storm. The gulls are flying round the lighthouse. How high the tide is! You must want your dinner. I wish you *would* see to Fanny; she is lording it over us all."

"Yes, yes, I will do it; you may depend on me. I will reign, and serve also."

"Oh, Cassandra, *can* you give up *yourself?*"

"I must, I suppose. Confound the spray; it is flying against the windows."

"Come in; your hair is wet, and your shawl is wringing. Now for a cold."

"I never shall have any more colds, Aunt Merce; never mean to have anything to myself—entirely, you know."

"You do me good, you dear girl; I love you"; and she began to cry. "There's nothing but cold ham and boiled rice for your dinner."

"What time is it?"

"Near three."

I opened the door of the dining-room; the table was laid, and I walked round it, on a tour of inspection.

"I thought you might as well have your dinner, all at once," said Fanny, by the window, with her feet tucked up on the rounds of her chair. "Here it is."

"I perceive. Who arranged it?"

"Me and Paddy Margaret."

"How many tablecloths have we?"

"Plenty. I thought as you didn't seem to care about any regular hour for dinner, and made us all wait, *I* needn't be particular; besides, I am not the waiter, you know."

She had set on the dishes used in the kitchen. I pulled off cloth and all—the dishes crashed, of course—and sat down on the floor, picking out the remains for my repast.

"What will Mr. Morgeson say?" she asked, turning very red.

"Shall you clear away this rubbish by the time he comes home?"

"Why, I must, mustn't I?"

"I hope so. Where's Veronica?"

"She has been gone since twelve; Sam carried her to Temperance's house."

I continued my meal. Fanny brought a chair for me, which I did not take. I scarcely tasted what I ate. A wall had risen up suddenly before me, which divided me from my dreams; I was inside it, on a prosaic domain I must henceforth be confined to. The unthought-of result of mother's death—disorganization, began to show itself. The individuality which had kept the weakness and faults of our family life in abeyance must have been powerful; and I had never recognized it! I attempted to analyze this influence, so strong, yet so invisibly produced. I thought of her mildness, her dreamy habits, her indifference, and her incapacity of comprehending natures unlike her own. Would endowment of character explain it—that faculty which we could not change, give, or take? Character was a mysterious and indestructible fact, and a fact that I had had little respect for. Upon what a false basis I had gone—a basis of extremes. I had seen men as trees walking; that was my experience.

"You'll choke yourself with that dry bread," exclaimed Fanny, really concerned at my abstraction.

"Where is my trunk? Did you unlock it?"

"I took from it what you needed at the time: but it is not unpacked, and it is in the upper hall closet."

She was picking up the broken delf meekly.

"Did you see a small bag I brought? And where's my satchel? Good heavens! What has made me put off that letter so? For I have thought of it, and yet I have kept it back."

"It is safe, in your closet, Miss Cassandra; and the box is there."

"Aunt Merce," I called, "will you have nothing to eat?"

She laughed hysterically, when she saw what I had done.

"Where is Hepsey, Aunt Merce?"

"She goes to bed after dinner, you know, for an hour or two."

"She must go from here."

"Oh!" they both chorused, "what for?"

"She is too old."

"She *has* money, and a good house," said Aunt Merce, "if she must go. I wonder how Mary stood it so long."

"Turn 'em off," said Fanny, "when they grow useless."

Aunt Merce reddened, and looked hurt.

"I shall keep *you;* look sharp now after your own disinterestedness."

I wanted to go to my room, as I thought it time to arrange my trunks and boxes; besides, I needed rest—the sad luxury of reaction. But word was brought to the house that Arthur had disappeared, in company with two boys notorious for mischief. His teacher was afraid they might have put out to sea in a crazy sailboat. We were in a state of alarm till dark, when father came home, bringing him, having found him on the way to Milford. Veronica had not returned. It stormed violently, and father was vexed because a horse must be sent through the storm for her. At last I obtained the asylum of my room, in an irritable frame of mind, convinced that such would be my condition each day. Composure came with putting my drawers and shelves in order. The box with Desmond's flowers I threw into the fire, without opening it, ribbon and all, for I could not endure the sight of them. I unfolded the dresses I had worn on the occasions of my meeting him; even the collars and ribbons I had adorned myself with were conned with jealous, greedy eyes; in looking at them all other remembrances connected with my visit vanished. The handkerchief scented with violets, which I found in the pocket of the dress I had worn when I met him at Mrs. Hepburn's, made me childish. I was holding it when Veronica entered, bringing with her an atmosphere of dampness.

"Violet! I like it. There is not one blooming yet, Temperance says. Why are they so late? There's only this pitiful snake-grass," holding up a bunch of drooping, pale blossoms.

"Oh, Verry, can you forgive me? I did not forget these, but I felt the strangest disinclination to look them up." And I gave her the jewel box and letter.

She seized them, and opened the box first.

"Child-Verry."

"I never was a child, you know; but I am always trying to find my childhood."

She took a necklace from the box, composed of a single string of small, beautiful pearls, from which hung an egg-shaped amethyst of pure violet. She fastened the necklace round her throat.

"It is as lucent as the moon," she said, looking down at the amethyst, which shed a watery light; "I wish you had given it to me before."

Breaking the seal of the letter, with a twist of her mouth at the coat-of-arms impressed upon it, she shook out the closely written pages, and saying, "There is a volume," began reading. "It is very good," she observed at the end of the first page, "a regular com-position," and went on with an air of increasing interest. "How does he look?" she asked, stopping again.

"As if he longed to see you."

Her eyes went in quest of him so far that I thought they must be startled by a sudden vision.

"How did you find his family?"

"Not like him much."

"I knew that; he would not have loved me so suddenly had I not been wholly unlike any woman he had known."

"His character is individual."

"I should know that from his influence upon you."

She looked at me wistfully, smoothed my hair with her cool hand, and resumed the letter.

"He thinks he will not come to Surrey with you; asks me to tell him my wishes," she repeated rapidly, translating from the origi-nal. "What do I think of our future? How shall we propose any change? Will Cassandra describe her visit? Will she tell me that he thinks of going abroad?"

She dropped the letter. "What pivot is he swinging on? What is he uncertain about?"

"There must be more to read."

She turned another page.

"If I go to Switzerland (I think of going on account of family affairs), when shall I return? My family, of course, expected me to marry in their pale; that is, my mother rather prefers to select a wife for me than that I should do it. But, as you shall never come to Belem, her plans or wishes need make no difference to us. If Cassandra would be to us what she might, how things would clear! Don't you think, my love, that there should be the greatest sympathy between sisters?"

I laughed.

Verry said she did not like his letter much after all. He evidently thought her incapable of understanding ordinary matters. It was well, though; it made their love idyllic.

"Let us speak of matters nearer home."

"Let us go to my room; the storm is so loud this side of the house."

"No; you must stay till the walls tremble. Have you seen, Verry, any work for me to do here?"

"Everything is changed. I have tried to be as steady as when mother was here, but I cannot; I whirl with a vague idea of liberty. Did she keep the family conscience? Now that she has gone I feel responsible no more."

"An idea of responsibility has come to me—what plain people call Duty."

"I do not feel it," she cried mournfully. "I must yield to you then. You can be good."

"I must act so; but help me, Verry; I have contrary desires."

"What do they find to feed on? What are they? Have you your evil spirit?"

"Yes; a devil named Temperament."

"Now teach me, Cassandra."

"Not I. Go, and write Ben. Make excuses for my negligence toward you about his letter. Tell him to come. I shall write Alice and Helen this evening. We have been shut off from the world by the gate of Death; but we must come back."

"One thing you may be sure of—though I shall be no help, I shall never annoy you. I know that my instincts are fine only in a self-centering direction; yours are different. I shall trust them. Since you have spoken, I perceive the shadows you have raised and must encounter. I retreat before them, admiring your discernment, and placing confidence in your powers. You convince if you do not win me. Who can guess how your every plan and hope of well-doing may be thwarted? I need say no more?"

"Nothing more."

She left the room. There would be no antagonism between us; but there would be pain—on one side. The distance which had kept us apart was shortened, but not annihilated. What could I expect? The silent and serene currents which flow from souls like Veronica's and Ben's, whose genius is not of the heart, refuse to enter a nature so turbulent as mine. But my destiny must be changed by such! It was taken for granted that my own spirit should not rule me. And with what reward? Any, but that of sympathy. But I muttered:

> " 'I dimly see
> My far-off doubtful purpose, as a mother
> Conjectures of the features of her child
> Ere it is born.' "[55]

The house trembled in the fury of the storm. The waves were hoarse with their vain bawling, and the wind shrieked at every crevice of chimney, door, and window. No answering excitement in me now! I had grown older.

CHAPTER XXXVI.

A few days after, I went to Milford with father, to make some purchases. I sought a way to speak to him about the future, intending also to go on with various remarks; but it seemed difficult to begin. Observing him, as he contemplated the road before us, grave and abstracted, I recollected the difference between his age and mother's, and wondered at my blindness, while I compared the old man of my childhood, who existed for the express purpose of making money for the support and pleasure of his family, and to accommodate all its whims, with the man before me,—barely forty-eight, without a wrinkle in his firm, ruddy face, and only an occasional white hair, in ambuscade among his fair, curly locks. My exclusive right over him I felt doubtful about. I gave my attention to the road also, and remarked that I thought the season was late.

"Yes. Why didn't Somers come home with you?"

"I hardly know. The matter of the marriage was not settled, nor a plan of spending a summer abroad."

"Will it suit him to vegetate in Surrey? Veronica will not leave home."

"He has no ambition."

"It is a curse to inherit money in this country. Mr. Somers writes that Ben will have three thousand a year; but that the disposal, at present, is not in his power."

I explained as well as I could the Pickersgill property.

"I see how it is. The children are waiting for the principal, and have exacted the income; and their lives have been warped for this reason. Ben has not begun life yet. But I like Somers exceedingly."

"He is the best of them, his mother the worst."

"Did you have a passage?"

"She attempted."

"I can give Veronica nothing beyond new clothes or furniture; whatever she likes that way. To draw money from my business is impossible. My business fluctuates like quicksilver, and it is enormously extended. If they should have two thousand a year, it would be a princely income; I should feel so now, if they had it clear of incumbrance."

"Do you mean to say that your income does not amount to so much?"

"My outgoes and incomes have for a long time been involved with each other. I do not separate them. I have never lived extravagantly. My luxury has been in doing too much."

A cold feeling came over me.

"By the way, Mr. Somers pays you compliments in his note. How old are you? I forget." He surveyed me with a doubtful look. "Are you thin, or what is it?"

"East wind, I guess. I am twenty-five."

"And Veronica?"

"Over twenty."

"She must be married. I hope she will cut her practical eye-teeth then, for Somers's sake,"

"He does not require a practically minded woman."

"What do men require!"

"They require the souls and bodies of women, without having the trouble of knowing the difference between the one and other."

"So bad as that? Whoa!"

He stopped to pay toll, and the conversation stopped.

On the way home, however, I found a place to begin my proposed talk, and burst out with, "I think Hepsey should leave us."

"What ails Hepsey?"

"She is so old, and is such a poke."

"You must tell her yourself to go. She has money enough to be comfortable; I have some of it, as well as that of half the widows, old maids, and sailors' wives in Surrey, being better than the Milford banks, they think."

I felt another cold twinge.

"What! are our servants your creditors?"

"Servants—don't say that," he said harshly; "we do not have these distinctions here."

"It costs you more than two thousand a year."

"How do you know?"

"Think of the hired people—the horses, the cows, pigs, hens, garden, fields—all costing more than they yield."

"What has come over you? Did you ever think of money before? Tell me, have you ever been in our cellar?"

"Yes, to look at the kittens."

"In the store-room?"

"For apples and sweetmeats."

"Look into these matters, if you like; they never troubled your mother, at least I never knew that they did; but don't make your reforms tiresome."

What encouragement!

In the yard we saw Fanny contemplating a brood of hens, which were picking up corn before her. "Take Fanny for a coadjutor; she is eighteen, and a bright girl." She sprang to the chaise, and caught the reins, which he threw into her hands, unbuckled the girth, and, before I was out of sight, was leading the horse to water.

"We might economize in the way of a stable-boy," I said.

"Pooh! you are not indulgent. Here," whistling to Fanny, "let Sam do that." She pouted her lips at him, and he laughed.

Aunt Merce gave me a letter the moment I entered. "It is in Alice's hand; sit down and read it."

She took her handkerchief and a bit of flagroot from her pocket, to be ready for the sympathetic flow which she expected. But the letter was short. She had seen, it said, the announcement of mother's death in a newspaper at the time. She knew what a change it had made. We might be sure that we should never find our old level, however happy and forgetful we might grow. She bore us all in mind but sent no message, except to Aunt Merce; she must come to Rosville before summer was over. And could she assist me by taking Arthur for a while? Edward was a quiet, companionable lad, and Arthur would be safe with him at home and at school.

"I wish you would go, Aunt Merce."

"Yes, why not, Mercy?" asked father. "Would it be a good thing for Arthur, Cassandra? You know what Surrey is for a boy."

"I know what Rosville was for a girl," I thought. It was an excellent plan for Arthur; but a feeling of repulsion at the idea of his going kept me silent.

"Is it a good idea?" he repeated.

"Yes, yes, father; send him by all means."

Aunt Merce sighed. "If he goes, I must go; I can be the receptacle for his griefs and trials for a while at least, and be a little useful that way. You know, Locke, I am but a poor creature."

"I was not aware of that fact, and am astonished to hear you say so, Mercy, when you know how far back I can remember. Mary shines all along those years, and you with her."

"Locke, you are the kindest man in the world."

"He feels fifty years younger than she appears to him," I thought; but I thanked him for his consideration for her.

"Veronica has had a letter to-day from Mr. Somers. What did you buy in Milford?"

"Mr. Morgeson," Fanny called, "Bumpus, the horse-jockey, is in the yard. He says Bill is spavined. I think he lies; he wants to trade."

He went out with her.

"Aunt Merce, let us be more together. What do you think of spending our evenings in the parlor?"

"Do you expect to break up our habits?"

"I would if I could."

"Try Veronica."

"I have."

"Will she give up solitude?"

"Bring your knitting to the parlor and see."

Veronica came in to tell me that Ben was coming in a week.

"Glad of it."

"Sends love to you."

"Obliged."

"Calls me 'poor girl'; speaks beautifully of his remembrance of mother, and—"

"What?"

"Tells me to rely on your faithful soul; to trust in the reasonable hope of our remaining together; to try to establish an equality of tastes and habits between us. He tells me what I never knew,— that I need you—that we need each other."

"Is that all?"

"There is more for *me.*"

I left her. Closing the door of my room gently, I thought: "Ben is a good man; but for all that, I feel like blind Sampson just now. Could I lay my hands on the pillars which supported the temple he has built, I would wrench them from their foundation and surprise him by toppling the roof on his head."

His arrival was delayed for a few days. When he came Surrey looked its best, for it was June; and though the winds were chilly, the grass was grown and the orchard leaves were crowding off the blossoms. The woods were vividly green. The fauns were playing there, and the sirens sang under the sea. But I had other thoughts; the fauns and sirens were not for me, perplexed as I was with household cares. Hepsey proposed staying another year, but I was firm; and she went, begging Fanny to go with her and be as a daughter. She declined; but the proposition influenced her to be troublesome to me. She told me she was of age now, and that no person had a right to control her. At present she was useful where she was, and might remain.

"Will you have wages?" I asked her.

"That is Mr. Morgeson's business."

My anger would have pleased her, so I concealed it.

"Your ability, Fanny, is better than your disposition. Me,—you do not suit at all; but it is certain that father depends on you for his small comforts, and Veronica likes you. I wish you would stay."

She placed her arms akimbo.

"I should like to find you out, exactly. I can't. I never could find out your mother; all the rest of you are as clear as daylight." And she snapped her fingers as if 'the rest' were between them.

"You lack faith."

"You believe that this is a beautiful world, don't you? I hate it. I should think *you* had reason, too, for hating it. Pray what have you got?"

"An ungrateful imp that was bequeathed to me."

She saw father in the garden beckoning me. "He wants you. I do *not* hate the world always," she added, with her eyes fixed on him.

I was disposed to trouble the still waters of our domestic life with theories. Our ways were too mechanical. The old-fashioned asceticism which considered air, sleep, food, as mere necessities was stupid. But I had no assistance; Veronica thought that her share of my plans must consist of a diligent notice of all that I did, which she gave, and then went to her own life, kept sacredly apart. Fanny laughed in her sleeve and took another side—the practical, and shone in it, becoming in fact the true manager and worker, while I played. Aunt Merce was helpless. She neglected her former cares; and father was, what he always had been at home,—heedless and indifferent.

One morning we stood on the landing stair—Ben, Veronica, and myself—looking from the window. A silver mist so thinly wrapped the orchard that the wet, shining leaves thrust themselves through in patches. Birds were singing beneath, feeling the warmth of the sun, scarcely hid. The young leaves and blossoms steeping in the mist sent up a delicious odor.

"I like Surrey better and better," he said; "the atmosphere suits me."

"Oh, I am glad," answered Verry. "I could never go away. It is not beautiful, I know; in fact, it is meager when it comes to be talked of; but there are suggestions here which occasionally stimulate me."

"Verry, can you keep people away from me when I live here?"

"I do not like that feeling in you."

"I like fishermen."

"And a boat?"

"Yes, I'll have a boat."

"I shall never go out with you."

"Cass will. I shall cruise with her, and you, in your house, need not see us depart. Eric the Red made excursions in this region. We will skirt the shores, which are the same, nearly, as when he sailed from them, with his Northmen; and the ancient barnacles will think, when they see her fair hair, which she will let ripple around her stately shoulders, that he has come back with his bride."

Verry looked with delight at him and then at me. "Her long, yellow hair and her stately shoulders," she repeated.

"Will you go?" he asked.

"Of course," I answered, going downstairs. I happened to look back on the way. His arm was round Verry, but he was looking after me. He withdrew it as our eyes met, and came down; but she remained, looking from the window. We went into the parlor, and I shut the door.

"Now then," I said.

He took a note from his pocket and gave it to me.

I broke its seal, and read: "Tell Ben, before you can reflect upon it, that *I* will go abroad, and then repent of it,—as I shall. Desmond."

" 'Tell Ben,' " I repeated aloud, " 'that *I* will go abroad. Desmond.' "

"Do you guess, as he does, that my reason for going was that I might be kept aloof from all sight and sound of you and him? In the result toward which I saw *you* drive I could have no part."

"Stay; I know that he will go."

"You do not know. Nor do you know what such a man is when—" checking himself.

"He is in love?"

"If you choose to call it that."

"I do."

All there was to say should be said now; but I felt more agitated than was my wont. These feelings, not according with my house-wifely condition, upset me. I looked at him; he began to walk about, taking up a book, which he leaned his head over, and whose covers he bent back till they cracked.

"You would read me that way," I said.

"It is rather your way of reading."

"Can you remember that Desmond and I influence each other to act alike? And that we comprehend each other without collision? I love him, as a mature woman may love,—once, Ben, only once; the fire-tipped arrows rarely pierce soul and sense, blood and brain."

He made a gesture, expressive of contempt.

"Men are different; he is different."

"You have already spoken for me, and, I suppose, you will for him."

"I venture to. Desmond is a violent, tyrannical, sensual man; his perceptions are his pulses. That he is handsome, clever, reso-lute, and sings well, I can admit; but no more."

"We will not bandy his merits or his demerits between us. Let us observe him. And now, tell me,—what am I?"

"You have been my delight and misery ever since I knew you. I saw you first, so impetuous, yet self-contained! Incapable of insin-cerity, devoid of affection and courageously naturally beautiful. Then, to my amazement, I saw that, unlike most women, you understood your instincts; that you dared to define them, and were impious enough to follow them. You debased my ideal, you con-fused me, also, for I could never affirm that you were wrong; forcing me to consult abstractions, they gave a verdict in your favor, which almost unsexed you in my estimation. I must own that the man who is willing to marry you has more courage than I have. Is it strange that when I found your counterpart, Veronica, that I yielded? Her delicate, pure, ignorant soul suggests to me eternal repose."

"It is not necessary that you should fatigue your mind with abstractions concerning her. It will be the literal you will hunger for, dear Ben."

"Damn it! the world has got a twist in it, and we all go round with it, devilishly awry."

I said no more. He had defined my limits, he would, as far as possible, control me without pity or compassion, thinking, probably, that I needed none; the powers he had always given me credit for must be sufficing. I could not comprehend him. How was it that he and Verry gave me such horrible pain? Was it exceptional? Could I claim nothing from women? Had they thought me an anomaly?—while I thought it was Veronica who was called peculiar and original? The end of it all must be for me to assimilate with their happiness!

"Well?" he said.

"Thank you."

Then Veronica came, swinging her bonnet. "The *Sagamore* has arrived, and I am going to stand on the wharf to count the sailors, and learn if they have all come home. Will you go, Ben?"

He complied, and I was left alone.

CHAPTER XXXVII.

When Ben left Surrey, I sent no message or letter by him, and he asked for none. But at once I wrote to Desmond, and did not finish my letter till after midnight. Intoxicated with the liberty my pen offered me, I roamed over a wide field of paper. The next morning I burnt it. But there was something to be said to him before his departure, and again I wrote. I might have condensed still more. In this way—

VESTIGIA RETRORSUM.[56]

CHARLES MORGESON.

When the answer came I reflected before I read it, that it might be the last link of the chain between us. Not a bright one at the best, nor garlanded with flowers, nor was it metal, silver, or gold. There was rust on it, it was corroded, for it was forged out of his and my substance.

I read it: "I am yours, as I have been, since the night I asked you 'How came those scars?' Did you guess that I read your story? I go from you with one idea; I love you, and I *must* go. Brave woman! you have shamed me to death almost."

He sent me a watch. I was to wear it from the second of July. It was small and plain, but there were a few words scratched inside the case with the point of a knife, which I read every day. Veronica's eye fell on it the first time I put it on.

"What time is it?"

"Near one."

"I thought, from the look of it, that it might be near two."

"Don't mar my ideal of you, Verry, by growing witty."

She shrugged her shoulders. "I guess you found it washed ashore, among the rocks; was it bruised?"

"A man gave it to me."

"A merman, who fills the sea-halls with a voice of power?"

"May be."

"Tut, Ben gave it to you. It is a kind of housekeepish present; did he add scissors and needle-case?"

"What if the merman should take me some day to the 'pale sea-groves straight and high?' "[57]

"You must never, never go. You cannot leave me, Cass!" She grasped my sleeve, and pulled me round. "How much was there for you to do in the life before us, which you talked about?"

"I remember. There is much, to be sure."

Fanny's quick eye caught the glitter of the watch. The mystery teased her, but she said nothing.

Aunt Merce had gone to Rosville with Arthur. There was no visitor with us; there had been none beside Ben since mother died. All seemed kept at bay. I wrote to Helen to come and pass the summer, but her child was too young for such a journey, she concluded. Ben had sailed for Switzerland. The summer, whose biography like an insignificant life must be written in a few words, was a long one to live through. It happened to be a dry season, which was unfrequent on our coast. Days rolled by without the variation of wind, rain, or hazy weather. The sky was an opaque blue till noon, when solid white clouds rose in the north, and sailed seaward, or barred the sunset, which turned them crimson and black. The mown fields grew yellow under the stare of the brassy sun, and the leaves cracked and curled for the want of moisture. It was dull in the village, no ships were building, none sailed, none arrived. But father was more absorbed than ever, more away from home. He wrote often in the evening, and pored over ledgers with his bookkeeper. Late at night I found him sorting and reading papers. He forgot us. But Fanny, as he grew forgetful, improved as housekeeper. Her energy was untiring; she waited so much on him that I grew forgetful of him. Veronica was the same as before;

her room was pleasant with color and perfume, the same delicate
pains with her dress each day was taken. She looked as fair as a
lily, as serene as the lake on which it floats, except when Fanny
tried her. With me she never lost temper. But I saw little of her;
she was as fixed in her individual pursuits as ever.

There were intervals now when all my grief for mother returned, and I sat in my darkened chamber, recalling with a sad
persistence her gestures, her motions, the tones of her voice, through
all the past back to my first remembrance. The places she inhabited, her opinions and her actions I commented on with a minute-
ness that allowed no detail to escape. When my thoughts turned
from her, it seemed as if she were newly lost in the vast and
wandering Universe of the Dead, whence I had brought her.

In September a letter came from Ben, which promised a return
by the last of October. With the ruffling autumnal breezes my
stagnation vanished, and I began my shore life again in a mood
which made memory like hope; but staying out too late one evening,
I came home in a chill. From the chill I went to a fever, which
lasted some days. Veronica came every day to see me, and groaned
over my hair, which fell off, but she could not stay long, the smell
of medicine made her ill, the dark room gave her an uneasiness;
besides, she did not know what she should say. I sent her away
always. Fanny took care of me till I was able to move about the
room, then she absented herself most of the time. One afternoon
Veronica came to tell me that Margaret, the Irish girl, was going;
she supposed that Fanny was insufferable, and that she could not
stay.

"I must be well by to-morrow," I said.

The next day I went down stairs, and was greeted with the
epithet of "Scarecrow."

"Do you feel pretty strong?" asked Fanny, with a peculiar accent, when we happened to be alone.

"What is the matter? Out with it!"

"Something's going to turn up here; something ails Mr. Morgeson."

I guessed his ailment.

"He is going to fail, he is smashed all to nothing. He knows
what will be said about him, yet he goes about with perfect calm-
ness. But he feels it. I tried him this morning, I gave him tea
instead of coffee, and he didn't know it!"

"Margaret's gone?"

"There must be rumors; for she asked him for her wages a day or two ago. He paid her, and said she had better go."

I examined my hands involuntarily. She tittered.

"How easily you will wash the long-necked glasses and pitchers, with your slim hand!"

I dropped into a mental calculation, respecting the cost of an entire change of wardrobe suitable to our reduced circumstances, and speculated on a neat cottage-style of cookery.

"I think I must go, too," she said with cunning eyes.

"How can you bear to, when there will be so much trouble for you to enjoy?"

"How tired you look, Cass," said Veronica, slipping in quietly. "What are you talking about? Has Fanny been tormenting you?"

"Of course," she answered. "But if am not mistaken, you will be tormented by others besides me."

"Go out!" said Veronica. "Leave us, pale pest."

"You may want me here yet."

"What does she mean, Cass?"

I hesitated.

"Tell me," she said, in her imperative, gentle voice. "What is there that I cannot know?"

"Now she is what you call high-toned, isn't it?" inquired Fanny.

Veronica threw her book at her.

"The truth is, ladies, that your father, the principal man in Surrey, is not worth a dollar. What do you think of it? And now will you come off the high horse?" And Fanny drummed on the table energetically.

"Did you really think of going, Fanny?" asked Veronica. "You will stay, and do better than ever, for if you attempt to go, I shall bring you back."

This was the invitation she wanted, and was satisfied with.

"I must give up flowers," said Veronica, "of course."

"I wonder if we shall keep pigs this fall?" said Fanny. "Must we sit in the free seats in the meeting-house? It will be fine for the boys to drop paper balls on our heads from the gallery. I'd like to see them do it, though," she concluded, as if she felt that such an insult would infringe upon her rights.

CHAPTER XXXVIII.

It was true. Locke Morgeson had been insolvent for five years. All this time he had thrown ballast out from every side in the shape of various ventures, which he trusted would lighten the ship, that, nevertheless, drove steadily on to ruin. Then he steered blindly, straining his credit to the utmost; and then—the crash. His losses were so extended and gradual that the public were not aware of his condition till he announced it. There was a general exasperation against him. The Morgeson family rose up with one accord to represent the public mind, which drove Veronica wild.

"Have you acted wrongly, father?" she asked.

"I have confessed, Verry, will that suit you!"

Our house was thronged for several days. "Pay us," cried the female portion of his creditors. In vain father represented that he was still young—that his business days were not over—that they must wait, for paid they should be. "Pay us now, for we are women," they still cried. Fanny opened the doors for these persons as wide as possible when they came, and shut them with a bang when they went, astonishing them with a satirical politeness, or confounding them with an impertinent silence. The important creditors held meetings to agree what should be done, and effected an arrangement by which his property was left in his hands for three years, to arrange for the benefit of his creditors. The arrangement proved that his integrity was not suspected; but it was an ingenious punishment, that he should keep in sight, improve, or change, for others, what had been his own. I was glad when he decided to sell his real estate and personal property, and trust to the ships alone, but would build no more. I begged him to keep our house till Ben should return. He consented to wait; but I did not tell Verry what I had done. All the houses he owned, lots, carriages, horses, domestic stock, the fields lying round our house— were sold. When he began to sell, the fury of retrenchment seized him, and he laid out a life of self-denial for us three. Arthur's ten thousand dollars were safe, who was therefore provided for. He would bring wood and water for us; the rest we must do, with Fanny's help. We could dine in the kitchen, and put our beds in one room; by shutting up the house in part, we should have less labor to perform. We attempted to carry out his ideas, but Veronica was so dreadfully in Fanny's way and mine, that we were obliged to entreat her to resume her old rôle. As for Fanny, she was happy—working like a beaver day and night. Father was much at home, and took an extraordinary interest in the small details that Fanny carried out.

When Temperance heard of these arrangements, she came down with Abram in their green and yellow wagon. Temperance drove the shaggy old white horse, for Abram was intrusted with the care of a meal bag, in which were fastened a cock and four hens. We should see, she said when she let them out, whether we were to keep hens or not. Was Veronica to go without new-laid eggs? Had he sold the cat, she sarcastically inquired of father.

"Who is going to do your washing, girls?" she asked, taking off her bonnet.

"We all do it."

"Now I shall die a-laughing!" But she contradicted herself by crying heartily. "One day in every week, I tell *you,* I am coming; and Fanny and I can do the washing in a jiffy."

"Sure," said Abram, "you can; the sass is in."

"Sass or no sass, I'm coming."

She made me laugh for the first time in a month. I was too tired generally to be merry, with my endeavors to carry out father's wishes, and keep up the old aspect of the house. When she left us we all felt more cheerful. Aunt Merce wanted to come home, but Verry and I thought she had better stay at Rosville. We could not deny it to ourselves, that home was sadly altered, or that we were melancholy; and though we never needed her more, we begged her not to come. Happily father's zeal soon died away. A boy was hired, and as there was no out-of-doors work for him to do, he relieved Fanny, who in her turn relieved me. Finding time to look into myself, I perceived a change in my estimation of father; a vague impression of weakness in him troubled me. I also discovered that I had lost my atmosphere. My life was coarse, hard, colorless! I lived in an insignificant country village; I was poor. My theories had failed; my practice was like my moods—variable. But I concluded that if *to-day* would go on without bestowing upon me sharp pains, depriving me of sleep, mutilating me with an accident, or sending a disaster to those belonging to me, I would be content. Arthur held out a hope, by writing me, that he meant to support me handsomely. He wished me to send him some shirt studs; and told me to keep the red horse. He had heard that I was very handsome when I was in Rosville. A girl had asked him how

I looked now. When he told her I was handsomer than any woman Rosville could boast of, she laughed.

October had gone, and we had not heard from Ben. Veronica came to my room of nights, and listened to wind and sea, as she never had before. Sometimes she was there long after I had gone to bed, to look out of the windows. If it was calm, she went away quietly; if the sea was rough, she was sorrowful, but said nothing. The lethargic summer had given way to a boisterous autumn of cold, gray weather, driving rains, and hollow gales. At last he came—to Veronica first. He gave a deep breath of delight when he stood again on the hearth-rug, before our now unwonted parlor fire. The sight of his ruddy face, vigorous form, and gay voice made me as merry as the attendants of a feast are when they inhale the odor of the viands they carry, hear the gurgle of the wine they pour, and echo the laughter of the guests.

There was much to tell that astonished him, but he could not be depressed; everything must be arranged to suit us. He would buy the house, provided he could pay for it in instalments. Did I know that his mother had docked his allowance as soon as she knew that he would marry Verry?

"How should I know it?"

I had not heard then that Desmond's was doubled, when she heard his intention of going to Spain.

"How should I know that?"

One thing I should learn, however—and that was, that Desmond had begged his mother to make no change in the disposition of her income. He had declined the extra allowance, and then accepted it, to offer him—Ben. Was not that astonishing?

"Did you take it?"

"No; but pa did."

All he could call his was fifteen hundred a year. Was that enough for them to live on, and pay a little every year for the house? Could we all live there together, just the same? Would we, he asked father, and allow him to be an inmate?

Father shook hands with him so violently that he winced; and Verry crumpled up a handful of his tawny locks and kissed them, whereat he said: "Are you grown a human woman?"

About the wedding? He could only stay to appoint a time, for he must post to Belem. It must be very soon.

"In a year or two," said Verry.

"Verry!"

"In three weeks, then."

"From to-day?"

"No, that will be the date of the wreck of the *Locke Morgeson;* but three weeks from to-morrow. Must we have anybody here, Ben?"

"Helen, and Alice, Cassandra?"

"Certainly."

"I have no friends," said Verry.

"What will you wear, Verry?" I asked.

"Why, this dress," designating her old black silk. Her eyes filled with tears, and went on a pilgrimage toward the unknown heaven where our mother was. *She* could only come to the wedding as a ghost. I imagined her flitting through the empty spaces, from room to room, scared and troubled by the pressure of mortal life around her.

"I shall not wear white," Verry said hastily.

The very day Ben went to Belem one of father's outstanding ships arrived. She came into the harbor presenting the unusual sight of trying oil on deck. Black and greasy from hull to spar, she was a pleasant sight, for she was full of sperm oil. Little boys ran down to the house to inform us of that fact before she was moored. "Wouldn't Mr. Morgeson be all right now that his luck had changed?" they asked.

At supper father said "By George!" several times, by that oath resuming something of his old self. "Those women can now be paid," he said. "If I could have held out till now, I could have gone on without failing. This is the first good voyage the *Oswego* ever made me; if another ship, the *Adamant,* will come full while oil is high, I shall arrange matters with my creditors before the three years are up. To hold my own again—ah! I never will venture all upon the uncertain field of the sea."

The *Oswego's* captain sent us a box of shells next day, and a small Portuguese boy, named Manuel—a handsome, black-eyed, husky-voiced fellow, in a red shirt, which was bound round his waist with a leather belt, from which hung a sailor's sheath-knife.

"He is volcanic," said Verry.

"The Portuguese are all handsome," said Fanny, poking him, to see if he would notice it. But he did not remove his eyes from Veronica.

"He shall be your page, Verry."

The next night a message came to us that Abram was dying. If we ever meant to come, Temperance sent word, some of us might come now; but she would rather have Mr. Morgeson. Fanny insisted upon going with him to carry a lantern. Manuel offered her his knife, when he comprehended that she was going through a dark road.

"You are a perfect heathen. There's nothing to be afraid of, except that Mr. Morgeson may walk into a ditch; will a knife keep us out of that?"

"Knife is good—it kills," he said, showing his white, vegetable-ivory teeth.

Verry and I sat up till they returned, at two in the morning. Abram had died about midnight, distressed to the last with worldly cares. "He asked," said father, "if I remembered his poor boy, whose chest never came home, and wished to hear some one read a hymn; Temperance broke down when I read it, while Fanny cried hysterically."

"I was freezing cold," she answered haughtily.

In the morning Verry and I started for Temperance's house; but she waited on the doorstep till I had inquired whether we were wanted. I called her in, for Temperance asked for her as soon as she saw me.

"He was a good man, girls," she said with emphasis.

"Indeed he was."

"A little mean, I spose."

I put in a demurrer; her face cleared instantly.

"He thought a great deal of your folks."

"And a great deal of you."

"Oh, what a loss I have met with! He had just bought a first-rate overcoat."

"But Temperance," said Verry, with a lamentable candor, "you can come back now."

"Can't you wait for him to be put into the ground?" And she tried to look shocked, but failed.

A friend entered with a doleful face, and Temperance groaned slightly.

"It is all done complete now, Mis Handy. He looks as easy as if he slept, he was *so* limber."

"Yes, yes," answered Temperance, starting up, and hurrying us out of the room, pinching me, with a significant look at Verry. She was afraid that her feelings might be distressed. "The funeral

will be day after to-morrow. Don't come; your father will be all
that must be here of the family. I shall shut up the house and come
straight to you. I know that I am needed; but you mustn't say a
word about pay—I can't stand it, I have had too much affliction to
be pestered about wages."

Verry hugged her, and Temperance shed the honestest tears of
the day then, she was so gratified at Verry's fondness. Before
Abram had been buried a week, she was back again—a fixture,
although she declared that she had only come for a spell, as we
might know by the size of the bundle she had, showing us one,
tied in a blue cotton handkerchief. What should she stay from her
own house for, when as good a man as ever lived left it to her? We
knew that she merely comforted a tender conscience by praising
the departed, for whom she had small respect when living. We felt
her brightening influence, but Fanny sulked, feeling dethroned.

Ben Pickersgill Somers and Veronica Morgeson were "published." Contrary to the usual custom, Verry went to hear her
own banns read at the church. She must do all she could, she told
me, to realize that she was to be married; had I any thoughts about
it, with which I might aid her? She thought it strange that people
should marry, and could not decide whether it was the sublimest
or the most inglorious act of one's life. I begged her to think about
what she would wear—the time was passing. Father gave me so
small a sum for the occasion, I had little opportunity for the splendid; but I purchased what Veronica wanted for a dress, and super-
intended the making of it—black lace over lavender-colored silk.
She said no more about it; but I observed that she put in order all
her possessions, as if she were going to undertake a long and
uncertain journey. Every box and drawer was arranged. All her
clothes were repaired, refolded, and laid away; every article was
refreshed by a turn or shake-up. She made her room a miracle of
cleanliness. What she called rubbish she destroyed—her old papers,
things with chipped edges, or those that were defaced by wear.
She went once to Milford in the time, and bought a purple Angola
rug, which she put before her arm-chair, and two small silver
cups, with covers; in one was a perfume which Ben liked, the
other was empty. Her favorite blank-books were laid on a shelf,
and the table, with its inkstand and portfolio, was pushed against
the wall. The last ornament which she added to her room was a
beautifully woven mat of evergreens, with which she concealed
the picture of the avenue and the nameless man. After it was done,

she inhabited my room, appearing to feel at home, and glad to have me with her. As the time drew near, she grew silent, and did not play at all. Temperance watched her with anxiety. "If ever she can have one of those nervous spells again she will have one now," she said. "Don't let her dream. I am turning myself inside out to keep up her appetite."

"Do you ever feel worried about *me,* Tempy?"

"Lord 'a marcy! you great, strong thing, why should I? May be you do want a little praise. I never saw anybody get along as well as you do, nowadays; you have altered very much; I never would have believed it."

"What *was* the trouble with me?"

"*I* always stuck up for you, gracious knows. Do you know what has been said of you in Surrey?"

"No."

"Then I shan't tell you; if I were you, though, I shouldn't trouble myself to be overpolite to the folks who have come and gone here, nigh on to twenty years,—hang 'em!"

A few days before the wedding Aunt Merce and Arthur came home. Arthur was shy at first regarding the great change, but being agreeably disappointed, grew lively. I perceived that Aunt Merce had aged since mother's death; her manner was changed; the same objects no longer possessed an interest. She looked at me penitentially. "I wish I could say," she said, "what I used to say to you,—that you were 'possessed.' Now that there is no occasion for me to comprehend people, I begin to. My education began wrong end foremost. I think Mary's death has taught me something. Do you think of her? She was the love of my life."

"Women do keep stupid a long time; but I think they are capable of growth, beyond the period when men cease to grow or change."

"Oh, I don't know anything about men, you know."

Temperance and I cleaned the house, opened every room, and made every fire-place ready for a fire—a fire being the chief luxury which I could command. Baking went on up to within a day of the wedding, under Hepsey's supervision, who had been summoned as a helper; Fanny was busy everywhere.

"Mr. Morgeson," said Temperance, "the furniture is too darned shabby for a wedding."

"It is not mine, you must remember."

"Plague take the creditors! they know as well as I that you turned Surrey from a herring-weir into a whaling-port, and that the houses they live in were built out of the wages you gave them. I am thankful that most of them have water in their cellars."

CHAPTER XXXIX.

The day came. Alice Morgeson, and Helen with her baby, arrived the night before; and Ben and Mr. Somers drove from Milford early in the afternoon. Mr. Somers was affable and patronizing. When introduced to Veronica, he betrayed astonishment. "She is not like you, Cassandra. Are you in delicate health, my dear!" addressing her.

"I have a peculiar constitution, I believe."

He made excuses to her for Mrs. Somers and his daughters to which she answered not a word. He was in danger of being embarrassed, and I enticed him away from her—not before she whispered gravely, "Why did *he* come?" I went over the house with him, he remarking on its situation, for sun and shade, and protection from, or exposure to, the winds; and tasting the water, pronounced it excellent. He thought I had a true idea of hospitality; the fires everywhere proclaimed that. Temperance had the air of a retainer; there was an atmosphere about our premises which placed them at a distance from the present. Then Alice came to my assistance and entertained him so well that I could leave him.

We had invited a few friends and relations to witness the ceremony, at eight o'clock. I had been consulted so often on various matters that it was dark before I finished my tasks. The last was to arrange some flowers I had ordered in Milford. I kept a bunch of them in reserve for Verry's plate; for we were to have a supper, at father's request, who thought it would be less tiresome to feed the guests than to talk to them. Verry did not know this, though she had asked several times why we were so busy.

It was near seven when I went upstairs to find her. Temperance had sent Manuel and Fanny to the different rooms with tea, bread and butter, and the message that it was all we were to have at present. Ben had been extremely silent since his arrival, and disposed to reading. I looked over his shoulder once, and saw that it was "Scott's Life of Napoleon" he perused; and an hour after, being obliged to ask him a question, saw him still at the same page. He was now dressing probably. Helen and Alice were in their rooms. Mr. Somers was napping on the parlor sofa; father was meditating at his old post in the dining-room and smoking. It was a familiar picture; but there was a rent in the canvas and a figure was missing—she who had been its light!

I found Verry sound asleep on the sofa in my room.

A glass full of milk was on the floor beside her, and a plate with a slice of bread. The lamp had been lighted by some one, and carefully shaded from her face. She had been restless, I thought, for her hair had fallen out of the comb and half covered her face, which was like marble in its whiteness and repose. Her right arm was extended; I took her hand, and her warm, humid fingers closed over mine.

"Wake up, Verry; it is time to be married."

She opened her eyes without stirring and fixed them upon me. "Do you know any man who is like Ben? Or was it he whom I have just left in the dark world of sleep?"

"I know his brother, who is like him, but dark in complexion—and his hair is black."

"His hair is not black."

I rushed out of the room, muttering some excuse, came back and arranged her toilette; but she remained with her arm still extended, and continued:

"It was a strange place where we met; curious, dusty old trees grew about it. He was cutting the back of one with a dagger, and the pieces he carved out fell to the ground, as if they were elastic. He made me pick them up, though I wished to listen to a man who was lying under one of the trees, wrapped in a cloak, keeping time with *his* dagger, and singing a wild air.

" 'What do you see?' said the first.

" 'A letter on every piece,' I answered, and spelt Cassandra. 'Are you Ben transformed?' I asked, for he had his features, his air, thought he was a swarthy, spare man, with black, curly hair, dashed with gray; but he pricked my arm with his dagger, and said, 'Go on.' I picked up the rest, and spelt 'Somers.'

" 'Cassandra Somers! now tell her,' he whispered, turning me gently from him, with a hand precisely like Ben's."

"No, it is handsomer," I muttered.

"Before me was a space of sea. Before I crossed I wanted to hear that wild music; but your voice broke my dream."

She sat up and unbuttoned her sleeve. *As I live,* there was a red mark on her arm above her elbow!

I crushed my hands together and set my teeth, for I would have kissed the mark and washed it with my tears. But Verry must not be agitated now. She divined my feelings for the first time in her life. "I have indeed been in a long sleep, as far as *you* are concerned; this means something. My blindness is removed by a dream. Do you despise me?" Two large, limpid tears dropped down her smooth cheeks without ruffling the expression of her face.

"I have prided myself upon my delicacy of feeling. You may have remarked that I considered myself your superior?"

"You are all wrong. I have no delicate feelings at all; they are as coarse and fibrous as the husk of a cocoanut. Do for heaven's sake get up and let me dress you."

She burst into laughter. "Bring me some water, then."

I brought her a bowl full, and stood near her with a towel; but she splashed it over me, and dribbled her hands in it till I was in despair. I took it away and wiped her face, which looked at me so childly, so elfish, so willful, and so tenderly, that I took it between my hands and kissed it. I pulled her up to a chair, for she was growing willful every moment; but she must be humored. I combed her hair, put on her shoes and stockings, and in short dressed her. Father came up and begged me to hurry, as everybody had come. I sent him for Ben, who came with a pale, happy face and shining eyes. She looked at him seriously. "I like you best," she said.

"It *is* time you said that. Oh, Verry! how lovely you are!"

"I feel so."

"Come, come," urged father.

"I do not want these gloves," she said, dropping them.

Ben slipped on the third finger of her hand a plain ring. She kissed it, and he looked as if about to be translated.

"Forever, Verry!"

"Forever."

"Wait a moment," I said, "I want a collar," giving a glance into the glass. What a starved, thin, haggard face I saw, with its border of pale hair! Whose were those wide, pitiful, robbed eyes?

I hurried into the room in advance to show them their place in front of a screen of plants. When they entered the company rose, and the ceremony was performed. Veronica's dress was commented upon and not approved of; being black, it was considered ominous. She looked like a 'cloud with a silver lining.' I also made my comments. Temperance, whose tearful eyes were fixed on her darling, was unconscious that she had taken from her pocket, and was flourishing, a large red and yellow silk handkerchief, while the cambric one she intended to use was neatly folded in her left hand. She wore the famous plum-colored silk, old style, which had come into a fortune in the way of wrinkles. A large bow of black ribbon testified that she was in mourning. Hepsey rubbed her thumb across her fingers with the vacant air of habit. I glanced at Alice; she was looking intently at Fanny, whose eyes were fixed upon father. A strange feeling of annoyance troubled me, but the ceremony was over. Arthur congratulated himself on having a big brother. Ben was so pale, and wore so exalted an expression, that he agitated me almost beyond control.

After the general shaking of hands, there came retorts for me. "When shall we have occasion to congratulate you?" And, "You are almost at the corner." And, "Your traveling from home seems only to have been an advantage to Veronica."

"I tell you, Cousin Sue," said Arthur, who overheard the last remark, "that you don't know what they say of Cassandra in Rosville. She's the biggest beauty they ever had, and had lots of beaus."

A significant expression passed over Cousin Sue's face, which was noticed by Alice Morgeson, who colored deeply.

"Have you not forgotten?" I asked her.

"It was of you I thought, not myself. I cannot tell you how utterly the past has gone, or how insignificant the result has proved."

"Alice," said father, "can you carve?"

"Splendidly."

"Come and sit at the foot of my table; Mr. Somers will take charge of the smaller one."

"With pleasure."

"Slip out," whispered Fanny, "and look at the table; Temperance wants you."

"For the Lord's sake!" cried Temperance, "say whether things are ship-shape."

I was surprised at the taste she had displayed, and told her so.

"For once I have tried to do my best," she said; "all for Verry. Call 'em in; the turkeys will be on in a whiffle."

Tables were set in the hall, as well as in the dining-room. "They must sit down," she continued, "so that they may eat their victuals in peace." The supper was a relief to Veronica, and I blessed father's forethought. Nobody was exactly merry, but there was a proper cheerfulness. Temperance, Fanny, and Manuel were in attendance; the latter spilled a good deal of coffee on the carpet in his enjoyment of the scene; and when he saw Veronica take the flowers in her hand, he exclaimed, "Santa Maria!"

Everybody turned to look at him.

"What are you doing here, Manuel?" asked Ben.

"I wait on the señoritas," he answered. "Take plumduff?"

Everybody laughed.

"Do you like widows?" whispered Fanny at the back of my chair. I made a sign to her to attend to her business, but, as she suggested, looked at Alice. At that moment she and father were drinking wine together. I thought her handsomer than ever; she had expanded into a fair, smooth middle age.

The talking and clattering melted vaguely into my ears; I was a lay-figure in the scene, and my soul wandered elsewhere. Mr. Somers began to fidget gently, which father perceiving, rose from the table. Soon after the guests departed. The remains of the feast vanished; the fires burnt down, "winding sheets" wrapped the flame of the candles, and suppressed gaping set in.

The flowers, left to themselves, began to give out odors which perfumed the rooms. I went about extinguishing the waning candles and stifling the dying fires, finished my work, and was going upstairs when I heard Veronica playing, and stopped to listen. It was not a pæan nor a lament that she played, but a fluctuating, vibratory air, expressive of mutation. I hung over the stair-railing after she had ceased, convinced that she had been playing for herself a farewell, which freed me from my bond to her. Mr. Somers came along the hall with a candle, and I waited to ask him if I could do anything for his comfort.

"My dear," he said with apprehension, "your sister is a genius, I think."

"In music—yes."

"What a deplorable thing for a woman!"

"A woman of genius is but a heavenly lunatic, or an anomaly sphered between the sexes; do you agree?"

He laughed, and pushed his spectacles up on his forehead.

"My dear, I am astonished that Ben's choice fell as it did—"

"Good-night, sir," I said so loudly that he almost dropped his candle, and I retired to my room, taking a chair by the fire, with a sigh of relief. After a while Ben and Veronica came up.

"It is a cold night, " I remarked.

"I am in an enchanted palace," said Ben, "where there is no weather."

"Cassy, will you take these pins out of my hair?" asked Verry, seating herself in an easy-chair. "Ben, we will excuse you."

"How good of you." He strode across the passage, went into her room, and shut the door.

"There, Verry, I have unbound your hair."

"But I want to talk."

I took her hand, and led her out. She stood before her door for a moment silently, and then gave a little knock. No answer came. She knocked again; the same silence as before. At last she was obliged to open it herself, and enter without any bidding.

"Which will rule?" I thought, as I slipped down the back stairs, and listened at the kitchen door. I heard nothing. Finding an old cloak in the entry, I wrapped myself in it and left the house. The moon was out-riding black, scudding clouds, and the wind moaned round the sea, which looked like a vast, wrinkled serpent in the moonlight.

I walked to Gloster Point, and rested under the lee of the light-house, but could not, when I made the attempt, see to read the inscription inside my watch, by the light of the lantern. I must have fallen asleep from fatigue, still holding it in my hand; for when I started homeward, there was a pale reflection of light in the east, and the sea was creeping quietly toward it with a murmuring morning song.

CHAPTER XL.

I looked across the bay from my window. "The snow is making 'Pawshee's Land' white again, and I remain this year the same. No change, no growth or development! The fulfillment of duty avails me nothing; and self-discipline has passed the necessary point."

I struck the sash with my closed hand, for I would now give my life a new direction, and it was fettered. But I would be resolute, and break the fetters; had I not endured a "mute case" long enough? Manuel, who had been throwing snowballs against the house, stopped, and looked toward the gate, and then ran toward it. A pair of tired, splashed horses dashed down the drive. Manuel had the reins, and Ben was beside him, reeling slightly on the seat of the wagon. I ran down to meet him; he had been on a trip to Belem, where he never went except when he wanted money.

"I have some news for you," he said, putting his arm in mine, as he jumped from the wagon. "Come in, and pull off my boots, Manuel." I brought a chair for him, and waited till his boots were off. "Bring me a glass of brandy."

I stamped my foot. Verry entered with a book. "Ah, Verry, darling, come here."

"Why do you drink brandy? Have you over-driven the horses?"

He drank the brandy. She nodded kindly to him, shut her book, and slipped out, without approaching him.

"That's *her* way," he said, staring hard at me. "She always says in the same unmoved voice, 'Why do you drink brandy?' "

"And then—she will not come to kiss you."

"The child is dead, for the first thing. (Cigar, Manuel.) Second, I was possessed to come home by the way of Rosville. When did your father go away, Cass?"

I felt faint, and sat down.

"Ah, we *all* have a weakness; does yours overcome you?"

"He went three days ago."

"I saw him at Alice Morgeson's."

"Arthur?"

"He didn't go to see Arthur. He will marry Alice, and I must build my house now."

A devil ripped open my heart; its fragments flew all over me, blinding and deafening me.

"He will be home to-night."

"Very well."

"What shall you say, Cassy?"

"Expose that little weakness to him."

"When will you learn real life?"

"Please ask him, when he comes, if he will see me in my room."

I waited there. My cup was filled at last. My sin swam on the top.

Father came in smoking, and taking a chair between his legs, sat opposite me, and tapped softly the back of it with his fingers. "You sent for me?"

"I wanted to tell you that Charles Morgeson loved me from the first, and you remember that I stayed by him to the last."

"What more is there?" knocking over the chair, and seizing me; "tell me."

His eyes, that were bloodshot with anger, fastened on my mouth.

"I know, though, damn him! I know his cunning. Was Alice aware of this?" And he pushed me backward.

"All."

An expression of pain and disappointment crossed his face; he ground his teeth fiercely.

"Don't marry her, father; you will kill me if you do!"

"Must you alone have license?"

He resumed his cigar, which he picked up from the floor.

"It would seem that we have not known each other. What evasiveness there is in our natures! Your mother was the soul of candor, yet I am convinced I never knew her."

"If you bring Alice here, I must go. We cannot live together."

"I understand why she would not come here. She said that she must see you first. She is in Milford."

He knocked the ashes from his cigar, looked round the room, and then at me, who wept bitterly. His face contracted with a spasm.

"We were married two days ago." And turning from me quickly, he left the room.

I was never so near groveling on the face of the earth as then; let me but fall, and I was sure that I never should rise.

Ben knew it, but left it to me to tell Veronica.

My grief broke all bounds, and we changed places; she tried to comfort me, forgetting herself.

"Let us go away to the world's end with Ben." But suddenly recollecting that she liked Alice, she cried, "What shall I do?"

What could she do, but offer an unreasoning opposition? Aunt Merce cried herself sick, fond as she was of Alice, and Temperance declared that if she hadn't married a widower herself, she would put in an oar. Anyhow, she hadn't married a man with grown-up daughters.

"What ails Fanny?" she asked me the next day. "She looks like a froze pullet."

"Where is she now?"

"Making the beds."

Temperance knew well what was the matter, but was too wise to interfere. I found her, not bed-making, but in a spare room, staring at the wall. She looked at me with dry eyes, bit her lips, and folded her hands across her chest, after her old, defiant fashion. I did not speak.

"It is so," she said; "you need not tear me to pieces with your eyes, I can confess it to *you,* for you are as I am. I love him!" And she got up to shake her fist in my face. "My heart and brain and soul are as good as hers, and *he* knows it."

I could not utter a word.

"I know him as you never knew him, and have for years, since I was that starved, poor-house brat your mother took. Don't trouble yourself to make a speech about ingratitude. I know that your mother was good and merciful, and that I should have worshiped her; but I never did. Do you suppose I ever thought he was perfect, as the rest of you thought? He is full of faults. I thought he was dependant on me. He knows how I feel. Oh, what shall I do?" She threw up her arms, and dropped on the floor in a hysteric fit. I locked the door, and picked her up. "Come out of it, Fanny; I shall stay here till you do."

By dint of shaking her, and opening the window, she began to come to. After two or three fearful laughs and shudders, she opened her eyes. She saw my compassion, and tears fell in torrents; I cried too. The poor girl kissed my hands; a new soul came into her face.

"Oh, Fanny, bear it as well as you can! You and I will be friends."

"Forgive me! I was always bad; I am now. If that woman comes here, I'll stab her with Manuel's knife."

"Pooh! The knife is too rusty; it would give her the lockjaw. Besides, she will never come. I know her. She is already more than half-way to meet me; but I shall not perform my part of the journey, and she will return."

"You don't say so!" her ancient curiosity reviving.

"Manuel keeps it sharp," she said presently, relapsing into jealousy.

"You are a fool. Have you eaten anything to-day?"

"I can't eat."

"That's the matter with you—an empty stomach is the cause of most distressing pangs."

Ben urged me to go to Milford to meet Alice, and to ask her to come to our house. But father said no more to me on the subject. Neither did Veronica. In the afternoon they drove over to Milford, returning at dusk. She refused to come with them, Ben said, and never would probably. "You have thrown out your father terribly."

"You notice it, do you?"

"It is pretty evident."

"What is your opinion?"

He was about to condemn, when he recollected his own inter-ference in my life. "Ah! you have me. I think you are right, as far as the past which relates to Alice is concerned. But if she chooses to forget, why don't you? We do much that is contrary to our moral ideas, to make people comfortable. Besides, if we do not lay our ghosts, our closets will be overcrowded."

"We may determine some things for ourselves, irrespective of consequences."

"Well, there is a mess of it."

Fanny had watched for their return, counting on an access of misery, for she believed that Alice would come also. It was what *she* would have done. Rage took possession of her when she saw father alone. She planted herself before him, in my presence, in a contemptuous attitude. He changed color, and then her mood changed.

"What shall I do?" she asked piteously.

I tried to get away before she made any further progress; but he checked me, dreading the scene which he foreboded, without com-prehending.

"Fanny," he said harshly, but with a confused face, "you mistake me."

"Not I; it was your wife and children who mistook you."

"What is it you would say?"

"You have let me be your slave."

"It is not true, I hope—what your behavior indicates?"

I forgave him everything then. Fanny had made a mistake. He had only behaved very selfishly toward her, without having any perception of her—that was all! She was confounded, stared at him a moment, and rushed out. That interview settled her; she was a different girl from that day.

"Father, you will go to Rosville, and be rich again. Can you buy this house from Ben, for me? A very small income will suffice me and Fanny, for you may be sure that I shall keep her. Temperance will live with Verry; Ben will build, now that his share of his grandfather's estate will come to him."

"Very well," he said with a sigh, "I will bring it about."

"It is useless for us to disguise the fact—I have lost you. You are more dead to me than mother is."

"You say so."

It was the truth. I was the only one of the family who never went to Rosville. Aunt Merce took up her abode with Alice, on account of Arthur, whom she idolized. When father was married again, the Morgeson family denounced him for it, and for leaving Surrey; but they accepted his invitations to Rosville, and returned with glowing accounts of his new house and his hospitality.

By the next June, Ben's house was completed and they moved. Its site was a knoll to the east of our house, which Veronica had chosen. Her rooms were toward the orchard, and Ben's commanded a view of the sea. He had not ventured to intrude, he told her, upon the Northern Lights, and she must not bother him about his boat-house or his pier. They were both delighted with the change, and kept house like children. Temperance indulged their whims to the utmost, though she thought Ben's new-fangled notions were silly; but they might keep him from *something worse.* This something was a shadow which frightened me, though I fought it off. I was weary of trouble, and shut my eyes as long as possible. Whenever Ben went from home, and he often drove to Milford, or to some of the towns near, he came back disordered with drink. At the sight my hopes would sink. But they rose again, he was so genial, so loving, so calmly contented afterward. As Verry never spoke of it either to Temperance or me, I imagined she was not troubled much. She could not feel as I felt, for she knew nothing of the Bellevue Pickersgill family history.

The day they moved was a happy one for me. I was at last left alone in my own house, and I regained an absolute self-possession, and a sense of occupation I had long been a stranger to. My ownership oppressed me, almost, there was so much liberty to realize.

I had an annoyance, soon after I came into sole possession. Father's business was not yet settled, and he came to Surrey. He was paying his debts in full, he told me, eking out what he lacked himself with the property of Alice. He could not have used much of it, however, for the vessels that were out at the time of the failure came home with good cargoes. I fancied that he had more than one regret while settling his affairs; that he missed the excitement and vicissitudes of a maritime business. Nothing disagreeable arose between us, till I happened to ask him what were the contents of a box which had arrived the day before.

"Something Alice sent you; shall we open it?"

I made no answer; but it was opened, and he took out a sea-green and white velvet carpet, with a scarlet leaf on it, and a piece of sea-green and white brocade for curtains. Had she sought the world over, she could have found nothing to suit me so well.

"She thought that Verry might have a fancy for some of the old furniture, and that you would accept these in its place."

"There's nothing here to match this splendor, and I cannot bear to make a change. Verry must have them, for she took nothing from me."

"Just as you please."

CHAPTER XLI.

"What a hot day!" said Fanny. "Every door and window is open. There is not a breath of air."

"It will be calm all day," I said. "We have two or three days like this in a year. Give me another cup of coffee. Is it nine yet?"

"Nearly. I ought to go to Hepsey's to-day. She wont be able to leave her bed, the heat weakens her so."

"Do go. How still it is! The shadows of the trees on the Neck reach almost from shore to shore, and there's a fish-boat motion-less."

"The boat was there when I got up."

"Everything is blue and yellow, or blue and white."

"How your hair waves this morning! It is handsomer than ever."

I went to the glass with my cup of coffee. "I look younger in the summer."

"What's the use of looking younger here?" she asked gruffly. "You never see a man."

"I see Ben coming with Verry, and Manuel behind."

"Hillo!" cried Ben, pulling up his horses in front of the window. "We are going on a picnic. Wont you go?"

"How far?"

"Fifteen or twenty miles."

"Go on; I had rather imprison the splendid day here."

"There's nothing for dinner," said Fanny.

"The fish-boat may come in, in time."

"Will three o'clock do for you? If so, I'll stay with Hepsey till then."

"Four will answer."

She cleared away my breakfast things and left me. I sat by the window an hour, looking over the water, my thoughts drifting through a golden haze, and then went up to my room and looked out again. If I turned my eyes inside the walls, I was aware of the yearning, yawning empty void within me, which I did not like. I sauntered into Verry's room, to see if any clouds were coming up from the north. There were none. The sun had transfixed the sky, and walked through its serene blue, "burning without beams." Neither bird nor insect chirped; they were hid from the radiant heat in tree and sod. I went back again to my own window. The subtle beauty of these inorganic powers stirred me to mad regret and frantic longing. I stretched out my arms to embrace the presence which my senses evoked.

It would be better to get a book, I concluded, and hunted up Barry Cornwall's songs.[58] With it I would go to the parlor, which was shaded. I turned the leaves going down, and went in humming:

"Mount on the dolphin Pleasure," and threw myself on the sofa beside—*Desmond!*

I dropped Barry Cornwall.

"I have come," he said, in a voice deathly faint.

"How old you have grown, Desmond!"

"But I have taken such pains with my hands for you! You said they were handsome; are they?"

I kissed them.

He was so spare, and brown, and his hair was quite gray! Even his mustache looked silvery.

"Two years to-day since I have worn the watch, Desmond."

He took one exactly like it from his pocket, and showed me the inscription inside.

"And the ruby ring, on the guard?"

"It is gone, you see; you must put one there now."

"Forgive me."

"Ah, Cassy! I couldn't come till now. You see what battles *I* must have had since I saw you. It took me so long to break my cursed habits. I was afraid of myself, afraid to come; but I have tried myself to the utmost, and hope I am worthy of you. Will you trust me?"

"I am yours, as I always have been."

"I have eaten an immense quantity of oil and garlic," he said with a sigh. "But Spain is a good place to reform in. How is Ben?"

I shook my head.

"Don't tell me anything sad now. Poor fellow! God help him."

Fanny was talking to some one on the walk; the fisherman probably, who was bringing fish.

"Do you want some dinner?"

"I have had no breakfast."

"I must see about something for you."

"Not to leave me, Cassy."

"Just for a few minutes."

"No."

"But I want to cry by myself, besides looking after the dinner."

"Cry here then, with me. Come, Cassandra, my wife! My God, I shall die with happiness."

A mortal paleness overspread his face.

"Desmond, Desmond, do you know how I love you? Feel my heart,—it has throbbed with the weight of you since that night in Belem, when you struck your head under the mantel."

He was speechless. I murmured loving words to him, till he drew a deep breath of life and strength.

"These fish are small," said Fanny at the door. "Shall I take them!"

"Certainly," said Desmond, "I'll pay for them."

"It is Ben in black lead," said Fanny.

We laughed.

At dusk Ben and Veronica drove up. Desmond was seated in the window. Ben fixed his eyes upon him, without stopping.

We ran out, and called to him.

"Old fellow," said Desmond, "willing or not, I have come."

Ben's face was a study; so many emotions assailed him that my heart was wrung with pity.

"Give her to me," Desmond continued in a touching voice. "You are her oldest friend, and have a right."

"She was always yours," he answered. "To contend with her was folly."

Veronica took hold of Ben's chin and raised his head to look into his face. "What dreams have you had?"

But he made no reply to her. We were all silent for a moment, then he said, "Was I wrong, Des.?"

"No, no."

While I was saying to myself, in behalf of Veronica, whose calm face baffled me, "Enigma, Sphinx," she turned to Desmond, holding out her right arm, and said, "You are the man I saw in my dream."

"And you are like the Virgin I made an offering to, only not quite so bedizened." He took her extended hand and kissed it.

Ben threw the reins with a sudden dash toward Manuel, who was standing by, and jumped down.

"Have tea with me," I asked, "and music, too. Verry, will you play for Desmond?"

She took his arm, and entered the house.

"Friend," I said to Ben, who lingered by the door, "to contend with me was not folly, unless it has kept you from contending with yourself. Tell me—how is it with you?"

"Cassandra, the jaws of hell are open. If you are satisfied with the end, I must be."

After I was married, I went to Belem. But Mrs. Somers never forgave me; and Mr. Somers liked Desmond no better than he had in former times. Neither did Adelaide and Ann ever consider the marriage in any light but that of a misalliance. Nor did they recognize any change in him. It might be permanent, but it was no less an aberration which they mistrusted. The ground plan of the Bellevue Pickersgill character could not be altered.

In a short time after we were married we went to Europe and stayed two years.

These last words I write in the summer time at our house in Surrey, for Desmond likes to be here at this season, and I write in my old chamber. Before its windows rolls the blue summer sea. Its beauty wears a relentless aspect to me now; its eternal monotone expresses no pity, no compassion.

Veronica is lying on the floor watching her year-old baby. It smiles continually, but never cries, never moves, except when it is moved. Her face, thin and melancholy, is still calm and lovely. But her eyes go no more in quest of something beyond. A wall of darkness lies before her, which she will not penetrate. Aunt Merce sits near me with her knitting. When I look at her I think how long it is since mother went, and wonder whether death is not a welcome idea to those who have died. Aunt Merce looks at Verry and the child with a sorrowful countenance, exchanges a glance with me, shakes her head. If Verry speaks to her, she answers cheerfully, and tries to conceal the grief which she feels when she sees the mother and child together.

Ben has been dead six months. Only Desmond and I were with him in his last moments. When he sprang from his bed, staggered backwards, and fell dead, we clung together with faint hearts, and mutely questioned each other.

"God is the Ruler," he said at last. "Otherwise let this mad world crush us now."

THE END.

NOTES

1. The anonymous *Northern Regions; or, Uncle Richard's relation of Captain Parry's voyages for the discovery of a north-west passage, and Franklin's and Cochrane's overland journeys to other parts of the world* (1827), a simplified account of selected polar explorations, pirated from a British work of similar title.

2. *The Saint's Everlasting Rest* (1650), by English Puritan divine Richard Baxter (1615–91), classic of Protestant devotional literature, well known in early nineteenth-century Congregationalist circles.

3. Richard Brinsley Sheridan (1751–1816), late neoclassical British playwright, was very popular in America. The works of Laurence Sterne (1713–68), including his picaresque semi-autobiographical narrative, *A Sentimental Journey Through France and Italy* (1768), had been much admired in late-eighteenth-century New England but by the 1820s, the time of this opening chapter, were increasingly considered improper. *An Account of a Voyage Round the World in the Years 1768–71* (1773) and other travel writings by James Cook (1728–79) were notable examples of a genre that because of its combination of the pleasurable and the utilitarian greatly appealed to contemporary New England readers. The list as a whole, however, makes the point that young Cassandra's reading is, by contrast to her mother's, emphatically secular and precocious.

4. John Hepburn, a British seaman renowned as the heroic, faithful companion of explorer John Franklin (1786–1847) during his 1819–21 trek through Canada's Northwest Territories. Plagued by cold and starvation, several members of the expedition ate shoe leather, along with deer skin and bones—but not in the Davis Straits.

5. Weekly Congregationalist newspaper (1816–67), published in Boston.

6. Tract by the popular British evangelical writer Hannah More (1745–1833), first issued in the series "Cheap Repository Tracts" (1795) and frequently reprinted in England and the United States during the first half of the nineteenth century. This is the kind of children's literature Cassandra's mother would like her to read, but if she likes such "good stories" it is for the "wrong" reasons.

7. Perhaps the closest approximation to a conventional love story in the Old Testament, Ruth 2–4.

8. Stoddard's fictionalization of her native village of Mattapoisett, on Buzzard's Bay, Massachusetts. To a degree, father, mother, and Veronica correspond to Elizabeth's parents and sister Jane.

9. *New Englands Memoriall* (1669), by Pilgrim father Nathaniel Morton (1613–85), the chief authority for early Plymouth history until the publication in full of its main source, William Bradford's *History of Plimouth Plantation* (1856).

10. Traditional term for Yankee domestic, reflecting the somewhat indistinct line between such retainers and regular family members. During the second quarter of the nineteenth century, relations between domestics and their employers were put increasingly on an economic basis, and native New England domestics were increasingly replaced by Irish immigrants, who were treated much more unequivocally as inferiors. *The Morgesons* reflects these trends, with some variations. See Faye E. Dudden, *Serving Women: Household Service in Nineteenth-Century America* (Middletown, Conn.: Wesleyan University Press, 1983).

11. Lady Teazle appears in Sheridan's comedy *The School for Scandal* (1777).

12. "Selah" is an obscure term, perhaps simply a musical notation, phonetically transliterated in the King James translation of Psalm 24:6, 10, the version Mrs. Morgeson would have read to the bored Cassandra.

13. A 1791 song by Robert Burns (1759–96), widely reprinted in nineteenth-century America.

14. First stanza of hymn by English Congregational minister Joseph Hoskins (1745–88). How Stoddard knew this text is uncertain, since its only American printings before 1862 had been in Dutch Reformed and Mennonite hymnbooks. Possibly the excellent library of her local pastor Thomas Robbins ("Dr. Snell"; see p. 256, n. 25) contained Hoskins' *Hymns on Select Texts of Scripture and Occasional Subjects* (1789). In any case, Stoddard would have regarded the stanza as epitomizing to the point of self-parody all that was most distasteful in Calvinism.

15. In Roman religion, household gods; here used, ironically, to suggest family disunity.

16. Boston edition of the British *Knight's Penny Magazine* (1832–46), published by the Society for Diffusion of Useful Knowledge.

17. Making a deep curtsey. To make a cheese was a schoolgirls' amusement, consisting in turning around rapidly and then suddenly sinking down, so that the petticoats were inflated all around somewhat in the form of a cheese (*Oxford English Dictionary*).

18. In satirizing her snobbish schoolmates for their misplaced pride in their ancestors, Cassandra implies that, in contrast to her own great-grandfather, their grandfathers made their fortunes through one form of disreputable sea trade or another. "Black Peter" was involved in slave-trading in Africa, and his later respectability did not extend to endorsing efforts to establish in Liberia a country for freed American blacks.

19. Touch me not.

20. Unidentified, perhaps imaginary, Gothic novel in the tradition of Ann Radcliffe and Matthew G. Lewis.

21. Popular song by Scottish songwriter Robert Tannahill (1774–1810), published in America by J. A. and W. Geib (1818).

22. The American Home Missionary Society (established 1816), the arm of Congregationalism devoted to domestic evangelizing, particularly in the Midwest.

23. A tailor's smoothing iron, called a goose because of the shape of its handle.

24. Reference to the elaborately polite deportment of the hero of *Sir Charles Grandison* (1753–54) by English novelist Samuel Richardson (1689–1761).

25. The library of the original Doctor Snell, Elizabeth Stoddard's pastor Thomas Robbins (1777–1854), *was* of regional note, amounting to three thousand volumes in 1832. Robbins was an antiquarian with a special interest in Puritan history. From Cassandra's perspective, however, his collection looks simply like that of an old-fashioned eighteenth-century gentleman, containing standard works by Addison and Steele, Fielding, and Goldsmith, with a run of the leading eighteenth-century London periodical, *The Gentleman's Magazine* (1731–1914), and with the sectarian *Boston Recorder* mentioned in a hasty afterthought as Cassandra searches in vain for a volume of poetry. Altogether, Snell's tastes look genteel, secularized, safe to the point of stuffiness—all of which was stereotypical of the generation of liberally educated "moderate" Calvinist divines displaced in the early nineteenth century by more sectarian, evangelical, seminary-trained successors. Like his historical counterpart, Snell is succeeded by a zealot "red hot from Andover" (p. 118).

26. *Histoire naturelle, generale et particuliere* (1749–1804), monumental forty-four-volume encyclopedia of natural history by Georges Louis Leclerc de Buffon (1707–88) and his successors.

27. Swiss French; a popular song sung by cattlemen as they lead their herds to pasture. Cassandra is being doubly impious by passing off her parody of a sermon as a popular song.

28. The pace at which Cassandra devours Byron's satiric *Don Juan* (1819–24) and melancholy *Childe Harold* (1812, 1816, 1818) is arresting, as is her failure to comment on the contrast in tone between the two works.

29. An inland Massachusetts county seat, possibly modeled on Worcester, Rosville is still provincial by comparison to what Cassandra will later encounter, yet secularized and liberal compared with what she has known before. The community's theological orientation, as indicated below, is Unitarian rather than the "moderate" Calvinism of the more conservative brand of Congregationalism in Cassandra's home town.

30. "Once on the raging seas he rode" is a slightly altered version of the opening of the third stanza of "The Star of Bethlehem" by English poet Henry Kirke White (1785–1806); the text appears in abridged form in several American hymnbooks. "Should these fond hopes" is from *Moore's National Melodies,* arranged by Sir John Stevenson and published in America by W. D. Dubois (1818).

31. The American Board of Commissioners for Foreign Missions (established 1810), the arm of Congregationalism devoted to international evangelizing.

32. According to nineteenth-century medical opinion, healthy women were passionless; female sexuality was viewed as an illness. In suggesting that Cassandra avoid physical stimulation, Dr. White is seeking to steer her clear of the potential for sexuality he perceives in her. But whereas in other nineteenth-century fiction by women, e.g., Charlotte Perkins Gilman's "The Yellow Wallpaper" (1892), doctors were portrayed as authoritarianly confining forces in women's lives, Stoddard shows Cassandra to be as oblivious to the medical profession's paternalistic efforts to restrict women as she is at this point in her life to other confining institutions.

33. Lines 87–88 of "A Dream of Fair Women" (1833), by Alfred Lord Ten-

nyson (1809–92). In the poem the reference, ironically, is to Helen of Troy, not to Cassandra.

34. *Agamemnon* (458 B.C.) is the first tragedy in the *Oresteia* trilogy by Aeschylus. Ben's translation begins at line 855. The play deals with the murder of Agamemnon, leader of the Greeks during the Trojan War, by his wife Clytemnestra, in revenge for his sacrifice of their daughter Iphegenia to the goddess Artemis. Clytemnestra also murders Cassandra, daughter of the Trojan leader Priam; Cassandra has become Agamemnon's slave and concubine. Cassandra, a prophetess, had been doomed by Apollo to utter predictions no one believes, because she had spurned his love for her. Ben shows off his classical education here, but Cassandra feels the ancient associations of her name do not apply to her. As she gains the upper hand in relation to Ben, the shift in dynamics is reflected in her claiming as her own the vision of the contemporary poet Tennyson, to whom Ben also introduces her at this point. Later she refashions from Tennyson's account of aspects of the Trojan War from a woman's viewpoint a covert statement about her refusal to take responsibility for Ben's life. See p. 219, no. 55.

35. Tennyson's "Fatima" (1833) is a poem spoken by a woman yearningly awaiting her lover, whom she will "possess or . . . die." Cassandra's attraction to the poem emphasizes the intensity of her response to Charles, as well as inaugurating her appropriation of Tennyson's poetic vision.

36. An 1807 novel by Anne Louise Germaine Necker de Staël (1766–1817), whose title character is arguably the first female protagonist in a major work of Western fiction conceived along something like feminist lines. Corinne and Oswald, the leading male figure, are analogues to Cassandra and Charles.

37. Generic name for horse-driver, after the biblical Jehu's feats of charioteering (2 Kings 9:20).

38. Shakespeare, *The Merchant of Venice*, V.i.3–6, 9–12. The lines in this section are spoken alternately by the lovers Lorenzo and Jessica, but Stoddard quotes Lorenzo only.

39. Felicia Hemans (1793–1835) was a late romantic poet whose mixture of piety and Byronism was widely imitated in antebellum America. Edward Young (1683–1765), whose *The Complaint; or, Night-Thoughts on Life, Death and Immortality* (1742–45) was the magnum opus of the pre-Romantic "Graveyard School" of poetry, was still read with interest a century later by elderly New Englanders of orthodox bent. Stoddard probably means here to juxtapose old- and new-fashioned examples of inflated rhetoric.

40. The eighteenth-century British poets Thomas Gray (1716–71), Alexander Pope (1688–1744), and James Thomson (1700–1748).

41. Historical romance (1841) about Toussaint L'Ouverture, by Harriet Martineau (1802–76), English writer and reformer.

42. Shetland Island landowner in *The Pirate* (1821), novel by Sir Walter Scott (1771–1832), Magnus Troil is the father of the two leading female characters.

43. Written by Stoddard herself. With a middle stanza and slightly altered third stanza, this poem appeared in her *Poems* (1895), entitled "A Summer Night." Edmund Clarence Stedman included it among the eight Stoddard poems he selected for his *An American Anthology* (1900).

44. Legendary figure doomed to a life of eternal wandering after mocking Jesus on his way to the crucifixion.

45. At the end of chapter 3 of *American Notes* (1842), British novelist Charles Dickens (1812–70) satirized the inevitable steak he was daily served for breakfast in Boston as "deformed . . . with a great flat bone in the centre, swimming in hot butter, and sprinkled with a very blackest of all possible pepper." The Curiosity Shop referred to by the waiter is kept by the protagonist's grandfather in Dickens' fourth novel, *The Old Curiosity Shop* (1840–41).

46. James Matlack argues persuasively that Belem is reminiscent of Salem, Massachusetts; that the Pickersgill family, into which Veronica and Cassandra are to marry, recalls the Forresters of Salem, with whom the Mattapoisett Barstows were allied by the marriage of Elizabeth Stoddard's uncle, a doctor who thereby made his fortune. Stoddard plays on the irony of the fact that the Forresters looked down on the Barstows yet were themselves considered parvenus by the older Salem gentility. See James Matlack, "Hawthorne and Elizabeth Barstow Stoddard," *New England Quarterly* 50 (1977): 295–300.

47. Miss Hiticutt appears newly aware of the fact that fiction had been for several decades the backbone of the major circulating libraries, private profit-making operations sometimes quite lucrative for the more enterprising proprietors.

48. First stanza of Ben Jonson's "Song. To Celia" (1616).

49. Lines 859, 861–63, of John Milton's *Comus* (1637).

50. Adaptation of line 1 of Tennyson's "The Palace of Art" (1833), in which the soul's self-centered construction of its pleasure house is seen as leading to spiritual corruption.

51. Johann Christoph Friedrich von Schiller (1759–1805), *Wallenstein* (1799), lines 3518–19.

52. "Pour prendre congé": to take leave. Written on visiting cards when one is about to depart.

53. In Shakespeare's *Antony and Cleopatra*, V.ii, Octavius Caesar seeks to strike a bargain with Cleopatra after Antony's death, to the effect that she will not commit suicide. Cassandra's analogy between herself and Cleopatra is one of her melodramatic pronouncements, with Caesar representing propriety. She soon resumes her more typically caustic stance.

54. Electricity was thought to have a healing effect on individuals suffering from neurasthenia (nervous exhaustion), and electrical gadgetry was used by respectable medical practitioners as well as quacks in order to "cure" patients. Cassandra's traveling companions are offended by her unconventionality and seek to put her in her place by suggesting that she is suffering from nervous disorders.

55. From Tennyson, "Oenone" (1833), lines 246–49. Oenone, a mountain nymph, was deserted by Paris after Aphrodite promised him the fairest and most loving wife in Greece. In Tennyson's poem, Oenone addresses her mother, the goddess Ida, in her grief but finally suspends her wish to die in favor of the hope for revenge suggested in the lines Cassandra quotes. She then resolves to go to Troy and "talk with the wild Cassandra," whose presentiments of destruction harmonize with her own vengeful visions. Cassandra Morgeson's quotation of the lines at this point in the novel suggests her resentment of the marriage of Verry and Ben, whose tranquillity will be bought at her expense, and identifies Cassandra with Oenone as well as her namesake. Oenone refused to heal Paris when he was mortally wounded, and Cassandra will do nothing to help combat

Ben's alcoholism. By implication, Tennyson, to whom Ben introduced Cassandra, now becomes the bard of the housc of Morgeson and she herself the keeper of the keys to the family history.

56. Literally "footsteps backward," from Horace, *Epistles*, I, 74–75. Horace here alludes to an Aesop fable in which a wary fox tells a sick lion that the footsteps frighten him because all point to the lion's den and none point backward ("quia me vestigia terrent, / Omnia te adversum spectantia, nulla retrorsum"). Stoddard's immediate source, however, is the lurid poem "Vestigia Retrorsum" by her husband's friend George Henry Boker (1823–90), in which a guilt-ridden speaker recalls the trysting-place where he seduced his beloved, who later died of grief (*Plays and Poems*, 1856, vol. 2).

57. Verry quotes Tennyson, "The Merman" (1830), line 10, to turn the subject of Cass's new watch into a fantasy, but Cassandra adapts line 18 of the poem to indicate her wish for a more pleasurable life.

58. *English Songs and Other Smaller Poems* (1832), by British poet and song writer Bryan Waller Procter (1787–1874), pseud. Barry Cornwall.

1901 *Preface to* The Morgesons

I suppose it was environment that caused me to write these novels; but the mystery of it is, that when I left my native village I did not dream that imagination would lead me there again, for the simple annals of our village and domestic ways did not interest me; neither was I in the least studious. My years were passed in an attempt to have a good time, according to the desires and fancies of youth. Of literature and the literary life, I and my tribe knew nothing; we had not discovered "sermons in stones." Where then was the panorama of my stories and novels stored, that was unrolled in my new sphere? Of course, being moderately intelligent I read everything that came in my way, but merely for amusement. It had been laid up against me as a persistent fault, which was not profitable; I should peruse moral, and pious works, or take up sewing,—that interminable thing, "white seam," which filled the leisure moments of the right-minded. To the *personnel* of writers I gave little heed; it was the hero they created that charmed me, like Miss Porter's gallant Pole, Sobieski, or the ardent Ernest Maltravers, of Bulwer.

I had now come to live among those who made books, and were interested in all their material, for all was for the glory of the whole. Prefaces, notes, indexes, were unnoticed by me,—even Walter Scott's and Lord Byron's. I began to get glimpses of a profound ignorance, and did not like the position as an outside consideration. These mental productive adversities abased me. I was well enough in my way, but nothing was expected from me in their way, and when I beheld their ardor in composition, and its fine emulation, like "a sheep before her shearers," I was dumb. The environment pressed upon me, my pride was touched; my situation, though "tolerable, was not to be endured."

Fortunate or not, we were poor. It was not strange that I should marry, said those who knew the step I had taken; but that I should follow that old idyl; and accept the destiny of a garret and a crust with a poet, was incredible! Therefore, being apart from the diversions of society, I had many idle hours. One day when my husband was sitting at the receipt of customs, for he had obtained a modest appointment, I sat by a little desk, where my portfolio lay open. A pen was near, which I took up, and it began to write, wildly like "Planchette" upon her board, or like a kitten clutching a ball of yarn fearfully. But doing it again—I could not say why—my mind began upon a festival in my childhood, which my mother arranged for several poor old people at Thanksgiving. I finished the sketch in private, and gave it the title of "A Christmas Dinner," as one more modern. I put in occasional "fiblets" about the respectable guests, Mrs. Carver and Mrs. Chandler, and one dreadful little girl foisted upon me to entertain. It pleased the editor of *Harper's Magazine,* who accepted it, and sent me a check which would look wondrous small now. I wrote similar sketches, which were published in that magazine. Then I announced my intention of writing a "long story," and was told by him of the customs that he thought I "lacked the constructive faculty." I hope that I am writing an object lesson, either of learning how, or not learning how, to write.

I labored daily, when alone, for weeks; how many sheets of foolscap I covered, and dashed to earth, was never told. Since, by my "infinite pains and groans," I have been reminded of Barkis, in "David Copperfield," when he crawled out of his bed to get a guinea from his strong box for David's dinner. Naturally, I sent the story to *Harper's Magazine,* and it was curtly refused. My husband, moved by pity by my discouragement, sent it to Mr. Lowell, then editor of the *Atlantic Monthly.* In a few days I received a letter from him, which made me very happy. He accepted the story, and wrote me then, and afterwards, letters of advice and suggestion. I think he saw through my mind, its struggles, its ignorance, and its ambition. Also I got my guinea for my pains. The *Atlantic Monthly* sent me a hundred dollars. I doubt but for Mr. Lowell's interest and kindness I should ever have tried prose again. I owe a debt of gratitude to him which I shall always give to his noble memory.

My story did not set the river on fire, as stories are apt to do nowadays. It attracted so little notice from those I knew, and knew of, that naturally my ambition would have been crushed. Notwith-

standing, and saying nothing to anybody, I began "The Morgesons," and everywhere I went, like Mary's lamb, my MS. was
sure to go. Meandering along the path of that family, I took them
much to heart, and finished their record within a year. I may say
here, that the clans I marshaled for my pages had vanished from
the sphere of reality—in my early day the village Squire, peerless
in blue broadcloth, who scolded, advised, and helped his poorer
neighbors; the widows, or maidens, who accepting service "as a
favor," often remained a lifetime as friend as well as "help;" the
race of coast-wise captains and traders, from Maine to Florida, as
acute as they were ignorant; the rovers of the Atlantic and the
Pacific, were gone not to return. If with these characters I have
deserved the name of "realist," I have also clothed my skeletons
with the robe of romance. "The Morgesons" completed, and no
objections made to its publication, it was published. As an author
friend happened to be with us, almost on the day it was out, I
gave it to him to read, and he returned it to me with the remark
that there were "a good many *whiches* in it." That there were, I
must own, and that it was difficult to extirpate them. I was annoyed at their fertility. The inhabitants of my ancient dwelling
place pounced upon "The Morgesons," because they were convinced it would prove to be a version of my relations, and my own
life. I think one copy passed from hand to hand, but the interest in
it soon blew over, and I have not been noticed there since.

"Two Men" I began as I did the others, with a single motive;
the shadow of a man passed before me, and I built a visionary
fabric round him. I have never tried to girdle the earth; my limits
are narrow; the modern novel, as Andrew Lang lately calls it,—
with its love-making, disquisition, description, history, theology,
ethics,—I have no sprinkling of. My last novel, "Temple House,"
was personally conducted, so far that I went to Plymouth to find
a suitable abode for my hero, Angus Gates, and to measure with
my eye the distance between the bar in the bay and the shore, the
scene of a famous wreck before the Revolution. As my stories and
novels were never in touch with my actual life, they seem now as
if they were written by a ghost of their time. It is to strangers
from strange places that I owe the most sympathetic recognition.
Some have come to me, and from many I have had letters that
warmed my heart, and cheered my mind. Besides the name of Mr.
Lowell, I mention two New England names, to spare me the fate
of the prophet of the Gospel, the late Maria Louise Pool, whose

lamentable death came far too early, and Nathaniel Hawthorne, who lived to read "The Morgesons" only, and to write me a characteristic letter. With some slight criticism, he wrote, "Pray pardon my frankness, for what is the use of saying anything, unless we say what we think? . . . Otherwise it seemed to me as genuine and lifelike as anything that pen and ink can do. There are very few books of which I take the trouble to have any opinion at all, or of which I could retain any memory so long after reading them as I do of 'The Morgesons.' "

Could better words be written for the send-off of these novels?

ELIZABETH STODDARD.

New York, May 2nd, 1901.

Short Fiction

Introduction

This section contains a sampling of Stoddard's short fiction written during her most productive period, the 1860s. Like the majority of her other stories of that decade, both works reprinted here appeared in *Harper's New Monthly Magazine*. After having achieved the greatest commercial success in American magazine history within a decade of its founding in 1850, *Harper's* (circulation 200,000 in 1860) had been temporarily set back by the Civil War, but it still continued to be an attractive outlet for aspiring writers. An illustrated magazine designed for middlebrow readership, with a literary department that included many famous names, steering a middle course in politics (i.e., no more than mildly pro-North), *Harper's* guaranteed its contributors a wider readership than its younger rival, the *Atlantic Monthly,* even if not quite the same degree of prestige.

Harper's made no special effort to encourage American talent. On the contrary, the mainstay of its fiction department was serialization of the works of the great Victorian novelists. The magazine's short fiction, however, was contributed almost entirely by Americans, who wrote in a variety of styles: Oriental allegory, domestic romance, travel narrative, and (increasingly) regional and specifically New England realism. In the same volume as "Lemorne *Versus* Huell" appeared stories by the woman's fictionist Caroline Chesebrough, the pioneer realist J. W. DeForest, and the local colorist Rose Terry Cooke, as well as installments of George Eliot's *Romola* and two minor novels by Anthony Trollope. In short, *Harper's* range, like Stoddard's taste, was Anglo-American and eclectic; the ability of many of *Harper's* regular contributors was high; and the quality of its best fiction was exceptional (Dickens' *Bleak House,* Thackeray's *The Newcomes,* Melville's "The Town-Ho's Story"). Stoddard undoubtedly turned to *Harper's* as a reasonably remunerative, sufficiently prestigious magazine that had previously shown itself hospitable to her poetry and nonfictional sketches.

The two selections included in this volume have been chosen both for intrinsic quality and for their value in illuminating Stoddard's work as a whole. The dramatic situation in "Lemorne" compares interestingly with the sexual combat between Cassandra and Charles, Ben, and Desmond in *The Morgesons*. A similarly laconic style of first-person narration, for example, is used in the case of "Lemorne" to dramatize the protagonist's lack of assertiveness. Furthermore, the characterization of the protagonist and the handling of plot can be seen as satirical inversions of the formulas of woman's fiction being employed straightforwardly elsewhere in the pages of *Harper's,* as in Louise Chandler Moulton's "A Wife's Story," (vol. 24, 1861, pp. 42–53). In Stoddard's story, the conventional protagonist's combination of external vulnerability and demure strength is transformed into a fragile veneer of apathetic cynicism, and the "happy ending" is a betrayal. Stoddard's literary and social satire is reinforced by the beautifully understated motif of Margaret Huell as fugitive slave.

"Collected by a Valetudinarian" is a more diffuse tale centering around the narrator's perusal of an obscure woman writer's diary that is in fact based on Stoddard's own unpublished journal of 1866, included as the last item in this volume. The story can thus be read as Stoddard's portrait of the artist as middle-aged unknown partly as she saw her actual situation, partly as a romanticization thereof. The journal entry for 3 September is perhaps the closest Stoddard ever came to an *ars poetica*. "Collected" can also be read as an ironic valedictory of sorts, being Stoddard's last really ambitious New England tale, though in later life she produced numerous other short stories and sketches.

In some respects, "Lemorne" and "Collected" give a skewed picture of Stoddard's work, the latter (like *The Morgesons*) being unusually autobiographical, and both being first-person narratives (again like *The Morgesons*). In general, however, the two stories typify the two most common narrative approaches favored by Stoddard in her short pieces. She likes either to play semi-satirical variations on romance formulas, as in "Lemorne," or to build skeletal plots on documentary bases as in "Collected." Of the first type, some further examples are "Tuberoses"(*Harper's,* 1863) and "The Prescription" (*Harper's,* 1864); of the second, "Captain Bond" (*Hearth and Home,* 1869) and "A Study for a Heroine" (*Independent,* 1885). "The Chimneys" (*Harper's,* 1865), a local color story about a somewhat Byronic rustic who wins a provincial belle despite socioeconomic barriers, illustrates the convergence of these two approaches, which taken together reinforce the image of Stoddard's liminal status between romanticist and realist modes.

Lemorne *Versus* Huell*

The two months I spent at Newport[1] with Aunt Eliza Huell, who had been ordered to the sea-side for the benefit of her health, were the months that created all that is dramatic in my destiny. My aunt was troublesome, for she was not only out of health, but in a lawsuit. She wrote to me, for we lived apart, asking me to accompany her—not because she was fond of me, or wished to give me pleasure, but because I was useful in various ways. Mother insisted upon my accepting her invitation, not because she loved her late husband's sister, but because she thought it wise to cotton to her in every particular, for Aunt Eliza was rich, and we—two lone women—were poor.

I gave my music-pupils a longer and earlier vacation than usual, took a week to arrange my wardrobe—for I made my own dresses—and then started for New York, with the five dollars which Aunt Eliza had sent for my fare thither. I arrived at her house in Bond Street at 7 a.m., and found her man James in conversation with the milkman. He informed me that Miss Huell was very bad, and that the housekeeper was still in bed. I supposed that Aunt Eliza was in bed also, but I had hardly entered the house when I heard her bell ring as she only could ring it—with an impatient jerk.

"She wants hot milk," said James, "and the man has just come."

I laid my bonnet down, and went to the kitchen. Saluting the cook, who was an old acquaintance, and who told me that the "divil" had been in the range that morning, I took a pan, into which I poured some milk, and held it over the gaslight till it was hot; then I carried it up to Aunt Eliza.

"Here is your milk, Aunt Eliza. You have sent for me to help you, and I begin with the earliest opportunity."

Harper's New Monthly Magazine, 26 (1863): 537–43.

"I looked for you an hour ago. Ring the bell."

I rang it.

"Your mother is well, I suppose. She would have sent you, though, had she been sick in bed."

"She has done so. She thinks better of my coming than I do."

The housekeeper, Mrs. Roll, came in, and Aunt Eliza politely requested her to have breakfast for her niece as soon as possible.

"I do not go down of mornings yet," said Aunt Eliza, "but Mrs. Roll presides. See that the coffee is good, Roll."

"It is good generally, Miss Huell."

"You see that Margaret brought me my milk."

"Ahem!" said Mrs. Roll, marching out.

At the beginning of each visit to Aunt Eliza I was in the habit of dwelling on the contrast between her way of living and ours. We lived from "hand to mouth." Every thing about her wore a hereditary air; for she lived in my grandfather's house, and it was the same as in his day. If I was at home when these contrasts occurred to me I should have felt angry; as it was, I felt them as in a dream—the china, the silver, the old furniture, and the excellent fare soothed me.

In the middle of the day Aunt Eliza came down stairs, and after she had received a visit from her doctor, decided to go to Newport on Saturday. It was Wednesday; and I could, if I chose, make any addition to my wardrobe. I had none to make, I informed her. What were my dresses?—had I a black silk? she asked. I had no black silk, and thought one would be unnecessary for hot weather.

"Who ever heard of a girl of twenty-four having no black silk! You have slimsy muslins, I dare say?"

"Yes."

"And you like them?"

"For present wear."

That afternoon she sent Mrs. Roll out, who returned with a splendid heavy silk for me, which Aunt Eliza said should be made before Saturday, and it was. I went to a fashionable dress-maker of her recommending, and on Friday it came home, beautifully made and trimmed with real lace.

"Even the Pushers could find no fault with this," said Aunt Eliza, turning over the sleeves and smoothing the lace. Somehow she smuggled into the house a white straw-bonnet, with white roses; also a handsome mantilla. She held the bonnet before me with a nod, and deposited it again in the box, which made a part of the luggage for Newport.

On Sunday morning we arrived in Newport, and went to a quiet hotel in the town. James was with us, but Mrs. Roll was left in Bond Street, in charge of the household. Monday was spent in an endeavor to make an arrangement regarding the hire of a coach and coachman. Several livery-stable keepers were in attendance, but nothing was settled, till I suggested that Aunt Eliza should send for her own carriage. James was sent back the next day, and returned on Thursday with coach, horses, and William her coachman. That matter being finished, and the trunks being unpacked, she decided to take her first bath in the sea, expecting me to support her through the trying ordeal of the surf. As we were returning from the beach we met a carriage containing a number of persons with a family resemblance.

When Aunt Eliza saw them she angrily exclaimed, "Am I to see those Uxbridges every day?"

Of the Uxbridges this much I knew—that the two brothers Uxbridge were the lawyers of her opponents in the lawsuit which had existed three or four years. I had never felt any interest in it, though I knew that it was concerning a tract of ground in the city which had belonged to my grandfather, and which had, since his day, become very valuable. Litigation was a habit of the Huell family. So the sight of the Uxbridge family did not agitate me as it did Aunt Eliza.

"The sly, methodical dogs! but I shall beat Lemorne yet!"

"How will you amuse yourself then, aunt?"

"I'll adopt some boys to inherit what I shall save from his clutches."

The bath fatigued her so she remained in her room for the rest of the day; but she kept me busy with a hundred trifles. I wrote for her, computed interest, studied out bills of fare, till four o'clock came, and with it a fog. Nevertheless I must ride on the Avenue, and the carriage was ordered.

"Wear your silk, Margaret; it will just about last your visit through—the fog will use it up."

"I am glad of it," I answered.

"You will ride every day. Wear the bonnet I bought for you also."

"Certainly; but won't that go quicker in the fog than the dress?"

"Maybe; but wear it."

I rode every day afterward, from four to six, in the black silk, the mantilla, and the white straw. When Aunt Eliza went she was so on the alert for the Uxbridge family carriage that she could have had little enjoyment of the ride. Rocks never were a passion with her, she said, nor promontories, chasms, or sand. She came to Newport to be washed with salt-water; when she had washed up to the doctor's prescription she should leave, as ignorant of the peculiar pleasures of Newport as when she arrived. She had no fancy for its conglomerate societies, its literary cottages, its par-venue suits of rooms, its saloon habits, and its bathing herds.

I considered the rides a part of the contract of what was ex-pected in my two months' performance. I did not dream that I was enjoying them, any more than I supposed myself to be enjoy-ing a sea-bath while pulling Aunt Eliza to and fro in the surf. Nothing in the life around me stirred me, nothing in nature at-tracted me. I liked the fog; somehow it seemed to emanate from me instead of rolling up from the ocean, and to represent me. Whether I went alone or not, the coachman was ordered to drive a certain round; after that I could extend the ride in whatever direction I pleased, but I always said, "Any where, William." One afternoon, which happened to be a bright one, I was riding on the road which led to the glen, when I heard the screaming of a flock of geese which were waddling across the path in front of the horses. I started, for I was asleep probably, and, looking forward, saw the Uxbridge carriage, filled with ladies and children, coming toward me; and by it rode a gentleman on horseback. His horse was rearing among the hissing geese, but neither horse nor geese appeared to engage him; his eyes were fixed upon me. The horse swerved so near that its long mane almost brushed against me. By an irresistible impulse I laid my ungloved hand upon it, but did not look at the rider. Carriage and horseman passed on, and Wil-liam resumed his pace. A vague idea took possession of me that I had seen the horseman before on my various drives. I had a vision of a man galloping on a black horse out of the fog, and into it again. I was very sure, however, that I had never seen him on so pleasant a day as this! William did not bring his horses to time; it was after six when I went into Aunt Eliza's parlor, and found her impatient for her tea and toast. She was crosser than the occasion warranted; but I understood it when she gave me the outlines of a letter she desired me to write to her lawyer in New York. Something had turned up, he had written her; the Uxbridges believed that they had ferreted out what would go against her. I told her that I had met the Uxbridge carriage.

"One of them is in New York; how else could they be giving me trouble just now?"

"There was a gentleman on horseback beside the carriage."

"Did he look mean and cunning?"

"He did not wear his legal beaver up, I think; but he rode a fine horse and sat it well."

"A lawyer on horseback should, like the beggar of the adage, ride to the devil."

"Your business now is the 'Lemorne?' "

"You know it is."

"I did not know but that you had found something besides to litigate."

"It must have been Edward Uxbridge that you saw. He is the brain of the firm."

"You expect Mr. Van Horn?"

"Oh, he must come; I can not be writing letters."

We had been in Newport two weeks when Mr. Van Horn, Aunt Eliza's lawyer, came. He said that he would see Mr. Edward Uxbridge. Between them they might delay a term, which he thought would be best. "Would Miss Huell ever be ready for a compromise?" he jestingly asked.

"Are you suspicious?" she inquired.

"No; but the Uxbridge chaps are clever."

He dined with us; and at four o'clock Aunt Eliza graciously asked him to take a seat in the carriage with me, making some excuse for not going herself.

"Hullo!" said Mr. Van Horn when we had reached the country road; "there's Uxbridge now." And he waved his hand to him.

It was indeed the black horse and the same rider that I had met. He reined up beside us, and shook hands with Mr. Van Horn.

"We are required to answer this new complaint?" said Mr. Van Horn.

Mr. Uxbridge nodded.

"And after that the judgment?"

Mr. Uxbridge laughed.

"I wish that certain gore of land had been sunk instead of being mapped in 1835."

"The surveyor did his business well enough, I am sure."

They talked together in a low voice for a few minutes, and then Mr. Van Horn leaned back in his seat again. "Allow me," he said, "to introduce you, Uxbridge, to Miss Margaret Huell, Miss Huell's niece. Huell *vs.* Brown, you know," he added, in an explanatory tone; for I was Huell *vs.* Brown's daughter.

"Oh!" said Mr. Uxbridge bowing, and looking at me gravely. I looked at him also; he was a pale, stern-looking man, and forty years old certainly. I derived the impression at once that he had a domineering disposition, perhaps from the way in which he controlled his horse.

"Nice beast that," said Mr. Van Horn.

"Yes," he answered, laying his hand on its mane, so that the action brought immediately to my mind the recollection that I had done so too. I would not meet his eye again, however.

"How long shall you remain, Uxbridge?"

"I don't know. You are not interested in the lawsuit, Miss Huell?" he said, putting on his hat.

"Not in the least; nothing of mine is involved."

"We'll gain it for your portion yet, Miss Margaret," said Mr. Van Horn, nodding to Mr. Uxbridge, and bidding William drive on. He returned the next day, and we settled into the routine of hotel life. A few mornings after, she sent me to a matinée, which was given by some of the Opera people, who were in Newport strengthening the larynx with applications of brine. When the concert was half over, and the audience were making the usual hum and stir, I saw Mr. Uxbridge against a pillar, with his hands incased in pearl-colored gloves, and holding a shiny hat. He turned half away when he caught my eye, and then darted toward me.

"You have not been much more interested in the music than you are in the lawsuit," he said, seating himself beside me.

"The *tutoyer*² of the Italian voice is agreeable, however."

"It makes one dreamy."

"A child."

"Yes, a child; not a man nor a woman."

"I teach music. I can not dream over 'one, two, three.' "

"*You*—a music teacher!"

"For six years."

I was aware that he looked at me from head to foot, and I picked at the lace of my invariable black silk; but what did it matter whether I owned that I was a genteel pauper, representing my aunt's position for two months, or not?

"Where?"

"In Waterbury."

"Waterbury differs from Newport."

"I suppose so."

"You suppose!"

A young gentleman sauntered by us, and Mr. Uxbridge called to him to look up the Misses Uxbridge, his nieces, on the other side of the hall.

"Paterfamilias Uxbridge has left his brood in my charge," he said. "I try to do my duty," and he held out a twisted pearl-colored glove, which he pulled off while talking. What white nervous fingers he had! I thought they might pinch like steel.

"You suppose," he repeated.

"I do not look at Newport."

"Have you observed Waterbury?"

"I observe what is in my sphere."

"Oh!"

He was silent then. The second part of the concert began; but I could not compose myself to appreciation. Either the music or I grew chaotic. So many tumultuous sounds I heard   of hope, doubt, inquiry, melancholy, and desire; or did I feel the emotions which these words express? Or was there magnetism stealing into me from the quiet man beside me? He left me with a bow before the concert was over, and I saw him making his way out of the hall when it was finished.

I had been sent in the carrriage, of course; but several carriages were in advance of it before the walk, and I waited there for William to drive up. When he did so, I saw by the oscillatory motion of his head, though his arms and whiphand were perfectly correct, that he was inebriated. It was his first occasion of meeting fellow-coachmen in full dress, and the occasion had proved too much for him. My hand, however, was on the coach door, when I heard Mr. Uxbridge say, at my elbow.

"It is not safe for you."

"Oh, Sir, it is in the programme that I ride home from the concert." And I prepared to step in.

"I shall sit on the box, then."

"But your nieces?"

"They are walking home, squired by a younger knight."

Aunt Eliza would say, I thought, "Needs must when a lawyer drives"; and I concluded to allow him to have his way, telling him that he was taking a great deal of trouble. He thought it would be less if he were allowed to sit inside; both ways were unsafe.

Nothing happened. William drove well from habit; but James was obliged to assist him to dismount. Mr. Uxbridge waited a moment at the door, and so there was quite a little sensation, which spread its ripples till Aunt Eliza was reached. She sent for William, whose only excuse was "dampness."

"Uxbridge knew my carriage, of course," she said, with a complacent voice.

"He knew me," I replied.

"You do not look like the Huells."

"I look precisely like the young woman to whom he was introduced by Mr. Van Horn."

"Oh ho!"

"He thought it unsafe for me to come alone under William's charge."

"Ah ha!"

No more was said on the subject of his coming home with me. Aunt Eliza had several fits of musing in the course of the evening while I read aloud to her, which had no connection with the subject of the book. As I put it down she said that it would be well for me to go to church the next day. I acquiesced, but remarked that my piety would not require the carriage, and that I preferred to walk. Besides, it would be well for William and James to attend divine service. She could not spare James, and thought William had better clean the harness, by way of penance.

The morning proved to be warm and sunny. I donned a muslin dress of home manufacture and my own bonnet, and started for church. I had walked but a few paces when the consciousness of being *free* and *alone* struck me. I halted, looked about me, and concluded that I would not go to church, but walk into the fields. I had no knowledge of the whereabouts of the fields; but I walked straight forward, and after a while came upon some barren fields, cropping with coarse rocks, along which ran a narrow road. I turned into it, and soon saw beyond the rough coast the blue ring of the ocean—vast, silent, and splendid in the sunshine. I found a seat on the ruins of an old stone-wall, among some tangled bushes and briers. There being no Aunt Eliza to pull through the surf, and no animated bathers near, I discovered the beauty of the sea, and that I loved it.

Presently I heard the steps of a horse, and, to my astonishment,

Mr. Uxbridge rode past. I was glad he did not know me. I watched him as he rode slowly down the road, deep in thought. He let drop the bridle, and the horse stopped, as if accustomed to the circumstance, and pawed the ground gently, or yawed his neck for pastime. Mr. Uxbridge folded his arms and raised his head to look seaward. It seemed to me as if he were about to address the jury. I had dropped so entirely from my observance of the landscape that I jumped when he resumed the bridle and turned his horse to come back. I slipped from my seat to look among the bushes, determined that he should not recognize me; but my attempt was a failure—he did not ride by the second time.

"Miss Huell!" And he jumped from his saddle, slipping his arm through the bridle.

"I am a runaway. What do you think of the Fugitive Slave Bill?"[3]

"I approve of returning property to its owners."

"The sea must have been God's temple first, instead of the groves."[4]

"I believe the Saurians were an Orthodox tribe."

"Did you stop yonder to ponder the sea?"

"I was pondering 'Lemorne vs. Huell.' "

He looked at me earnestly, and then gave a tug at the bridle, for his steed was inclined to make a crude repast from the bushes.

"How was it that I did not detect you at once?" he continued.

"My apparel is Waterbury apparel."

"Ah!"

We walked up the road slowly till we came to the end of it; then I stopped for him to understand that I thought it time for him to leave me. He sprang into the saddle.

"Give us good by!" he said, bringing his horse close to me.

"We are not on equal terms; I feel too humble afoot to salute you."

"Put your foot on the stirrup then."

A leaf stuck in the horse's forelock, and I pulled it off and waved it in token of farewell. A powerful light shot into his eyes when he saw my hand close on the leaf.

"May I come and see you?" he asked, abruptly. "I will."

"I shall say neither 'No' nor 'Yes.' "

He rode on at a quick pace, and I walked homeward forgetting the sense of liberty I had started with, and proceeded straightway to Aunt Eliza.

"I have not been to church, aunt, but to walk beyond the town;

it was not so nominated in the bond, but I went. The taste of freedom was so pleasant that I warn you there is danger of my 'striking.' When will you have done with Newport?"

"I am pleased with Newport now," she answered, with a curious intonation. "I like it."

"I do also."

Her keen eyes sparkled.

"Did you ever like anything when you were with me before?"

"Never. I will tell you why I like it: because I have met, and shall probably meet, Mr. Uxbridge. I saw him to-day. He asked permission to visit me."

"Let him come."

"He will come."

But we did not see him either at the hotel or when we went abroad. Aunt Eliza rode with me each afternoon, and each morning we went to the beach. She engaged me every moment when at home, and I faithfully performed all my tasks. I clapped to the door on self-investigation—locked it against any analysis or reasoning upon any circumstance connected with Mr. Uxbridge. The only piece of treachery to my code that I was guilty of was the putting of the leaf which I brought home on Sunday between the leaves of that poem whose motto is,

"Mariana in the moated grange."[5]

On Saturday morning, nearly a week after I saw him on my walk, Aunt Eliza proposed that we should go to Turo Street on a shopping excursion; she wanted a cap, and various articles besides. As we went into a large shop I saw Mr. Uxbridge at a counter buying gloves; her quick eye caught sight of him, and she edged away, saying she would look at some goods on the other side; I might wait where I was. As he turned to go out he saw me and stopped.

"I have been in New York since I saw you," he said. "Mr. Lemorne sent for me."

"There is my aunt," I said.

He shrugged his shoulders.

"I shall not go away soon again," he remarked. "I missed Newport greatly."

I made some foolish reply, and kept my eyes on Aunt Eliza, who dawdled unaccountably. He appeared amused, and after a little talk went away.

Aunt Eliza's purchase was a rose-colored moire antique, which she said was to be made for me; for Mrs. Bliss, one of our hotel acquaintances, had offered to chaperon me to the great ball which would come off in a few days, and she had accepted the offer for me.

"There will be no chance for you to take a walk instead," she finished with.

"I can not dance, you know."

"But you will be *there*."

I was sent to a dress-maker of Mrs. Bliss's recommending; but I ordered the dress to be made after my own design, long plain sleeves, and high plain corsage, and requested that it should not be sent home till the evening of the ball. Before it came off Mr. Uxbridge called, and was graciously received by Aunt Eliza, who could be gracious to all except her relatives. I could not but perceive, however, that they watched each other in spite of their lively conversation. To me he was deferential, but went over the ground of our acquaintance as if it had been the most natural thing in the world. But for my life-long habit of never calling in question the behavior of those I came in contact with, and of never expecting any thing different from that I received, I might have wondered over his visit. Every person's individuality was sacred to me, from the fact, perhaps, that my own individuality had never been respected by any person with whom I had any relation—not even by my own mother.

After Mr. Uxbridge went, I asked Aunt Eliza if she thought he looked mean and cunning? She laughed, and replied that she was bound to think that Mr. Lemorne's lawyer could not look otherwise.

When, on the night of the ball, I presented myself in the rose-colored moire antique for her inspection, she raised her eyebrows, but said nothing about it.

"I need not be careful of it, I suppose, aunt?"

"Spill as much wine and ice-cream on it as you like."

In the dressing room Mrs. Bliss surveyed me.

"I think I like this mass of rose-color," she said. "Your hair comes out in contrast so brilliantly. Why, you have not a single ornament on!"

"It is so easy to dress without."

This was all the conversation we had together during the evening, except when she introduced some acquaintance to fulfill her matronizing duties. As I was no dancer I was left alone most of the time, and amused myself by gliding from window to window along the wall, that it might not be observed that I was a fixed flower. Still I suffered the annoyance of being stared at by wandering squads of young gentlemen, the "curled darlings" of the ballroom. I borrowed Mrs. Bliss's fan in one of her visits for a protection. With that, and the embrasure of a remote window where I finally stationed myself, I hoped to escape further notice. The music of the celebrated band which played between the dances recalled the chorus of spirits which charmed Faust:

> "And the fluttering
> Ribbons of drapery
> Cover the plains,
> Cover the bowers,
> Where lovers,
> Deep in thought,
> Give themselves for life."[6]

The voice of Mrs. Bliss broke its spell.

"I bring an old friend, Miss Huell, and he tells me an acquaintance of yours."

It was Mr. Uxbridge.

"I had no thought of meeting you, Miss Huell."

And he coolly took the seat beside me in the window, leaving to Mrs. Bliss the alternative of standing or of going away; she chose the latter.

"I saw you as soon as I came in," he said, "gliding from window to window, like a vessel hugging the shore in a storm."

"With colors at half-mast; I have no dancing partner."

"How many have observed you?"

"Several young gentlemen."

"Moths."

"Oh no, butterflies."

"They must keep away now."

"Are you Rhadamanthus?"

"And Charon, too. I would have you row in the same boat with me."

"Now you are fishing."

"Won't you compliment me. Did I ever look better?"

His evening costume *was* becoming, but he looked pale, and weary, and disturbed. But if we were engaged for a tournament, as his behavior indicated, I must do my best at telling. So I told him that he never looked better, and asked him how I looked. He would look at me presently, he said, and decide. Mrs. Bliss skimmed by us with nods and smiles; as she vanished our eyes followed her, and we talked vaguely on various matters, sounding ourselves and each other. When a furious redowa set in which cut our conversation into rhythm he pushed up the window and said, "Look out."

I turned my face to him to do so, and saw the moon at the full, riding through the strip of sky which our vision commanded. From the moon our eyes fell on each other. After a moment's silence, during which I returned his steadfast gaze, for I could not help it, he said:

"If we understand the impression we make upon each other, what must be said?"

I made no reply, but fanned myself, neither looking at the moon, nor upon the redowa, nor upon any thing.

He took the fan from me.

"Speak of yourself," he said.

"Speak you."

"I am what I seem, a man within your sphere. By all the accidents of position and circumstance suited to it. Have you not learned it?"

"I am not what I seem. I never wore so splendid a dress as this till tonight, and shall not again."

He gave the fan such a twirl that its slender sticks snapped, and it dropped like the broken wing of a bird.

"Mr. Uxbridge, that fan belongs to Mrs. Bliss."

He threw it out of the window.

"You have courage, fidelity, and patience—this character with a passionate soul. I am sure that you have such a soul?"

"I do not know."

"I have fallen in love with you. It happened on the very day when I passed you on the way to the Glen. I never got away from the remembrance of seeing your hand on the mane of my horse."

He waited for me to speak, but I could not; the balance of my mind was gone. Why should this have happened to me—a slave? As it had happened, why did I not feel exultant in the sense of power which the chance for freedom with him should give?

"What is it, Margaret? your face is as sad as death."

"How do you call me 'Margaret?'"

"As I would call my wife—Margaret."

He rose and stood before me to screen my face from observation. I supposed so, and endeavored to stifle my agitation.

"You are better," he said, presently. "Come go with me and get some refreshment." And he beckoned to Mrs. Bliss, who was down the hall with an unwieldly gentleman.

"Will you go to supper now?" she asked.

"We are only waiting for you," Mr. Uxbridge answered, offering me his arm.

When we emerged into the blaze and glitter of the supper-room I sought refuge in the shadow of Mrs. Bliss's companion, for it seemed to me that I had lost my own.

"Drink this Champagne," said Mr. Uxbridge. "Pay no attention to the Colonel on your left; he won't expect it."

"Neither must you."

"Drink."

The Champagne did not prevent me from reflecting on the fact that he had not yet asked whether I loved him.

The spirit chorus again floated through my mind:

> "Where lovers,
> Deep in thought,
> *Give* themselves for life."

I was not allowed to *give* myself—I was *taken*.

"No heel-taps," he whispered, "to the bottom quaff."

"Take me home, will you?"

"Mrs. Bliss is not ready."

"Tell her that I must go."

He went behind her chair and whispered something, and she nodded to me to go without her.

When her carriage came up, I think he gave the coachman an order to drive home in a round-about way, for we were a long time reaching it. I kept my face to the window, and he made no effort to divert my attention. When we came to a street whose thick rows of trees shut out the moonlight my eager soul longed to leap out into the dark and demand of him his heart, soul, life, for *me*.

I struck him lightly on the shoulder; he seized my hand.

"Oh, I know you, Margaret; you are mine!"

"We are at the hotel."

He sent the carriage back, and said that he would leave me at my aunt's door. He wished that he could see her then. Was it magic that made her open the door before I reached it?

"Have you come on legal business?" she asked him.

"You have divined what I come for."

"Step in, step in; it's very late. I should have been in bed but for neuralgia. Did Mr. Uxbridge come home with you, Margaret?"

"Yes, in Mrs. Bliss's carriage; I wished to come before she was ready to leave."

"Well, Mr. Uxbridge is old enough for your protector, certainly."

"I *am* forty, ma'am."

"Do you want Margaret?"

"I do."

"You know exactly how much is involved in your client's suit?"

"Exactly."

"You also know that his claim is an unjust one."

"Do I?"

"I shall not be poor if I lose; if I gain, Margaret will be rich."

" 'Margaret will be rich,' " he repeated, absently.

"What! have you changed your mind respecting the orphans, aunt?"

"She has, and is—nothing," she went on, not heeding my remark. "Her father married below his station; when he died his wife fell back to her place—for he spent his fortune—and there she and Margaret must remain, unless Lemorne is defeated."

"Aunt, for your succinct biography of my position many thanks."

"Sixty thousand dollars," she continued. "Van Horn tells me that, as yet, the firm of Uxbridge Brothers have only an income— no capital."

"It is true," he answered, musingly.

The clock on the mantle struck two.

"A thousand dollars for every year of my life," she said. "You and I, Uxbridge, know the value and beauty of money."

"Yes, there is beauty in money, and"—looking at me—"beauty without it."

"The striking of the clock," I soliloquized, "proves that this scene is not a phantasm."

"Margaret is fatigued," he said, rising. "May I come to-morrow?"

"It is my part only," replied Aunt Eliza, "to see that she is, or is not, Cinderella."

"If you have ever thought of me, aunt, as an individual, you must have seen that I am not averse to ashes."

He held my hand a moment, and then kissed me with a kiss of appropriation.

"He is in love with you," she said, after he had gone. "I think I know him. He has found beauty ignorant of itself; he will teach you to develop it."

The next morning Mr. Uxbridge had an interview with Aunt Eliza before he saw me.

When we were alone I asked him how her eccentricities affected him; he could not but consider her violent, prejudiced, warped, and whimsical. I told him that I had been taught to accept all that she did on this basis. Would this explain to him my silence in regard to her?

"Can you endure to live with her in Bond Street for the present, or would you rather return to Waterbury?"

"She desires my company while she is in Newport only. I have never been with her so long before."

"I understand her. Law is a game, in her estimation, in which cheating can as easily be carried on as at cards."

"Her soul is in this case."

"Her soul is not too large for it. Will you ride this afternoon?"

I promised, of course. From that time till he left Newport we saw each other every day, and though I found little opportunity to express my own peculiar feelings, he comprehended many of my wishes, and all my tastes. I grew fond of him hourly. Had I not reason? Never was friend so considerate, never was lover more devoted.

When he had been gone a few days, Aunt Eliza declared that she was ready to depart from Newport. The rose-colored days were ended! In two days we were on the Sound, coach, horses, servants, and ourselves.

It was the 1st of September when we arrived in Bond Street. A week from that date Samuel Uxbridge, the senior partner of Uxbridge Brothers, went to Europe with his family, and I went to Waterbury, accompanied by Mr. Uxbridge. He consulted mother in regard to our marriage, and appointed it in November. In October Aunt Eliza sent for me to come back to Bond Street and spend a week. She had some fine marking to do, she wrote. While there I noticed a restlessness in her which I had never before observed, and conferred with Mrs. Roll on the matter. "She do be awake nights a deal, and that's the reason," Mrs. Roll said. Her manner was the same in other respects. She said she would not give me any thing for my wedding outfit, but she paid my fare from Waterbury and back.

She could not spare me to go out, she told Mr. Uxbridge, and in consequence I saw little of him while there.

In November we were married. Aunt Eliza was not at the wedding, which was a quiet one. Mr. Uxbridge desired me to remain in Waterbury till spring. He would not decide about taking a house in New York till then; by that time his brother might return, and if possible we would go to Europe for a few months. I acquiesced in all his plans. Indeed I was not consulted; but I was happy— happy in him, and happy in every thing.

The winter passed in waiting for him to come to Waterbury every Saturday; and in the enjoyment of the two days he passed with me. In March Aunt Eliza wrote me that Lemorne was beaten! Van Horn had taken up the whole contents of his snuff-box in her house the evening before in amazement at the turn things had taken.

That night I dreamed of the scene in the hotel at Newport. I heard Aunt Eliza saying, "If I gain, Margaret will be rich." And I heard also the clock strike two. As it struck I said, "*My husband is a scoundrel,*" and woke with a start.

NOTES

1. Newport, Rhode Island, was one of nineteenth-century New England's most fashionable seaside resorts.

2. Literally "to speak familiarly to" (to *tu*), *tutoyer* is here appropriated as an *ad hoc* musical term to describe the singer's tone of voice.

3. Margaret here elicits from Uxbridge the proper conservative Yankee reaction to the Fugitive Slave Law.

4. Margaret here adapts the first line of "A Forest Hymn" (1825), by American poet William Cullen Bryant (1794–1878): "The groves were God's first temples." This is one of the few allusions to American poetry in Stoddard's fiction.

5. "Mariana" (1830) by Alfred Lord Tennyson (1809–92). The motto is from Shakespeare, *Measure for Measure*, III.i. Shakespeare's and Tennyson's Marianas both await lovers who have deserted them.

6. Johann Wolfgang von Goethe (1749–1832), *Faust*, Part I (1808), ll.1463–69, an excerpt from the Chorus of Spirits that, summoned by Mephistopheles in Part I, lulls Faust to sleep in his study; translation unidentified. The motif of enchantment and the correspondence of names between Stoddard's heroine and Faust's love/victim Gretchen (also called Margaret) suggests other Goethean allusions in "Lemorne," e.g., between the pacts made by Faust with Mephistopheles, by Margaret with Uxbridge, and Uxbridge with Aunt Eliza.

Collected by a Valetudinarian*

Traveling this year in search of something lost, *i.e.,* health, and to appease a heart disquieted by grief, I revisited an old village on our sea-board for the first time in many years. Its mild and melancholy atmosphere accorded with my mood, and I determined to remain as long as the perturbed ghosts, my present rulers, would permit. The docks were empty, the wharves fallen to decay, the streets were bordered with burdock and plantain, and, for the most part, the houses looked as if life and thought had gone away:

> "Through the windows I might see
> The nakedness and vacancy
> Of the dark, deserted house."[1]

At intervals an ox team dragged its slow length along the roads, or a dilapidated chaise rumbled by, or the butcher's cart rattled on. A child, a dog, a cat sometimes made themselves visible and brightened the scene; an occasional woman, shawl wrapped, now and then appeared; and a few men, either with or without business, moved here and there; a sailor, a carpenter, the doctor, an old man with a cane, and the young gentleman of the place in a smart dress and with a preoccupied air.

It was already May, warm enough on sunny days to go into the pastures where the anemone was blowing—spring's earliest flower this way—lovely with its feathery foliage and tinted blossom; and the stunted blue violet, just breaking through the cold, gray sod; curious grasses also were springing up beside the rivulets and ditches, almost flower-like in form and color. I engaged a room at the lonesome hotel—with an ignominious rear and an imposing Doric or Corinthian front—which was managed by Mr. Binks, a retired stage-driver. As I settled my belongings I attempted to

*Harper's New Monthly Magazine 42 (1870): 96–105.

make myself cheerful by recalling early associations, and testing them in a philosophical crucible. However old *I* had grown, and whatever *my* past had been, surely the material universe must have remained the same as of yore, and it ought to prove a resource to the seeker. I remembered the words of a sad and sensitive writer, Châteaubriand. "It is," he said, "a natural instinct of the unhappy to seek to recall visions of happiness by the remembrance of their past pleasures. When I feel my heart dried up by intercourse with other men I turn away and give a sigh of regret to the past. It is in the midst of the immense forests of America that I have tasted to the full these enchanting meditations, these secret and ineffable delights of a mind rejoicing in itself. When I have found myself alone in an ocean of forests a change took place in me. I said, 'Here there are no more roads to follow, no more towns, no narrow houses, no presidents, no republics, or kings; above all, no more laws and no more men.' "[2]

Though neither oak nor maple leaf was unfolded, and the boughs were thin and brown, I could lose myself in the pine woods, which gave the northern part of the country a verdant, grand, and solitary expression. How well I knew them and their sand barrens, where were found arrow-heads, and the Indian skulls which premeditated them! I fondly wished for all the books written on solitude, retirement, communion with nature, and upon that text which the medieval Balzac calls *"Hide your life."* It was he who said, so ingeniously, that when he had any auditors about him he cried with all his might: "Let us go and live in the country; not only to make sure of rest, but also to make sure of salvation. Let us seek Jesus Christ in the way that He himself has directed us. He did not say that He was the gold of the palace, the purple of the court. He said that He was the flower of the field, and the lily of the valley."[3]

Who has written better on solitude, and the pleasures of the past, than the true Parisian authors—the fops and rakes of fashion and the court?

But I brought no books; indeed a bookish reminiscence was a resuscitation, for it had been months since I had read a printed page.

Yes, I had chosen the right spot; neither laws nor men could trouble a solitary stranger. Of the present generation inhabiting the village of course I knew nothing. Feeling as I did, it was no regret that my contemporaries had passed away. The very house I was in proved that every body who might have any knowledge of me was either dead or moved into some other place. It had been built and occupied by a family with which my own had been connected in a commercial way. As a child I had visited the old family. The house was worse than a ruin now, in my opinion, for it had been "fixed up" by a vulgar taste, which dictated monstrosities in form and color; scroll patterns every where in red and yellow. Happily my room, on one side of the house, had not been retouched; the old paper was on the walls, a satin gray with pink dots, and the chimney-place had not been bricked up according to modern fashion for an ugly stove. Mr. Binks was astonished at my choice of a room, and still more astonished when I proposed having a wood-fire. Nobody had wood-fires in the whole place, he insisted. I persisted; I wanted to watch the blaze, and I wanted to arrange and disarrange the sticks and brands at my own good pleasure and that of the tongs.

"A willful woman must have her way," he said; "and I expect you are sick, and maybe won't stay long." So he gave way, and made my room cheerful with birch and hickory fires, and after a little owned that it was the neatest spot in the house.

"It's dreadful dull out the window here," he remarked. "A crow or a robin is all you'll see."

"Swallows, and the grass, and the sky over the fields, also, Mr. Binks, and the three tall pines yonder."

"Well, I'll give up! You are too much for me, marm; them 'ere pines are about as aged as any thing since the flood."

All necessity for exertion being over, no demand of any sort to be made upon me, I fell into a lethargy; thought nothing and felt nothing for several days; dozed over my fire, or stared vacantly at the fields. Mr. Binks had a housekeeper; but she remained in the dark and backward abysm of the kitchen, and he waited upon me with a magisterial air which dignified the tray he brought to my door three times a day, with a kind, set little speech.

"Here is your meal, marm; may you relish it! The weather is softening; the wind is milder—more favorable for invalids. Sartinly you will be round by to-morrow." At last I did get round; that is, I crept down stairs, and Mr. Binks dragged his housekeeper into the parlor to look at me.

"Didn't I say so, Mary Jane? Ain't she down stairs? She hasn't died on my hands has she?"

"Mr. Binks," said Mary Jane, "always looks on the bright side of things, and you must excuse him."

If he was glad to have me down stairs, he was more rejoiced to have me sit at his table. There, to my surprise, I discovered another boarder, who bore a shadowy resemblance to myself, inasmuch as she was dressed in mourning, and looked delicate and feeble. When she saw a purpose of introduction in Mr. Binks's eye, she fluttered and turned her head, but in vain. In a loud voice he said:

"This is Mrs. Hobson; been with me, off and on, nigh to six years—haven't you, Mrs. Hobson?—and going all the time."

"Yes, Mr. Binks," she answered, gently inclining her head toward me, with a twinkle of humor in her eyes.

"Birds of a feather flock together," added Mr. Binks. "By your looks I conclude you have them 'ere mysterious complaints which make women so unaccountable. My wife was the same; first and last, she cost me a couple of hundred in patent medicines. She would try every individual one."

Mrs. Hobson and I exchanged looks, and both of us laughed; the laugh melted the frost between us, and we became friends. Take her for all in all, she was the most self-contained, heroic, patient creature I ever knew. She had come to that pass in life when nothing comes from nothing; consequently she reconstructed trifles into matters which filled up the hours—those slow serpents to people who have exhausted or lived out all illusion and enchantment. She had learned, she told me, to be more interested in a flower-pot than in a garden; to derive more satisfaction in the chairs and tables in her own room than she had formerly felt in setting up a whole house.

"Every small thing tells," she said, "when one becomes isolated; the soul comes out of it under observation. As for change, that which is good for us we have; it is in the atmosphere—its storms and sunshine; in the sky—its sunrise and sunset, its trailing clouds of glory and of gloom. In the sea too—so fixed and ever-varying."

Mrs. Hobson never told me her history; I never asked it. Having no wish to reveal mine, why should I demand hers? Mr. Binks, uneducated as he was, and as native as an oyster to the place which gave him birth, was delicate and refined in his care of her. He told me, soon after I made her acquaintance, that if ever there was a saint upon earth, she was one; that when she died she ought to have a monument equal to Washington's; that she had come to his house in the dead of winter, accompanied by a young man he thought to be a lawyer's clerk, and a great deal of baggage. In conclusion, he said: "Mrs. Sinclair, marm, I expect you have guessed

I am an inquisitive man, but I never asked Mrs. Hobson a question, and I am never going to. She is as good as gold, and as sick as Lazarus.[4] I don't mean that she has any irruption, for she hasn't. She gives fifty dollars every New-Year's to the poor, and pays me every Saturday, reg'lar as clock-work. She has property here."

When I began to ramble about the country, Mrs. Hobson accompanied me. She professed gratitude for an opening in her accustomed ways; the small area of wood and field surrounding the village she had never explored. I taught her the names and habits of wild flowers; how to gather and preserve various delicate plants, and how to watch the various and minute laws which are opened to the eye of the student in the book of Nature, which I had learned from *ennui*. It was "Eliza" and "Helen" between us soon. One day, when perhaps infected by my enthusiasm at the discovery in the woods of a fragrant and delicious flower, she said:

"Eliza, you should have known my cousin Alicia Raymond. Of all the persons I ever knew, you might have understood and aided her. I am foolish that I have never told you the chief reason of my coming to this wild place after my widowhood. Here for some years lived, and died, a woman of genius. Behind yonder point on which stands the lighthouse is an old house, belonging to me now, where she lived. To-morrow we will go there."

"Alicia Raymond! surely I have heard the name. Is she not in some literary complication—a book of the time—or literary dictionary?"

"I dare say; her father, Commodore Raymond, was proud of her, and published some of her childish performances. His house was frequented by all the distinguished people of his time; but when he died she was forgotten. Talk about Chatterton and Keats— if they did not live in their lifetime, they do now, while Alicia's memory only exists in mine and that of her brother.[5] Mr. Binks continually says, one half the world does not know how the other half lives. I say, what a mockery the life of genius is! What half of a community knows it? What does even the nearest neighboring soul know of it?"

Helen's passion astonished me. A hectic flush rose in her cheek, and she gesticulated with vehemence.

"It is all luck," she cried. "After old Brontë had lived a starving life—and God knows what his wife passed through in suffering, aspiration, and contemplation!—and after the daughters had starved every way—most of all, starved for Beauty—fame came to them.

Eliza, what a tragedy was the life of Charlotte Brontë! Do you know that I have a scrap of her handwriting? She did not have paper enough to scribble on—think of that! But I am convinced, from my own experience in this narrowish way of life, where there is nothing which may be called rank, where no one possesses fortune, where all the paraphernalia of living is limited to that which supplies bread and clothing, that this gifted woman, Alicia, discerned a world of beauty and truth that made an everlasting happiness for her great soul, as did Charlotte Brontë."[6]

"Dear Helen, how shall we idlers be taught this ideal happiness?"

"As soon as we can be made to believe that what is called material or positive happiness is no more truthful or exact than that named visionary or romantic happiness."

Mr. Binks, without being aware of a sense of the comic, called us a "game pair," when he met us strolling the by-roads; and so we were to the ordinary eye, for who would have guessed that any fire burned in our ashes? We were a couple of faded, middle-aged women, clad in black garments. Why should such indulge in aspirations for happiness, or the expectation of doing any farther [sic] work in this gay world?

In a day or two after Helen's mention of Alicia Raymond, on a calm, sombre afternoon, we took our way toward the light-house.

"We will go," said Helen, simply, "to the house Alicia last lived in. She gave it to me; the spot, worthless as it is, has chained me; the ground about it is barren; nobody would think of bringing it under cultivation, for it is a mixture of swamp and sandy beach; mullein, briers, sedge, and the beach pea dispute pre-eminence. Suppose, Eliza"—and Helen brightened at the thought—"that you and I should occupy the house?"

"But we should have to leave out the genius which has made such an impression upon you, and, I confess, upon me also. I have a lively curiosity concerning this Alicia and her surroundings."

We toiled in silence among the coarse pebbles of the beach, and climbed over the boulders scattered here and there on our way. The village grew distant, and the landscape solitary; on the left were swampy pastures, wild thickets, and borders of desolate woods; on the right, the wide bay, with distant headlands and islands uprising in the air. The waves came from afar, spent in their sounding fury, and fell in soft foam round the rocks and the pale smooth sand. The beautiful sea-swallow hovered near us, uttering its wild cry, and the little sand birds ran fearlessly before us.

"No wonder she lived here, Helen!"

"I knew you would like the scene; we are almost there—see!"

We had turned the point now on which the light-house stood, and I saw a large old-fashioned house standing in the middle of a natural lawn; two or three cherry-trees were in front of it, and a few fir-trees, indigenous to the soil, twisted and gnarled, but vigorous, were scattered over it. Helen took a key from her pocket as we went up a little path.

"How thick the butter-cups are!" she said, gayly; but I saw that she was deeply moved.

"Yes," I replied; "and the woodpecker is busy also; look at the hole under the eaves by the window-frame! How rank the flags are by the granite step! the ugly things flourish every where. No matter what happens, year after year their dull yellow flowers vulgarly blow."

"Year after year," she repeated, turning the key and opening the door. "So uniform was Alicia's life that it seemed eternal till it came to an end; then it was like a vision. Come in now; you will not see bats nor owls, for after a while it became my recreation to keep the house in order. I have given it sun and air; in the summer I pass half my time here. Has it not an occupied air?"

It was a plain common house; on one side a small parlor, on the other a large one. There was little furniture in either room. A table, a few chairs, book-cases with wide gaps in the shelves, a sofa, a desk, and some portraits on the dingy walls of literary people. I was surprised, however, to see the excellence of said portraits—Raeburn's Scott, Holmes's portrait of Byron—the one Byron himself preferred—Severn's portrait of Keats, a fine engraving of George Sand by Calomme, one of the young Mozart, one of the boy Chatterton, and a few delightful water-colors.[7]

"Do you mean to say," I asked, "that your friend Alicia was perfectly obscure?"

"Except to a few men and women of letters with whom she corresponded. Look over this desk, please; you may comprehend her taste. She *was* happy without fame, I believe."

"I might take her life for a text, and preach a sermon for these crusading days, when women assume so much, and so ardently desire that every assumption should be made public."

"Do so, if you dare. Every day of Alicia's life was made beautiful for the sake of beauty. She taxed all things for this purpose. A bit of moss, a bird's feather, an autumn leaf, a spray of grass served her. Her means went far to suit her artistic habits and tastes. She lived here six years in all. Her only brother returned from the East Indies with an obstinate disease, and was ordered to pass a year or two in the country. He selected this, where his mother was born."

"This desk is curious," I said; "have you examined it?"

"Only in a general way; but look over it. I think, now, I'll give up the place, having been long enough sentimental over it; and it is a trouble to fight with mould and moth."

I opened some little drawers; they were full of nick-nacks, ivory boxes, ornaments in agate and marble, pearl and shell carvings, paper-knives, gypsum figures, clay vases and boxes, Chinese toys, bits of fine china, engravings, and a hundred other articles. One of the prettiest was a green crystal basket in a gold frame. A minute nest was in the basket, and several rose-colored eggs with chocolate spots; a bit of paper was tied to the handle, on which was written—"Robbed May 20, '64."

"They were a queer couple, this brother and sister," said Helen.

Poking into the deep pigeon-holes of the ancient desk, I came upon a book with a brass lock; it was fastened, but on the cover was printed with a pen:

"He who does not run may read."

"Where is the key, Helen?"

"I have it, and you may read the diary; I never have. Let us go back, it is nightfall nearly. Mr. Binks thinks my mind is unsettled about this house; he will come for us with a lantern if we wait."

As we walked slowly homeward, Helen gave me some particulars of her cousin's life. If she had a mania, it was for composition; there were several manuscript volumes in existence, upon which months of labor had been bestowed. Her literary habits were as industrious and methodical as if her work had the market value of a Thackeray or a Dickens. But she had the most self-contained, self-sustaining soul that ever existed, requiring neither praise nor appreciation to feed an ambition perfectly pure and lofty in its aims. If she had lived, she might have given her work to the world.

"Look over the little diary by yourself," Helen said, while we were at our supper, and beamed upon by the genial Binks. In my room I opened Alicia's volume, and soon felt its fresh, natural atmosphere.

April 22, 1864.—House on the beach at Bront's Point just taken possession of by Brother Alton and myself, in the township where our beautiful mother died in our childhood.[8] Nothing threatens recollection of our last city campaign. One Julia—sweet girl—may enter into *his* dreams; *my* vision will be disturbed by no apparition of tulle, Neapolitan ice-cream, or the waltz band. I know he left the pretty creature to be with me. Ten rooms, up stairs and down, every one shabby and delightful. The rude lawn is full of clover and blooming grasses, and under the lonely stone walls, old as Adam, nicest brambles grow. We pulled down the paling this afternoon before the front of the house. Put up our Mexican hammock between the door and cherry-tree. Such a pretty view from said hammock: the lawn running to the beach, which is smooth, for it is the edge of the cove rounding in between two gravelly points, and looks quite lake-like; near the shore it is blue and smooth, when outside it is gray and rough under the beating winds.

The waves curve in and fall upon the sand, leaving soft bubbles and silky weeds, bits of drift-wood, snowy and silvery shells, and all the mysterious *débris* of the sea, daily tossed upon a hundred shores by the relentless tide. On each side of this secluded, fairy-like cove are groups of richly stained rocks. Above all this sea and shore I can watch the sunrise and sunset. But what civilized being ever sees a sunrise? The room with windows commanding this view I have named my own—this where I at this moment am. Funny gray paper on the walls, with sepia pictures—elegant fox-hunters on high-bred horses, hounds, whippers-in, a pleasant wood, and an impossible fountain. I have hung red curtains before the windows, and filled the mantel-piece with Indian china; matting is laid upon the floor, and the furniture is covered with Alton's Indian chintz—peacocks, parrots, birds of paradise, all so lively that I expect them to scream at any moment. A wood-fire burns in the chimney; Alton sits on the brick hearth beside it, a novel in his hand, his booted legs crossed, and he tugs at his mustache perfectly abstracted. *"Julia,"* I cry, from some impulse of mischief. He starts, drops his book, and says:

"Confound you, Alicia! Is she at the shutters? I thought I heard a woman whimper."

"It is only the water lapping the shore, Alton; better music than that of a woman's tongue."

"Shut yours, then, and go on with your pen. Its scratching is an opiate. I dare say what you write would prove a sleeping-draught to your reader."

Alton picks up his book, rustles a page or two, then lights a cigar, and resumes his musings. As I scribble on he rouses once more, winking his long black eyelashes, and says:

"Sis Alicia, literary people, after all, are only coral worms. It takes a million to make a little reef in the ocean."

"But the reef is there, Alton."

"Yes; and how much drifts to the patient minute structure!—weeds; all the refuse of the violence of the deep; weary sea-birds, with seeds of plants in their crops; the tangle of strong currents from pole to pole—and a world is made! I have half a mind to call you Coralline."

"Go to bed, my boy, or how shall I ever write a proper description of this house!"

"I'll go, my love, and snore to the breakers of Bront's Point. The air is superb coming through the shattered panes. And I shall be so hungry in the morning. What have you in the larder?"

"Nothing; I will watch for a fisherman."

Exit Alton with a grimace and loud yawn. Yes, this room suits me—at midnight—the present hour. Here is my new patent ink-stand, which promises to be a failure, and a paperweight with a bird on it unlike any known species of bird, and my comfortable port-folio under the shaded lamp. I have filled up the china closet with illustrated books. Their gold, red, and green backs glisten behind the glass door. What friends they are! A dead author is better than a live friend: the one can not change nor fail, the other may. Rogers, Gray, Bloomfield, Goldsmith, Béranger, Tennyson, my goodly company![9] The last brand has fallen on the hearth, and the white ashes cover the coals. The bay gives tongue under the moon. A journal is a good thing—to express that which is neither in the heart nor brain! By-the-way, in rummaging my brain to-day I believe that I thanked God for suddenly feeling virile; I mean that I emerged from my fog. Why is Alton tramping overhead? Pooh! what is the feeling of a restless heart?

April 28.—East wind. The chimneys have smoked. We had trout for dinner to-day. Alton caught them in a brook a mile above us, on the other side of the high hill at the back of the house, where the sun seems to sit down and rags of clouds gather and hide. Spying inside and outside of myself for the fashion of my novel. The hero is vital. What name can I give him—Greek, Oriental, or English? Cleon, Hafiz, John! Come, let me clutch thee! Lonely old town this. Nobody comes to see us; evidently there is no social system in vogue. Somebody went by, though, to-day—a man with a horse, cart, and pitchfork; all went over our lawn straight to the beach. When I saw his purpose—that of gathering sea-weed—I went out and helped him; that is, I poked over the long green ribbons dashed up by the tide, and discovered shelly crea-tures on their first voyage from home, bright and smooth pebbles, and umber tufts of fat weeds. I hope Helen Hobson will visit us soon. So much of society as she can give I require.

I laid the diary down and sought Helen.

"I have left off at the mention of your name, Helen."

"Do you wonder at my permitting you to read a private record? I shrink from it. Will you go through with it? Since you came I have decided to settle my affairs so far as that old place is con-cerned. When Alicia's papers are looked over and every thing removed, I will sell the house. When you leave the town I will go also, for I can no longer endure it. We will not precisely play Naomi and Ruth, but I trust we may not live far apart."[10]

"What about the brother Alton?"

"He will never return here. Nothing could induce him to look at any thing which might remind him of the lost Alicia, the sister he loved so wonderfully well. The delay is owing to him. Many letters have passed between us on the subject of Alicia's papers and possessions, and the house which she gave me. He has refused over and over again to have any thing to do with them, and at last, thanks to you, I have decided for myself. Read the fragmentary journal, and then give me your opinion whether any of her manu-script should be published."

"I should not imagine her a solitary or eccentric person from the little I have read."

"She was alive and at home with every thing except human companionship; but I never understood her."

"I dare say; no one understood her. Have you thought of that as a reason for her isolation? What should drive one into solitude, if a lack of comprehension of one's sincerest feelings and motives can not? And then, what strange modes of expression pride of soul will take! There are those, even in this jostling, crowded world, whose virgin hearts take alarm at the least approach to or necessity for revelation. They wait for some other world to be developed in—some unknown deity to govern them. I like this Alicia; she has her own atmosphere. Maybe I am sent here to be aided by her."

Helen's eyes glistened.

"Be, then," she exclaimed, "my atonement. Your mind is nearer hers than my futile, vacillating one was. Alicia is one of my dearest memories. Teach me to hope that she forgave me for every short-coming of obtuseness, ignorance, and habit. What wretchedly imperfect, unfinished creatures we are! The flood did not wash us right, after all."

Some occult influence led me the next calm, cloudy afternoon to the old house by the sea, Alicia's home. I was glad to be alone. The grass on the lawn waved me a welcome; butter-cups glistened in it; bees and butterflies hummed and hovered every where. The wind sounded a fitful melody round the eaves, and shook the tall cherry-trees before the door. I had Alicia's diary with me. Taking a seat on the granite gate-sill, I opened it; as I read, shadows flickered over the page, the wind fluttered the leaves, stalks and unripe cherries fell into my lap, and birds constantly twittered over my head. I was Alicia, or I was the dream of myself—which? I looked toward the vague, blue horizon where land and water blended, and should not have been surprised to see a colossal reflection of either uprising in the distance.

May 6.—My birthday. Alicia, the child of an unhappy mother, is twenty-eight to-day. Sho! The gray water laps the paler sand, glimmers and trembles; the purple clouds glide by. Insidious Spirit of Beauty, dark or bright, you lurk every where.

May 8.—Poor fellow! his grave is nameless. So shall mine be.

May 10.—Happy again under this sky, before this sea. Is happiness atmospheric? Read Victor Hugo's novel, "The Toilers of the Sea." A Greek poem in French.[11] Greek—a little distracted.

May 15.—Happier perhaps for being wrapped in a cloud of illness. Civilized people for the most part have nurses when they are ill. The black woman in the kitchen does not care for me, and while I suffer Alton stays in the woods. There is a deep frown on his face; I know what it means. He does not know how to approach me.

June 3.—I am gay. A box of books came to-day. So much good reading in so much good solitude. I see why Alton likes "Faith Unwin." The lonely, pathetic, simple tenor of human feeling suits him. Alas! why and for what should I torture my genius?[12] Let it be in its afrite box—small, neat, compact.[13] It need not rise in a cloud of smoke and assume in some kindred imaginative mind shape and meaning.

June 10.—I watched the road for Helen Hobson this morning. She did not come. Walked out and picked field flowers, so gay now every where.

June 11.—Helen came with a pair of amethyst ear-rings for me, a sketch by M'Entee—so like my friend—a bower of trees, a glimpse of blue, and a solitary wanderer beneath the boughs.[14] Art is better than nature. We talked, at first, about newspapers and religion. Helen ate a great deal. Next day we "parted at the gates of Ispahan"[15]—that is, Alton drove us to the railway station, six miles away. He made us swallow a mouthful of whisky from his flask, and muttered something which made Helen color. I did not understand him; but a moment after I discovered tears on my face. Suppose I was intoxicated. Heavens! What does it all mean? Are we wretched? What are we playing at, in this mechanical way? Shadows over the scene—death-ripples, gliding over the surface so glassy and hard! All forgetfulness must be intoxication.

June 12.—Summer drops in for a few hours on our bleak coast daily. Threw stones into the water to-day. Saw in the sand vermilion spiders, and black, swift-gaited ones. The blue scentless violet still blooms near the dead sea-weed, and the vivid yellow cinque-foil. Read the cook-book. Dashed into the opening of my novel. First line—very striking: *"On an autumn morning—"*

June 20.—I like old boggy fields. The sweetest flowers grow there, the greenest moss; there birds congregate, and the frog doth flourish. I brought home from said bogginess a bunch of delicious white violets, and put them to Alton's nose. He was lying in the hammock, with his hat pulled over his eyes. He caught my hands, and drew my face to his.

"Alicia, my love, how are you? Tell me, do you suffer?"

"One way, yes; two ways, no. And how are you, master?"

"Bored one way; two ways, no."

"How handsome you are, my dear!"

"Ain't I? Bring out the big looking-glass, quick!"

He kept my violets; where they went to I could not discover. No letters have come to him. Where is that heartless girl? Pooh! she is not heartless.

June 21.—The sea is awfully full to-night. "It runneth here, it runneth there," crowding round all the points, pressing up every pier, and wave kisses wave. Read "Tom Cringle's Log"—a first-rate nautical novel.[16]

June 27.—Telegram scared us to-day. Alton is summoned to the city upon some Indian business. He looked so wistfully at me when he came for a good-by that I said, "See Julia, by all means, and give her my love."

"Can you love her?" he asked, eagerly.

"I'll try."

"You never will, Alicia; I am a fool to ask it."

Cried, and made a beautiful loaf of cake after he left. Then fell to reading. Wordsworth is a good doctor for the mind.

June 28.—It struck me just now that I should never be happier. I am alone with my own power. What I decide to be, that I am for myself. So long as I am solitary, how can I be convicted of error? Last night I sat in Alton's deserted room and watched the orange sunset waning slow. The moon rose, and I saw spectral sails gliding down the bay and vanishing beyond a range of purple cloud. The sea grew wild as the moon rode up the sky; its tumult filled the air. Nothing in nature can be finer than these scenes in these hours. From nature, went to Wordsworth again; he is a teacher, as many painters and musicians are.

July 1.—Droning on my novel with faith and a tormented conscience. Shall I dare tell the truth about men and women? Can any wild invention excuse me for bringing to light that which exists with reason and with passion? Who may speak if I can not? I fear not my unborn publisher. No feat of my mind can deprive me of the fixed income which provides me bread; nothing can separate me from my sole living love—Alton—nothing from my sole friendship with Helen Hobson. As for opinion, criticism, admirers, enemies—how can I be reached *here,* or farther on—the grave? One may be egotistical on waste paper, as this is; and I assert that I have an experience in the life of love, enjoyment, and suffering which, frankly expressed and described, should teach timid and ignorant hearts their capacities and their limits. Have I the power? Shall I build better than I know, if I go on? *On,* I mean so; but must leave my pen and paper behind me, then.

July 2.—My woodland walks are perfect now. The lady's slipper is blooming above the pine needles; its pink-veined hanging
bells, between two pointed green leaves, looked so pretty in the
dry underbrush this afternoon. I dreamed away several hours under an aged, flat-topped yellow pine; the air was indescribably
delicious; every time I looked about me found some new flower,
among them the dwarf Solomon's-seal—an emerald, grooved leaf,
with tiny dots of white flowers on the tiny stalk. Numerous grasses
are in bloom, attractive in form, and dull, delicate in shade. Came
home and found Alton drinking claret out of the pale Bohemian
glasses, that is, one glass. Talk about writing novels and speaking
the truth! Here we two were together, kindred souls at that, in
utter ignorance of each other's moods and circumstances, having
been parted a day or two, and as shy as strangers.

"Where have you been, Alicia?"

"In the woods."

"You mean tree woods?"

"Yes; the breezy, aromatic, uninterfering woods."

"Go with me now there; sunset will not come off this two
hours. Besides, there is no more beautiful moment than that when
the sun's last rays drop below the level trunks. The birds sing their
even song; and the insects, creatures of night, begin their oratorio.
Then, for greeting, too, the shrubs send up odors to mingle with
the flying crimson clouds."

So we started. I continually said to myself, "Poor moth, glow-
worm, vain banging beetle, seeking the light and prating about
novels!" Whatever Alton's thoughts were, he showed no distur-
bance, looked from right to left, and at last said, "Hist, hush!" We
stood still, and presently heard the whir of wings and stifled chirps.

"Come out of the path, under the scrub oaks," he said; "it is
dry. Here is the moss, with its red eyes. See here, with such things
in it, Alicia, the world is pretty."

I looked into a holly-bush, as he directed, and close to the
ground was a thrush's nest—four little chocolate-colored birds in
it. The father and mother, with square cinnamon tails, kept near
us, with distressing cries.

July 6.—Read Emerson, who makes apparent the originality of
other authors. Read the "Simon" of George Sand.[17] Her case gives
me despair. I was alone in to-night's deepening dusk, still and
unoccupied; the walls of an invisible, fearful destiny I felt to be
slowly closing round me. The cold gray sea, monotonously roar-

ing, typified it. Horrible existence, now serene enough to contem-
plate inevitable death.

July 8.—The tissue complains to the brain. One's organs will
not be subservient to intellectual action. They shall be, though.
Wish I could get some black ink. Made a raid in the shops on Main
Street for it, and that put me in better spirits. Saw blue yarn, eggs,
but no ink. Lighted on a piece of lovely chintz, and bought it for
Alton's windows.

July 10.—Two military officers arrived. Wore my violet grena-
dine and black lace. Alton's eyes beamed when I came in to dinner.
Had roasted chickens, and the gold brand Champagne. The ice
was slightly troubled with roots. Wondered whether they were the
filaments of the Arethusa pink, or the adder's-tongue. Officers
talked about icebergs being at the north yet. Also cursed war
movements. Ate up all the dinner. Smoked terribly, and went away
with inane compliments.

July 18.—"My days go on." No motive for writing. The moth-
millers distract me. The beetles fly about greatly o' nights also.
Full-blooded summer swells the sea and is in my veins. Let me
sew a womanly seam. Who am I to summon giants? I remember
a fine, sacred soul—vanished. He had the best of mine, yet left
me. Eternally my heart is his. How frail and rapid my memorials
recalling him—the western wind blowing after sunset, when the
sky is still emerald and amber, and distant shrub and flowers send
their odors to me, when the white water is motionless, and the
crescent moon gives me silvered beams, where we often were,
Arnold and I.

July 20.—The fields are wonderful, a mass of white, yellow,
and blue blossoms in the deep, waving beds of green. Alton makes
my heart ache. His eye passes me by, even when his smile is most
pleasant, his voice most kind. Somebody sent me a bunch of white
roses to-day. A friend came unexpectedly. Alton is playing cards
with him in the east room. I saw this friend for the first time in
November last. What is he here for? I wish I could fall in love with
him. It might amuse us this summer weather.

Two hours afterward.

"Sir—Mr. Dresden," I asked, "do cards amuse you?"

"Not in the least. I came all these miles to see your ladyship,
and your indifference is killing."

"So I was afraid. I wish to make amends, and beg you to talk
with me. Alton, go away. Leave Mr. Dresden and myself together.

I am forgetting human beings, among all these waves, grass, and insects."

Shrugging his shoulders, and giving a pitying smile to Dresden, he sauntered off, candle in hand.

Mr. Dresden and I looked at each other and laughed.

"Tell and teach me, Miss Alicia," he begged. "I am but a baby of thirty-five, you know. You can mention insects."

"I am old too. Look at my hair."

With sudden passion he kissed the band on my forehead.

"Oh, Alicia, do not be such a heavenly icicle. What can I do to please you? Give up your dreadful isolation, or let me share it with you. Come; let me carry your camp-stool and your umbrella. I'll mend your pens to my dying day, learn botany—any thing. Or, better—" and here he caught my hands—"come out into my world, be my wife! Don't you know that my father has lately left me a large fortune? Alton knows it. I have his best wishes. We three shall never separate. I love you, Alicia. I am worthy even you."

"What! Does Alton know that you would marry me? Will he give me away?"

"No away about it. Visionary, Quixotic girl, yes! My love, let us go to the Old World, cities whose legends enchant you, to the birth-place of the genius you worship, the cradle of the arts you revere."

Oh, the pictures that flashed across my soul as he spoke the glowing vision of life without being aware of it! I put my hand in his; he saw tears in my eyes.

"Alton!" he shouted.

Instantly, like a ghost, Alton stood in the doorway.

"Do you mean for me to marry Dresden?" I asked.

"I mean that you shall do as you choose to do," he answered, stamping his foot. "But I like Dresden; he is good, strong."

"I can not die abroad. Somehow I can not fall in love, either. I wished most seriously to love you, Mr. Dresden. What's the matter with me? I am fond of you. But you must leave me."

"Alicia, you are a fool!" said Alton. "Come away, Dresden."

"Not I; I intend to talk with Alicia; you can take leave again of me. I begin to understand your sister."

And we did talk deep into the night. I like him better, much better; but what would become of my literary career? A strong man's love must interfere with my hero; and my heroine might interfere with him.

July 23.—He has gone. I feel free. What a perfect sunset we had!—purple drifts, crimson bars suffusing the sea, and then grew clearest light in the sky, with Venus, red and diamond-pointed, beside the young moon. I found to-day a great lunar moth sticking to a bush; splendid creature; hid him in my handkerchief, brought him home, administered chloroform, and pinned him on the curtain.

"Poor Dresden," said Alton, who was watching me.

"Kiss me, brother dear; I am lonely."

He complied, and then heaved a sigh. I continued:

"It need make no difference to you—"

Alton put his hand over my mouth.

"Hush! the lunar is kicking still, Alicia."

July 30.—Brought home a bunch of the wax-like flowers of the round-leafed winter-green. It has a penetrating odor, resembling that of the tuberose. More than "the glory in the grass, the splendor in the flower," I long for; their beauty suggests that which I require.[18] The evening is profoundly quiet; the shield of the full moon shines in the water. Alton is floating upon it; I see the sail of his boat on the edge of the moon's wake, where the water is dark; the sail is motionless. I am going out to walk—have had the heartache before in moonlight nights, and out-of-doors too. After a while my heart will be uplifted; something from the mysterious stars, far off as they are in the void, will come down to my aid.

August 1.—Gathered fresh immortelles to-day from the sand-banks between here and Gilford. Filled Arnold's glass—the one he drank from last—which I keep by me always. Arnold! Why should I dream of other love, either in speaking or writing? By-the-way, Alton and I have read six novels this week, full of conventional white-kid love.

August 21.—Blank to me, and all out-of-doors looked blank.

September 3.—Dog-days.

Goethe says: "The highest problem of every art is, by means of appearances, to produce the illusion of a loftier reality. That is, however, a false effort which, in giving reality to the appearance, goes so far as to leave in it nothing but the common everyday actual."[19] Wordy, this; and yet when I think how I lie about *Lucretia,* the heroine of my novel—that is, how I enlarge and diverge from the slender stock of the real experience from which I derive my *Lucretia*—I perceive that Goethe, the calculating, is right. I *am* afraid, after all. Or do I follow the principle governing the universe, that every flower must have an ugly root—that behind or back of all beauty is the black, rough, coarse structure? Who has ever looked thoroughly into the lining of things? First rough beams to support our dwellings; then rough laths and mortar; then delicate, beautifully colored papers, or fresco painting; and upon that pictures, the culmination of art!

September 10.—Dog-days have a merit of their own, a variety. Excellent aromatic fogs; vivid sunshine to ripen wild, luscious berries; heavy dews to comfort the dying grass and hardy, lowly herbs, and to moisten the painted leaf before it drops to the cold, waiting earth. I wander on; pretend to be artistic and intellectual, and all that, when I know that Alton's life beats loudly for Julia, the woman he loves. I shall have to send for her. If she has a heart she must love this spot. I say that, although it is on the New England coast, near Plymouth Rock—throne of the exalted Puritans—it is beautiful. Yes, I would have her here already. I cough so, I suppose that I must die soon, and I do not want to leave Alton alone. For, let him start at the hour of my death, for any spot on any continent, he would be alone unless some kind, loving woman should accompany him, to watch and guard him.

September 20.—Autumn days, autumn fields—*not* happy autumn fields. The days that are no more are not between us yet.[20] We tremble, we suffer; still our eyes behold them. What trivial things we say to each other daily—about the wind, weather, flowers, each other! Oh, my poor boy—my brother!

September 26.—Marsh marigold, and goldenrod, and wild asters, star-like, white, and lavender blossoms thickly strewing every path. Well, flowers make me believe in God. In the most secret and waste places they bloom. In the ditch, thicket, swamp, beneath the trees choked with thorns and thistles. Still, God need not convict us if we do not choose to watch and follow nature. Oh, miserable, canting generation, groveling in the ignorance of your forefathers! And why should the forefathers be reproached? Cain killed Abel, and nobody has excused Cain. Where did his vice come from?

September 28.—Now the days are inclined to thin mist. The crows are busy between shore and wood, cawing perpetually. The crickets chirp day and night; they creep into the house, under the hearth, into the wall, into every crevice. I like the unfeeling cricket. If we are very sad, we do not heed his voice; if we are merry, we say, "how sociable and friendly the cricket is." The grass has changed.

The sedge through which the tide washes is brown and sere. All these months gone, with bud, blossom, and fruit, and I have done nothing. Thirty chapters in my novel—all wrong, maybe. At any rate, I walked the room and felt my eyes water over the last one. Here's my journal, any how. How may we impart to each other the *ineffable?*—poor, poor word! How shall we help our neighbor souls with our nameless self-exaltations, which, noble and generous, do not seem to belong to our personality? They are not actions, nor resolves even. Yet, what moves and governs the world? By this prating I do not mean to say that I have done the ineffable with my pen.

September 30.—The brake along our rough granite walls is rich red-brown, pale amber, yellow-brown. Cheery autumn, dying so richly—loving summer, while reaching toward winter. This ineffectual record must end. Helen Hobson may read it; perchance, some person she loves, for Helen never liked trouble of any sort. October is at hand. Leaves lie on the grass already with decay's many tints.

"You shall not stay beyond the first frost, Alicia," orders my dear Alton, this evening.

"Oh, my darling, think of the Indian summer; let me stay!"

"I have written to Dresden. We are all going to the country you have dreamed of—Italy."

I pretended not to hear him.

"Won't you shoot any this month? Somebody says—

'For solemn autumn came with yellow wing.'

I take it to be snipe or plover; black wings and yellow legs, you know."

"Dear Alicia, I love you so that I will allow you to kiss me. Poor Dresden—a better fellow than I am; got more money."

I pull the boy's yellow mustache, and he nips my cheek.

"Don't be a goose," he continues, "but get ready and go, just as any sensible girl would.

" 'Let you and I, fair sister, look
Into the future's radiant book,
And learn its lessons, and the scope
It offers to the hearts that hope;
And *we* will hope; for, sister, mark,
To-morrow is not always dark!' "

"Alton, Alton!"

In a moment I am in his arms, and we are weeping together. We say no more about departure. I determine to send for Julia Beaufort. How can I endure her? I must, though, for she will come.

October 8.—A delicate frost. It gave me a cold. Alton has been savage to-day. Pulled a few autumn-stained maple leaves at eve, and saw that the lady-birch was growing yellow fast. The children brought us berries—the last, they said. I asked Alton should I preserve them for his sweet tooth. He answered, "Yes," and I went to him. Tears were in his beautiful eyes.

"Alicia, darling, am I a brute?"

"No, dear; you are angry because I can not live."

"You shall live, by Heaven! you shall live. What does God mean by all this daily agony? My love, ever since we have been in this secluded spot, do you know that I have seen young men and women, idols to somebody, dying with your insidious, treacherous, terrible disease? I *can not* bear it. There is no reason about it. Talk about 'chastening' and 'discipline;' these things, destroying life and happiness, make us infidels."

"Yes, I know it, dear. I have a note from Julia; she will be here in a day or two."

He did not speak a word, but kissed me repeatedly, and then went away.

October 20.—Julia Beaufort has been here a few days; she is quite a child, but she has never suffered. How pretty she is! I like to watch her. What a lover Alton is! his eyes continually stray in my direction; if I leave the room he follows me. Sometimes he sits at Julia's feet, sometimes beside her, with his arm about her, but he always appears absent, dreaming, and asks her, "Am I not dull, missy? You do not really think me worth the having, I know; if you do, what will happen? I only know how to care for old Alicias—ailing sisters. Let me go, Julia."

"I would, if it were not for parting from this same Alicia. I have accepted you on her account; she is dearer than you to me."

"Then I love you, child."

And I know that *they* love each other with a gentle affection, though there is a shadow upon it; but that will pass. Love will have its way, George Sand says, upon the bones of the dead, or upon a bed of roses, it is all the same to lovers. The drama here refreshes me. One way I see that I have failed in the story I am writing; that is, they teach me so. Alton loves Julia enough to make her his wife and the mother of his children; the desire to possess another woman will not enter into his heart. Yet, deep in the core of that noble heart is an undying love and regret for *me*. Every fibre of his soul recognizes me as his mate. What a pity! Yet he will be happy. Farewell, children; you have not seen me cry.

October 28.—Gray skies, gray sea, gray boughs. The winds rise and wail so, and we have long dull rains. Julia went away yesterday. The wedding is arranged. She cried terribly when she kissed me, and said she had never been so happy—what a girl's reason for weeping! I promised to be with her; but I have a conviction that if I leave this house I shall never return to it. What does that matter, though? I am on the last chapters of my book; I ventured to read two or three of the later ones to Julia. She clapped her hands at first, then grew silent; as I read on her delicate cheek crimsoned, her eyes blazed, she moved near me, took my hand, and kissed it. I refused to read her more.

"Oh, sister!" she cried, "how dare you tell the truth about us women? And, where have you lived, what have you done?"

"Does knowledge imply a wandering up and down the space of continents, and the speaking of French and Italian?"

"Not that," she stammered; "but I thought that you had been so entirely apart every way from the common herd. I did not know that one could create without experience."

"Nor can one; like Ulysses, I am a part of all that I have seen; and much good it has done me, hasn't it?"[21]

"I do not understand you, dear Alicia; does Alton?"

"Yes."

"Oh, I am so afraid of him—and you too. Thank you for giving me your written thoughts, though; I shall never forget them."

Now I am glad that she knows a thought of mine. I went about the house after she had gone, Alton having taken his departure for the woods with his gun, and never liked the rooms so little, they were so empty, desolate, and dark. I shut two or three entirely. "Next year," I said to myself. Then I packed some boxes of nick-nacks and put labels to them—that was dreary too; and I was glad to hear Alton's tramp and cheery whistle.

November 2.—Alicia Raymond—her mark.

Suddenly Alton ordains that we leave. Into a pigeon-hole goes this journal. I shall leave this room habitable—that is, I will have nothing set in order. Helen may do that for me.

This was Alicia's last record.

* * * * *

Helen told me that Alicia died abroad. When her brother Alton returned to this country she, Helen, was sent for, and the old house, with Alicia's papers and last wishes, given to her.

"You should have seen," said Helen, in conclusion, "Alicia's room—the one where you found her journal. When I opened the shutters to let the light in I could not for a moment persuade myself that Alicia or Alton would not presently enter, the bustle and presence of an occupation were so evident. Alton's cigar ashes and newspaper and an open book were on one table. At another I saw Alicia's little work-basket, with bits of muslin hanging from it; a vase of flowers arranged by her hands the day she left, probably, now black and rough; a pair of slippers were under her chair beside it, with blue rosettes. At the desk were loose papers, letters, boxes, and a tied-up bunch of grasses—fallen to seed and scattered like dust; the chairs were opposite each other, or in groups, as if company had lately sat in them, and the sofa-pillows were tumbled where some one had been resting. It was like a mirage. Then it grew terribly painful. It was a long time before I threw away the flower-stalks even; but you know that some material things must be taken care of, and I was forced to let in air and sunshine. As you know, also, I have never looked into Alicia's papers. Now what do you think of her?"

"I think if there were more minds among us equal to themselves, as hers appears to have been equal to *her* highest needs, we should have a better literature. I doubt whether she would ever have been induced to publish any thing."

"But is it not a pity she should be lost to the world?"

"She has her world in Alton, in you, and will have in me. Did Alton marry Julia?"

"Yes; and she cherishes Alicia's memory tenderly."

"That is enough."

NOTES

1. "The Deserted House" (1830) by Alfred Lord Tennyson (1809–92), lines 10–12.

2. Opening sentences of the final chapter of *Essai historique, politique et moral sur les révolutions anciennes et modernes* (1797), by François René de Chateaubriand (1768–1848). An English translation of the chapter "A Night Among the Savages of America" had been published in America as early as 1816, but the present translation is probably Stoddard's own.

3. From the concluding section of "Entretien I" of Jean-Louis Guez de Balzac's *Les Entretiens* (1657), the "medieval" Balzac as opposed to the better-known nineteenth-century novelist.

4. The poor invalid covered with sores (hence "irruption") in the parable of Dives and Lazarus (Luke 16:19–31), designed to show the divine retribution that overtakes the rich who, like Dives, neglect the indigent.

5. British Romantic poet John Keats (1795–1821) and the precocious late eighteenth-century poet-forger Thomas Chatterton (1752–70) were often linked together in the nineteenth century as examples of the tragic neglect of poetic genius.

6. To liken Alicia to English novelist Charlotte Brontë (1816–55) as an example of genius flowering in the provinces was in Stoddard's mind to pay the ultimate compliment.

7. The artists alluded to here are Scottish painter Henry Raeburn (1756–1823), English painter James Holmes (1777–1860), English painter Joseph Severn (1793–1879), and probably Italian artist Luigi Calamatta (1802–69), whose 1840 engraving of the French novelist George Sand (1804–76) was well known.

8. At this point, the story begins making use of selections from Elizabeth Stoddard's manuscript journal, included in this volume, pp. 347ff.

9. In addition to Tennyson, the poets referred to here are the British pre-romantics Samuel Rogers (1763–1855), Thomas Gray (1716–71), Robert Bloomfield (1766–1823), and Oliver Goldsmith (1730?–74), and French poet Pierre-Jean de Béranger (1780–1857). This list, however, bears a very limited resemblance to the list of writers quoted or discussed in the story.

10. In Ruth 1:16, Ruth elects to remain the companion of her Hebrew mother-in-law Naomi rather than return to her Moabite home.

11. An 1866 novel by Victor Hugo (1802–85).

12. See p.358, n. 7.

13. An "afrite" box would be a box with an evil demon ("afrit") in it (cf. Worcester's *Dictionary of the English Language,* 1860 edition).

14. Jervis McEntee (1828–91) was an American landscape painter.

15. Province and city in central Iran that carried with it romantic associations for the nineteenth-century Anglo-American mind. Exact source unidentified.

16. A novel (1829–33) by Scottish writer Michael Scott (1789–1835).

17. An 1836 novel by Sand.

18. "Ode: Intimations of Immortality" (1807) by William Wordsworth (1770–1850), line 179; misquoted slightly.

19. Johann Wolfgang von Goethe (1749–1832), *The Auto-Biography of Goethe. Truth and Poetry* (1811–32), trans. and ed. Parke Godwin (New York: Wiley & Putnam, 1846–47), Part III, Book XI, p. 35. Stoddard uses this quotation from the first American translation of *Dichtung und Wahrheit* also in her 1866 journal (below, p. 357). It expresses her own artistic credo: to represent daily life by revealing its underlying passions, conflicts, and ideals.

20. Cf. Tennyson, "Tears, idle tears" (1847), lines 4–5: "In looking on the happy autumn-fields, / And thinking of the days that are no more."

21. Cf. Tennyson, "Ulysses" (1842), line 18: "I am a part of all that I have met."

Early Journalism

Introduction

The following selections of Elizabeth Stoddard's work as the *Daily Alta California*'s "Lady Correspondent" are representative of her semi-monthly columns for that San Francisco newspaper, "the first genuine daily in the West,"[1] in a city fast becoming "the cultural center of the whole region west of the Rockies."[2] The excerpts printed here bear the individualistic stamp of Stoddard's best work. Nominally the letters from a Lady in New York City, they actually take the form of the public journal of a witty, sophisticated, often acerbic woman-on-the-move. They contain cultural and political observations, insiders' talk from the publishing world, reviews of literature, theater, and musical events, satiric travelogues, and commentary on contemporary personalities; and they feature the shrewd, entertaining, sometimes judgmental personality of the Lady Correspondent almost as much as they do her subject matter.

Not surprisingly, Stoddard's *Alta* columns are literary anomalies. Though written for a popular audience, they are far more probing and pointed than most popular literary journalism of the day. For example, the work of "Ik Marvel" (Donald Grant Mitchell)—still remembered for his *Reveries of a Bachelor*—usually takes the form of rather diffuse musings. Marvel, and such other literati as Nathaniel Parker Willis and George William Curtis, specialized in sketches of people, cultures, regions, and events that had an anecdotal, impressionistic, associative quality generally free of intellectual pressure or steadily informing opinion. Stoddard's columns are also quite unlike the similarly opinionated and often biting works of the day's most popular female literary journalist, "Fanny Fern" (Sara Payson Willis Parton), who, although she reviewed books and wrote about religion, concentrated on domestic problems such as the burdens of housework, children's rights, and double moral and economic standards for men and women. Stoddard's breadth of subject matter, virtual silence on domestic matters, and refusal to identify herself with women writers suggest that she envisioned her *Alta* work as the beginning of a literary career in which she hoped to buck convention by succeeding as a literary woman who did not write for a predominantly female audience.

Because of their tone, scope, and thoughtfulness, the *Alta* letters bear some resemblance to the journalism of Margaret Fuller. In fact, the columns may be said to combine some of the depth of Fuller's book reviews and occasional essays in the *New York Tribune* in the early 1840s with the acuteness of cultural observation of her European letters to that paper later in the decade. Unlike Fuller, however, Stoddard was not writing for an audience living in the nation's political and cultural centers; she was not writing as an acknowledged spokeswoman for cultural and moral standards; she was not even writing in a medium that commanded the same kind of respect that the *Tribune* had had, for by 1854 the most widely read cultural commentaries were already being published in the new magazines like *Harper's* and *Putnam's*. Yet with aplomb and zest, Stoddard turned the potential drawbacks of her situation to her advantage, using the freedom evidently given the Lady Correspondent to fashion a mode of commentary appropriate to fostering her own interests and development. Her wide-ranging, freewheeling format is borrowed from the "Editor's Easy Chair" of *Harper's* (written in the early 1850s by Ik Marvel himself), but the amused, detached editorial "we" is usually discarded in favor of a sharp, analytic "I" for whom writing a sketch of New York or New Bedford is inseparable from making a point—be it about New York rents or Massachusetts provincialism. She writes to experiment with tone, to inform and delight an appreciative audience, and above all to express herself.

Printed on the *Alta's* front page, Stoddard's pieces were very popular—the one popular success of her career. A number of readers sought her out when they returned East. Such interest undoubtedly spurred her on to analyze her literary preferences and continue her outspoken ways. Explicitly writing as a woman, she also tests the boundaries of possibility for women writers by playing with various personae, by experimenting with *bon mot*, with parody of political and other formulaic rhetoric, and with the potshot. Observing that American women, seldom given the serious criticism which results from intellectual respect, were generally content with writing second-rate fiction, she also insinuates that she herself has set more ambitious standards for the fiction on which she was already at work. If her later career did not fulfill her hope that she could attain literary success while circumventing existing conventions, the *Alta* columns nevertheless show how inventive—and invigorated—she was when she initially set out to make her mark while writing against the grain.

NOTES

1. Franklin Walker, *San Francisco's Literary Frontier* (New York: Alfred A. Knopf, 1939), p. 21.
2. James H. Matlack, "The *Alta California*'s Lady Correspondent," *New-York Historical Society Quarterly* 58 (1974): 284.

From "Our Lady Correspondent"'s Column, *Daily Alta California*, 1854–1858.

[8 October 1854]
This being my first essay to establish myself in the columns of your paper as one of "our own," I debate in my mind how to appear most effectively, whether to present myself as a genuine original, or adopt some great example in style; such as the pugilism of Fanny Fern, the pathetics of Minnie Myrtle, or the abandon of Cassie Cauliflower.[1] Perhaps your young republic is too ascetic to appreciate the grace of celebrated authors, possibly they are already elevated on pedestals, for I remember you are given to heroics; witness your theatrical furors. On the whole I conclude not to attempt the ornate at present, but to send you letters containing facts and opinions; and as I affirm most of them shall emanate from worthier minds than mine, I hope you will agree with me in thinking there may be "solid chunks of wisdom" therein.

* * * * *

If my limits would allow, the Book I would most like to expatiate upon, would be Thoreau's "Walden, or Life in the Woods," published by Ticknor & Fields, Boston.[2] It is the result of a two or three years' sojourn in the woods, and it is a most minute history of Thoreau's external life, and internal speculation. It is the latest effervescence of that peculiar school, at the head of which stands Ralph Waldo Emerson. Of Walden, Emerson says that Thoreau has cornered nature in it. . . . Notwithstanding an apparent contempt for utility, he seems a sharp accountant, and not a little interest is attached to his bills of expense, they are so ludicrously small. Coarse bread, occasional molasses and rice, now and then a

fish taken from Walden Pond, and philosophically matured vege-
tables, (he sold his beans,) were his fare. His ideas of beauty are
positive, but limited. The world of art is beyond his wisdom.
Individuality is the altar at which he worships. Philanthropy is an
opposite term, and he does not scruple to affirm that philanthropy
and he are two. The Book is full of talent, curious and interesting.
I recommend it as a study to all fops, male and female.

[22 October 1854]
Before commencing my book notices, I would say that I am deeply
interested in the development of the woman mind. I am anxious
to discover the innate inferiority to the mind masculine, or its
equality with it. I will not go into the old and vexed question, but
speak of what is now-a-days with us. All the women in this country can follow out their fancies, as far as book making is concerned. No criticism assails them. Men are polite to the woman,
and contemptuous to the intellect. They do not allow woman to
enter their intellectual arena to do battle with them. Hence the
intolerable vanity of our female writers. Eight out of ten books
that have been published in the last year in New York, have been
written by women. We have their reasons for publishing in the
prefaces. This one has a "spontaneous up-gushing" that must be
spoken. Another has a "mission," although her book does not
explain it. Another has no reason, except that she was "willed to
publish." The real reason is, an insane egotism or a desire to make
money. Money goes half in half with fame. Our truly excellent
female writers have been jostled aside. They are not "fast"enough;
having no inner meanings, they attempt nothing beyond the scope
of their clear sense. We have some fine books that belong to the
objective school of writing. But no one book has been written by
a woman of erudition; no metaphysical tale, novel or poem; no
story that holds in analysis the passions of the human heart. We
have no Elizabeth Browning, Bronte [sic], George Sand or Miss
Bremer, to offer to our enemies, the critics.[3] The eight books in
ten are written without genius; all show industry, and a few talent.
Their authors are Bedouins: Hagar should be the name of some,
and some should be nameless.[4]

    * * * * *

Madam George Sand is about to commence the publication of
her autobiography in *La Presse*.[5] It is to extend to five volumes,
and she is to receive a hundred thousand francs for it. It will

doubtless end with her religious scheme of retirement. Parisian gossip accuses her of having sufficient reason for it, in the friendship of a jurist, who lives near the cloister. Devotion, according to tradition, is the last resource of a fast Frenchman. But I cannot believe that George Sand has so exhausted life that she has no further need for it, save to patter prayers and count beads. We have no surplus women of her genius and passion that we can spare the intellectual revelations of one who has dared to live her own way.

[29 January 1855]
A friend writes me that my letters are his Sunday morning reading. Alas! should I not reproach myself because there is no echo of the church-going bell in them; that I have never cried aloud to the wicked San Franciscans—"Repent! Repent!" But, sinner that I am, I confess to secular habits entirely. When I was young, I was fed on the strong dish of New England polemics. God, my teachers said, did not reside in the natural heart of man, which fact I must learn through some process that my soul refused to understand. When I go to church, I read the sermon from the congregation; that from the pulpit is a tiresome reiteration, or a mistaken assertion. Mrs. Wardentry Covell preaches to me with her rouged cheeks, and her Brussells lace. I see Mr. Abraham Large reading "1000 N.J. Con. R. R. B. C. 3–90" from a velvet prayer book. I hear Madame Wallace singing an air from the *Barber of Seville*, to the words "Praise the Lord." Now what kind of a knocking at heaven's gate is this? Will Saint Peter open it? or will he reply in the words of that distinguished Ethiopian, Mr. Christy, "stop that knocking?"[6]

[19 March 1855]
The yearly epidemic of house letting and house hunting has attacked the city. Little placards, "To Let," come out like plague spots on the fronts of houses, and the maniac class of women, who revel in spying out the domestic affairs of the world generally, are in full cry. They are furniture ghouls—rent vampires. But in fact, moving is an important item in the life of a small-incomed New Yorker. It is a relief to go from one disagreeable place to another. Every year I move. The house I leave seems no longer supportable. Yet I have scarcely vacated it before some one else rushes in, equally wretched in his old place and hopeful of his new.

* * * * *

No man can deny that Poe was a man of great original and peculiar genius. His friends affirm in his behalf that his nervous system was so delicate that coffee would intoxicate him, and that a glass of wine would sometimes excite him to frenzy. Whether a man's organization atones for his faults, is a nicer problem than I can solve. I am inclined to think sin a physical matter, because when I eat too many buckwheat cakes, I am bad tempered; when I drink champagne, I am a patriot, and gin—the real Scheidam— gives me the spirit of a martyr! So it would seem vice and virtue are stomachic.[7]

[19 May 1855]
We have a topic now that promises much—the Maine Liquor Law— which is to be enforced in this city on the 1st of July. The *Tribune* is its grandfather, Gov. Clark its father, and Neal Dow, of Portland, its original Adam.[8]

I have now an opportunity for a sermon, taking for my text this passage from the philosophy of the past—

"The masses are influenced, and led by the obvious."

The cup is thrust from the lips of the drunkard: he is saved. The rum seller receives his reward for evil-doing; wives will cease to mourn; and children will grow up virtuous. I doubt, Tribunely speaking, whether there will ever be any more orphans. We may expect that all unlawful appetites will be entirely eradicated from the citizen of the temperance zone.

* * * * *

Some believe that the passage of the Maine Liquor Law is unconstitutional—myself among the number. As I have intimated a doubt whether purity can be legislated into men by the imprisonment of lewd women, so do I doubt whether law can keep a man sober. Physical excess can no more be gauged than intellectual. The tendency of all life is to excess; and if a man is cribbed and confined one way, he will break out into another. The awful intolerance of human nature curses it. The man of one appetite hates another with a different one. The cannibal eyes you with suspicion and disgust because you refuse the baby stew or the warrior soup he offers you. The vegetarian will tell you that the Crimean War is owing to the consumption of frogs and beefsteaks by the French and English. So it goes.

[2 June 1855]
I am sure the mention of one event which has lately occurred, will create an interest and sorrow. "Currer Bell" is dead.[9]

The hand that guided a powerful pen lies on a pulseless heart, and the intellect so brilliant and mature in this world has become simple and childlike in another. Now she is learning something beyond all her teachings here.

Miss Charlotte Bronti [sic], better known as "Currer Bell," became famous by writing that leaf of heart life—"Jane Eyre," a daring and masculine work. Some little time before "Jane Eyre" was written, her sisters, Ellis and Ashton Bell [sic], published "Wuthering Heights," and "The Tenant of Wildfield Hall" [sic], both singularly original novels. They died soon after, and Charlotte living within the shadow of their graves, in complete and strange isolation, wrote "Shirley," and Vellette" [sic], her last book.

Although she is neither the heroine of "Jane Eyre," or "Villette," some portions of both are biographical. She was a governess at Brussels, the scene where "Villette" is laid, and was either teacher or scholar at Mr. Brodhead's [sic] school, so painfully described in "Jane Eyre." For a long time "Currer Bell" remained unknown. Fame and money were not her incentives, she wrote, she says, because she felt it "needful to speak," and what she experienced in her own life, or what she saw in the life of others she expressed.

She was a little, frail body; sensitive and perhaps morbid, yet possessing more moral strength than the government and gunpowder heroes of the day. . . .

[19 June 1855]
. . . Miss Lucy Stone has recently married a Mr. Blackwell, brother of Dr. Elizabeth Blackwell, and Miss Blackwell, the translator of George Sand's "Jacques," homely and honorable women all.[10]

Miss Lucy Stone and Mr. Blackwell made a public protest against marriage, and took sundry precautions, one against the other, by contract beforehand. The Evening Post says that the unusual precautions they took not to be cheated in the bargain, doubtless had their origin in an acquaintance with each others character and propensities, which the public does not possess. Dry old Post!

I think a miserable egotism was at the bottom of the whole affair, a desire to gain notoriety. Or was the habit of virtue more powerful than their adopted beliefs? They have proved neither high-souled to each other, nor courageous before the world.

George Sand, a true prophet of what a woman can be, has lived consistently with her theory. Her religion and her philosophy are of the heart. Her senses have led her astray, but only to give her a truer knowledge, however sad, of the benevolence to be exercised toward the frailties of human nature. When Chopin, the musician, ceased to be her lover, and she his mistress, they remained friends, and, from their position, certain duties belonged to him which she nobly fulfilled.

But long life to Mr. Blackwell. I wear a portrait of Miss Lucy Stone on my imagination. I saw her first at a rail-way depot; she was conversing with a number of colored gentlemen. Dirty white woolen stockings characterized her feet, and a shabby straw bonnet her head. Mousseline de laine pantalettes were an obvious part of her costume; she weilded [sic] an immense cotton umbrella; either that, or Miss Lucy had a damp, mouldy smell. She was accompanied by a tall delicate woman with a razor-like mouth, who owned a husband that appeared to be utterly extinguished; but he paid the fare, and had just enough strength to carry the carpet bag.

[24 October 1855]

A Village on the Sea Shore[11]

I too am a pilgrim and a sojourner, but not a fashionable one; for I have come, with a small trunk and no bank-boxes, into a little village, where the foot of traveler some times strays, but never stays. "An ancient and fish-like smell" is apt to pervade its premises; its inhabitants catch fish, eat fish, and spread fish on the sterile land, and, if I am not mistaken, clothe themselves in fish skin. They are in fact a scaly set. Some few make small attempts at farming. Verdant beds of cabbages grace the landscape, and rows of corn alternate with rows of rock. The ploughman wonders why the "granite soil of New England" should be a favorite phrase with orators: he and his oxen think it a deuced bore. There is a chronic complaint of ship-building in this small spot, and here originated, according to my antiquarian researches, the saying,—"as smiling as a basket of chips," chips being the natural consequence of timber, timber of ships, and ships of employment: hence smiles! A puritanic flavor mingles with the saline qualities of the atmosphere. There is a meeting-house on my right, and a meeting-house on my left and a little farther back is a meeting house! But the latter need not be mentioned as it is Baptist, and has no bell.

But to come to the truth and beauty of my surroundings. Here rolls the everlasting sea. On the day of my birth its voice was uplifted; on the day of my death, its song will be the same. The sandy soil of the village grave yard hides generations of my race. The old slate stones level with their mounds, and covered with moss, the upright marble slabs with their names freshly cut have neither age nor date to the deaf and sightless sea. But unpitying as it is, I am drawn to it by a resistless fascination. Ever in motion, yet within impassible [sic] barriers, it seems a type of the soul on earth, fretted by and chained to the body. If it be true that we are in conformity with the configuration of the country and climate, in which we are born, I arrive at the conclusion that I am full of dents; that my disposi[tion] is a "nor-wester," that my intellect is misty, and that I am a queer *cove* generally.

On my journey thitherward, I passed through New Bedford. As this town is the birth-place of many commercially-famous Californians, I give it a passing notice. New Bedford is distinguished for ready-made trowsers; long lines of them swing through the streets, from some kind of fixture in shop doorways, suggesting very unpleasant ideas of hanging, and of drowned sailors. The inhabitants live in large, square boxes, painted dun color; these boxes are ornamented with strange devices, that appear to be glued on wherever there is a plain space. This order of architecture took its rise in whale oil. The citizen that happens by family estate to own a house with a sloping roof, paints it over dun color, and hides the disgrace of eaves, by putting on the devices. A few houses stand apart in the dignity of granite, but they belong to the Princes Royal, who know what it is to have a grandfather, and must not be touched with an irreverent pen. There are remarkable gradations of aristocracy in this city. The Ap-Morgans look down on the Allings; the Allings feel a contempt for the Barkings, and the Barkings despise the Smiths and the Browns. The Smiths and the Browns are miserable, without knowing what ails them; the Allings and Barkings are miserable, and do know what ails them. Both feel the need of having the Ap-Morgans recognise that their "flesh and blood is at as good as anybody's." The last great work of the city is a graded road round Clark's Point, making a beautiful drive, and opening a fine sea view. The condition of the poor is greatly ameliorated by the construction of this road. Every day they can have their taste gratified by seeing fast horses and easy wagons whirl along in noble emulation of each other! The literary miasma in the atmosphere of New Bedford is never powerful enough to agitate the brains of its natives. Their libraries are composed of ledgers, and for light reading they have the *Whalemen's Shipping List*. There are no poets, orators or artists. The times are represented by two papers: the *New Bedford Mercury*, which is somewhat paralytic from its intense respectability, but a good journal nevertheless, and the *Evening Standard*, which is devoted to a minute diffusion of local news. The style of the latter is this: "We stop the press to announce that a fishing boat arrived fifteen minutes ten seconds ago, with three bushels of tautog, caught by Capt. Ichabod Nye. Our readers may anticipate an epicurean repast." "Mr. H—— presented us yesterday with a pumpkin weighing eighteen pounds. Mr. H—— is an intelligent farmer, from Dartmouth."

Doubtless I should have made a clearer observation of New Bedford, if it had not been so early in the morning when I passed through, (it was not daylight,) and if I had not been accompanied by an infant, in whom I take a friendly interest, and who required exact attention from his travelling companions. One of them was devoted to keeping his socks on, as he manifested a strong inclination to kick them off; another was a committee to keep his hat from strangling him, getting over his eyes, or smothering him generally. A third kept up a skirmishing kind of warfare, surprising him by loud chirrups, stunning him by shrill whistlings, trotting the life out of him, and sundry other baby-pleasing manoeuvers. I was subjected to a close and fatigueing inquiry from the various mamas that infested the boat whereon I passed the night; "Is he troubled with wind?"—"Does he cut any teeth?" "Is he good nights?" "Is he a fractious child?" I in turn asked the like questions about their phenomena. So if I fail as tourist, my circumstances must excuse me.

[18 November 1855]
An Account of a Voyage across the Long Island Sound,
in search of the Waters of Peace and Comfort

I left an admiring crowd of the democracy on the pier at New York, and sailed away in the *Bay State*, with three peaches, a piece of mince pie (I believe that was its name), the daguerreotypes of all my family, a small sum of money in my pocket, and a princely revenue of tender recollections in my heart.

The steamboat world, its estates, colonies and dependencies, shall have as full justice in this marine narrative as my limits will allow, this not being a royal octavo. I cannot give a chemical analysis of steamboat atmosphere (thank Heaven, the gases are beyond the comprehension of the female mind); I only know that when I enter it I become a different being. Its smell, taste and feel are indescribable. Its effect on the traveller is transient, but its natives—the captains, clerks, waiters and stewardesses, are a marked and isolated race. On land they are what we are in the water. An omnibus is a terror to them, a wide bed a discomfort, and Cologne water an absolute stink. Their clothes are full of fine wrinkles, which give them a web-footed sort of air, and their fine things, shirts, collars and chemisettes, are apt to be "done up" yellow.

The steamboat *cuisine* is also a peculiar institution. Its *table d'hote* defines incongruity. Wo to the dyspeptic, and dismay to the epicure, who sit at these feasts! Indigestion is the skeleton guest of the banquet, hid in paper flowers, pyramids of butter and beet juice decorations. The Captain commands a dish of beefsteak, which he "pays out" to the larboard and the starboard, to the unprotected females, which tradition assigns as his especial charge. With hungry rage a row of men glare at a row of women; the latter are entitled to grab first. A line of galvanic, copper-colored waiters constantly jerk to and fro heavy pieces of crockery. The bill of fare is highly imaginative, and never varies. I believe that there are secret crypts, where what is left is being made over, rehashed, and remoulded, from one meal to another; the table always presents the same appearance. Vase of flowers—an infant bird on shavings. Vase of flowers—a small fish in a buttery element. Vase of flowers—fearfully and wonderfully made gimcracks. Vase of flowers —fish balls enough to cannonade Sebastopol. Vase of flowers—an egg laid on a sprig of parsley—and so on, out of sight! The combination of fried lobster and calf's-foot jelly, sponge cake and boiled ham, does not tickle my palate; so I took a shilling's worth of cold tea, with other lone tabbies. The stewardesses are in a general league to ignore the fact of passengers. They exhibit, however, a faint alacrity when collecting the above-named shillings for tea. They sleep well, and we are expected not to disturb them; and they carry with great dignity immense hoop earrings.

The occupant of a steamboat berth is an example of the extreme feebleness and impotence of the human creature in narrow circumstances. If he raises his head he bumps it against the slats above him; if he turns over he carries the "Bay State" blanket, and the damp linen skin, called in the vernacular a sheet, with him; if he draws his curtain with an insane idea of retirement, the fellow above, or below him, rattles it back. If he has an under berth, he sees like Jacob, shining ones in white, ascending and descending small ladders.[12] If he has an upper berth, he is beyond assistance; the waiters never hear anything from that height. He wishes to come down but the ladder is gone, and the boat in!

But my journey is ended. When I get out a revised edition of my voyage, I shall give a chapter to Captains; their rise, progress, and decline. For your famous Captain, is apt to decline from the happy recipiency of silver trumpets, and tea-services, to the merest old sea dog, without a ship at sea, or a house on land.

[3 December 1855]
A critic in *Putnam's* says that the women-novels contain puppets, instead of characters. I have a curious infatuation about such books. Their covers are pretty, and the print is clear; perhaps that is *the* attraction. With pertinacity I often waste time and taste reading on and on to the end. "Juno Clifford," a late affair, was the last of the kind I refer to.[13] I read it with scorn and derision, wondering at the same time at its ease of style. Juno is a preposterously rich and beautiful woman, inhabiting a "lofty" house on Mount Vernon Street, and drinking coffee from Sevres china at ten o'clock in the morning. Her husband is a broker of forty-five, an extraordinary business man, (though he takes his breakfast at ten o'clock, too,) with a "good deal of romance stored away."—Twice in seven years does Juno Clifford bestow a token of affection on the brow of said broker, in the shape of two faint kisses. They go to Europe, and Mrs. Clifford, after getting weary of triumphs there, sends back the architect and gardener of a certain prince, who build a villa and plant a garden against her return. The trees are fully grown when the divided pair arrive at their palatial mansion. Mrs. Clifford, the coldly proud, and the proudly cold, falls in love with her adopted son[;] he shrinks back with horror at her confession; says "Mother," and flees away to marry the young girl who had been separated from him by the mean tricks of Juno, and who in the meantime had married, had a baby, became a widow, wrote a book whose success was so great that she made five thousand dollars right off! On the last page Juno still reigns a queen of beauty, and gives

fashionable parties. This is the kind of stuff publishers are confident of selling ten thousand copies of.

[20 January 1856]
Then there's the literary visit. A finds B writing a poem. A insists on B's reading it. B reads and A says "glorious." Then A takes a manuscript from his pocket, which B insists shall be read. A reads and B says "glorious." A asks if B has seen his last squib in Young America. B asks if A has seen his last review of that book by Muggins. Each man puts his feet on the sofa (no, literary people don't have sofas)—somewhere above his head—and then Tennyson, Browning, Longfellow, and their faults are discovered.[14]

[17 February 1856]
Some officious person has suggested to me that perhaps I make these letters too personal; that the readers of the *Alta* might like more information:—in fact, that it would be better to make myself more newspaperish. I own I am an egoist. I had much rather look at my own daguerrcotypc than that of anybody else. And I do think my affairs are of more importance than the affairs of other folks.

[9 March 1856]
I remember well our Congregational fast days in New England. Instead of the ordinary noon-day meal, the folks had only pies and cakes, and cold coffee in mugs. This refreshment was not spread on a table, but eaten from the shelves of a dark pantry on the north side of the house. But at sundown the pious but rejoicing village sat down to a Yankee tea, the like of which can never be had out of New England. A Yankee sea-coast tea differs from an inland or mountainous tea. With mournful smacks of the mouth, I recall the former: small quohogs with melted butter poured over them; creek oysters in the shell; broiled split eels; hot biscuits; pan cakes; plum jelly; pound cake, and green tea. Happy days of youth and unsated appetite, forever fled! Cream toast, stewed lobster, grilled swordfish, fried tautog, have fled with them. Things with the same names but without the taste, sometimes appear on my table, but they are flat, stale and unprofitable.

[8 June 1856]

The undersigned, having farmed out the baby for three months, dismissed her landlady, and retired within the shelter of that protecting arm of the sea, "Buzzard's Bay," is desirous of obtaining a literary situation. Has no objection to writing bogus book notices for publishers, and inserting them in the advertisements as quotations from the *Indianapolis Banner*, the *Minnesota Chronicle*, the *Galveston Register*, or any other remote paper or magazine; is perfectly willing to write immoral articles for Sunday papers, or religious lies for Sunday School publishing houses; would also sit as a "notorious criminal" for a pictorial, and write a memoir to suit the expression of countenance. . . . Poems in the style of Hiawatha and Don Juan,[15] for hatters, manufacturers of hair dye, and cosmetics, on hand. Editorials for rival newspapers done up in the highest vituperative style. All this is to be paid for in advance!

* * * * *

I find things at Buzzard's Bay much the same as when I left them. There is another board out of the doorsteps of the Universalist Church, which shows the decay of vital piety, or that the evil one is being vanquished, just as one believes. This is the herring season. Everybody's yard is graced with four hundred herring, with birch sticks poked through their eyes. I eat as many as I can, to prove myself not entirely dead to my native instincts. I have only seen two turkey gobblers, one "bossy" calf, several antique relatives, a copy of Webster's Dictionary, and the gentlemanly editor of the New Bedford *Mercury*, since my arrival. I have half a mind to commence a serial novel in this letter, and entitle it "The Solitary of the Salt Pits," or "The Beauty of the Briny." The first chapter opens thus: "It was early candle-light when two-and-twenty boats, with twenty-two men between twenty-two and three years of age, might have been seen mysteriously rowing up and down the river." I want to do something to elevate myself above a mere correspondent. The *Alta* has such a corresponding army, that one feels a desire to accomplish incredible smartnesses.

[20 July 1856]

I am going into politics. I shall take up the great national question, sir, which should agitate every thinking man and woman, sir, in this great country, this vast country, on which the eyes of the small remainder of the world are fixed, sir! But I am on both sides. My soul is stirred by the disinterested patriotism of both parties; and my sense of the ludicrous, too.

The day after the Democratic nomination, "The Buchanan Hair Dye" was offered for sale in Broadway.[16] It is to be applied to the heads of office-seekers.

* * * * *

We are having Free Kansas meetings now all over the country. Monies are being collected in them for some good purpose; killing, I suppose. What a curious individuality runs through political speeches; Did you ever read one that did not have a scriptural quotation in it ?

* * * * *

This mail brings you the Republican nomination of John C. Fremont. In the new photograph by Root, the "Champion of Freedom" wears his hair parted in the middle of his forehead, but otherwise looks manly and well. His "Life and Times" are published also. His times prove him to be a remarkable man, even in the country of remarkable men. Some paper calls his wife remarkable, too. It is a sign of the times that the wife of a public man should be thought of. I feel much obliged, in behalf of my sex, to the generous man that has given Mrs. Fremont a newspaper notice.

In view, perhaps, of the wants of travellers, Ticknor & Fields have just issued a charming pocket edition of Tennyson. Just think that you can carry the whole of Tennyson in the basket with your sandwiches, or in your coat pocket with your cigars! This small edition meets with great approbation. . . . Tennyson is a monstrous fine poet. We all try to imitate his sweet, laborious art; but we fail.

[3 August 1856]

We have quite as many goodish books as usual. Among them, and more noticeable than the most of them, is Caroline Chesebro's "Victoria, or the World Overcome."[17] After the title (for why should the world be "overcome?") Miss Chesebro's dogmatic and pious ideal of a woman assails me in reading her book. I object to the position she takes in regard to the reader—that of a teacher. The morality is not agreeable, and quite impossible. It is only women of the brain that possess "the wisdom of the world and the virtue of the saint." Why will writers, especially female writers, make their heroines so indifferent to good eating, so careless about taking cold, and so impervious to all the creature comforts? The absence of these treats compose their good women, with an external preachment about self-denial, moral self-denial. Is good-ness, then, incompatible with the enjoyment of the senses? In read-ing such books I am reminded of what I have thought my mission was: a crusade against Duty—not the duty that is revealed to every man and woman of us by the circumstances of daily life, but that which is cut and fashioned for us by minds totally ignorant of our idiosyncrasies and necessities. The world has long been lost in a polemical fog. I am afraid we shall never get into plain sailing.

[9 November 1856]
I love New York, stiff, ugly and incongruous as it is. I love to be in the thick of my fellow-men.

Speaking of my fellow-men reminds me that I saw, at the win-dow of Fowler & Wells, in Broadway, on my memorable ride up, the sign of "Leaves of Grass," by Walt Whitman. This must be a new edition of a book published last year by "Walt," through Fowler & Wells.[18] It was neither read nor noticed much; but it made some sensation. Everything that convention says shall not be said, is spoken in that book. It is the experience of a thoughtful, talented, licentious man. What he knew he wrote, and he knew a great deal that may be called immensely nasty. Emerson wrote a letter to Whitman about his book, which he printed—showing no lack of vanity by doing so. You may see Walt Whitman any day in Broadway, with a red flannel shirt and black trowsers, a singular hat, and stiff beard. He is a printer. I do not think he will write anything more. He has put the whole of himself into "Leaves of Grass.". . .

[11 January 1857]
I attended the Woman's Rights Convention, which came off at the Tabernacle on the 25th and 26th [of November].[19] . . . All the conventional formulas were used, to my amusement; there was more formula than convention. [Convention President] Lucy Stone left out her Blackwell name, but not wishing to cast too great a reflection on her husband was introduced as *Mrs.* Lucy Stone. This lady has improved in looks and manner since I saw her, when she was newly fledged in the cause. Her dress was a respectable black silk, trimmed with velvet. She wore no hoops. Her hair was rather high up behind; this, with her *retrousse* nose, gave her an air *à là*

grisette. Her voice is low and fine toned; her intellect on a par with that of a man.

* * * * *

[Speaker Mary Davis] began in a high, squeaky nasal voice, at the beginning of the world, and brought woman down on the torrent of her discourse from Eve to herself; praising her as the Saviour of man, and calling her the Beautiful and Purifier of the Universe. Examples were given of excellent and splendid women, from Semiramis to Mrs. Mowatt![20] I thought if a man-orator should harangue us so on the virtues and beauty of his sex, he would be called egotistical and silly. I felt ashamed to hear from a woman such wholesale laudation of woman. The pronunciation of Mrs. Davis was bad; her rhetoric was false and confused, and her com-position barely equal to that of a schoolgirl. After skirmishing up and down the ages, packing in geological, geographical, and floral similes, she dropped suddenly on the core of her subject. Here she became worth the listening. Taking for a text an opinion of Judge Reeves, "That a woman should have no individual rights, because her husband has the right of possession of the person of his wife"—[21] she came down on the audience with Thor's hammer. She talked with a daring tact. Women, she said, were the victims of legalized prostitution. Forced by the lust of men into false and inharmonious relations with themselves, compelled to wear the painful honors of maternity, and to bring half-made wretches into the world, sapped in health and strength, their lives loathingly bitter and bur-densome. Therefore, she argued the right of self-possession on the part of wives; and ended her discourse. . . . My own impression is, that Mrs. Davis was not fully endorsed by her co-mates. Mrs. Lucretia Mott said that the place was not one for the display of rhetoric; they had not come there to talk, but to work. However, Mrs. Davis is right for all that; I am glad to get the truth anywhere.

These Conventions make people think, after they have done laughing. The getters-up of them have some right ideas too. Among these ideas, is an extension of the means of honorable and *honored* employment for women, and the enjoyment of property rights, and legal power to retain or dispose of property.

To become worthy of what they ask at the hands of men, women will educate themselves, and step out of the narrow boundaries which custom has assigned them. The idea of women casting votes is very much laughed at; but is it so laughable a case when the mass of men voters is looked into, and an opinion formed of their political intelligence? Your correspondent, despite a hideous tendency to laugh at strong-mindedism, which she traces to the unfortunate influence of her male friends, takes an humble place in the ranks of Women's Rights and Women's Shall Haves, especially in the latter.

Horace Greeley in an able letter to the Convention, says that he deems "the intellectual, like the physical capacities of women, unequal in the average to those of men." I am forced to agree with him. If women were equal to men, there never would have been these nineteenth century conventions. . . .

[22 March 1857]
[On Emerson's lecture "The Conduct of Life."][22]

Fine society, he says, is an "unprincipled decorum." I wish I could remember better what he said. Fifth Avenue and West End were sarcastically snubbed. I felt ashamed of the little longings I sometimes have for diamonds and earrings, and the stepping-on-your-toes air which so many fine ladies possess. I inwardly prayed that no mortal might ever discover my weakness. Alas! innate dignity goes such a very little ways in this world! We worship accessories, not facts. Emerson is the only literary nobleman I know of. He despises the masses as much as he does fine society, and says the world is divided into two classes—"benefactors and malefactors."

[26 July 1857]
Our poetical illusions and mirages of the heart must, of course, vanish with the years. But it is hard to lose faith in the wonderful material fables of the creation. It is best for us to continue in the belief that Eve actually ate an apple, and immediately ruined Adam in consequence! I like this belief, too, it speaks so well for the progressive power of women.

    * * * * *

The balance of power between men and women is swaying somewhat, I think. What will the world come to if an even intellectual basis is established between us? Every man of you knows that (sub rosa) we women pull the wires of your physical and moral natures. What you are in character, for good or bad, depends on the little inferior creatures you chuck under the chin, or tuck under the arm, or beat black and blue, or slobber with kisses.

To come back to the subject of the weather: I have been trying to say how unhappy the weather makes me. It gives me rheumatic pains in each individual limb; clogs my brain, and weighs on my heart. Unhappily for my present state of mind, our neighborhood is famous for coffin warehouses. I cannot help seeing more coffins than anything else. A strong sense of the fitness of things possesses the owners of these establishments. On the curtain of the window of one of them is painted a large hearse, highly plumed, and with a pair of horses that look as if they would be delighted to prance me off to Greenwood any day most convenient to me! On the window shelf stands a minature coffin, studded with silver nails, made for pastime probably in the leisure moments of the under-taker, and ultimately intended for his children to bury their dolls in. Over the way is another warehouse. This is simply filled with coffins standing on end—a frightful show. Passing this place one evening I observed a woman walking about the coffins with a young child in her arms. It reminds me of what George Sand says—"Love asserts its happiness over the bones of the dead as well as on beds of roses."

Is it right that the main feeling of life should be a defiance of death, or should we feel that the meaning of life is to die? You see what the weather does for me in the way of metaphysics.

The earth-worms and the fish in the sea are the only living things that can enjoy perpetual damp. The birds do not sing now. The flowers that are forced to bloom, come out with wicked leaves; the butterflies are saving up the dust on their wings in some dry holes or corners. Not a fly buzzes; the mosquitoes are not born; the bumble bee cannot find any pollen, and contemplates some other calling beside that of honey making.

[6 September 1857]
What is a neutral newspaper? Does neutrality mean a sharp eye to the subscription list? I know the editor of a popular paper here, who suffers mortal apprehensions, lest some book review, some personal item, or some political reference may creep into his paper and offend somebody at the North or the South. His business is to emasculate all the paragraphs, and his paper is in consequence devoid of vitality. All thinking people despise it. Even if a paper does not profess to be whig or democrat, it might, I think, win approval from both sides, by a fearless expression of opinions.

NOTES

1. Pseudonymous American women literary journalists of the period, whose vogue Stoddard was seeking to rival and surpass. "Fanny Fern," the most famous, was Sara Payson Willis Parton (1811–72), author of *Fern Leaves from Fanny's Portfolio* (1853), originally published piecemeal in the *Home Journal*. "Minnie Myrtle" was Anna C. Johnson (1818–92), author of the recently collected *The Myrtle Wreath, or Stray Leaves Recalled* (1854). As her epithets suggest, Stoddard wished to cultivate a more dryly reserved style than her counterparts.

2. Stoddard's review is broadly typical of the brief appreciative journalistic squibs that greeted Thoreau's recently published masterpiece. The following details reflect her particular temperament and situation, however: the seriousness with which she takes Thoreau's economic experiment, her apparent relish of his prickly individualism, and her condescension toward his idea of art.

3. Elizabeth Barrett Browning (1806–61), Victorian poet; Charlotte (1816–55) or perhaps Emily Brontë (1818–48), contemporary British novelists; George Sand (pseud. of Amandine Aurore Lucile Dupin, Baronne Dudevant [1804–76]), French novelist; Fredrika Bremer (1801–65), Swedish novelist and travel writer. All but the last appear frequently in Stoddard references to women writers she admires.

4. Bedouins, Arab nomads, were popularly supposed in nineteenth-century Protestant thinking to be the descendants of Ishmael, son of Hagar, Abraham's bondservant concubine whom he dismissed at the request of his wife Sarah after the birth of a legitimate heir, Isaac (Genesis 21:9–21).

5. Liberal Paris daily, one of the few significant newspapers of democratic sympathies during the Second Empire. The work referred to is *Histoire de ma vie* (1854–55).

6. Edwin P. Christy (1815–62), founder of the Christy's Minstrels, the group that set the pattern for the popular minstrel show—"Ethiopian" because such shows were performed by white entertainers in blackface.

7. Stoddard here replays and parodies the defense by friends of Edgar Allan Poe (1809–49) against the charge that he was an alcoholic.

8. An act regulating the sale of liquor, much weaker than Maine's, had previously passed the New York state legislature with the backing of new governor Myron H. Clark and the New York *Tribune*, edited by the reform-minded Horace Greeley. Neal Dow (1804–97), prominent American prohibitionist, drafted the Maine liquor law while he was mayor of Portland. Stoddard, as usual, succumbs to the temptation to poke fun at organized reform, although in this case, unlike the case of the feminist movement, she disagrees on first principles as well.

9. Pseudonym of Charlotte Brontë, author of *Jane Eyre* (1847), *Shirley* (1849), and *Villette* (1853). She and her sister Emily ("Ellis Bell"), author of *Wuthering Heights* (1847), were the novelists Elizabeth Stoddard most admired during this period of her life. Their often passionate and ambitious heroines and forceful styles of writing suggest Stoddard's own fiction; all three women were sometimes labeled coarse and unladylike by contemporary readers. "Acton Bell" was a third Brontë sister, Anne (1820–49), whose two novels were *Agnes Grey* (1847) and *The Tenant of Wildfell Hall* (1848).

10. Lucy Stone (1818–93) was a pioneer feminist and abolitionist who married into a family of iconoclasts, including her spouse Henry Brown Blackwell (1825–1909), who later co-edited with her the longest-lived women's rights newspaper (*Women's Journal*); his elder sister Elizabeth Blackwell (1821–1910), the first American woman physician; and his eldest sister Anna (1816–1901), journalist, poet, and translator, who had expatriated to France (1849) in part as a result of her interest in utopian socialism of the Brisbane-Fourier stamp. Stoddard mentions Anna Blackwell's 1847 translation of George Sand's novel *Jacques* (1834) in order to draw an ironic contrast between what Stoddard is pleased to regard as the forthrightness of Sand's extramarital affair with the composer Frédéric Chopin (1810–49) and the hypocrisy of the Stone-Blackwell marriage contract, in which Stone stipulated that she would keep her maiden name and both partners drew up a joint protest against the legal restrictions that marriage then imposed on the American woman. The contrast between Stoddard's anticonventional approval of Sand and her putdown of American feminism is characteristically inconsistent.

11. This sketch describes, in a stylized manner, a vacation visit to Elizabeth Stoddard's birthplace, Mattapoisett, Massachusetts, a little to the east of New Bedford. The sketch did not endear Elizabeth to her former neighbors.

12. An allusion to Genesis 28:10–15, Jacob's dream about the ladder reaching to heaven on which angels were ascending and descending.

13. *Juno Clifford* (1855) was a novel by Louise Chandler Moulton (1835–1908), a New England writer who later became a friend and correspondent of Elizabeth Stoddard.

14. Stoddard chooses for her triad of literary notables the three most prestigious names in Anglo-American poetry at mid-century: Alfred Lord Tennyson (1809–92), from whose work Stoddard frequently quotes; Robert Browning (1812–89); and Henry Wadsworth Longfellow (1807–82).

15. Longfellow's pseudo-Indian saga *The Song of Hiawatha* (1855) and the mock-epic *Don Juan* (1819–24) by George Gordon Lord Byron (1788–1824), a whimsically disparate duo.

16. James Buchanan (1791–1868) was twenty-two years older than the Republican candidate John C. Frémont (1813–90), whom Stoddard favored, although she did not, as we see below, favor the militant abolitionism of those radical Republicans who supported guerrillas like John Brown in the fight for political control of Kansas.

17. *Victoria* (1856), by Caroline Chesebrough (1825–73), was another work of woman's fiction by a writer with whom Elizabeth Stoddard later made friends (see below, p. 353). Throughout her most creative years, Stoddard was an avid if critical reader of popular domestic novels.

18. Stoddard is reacting to the second (1856) edition of *Leaves* by Whitman (1819–92), published the year after the first, which she had apparently looked into. The notice of Whitman is ironic in view of the Whitmanian sentence with which the previous paragraph ends.

19. The Seventh Annual Woman's Rights Convention, held at the Broadway Tabernacle in New York City. A wide range of issues was addressed, including women's right to own property, equal wages for women, women's access to education, marriage, and suffrage. The account of the convention in volume 1 of *History of Woman Suffrage*, edited by Elizabeth Cady Stanton et al. (Rochester, 1881–86), makes no mention of Mary Fenn Davis' speech. Davis (1824–86), a

spiritualist lecturer and reformer active also on behalf of women's rights, addressed later conventions on the issue of suffrage. In 1856 she apparently focused on women's ability to control sexual relations with their husbands as the key to women's rights.

20. Semiramis was an Assyrian queen of the ninth century B.C., legendary for beauty and valor; Anna Cora Mowatt (1819–70), a contemporary New York writer and actress known for her play *Fashion; or Life in New York* (1850) and her *Autobiography of an Actress* (1854).

21. The reference would seem to be to *The Law of Baron and Femme* (1816), the then-authoritative analysis of laws having to do with domestic relations, by American jurist and legal educator Tapping Reeve (1744–1823). Reeve stresses that "it will be found difficult to ascertain, with exactness, what power the husband has over the person of his wife," but opines that he may forcibly restrain her from elopement or from squandering his property (pp. 141–42 of 3d ed. [Albany: Gould, 1862]).

22. Undoubtedly Stoddard is reporting on Emerson's lecture of 12 February at the Young Men's Christian Union; the six-week delay before printing was normal, given the logistical problems of the transcontinental mail service.

Manuscripts

Letters to
Edmund Clarence Stedman

The Stoddards were close friends with Edmund Clarence Stedman (1833–1908) and his wife Laura. Stedman, like Richard Stoddard, was a poet-critic-essayist-anthologist, but also a successful Wall Street broker. With Edmund, Elizabeth Stoddard had an intense relationship that went beyond the merely intellectual, though it fell short of being explicitly amorous. With Laura she was also friendly, but less close. These relationships were sometimes threatened by Elizabeth's touchiness (as when Edmund's lack of enthusiasm for Richard's poetry provoked fulminations from Elizabeth that would dismay Edmund and anger Laura), yet their intimacy was lifelong. Elizabeth was especially grateful for Stedman's approval and support of her work, in which regard he was, or so she averred, more consistent than Richard, who eventually gave up on her. "In the entire suppression of any recognition [of my work]," she wrote him, "you have held to some faith in me."[1] Although most of her letters to Stedman dwell on minutiae, some are arresting examples of literary self-dramatization, especially some passages from the first and last stages of their correspondence, the periods represented here. For permission to reprint them, we are grateful to the Manuscript Department, William R. Perkins Library, Duke University (letter of 4 May 1860) and the Rare Book and Manuscript Library, Columbia University (remaining letters, in the Edmund Clarence Stedman Papers).

[4 May 1860]

Dear Stedman,

What a good letter you have sent me! I fully agree with you in what you say about my writing. You mentioned, Wuthering Heights[;][2] that book made more impression upon me than any book I ever read perhaps. The directness, truth, & isolation & individuality are wonderful. You have noticed what I have done closely, & I thank you for it. . . . I have had since I have been here, a fine letter from Lowell,[3] wherein he sets forth his "creed of life and letters." He is *purity* in both. In me he detects a tendency towards the *edge of things* & warns me against it. He objects strongly to the realistic tone of our present literature. Alas. I am coarse and literal of nature, what shall I do? My sensual perceptions react on my brain and I am a meek small, well disposed woman! I have been looking over Leaves of Grass.[4] The author leaves himself no privacy and I think he is very nasty and laughable. What you say about Dick—I feel. You will find no change in him—his faults are all on the surface & find vent in his, "Goddamn yes." He is an honorable, artistic man faithful to his notion of art—and generous to all real artists. We love each other as you know, though very different. . . .

[June 1861]

Be sincere with me I beg of you. Sincerity I must have, or I am a savage—a denizon of that forest where the passions walk free and naked. And then again, you must understand me. I admit that I feel *bad,* that is, irresponsible at times, but I *behave* well, keeping honor and justice in view. I sometimes think it a pity that I am a woman, then again I realize that I am thoroughly womanly and do not wish it. You must promise to let me see you often when you return. I cannot promise you that I will never say cruel things to you—but you will forgive me if I do. Write some fine poems by and by—perhaps I shall. We can at least look on each others tombstones with " $\left(\begin{array}{c}\text{she too}\\\text{he too}\end{array}\right)$ was an Arcadian." The life the gods live—after all—is the life of the brain. If they drank of that cold, sparkling firey [*sic*] cup, lust, in ancient times, they came down from Olympus—but then they always went back. Let us, good folk, play that we have gone back for good, to our Olympus. Do write me when you can. I kiss you, and I give you just one large full look.

Yours

EDBS

[22 June 1862]

Dear Stedman

I am confined to my bed & cannot write you much. I am now under the influence of brandy and *assafoedity,* & have sat up "in end" to send you a word. Do you know how I have suffered in the last six months? This time I have been ill ~~five months~~ five weeks. Nervous prostration the doctor calls it. I call it *Life,* it is too much for me. He says I shall get well, I hope to for I dread suffering & the act of dying, not death. I have had many blows the last year. All my friends are away, if they were here now, I should feel different I know—we are *deserted.* Come back can't you? The horrors of the war affect me deeply, when will it be over. As for my book did you *like* it?[5] I feel dreadfully nervous about it, it seems very poor to me now. I indeavored [*sic*] to make a plain transcript of human life—a portion as it were of the great panorama without tacking on a moral here or an explanation there. Perhaps I have failed. Indications are that it will be misunderstood. . . .

[12 July 1863]

I *am* writing a novel—trying to write the history of a man this time.[6] It is an awful task and I write it by the square inch—I do not seem to gain any facility in composition with practice. It must be so I suppose. Your "picture" way of writing your poems is a lazy way after all, a novel cannot be done so, details however are my destruction. I despise them, and do not manage them well—however I may do something with this book—if slow hard labor can compel success—I shall have a little. I have a reputation now—but it is one that makes every body cock their heads to one side when I am mentioned. By the way your review of the Morgeson's was terrific[.][7] I felt myself a monster when I read it. How is it that I inspire love as a woman Edmund,[8] with those terrific qualities—men and women *still* love me with a headlong feeling that sends them into an exaltation. . . .

[21 August 1891]

The failure of my novels to sell is always the 'black drop,' when they are praised, and it chokes me into silence. The other day I was accosted in the street by a woman who introduced herself as Mrs. Col Crawford of Georgia, she had heard we were here, and knowing my 'works,' was most desirous to meet me—In the South, she said, it was thought the re-publication of my books was most remarkable—that they were written for *now* &c My name ranked with Hawthorne &c—What could I say to her, except—

'Madam my books are never bought, they are borrowed, or taken from libraries' as it was I said nothing— . . .

Since all women look handsome to you, may I lie in your road-way soon, never will the brands of passion die out in my nature, through their blackness, the red fire will suddenly appear, and run like a serpant [sic]—I have constantly to struggle between the feeling of others, that I am an old woman to be set aside, while the young bachantes [sic] whirl by with uplifted arms in the dance of life—and my own feeling of my inward power of life, and achievement. I remind myself of that celebrated Irish gentleman who died lately, he was without arms and legs, but he left eight children!

[30 June 1892]

haven't I said to Stoddard and to my self, that you should have been married to *me* in some respects suiting me, as he does not, we should have been hand in hand in more ways than one—Alas, I am 'past master' in everything I have knocked under this year, and own that I am an old woman. I dont feel so behind my skeleton.

NOTES

1. Elizabeth Stoddard to Stedman, 8 October n.y. (probably late 1880s) (Columbia University).

2. Novel (1847) by Emily Brontë (1818–48). See p. 330, n. 9.

3. James Russell Lowell (1819–91), poet, critic, editor of the prestigious *Atlantic Monthly,* which had, to Elizabeth Stoddard's delight, accepted "My Own Story" for the May issue after the sexual dimension had been toned down.

4. Elizabeth Stoddard had noticed the second (1856) edition of Walt Whitman's poems for the *Alta* on 9 November 1856 (see p. 326). The third (1860) edition was imminent but was not printed until later the same month. Stoddard's combination of disdain for Whitman and anxiety about Lowell's opinion illustrates as well as anything in this volume the insecurity underlying her individualism, an insecurity that lessened but did not vanish when she became more experienced as an author.

5. *The Morgesons,* just published.

6. *Two Men* (1865).

7. *Philadelphia Evening Bulletin,* 24 June 1862.

8. Possibly Stedman, possibly the villain in Shakespeare's *King Lear.*

Letters to a Younger Literary Friend

Stoddard's surviving correspondence includes sizable batches of letters to a half-dozen other American women writers, all less talented than she, with whom she was at least briefly intimate. These friends helped supply her need for companionship, for an audience, for complaint. Often the relationship was interrupted or broken off by Stoddard's waspish temper, which at the same time helps to make her letters strikingly uninhibited and dramatic. At best they are artistic performances in themselves.

One of the fullest records of such a friendship is a collection of forty-two letters to Elizabeth Chase Akers Allen, portions of which are printed below by the kind permission of the Special Collections Division, Colby College Library, Waterville, Maine.

Elizabeth Allen (1832–1911) was a Methodist preacher's daughter and minor poet from Maine, once divorced, once widowed, and remarried (1865) to a New York merchant when Stoddard knew her. The Allens and the Stoddards probably met when the former resided briefly in New York in 1873–74. In 1874, when Elijah Allen took an extended business trip to England, Elizabeth Allen settled in Maine as an associate editor of the *Portland Transcript,* for which she had worked years before. In the early 1880s the couple returned to the New York area.

The majority of Stoddard's letters to Allen were written during the time of their first acquaintance and during the first few years of separation, but they extend over approximately two decades, beginning in 1873. In the 1880s, Stoddard's tone becomes markedly chillier, apparently because of what she considered unjustified criticism by Allen of the neglect of her work in an anthology Richard co-edited. (Stoddard's position was that the collaborator had control over the contents and that Allen had impugned Richard's integrity by presuming, in effect, that he had changed his previously expressed high opinion of her work.) The relationship was never quite the same: "Elizabeth" becomes "Mrs. Allen" thenceforth. But from the start Stoddard must have been a difficult friend, for she was often touchy, blunt, and insensitively self-indulgent. She responded, for instance, to Allen's periodic complaints about loneliness, exhaustion, and finances by insisting that her own problems were far greater. For the

modern reader, however, this resulted in some fascinating, if not altogether flattering, glimpses of a complex personality and her literary and
social milieux.

27 [December 1873]

With me, if you start on a friendship, you will have to begin and
go on—with entire, perhaps disagreeable truth, candor, sincerity.
There is not one particle of "nonsense" about me. I cannot stand
blarney, roundaboutness. As I have not many good qualities of
disposition I feel sure of this; which as many a member of my
family have told me, makes me often hateful. My father said once
he never saw any human being with such a talent for the disagreeable. . . .

[1873–74]

Dear Elizabeth,
    Is it not borne in upon us all—that life is a waste—or, a negating
platform for us all. My life is so welded a mass of black and white
that I cannot separate it. No hour has been without its alloy—but
a few even pleasant wholly. I percieve [sic] that you are like me,
men love us more than women, because we are stronger than men,
not as weak as women. This will not seem a horrible egotism to
you, because you cannot help understanding me. I can speak freely
and truly with you. When I went to see Mrs. Dorr[1] the writer,
this summer, whom I had never met—upon the second day, I
think of my visit—she came close to me, and, said—"May I love
you." I blunderingly answered yes, and broke away. I could not
reply that—I love you. I cannot even like people unless I know
them. Love with me, means mutual understanding, experience,
mutual sorrow, hope, interests. God knows I am sentimental—
but it takes time for me to love—even my husband, and then it is
forever. I already like and respect you, more, I admire you and so
does Stoddard[;] if we can help you over the dark inevitable small
moments of life we will. But, if you say again, that you are poorer
than we are, I won't play with you anymore. Upon that lame right
wrist of R. HS our bread depends. We have never known how to
prepare for that celebrated rainy day. Consequently as the clouds
have risen—we percieve [sic] we haven't got any umbrella. But

who can put us out of life because we are poor. Oh, how I love power and luxury! how I would crush my enemies and reward my friends.

It seems to me now that if I could have health, that I could do noble intellectual work. I think you ought to give your attention to prose. Not stories perhaps, but essays, and the numerous subjects which might come to any trained and reflective intellect. I do wish you might associate with your peers—*I* have been made the little that I am, by my association with literary men. Keep up good heart. Stedman[2] said the other day, when we were condoling about poverty, "Every year I grow easier in—feeling, for seeing I have expected to be a disgrace to my family, to get into jail, lose all my friends for the want of money, yet every year I find I *have* lived in decency and comparitive [*sic*] comfort, and maintained my relations. Mr. Allen was kind to come here today, he looks delicate—isn't he good? Stoddard *never* speaks my name—*old woman, that person—she. Mama.* I hope to see you next week. If you make the least *trouble* to have us, there will be another N Jersey murder.

Yours truly Elizabeth

I have not half answered your letter. I am struggling to write a critical paper on the habits of Sir Walter Scott's novels awful work & I am half alive.

E—

7 June [1874]

I am sorry you said what you did about your notice of Celia Thaxter's poems.[3] My faith and reverence for literature is such that no *personal* feeling should move me one atom. If my enemy writes well I can praise him, if my friend writes ill I *must* condemn him. This *personal* reasoning is the curse of our literature—we shall never have a worthy literature until we have a worthy criticism[.] Look at the venal Tribune—George Ripley[4] has been a blight and blot upon our literature for the last twenty five years. . . . Why should you, a high-minded intellectual woman be accused of envy if you write a discriminating notice?

Mattapoisett. Mass.
29 Aug. [1874?]

Dear Elizabeth

I must give you a word not an answer to your welcome letter. I like you. If you could only come into this heavenly sea place. I think we should just kill ourselves with talk. We have been here a week. Stoddard is still ill—*What* will become of us—his right hand *keeps* useless, and he is more discouraged than I ever saw him. Mr. Benton⁵ came to see me a few days before we left—he does confound me by talking about my books—I feel ashamed that I have done so little when I see how earnest he is. He asked me to visit him. If he had no wife I would go right off—These wives are awful, they always stand between me and the men I could serve and make happy. I hope you will come back to NY, or near. I have been out of doors all the week till I am burned and done, but Oh how much better I am smack with nature, than twiddling my thumbs in the city. Don't think I bought this paper, a man sent me *reams* of it, monogram and all.⁶ A man I love dearly too. I will write you again soon, but don't wait for me. Stoddard sends his regards to you. Lorry⁷ is with us, he is a lovely child—better than his parents, but he is *ours*. The *double* element finishes him. How is your sweet Grace⁸—she is a peculiar child—how could *you* have one otherwise. Keep up heart and courage—You are one of the few great women we have—As for the others, who *fuss* and *fume* God help them—only his goodness will—As for Beecher—I believe that he did as he pleased with that lying weak fool Elizabeth Tilton—I can tell you something.⁹ I hope you can read this.

Yours EDBS

31st Oct [1874]

Dear Elizabeth—

It is like a game of pins between you and I—it may be heads or points, but the *pins* are the same. Letters are poor things to convey all the truth. I could write you a quire, but have not the *power*—how I wish I could talk with you. I wonder if you are so dreadful alone so far as womanly friendship and sympathy go—The one early woman friend I have living as far away and is as separate in common mutual interest as you are from me. When I got your last letter how I wished for you and wondered if I could confide to you my complex nature and life—it seems to me you are strong, but the question is are you weak. I am. You might knock me down by your strength, but I must be raised by your weakness. I am something so driven by circumstances that I feel at bay. I stamp my feet, shake my mane at anybody who looks at me through my bars.

Stoddard is no better in his wrist, the constant pain weakens and wears upon him, but his patience is angelic—he frightens me by it, and by his absolute clinging to me—his life is a constant prayer of passion for me. I also am shattered everyway. Are you beginning to feel that shaking up of our Eve-like constitution, which has nearly killed me. . . .

12th Feb. [1876?]

Dear Elizabeth,
What a wry world this is—If I did not know our own experience I could not possibly understand how a woman of your ability could be so situated as you appear to be. Did you ever think that our *results* may be owing to ourselves our idiosyncrasies, faults, that our misfortunes are not wholly due to circumstances outside us? I judge myself so in a degree and so I do Stoddard. With patience, charity, unrelenting self-discipline, with unselfishness, high intellectual endeavor I see that to day all these forces kept in operation I should be much more a success. But I have been too high tempered, censorious, had a contempt for my kind, made people fear instead of love—I went to Dr. Hollands' day reception last week,[10] the first time I have been out really and there I was conscious of being an object of curiosity and fear rather than affection. I do wish I could hear some good news from you. How is Mr. Allen— is he still unfortunate—you are both lonely. . . . My husband and child love me I am that worth[y]. By the way I never was in love with the former. I love him and am bound to him—perhaps his death would kill me, but to my *ideal* of my love, I never approached with him. Do write me when you are in the mood— would that I could lift the burden *one* inch.

Ever yours
Elizabeth

NY April 13th
[1876]

I can venture to preach a little because I am not a success. No one knows what a literary ambition I had, nor how my failure has broken me. S and I have had a hand to hand fight to keep hold of our modest position, and we have had to shape devise and change according to our present powers, in the smallest matters, not the grand heroic Homeric Sacrifice but such a sacrifice as eating a pork chop instead of a porterhouse, wearing Lisle thread gloves instead of 3 buttons, and walking out with boots down at the heel and a cotton umbrella. My taste which is a curse has been excoriated for twenty years. What strong minded people consider trifles have been boils, ulcers, cramps to me. For all I can still feel that I have much to value and love and like—you my poor girl seem to have little just now. But for one thing why should you not have a few days out, like other newspaper folks, surely any decent employee must fall into the ordinary habits of his class. I do think, knowing you[r] fine intellectual ability think it is owing to yourself in a degree that you cannot shove destiny more to your will. You know I respect and like you so well that I will be nothing but candid. If I had not known you, if I had the power to serve you, when I read your last long letter, I should [have] felt repelled and not inclined to help you, not because you complained of your hard fortune, but because you seemed to believe that if you could be false as the rest of the world, speak with a smooth tongue, flatter and follow you too could be [as] fortunate as they—but enough of sermon. . . .

[summer, 1876]

We are not quite so bad off, for in the last pinch something turns up and lets us off the rack.[11] It is the suspense, the doubt, the imperative necessity of wresting out our daily life by work and management [that is] so hard. Sometimes we get down to one dollar, 25 cts o for a day. Then I sit still and read and go without anything till money comes. My lodger paid me two month's rent several days ago, that tides over towards the next Providence. When Stoddard was in bed I got down to o and borrowed five dollars which he did not know, when that was gone he got up &

went to work. He earns a great deal of money, but having no foundation it all goes[.] We took this house on an income of 5000—that went, and so we struggle on. I have an order for three stories but I cannot write no mind, I envy you your courage and capacity, and I am glad you could lend a "ewe-lamb" of 50—I cant keep money and I am a poor manager—I love spring chicken. Lorry's appetite and mine are fragile and expensive neither of us can eat coarse or badly cooked food. You would never imagine we were poor. Our house is much prettier than ever, one of Stoddard's friends whom he did a favor—sent a man and paper to us to paper our library, the paper is an imitation of stamped leather gold and scarlet figures—The room is lovely, we have had three beautiful landscape pictures given us, and I personally have had presents given me within three or four months, the value of which would run the house six months—On my birth day I received a set of lace the like of which I never had—jabot, frill, pocket half, cuffs and a wide scarf two yards long of exquisite Valenciennes[.] Are you woman enough to like such gossip—We have lots of wine fruits &c sent us muscatel and Hamburg grapes a dollar or two a pound—Yet sometimes one [of] us so needs an article of common apparel that it seems to me I shall simply go mad—The want of money cramps and paralyzes me. I can only fold my hands and stare into the present. It is droll though my gifts[;] Friday a friend sent me a lovely shill comb and a pair of silk stockings (all my cotton ones are darned). . . .

20 January 1880

I live a lazy busy life, times flies, I feel I live, but what do I do, what help am I to anybody—there is no power of likefulness in me—I feel all the virtue gone out of me, because I percieve [sic] I never had any! I feel my age terribly, its ugliness is so disgusting—I cant write any more, if I try, such poor stuff stares me in the face that I destroy it. I do not see one single sweet, worthy thing in me, but one, I would like to do good to others, and I do not feel I am selfish—I am sure I am too much alone, I need the companionship of a woman, one I could love, and who would love me, but as poor a thing as I feel myself I am exacting—now you have my confession which no one would guess I could make.

NOTES

1. Julia Caroline Ripley Dorr (1825–1913), minor Vermont poet, long-term acquaintance and correspondent of Elizabeth Stoddard.

2. Edmund Clarence Stedman (1833–1908), critic, businessman, editor, minor poet, close friend of Elizabeth Stoddard and Richard.

3. Celia Laighton Thaxter (1835–1894), New Hampshire writer, best known for her prose sketches *Among the Isles of Shoals* (1873), a classic of New England local colorism. Her poetry is less impressive. Stoddard no doubt refers to a notice by Elizabeth Allen of Thaxter's *Poems* (1872), her first volume.

4. George Ripley (1802–80), Transcendentalist minister and organizer of Brook Farm, later the successor to Margaret Fuller as literary critic of the *New York Tribune*. Although Ripley's reviews (see "Guide to Writings," Section III, above, p. xxviii) praised Stoddard, she was annoyed that he preferred "to analyze my mind instead of my books" (Elizabeth Stoddard to Caroline H. Dall, 11 February 1868, quoted in James Matlack, "The Literary Career of Elizabeth Barstow Stoddard" [Ph.D. diss., Yale University, 1967], p. 443).

5. An otherwise unidentified admirer of Elizabeth Stoddard.

6. Matlack, "Literary Career," p. 514, suggests that the mysterious donor was one Edward Smith, who was Elizabeth Stoddard's "patron, consoler, and companion from about 1874 until at least 1880" (p. 513).

7. Elizabeth Stoddard's third and only surviving son Lorimer (1863–1901).

8. The Allens' only child.

9. Spouse of the Stoddards' friend editor Theodore Tilton (1835–1907); implicated in a famous adultery scandal involving the Rev. Henry Ward Beecher (1813–87). The alleged incident was in 1870, but the case came to a head in 1874–75, ending with Beecher's acquittal through a hung jury.

10. Josiah Gilbert Holland (1819–81), journalist, minor poet and novelist, then editor of *Scribner's Monthly*.

11. Apparently Allen had lent or given the Stoddards fifty dollars (see "ewe-lamb" reference, below) and offered more. Note that although Elizabeth Stoddard is thankful, she goes to great lengths to show that the Stoddards are no beggars. It is interesting to imagine Allen's response to Stoddard's catalog of luxuries.

Journal, 1866

The following journal, printed here in its entirety, was kept between April and October 1866, when Stoddard was living with her son Lorimer (Lorry) and her younger brother Altol in a rented house at their native Mattapoisett, with her husband Richard and favorite brother Wilson in residence for different periods.

As the self-conscious first entry shows, Stoddard's goal was to work on her third novel, *Temple House* (1867), and the diary was to be a writer's journal. These plans did not quite work out. The novel lagged, and the journal became (in the author's view) an "ineffectual record" of desultory perceptions. In addition to being interrupted by domestic cares, sickness, and vacillating moods, Stoddard found the journal form itself somewhat awkward. The result is a less spontaneous document than her letters.

It has great interest nonetheless. It reveals a good deal about her feelings toward her husband, her dead and living sons, and her brothers; about her literary opinions; about her responsiveness to nature, particularly flowers and the sea (*vide* Cassandra Morgeson); about her ambivalence toward her native place. From a literary standpoint, the journal is significant, in one respect, as background material for the story that grew out of it, "Collected by a Valetudinarian" (p. 285), comparison with which tells one a good deal about the autobiographical bases of some of Stoddard's art. But it will also stand on its own as an artistic performance. Stoddard's characteristic eye for surface detail, as well as her impatience with *mere* surface detail, are both strongly evident here. Beyond this, the journal, partly because of its author's sense of the artificiality of the journal medium, is to a remarkable extent an aesthetic whole: a story of disappointed expectations on the part of a troubled soul conscious of not being able consistently to realize the "power" which fills her in moments of greatest strength and clarity. As in her letters, so in this journal Stoddard managed to convert even the frustrations of her life into art.

The manuscript of Stoddard's 1866 journal is in the Stedman Papers in the Rare Book and Manuscript Library of Columbia University, to whom we are grateful for permission to publish.

347

1866
Sunday Evening
22^d April

House on the beach at Mattapoisett in which I have one room that can be called handsome. I am in this room and have just now finished the arrangement of my writing table. Its fixtures are good. First the beautiful portfolio which Stoddard gave me last Christmas, second my new china patent inkstand which threatens to be a nuisance, third my new walnut box for pens and pencils, then the paper knife with autumnal leaves, and the paper weight with a bird unlike any real bird upon it, and lastly the little desk for which I sold "Eros and Anteros,"[1] to buy, or rather I sold the sketch and thought of the desk afterwards. Lorry[2] has dropped asleep in the chamber overhead, Altol[3] sits by the fire with a novel—the snapping of the coals, the coarse tick of the clock from the kitchen and the scratching pen concert together to make noise enough to disturb the silence. The fog which has rolled in from sea for three nights stays outside the bay tonight, and a weak, watery moon stands guard over my roof. Just the hour to write in one's journal—that which is neither in the heart nor brain. In rummaging my brain, I think I thanked God when I walked out this afternoon for suddenly feeling virile. By virile I mean that I came to myself for an instant, the kingly power asserted itself. It is very pretty here, my dear old pictures never looked better than they do on the yellow or buff paper, behind the glass door of the closet are some of the familiar illustrated books, my vases, boxes, boxes, ornaments are round me, but how I have labored to place them, and how I have counted the money it has cost Stoddard to bring me here!

It is all done newly[;] when the books are arranged, I shall be ready to write my book, and the method of my life will be tantalizing, unique, picturesque, unsocial, sad, incomplete.

23d.

Splendid spot to read & write in, but Lorry will not allow either[.] The chimneys have smoked me frantic in the East wind, but how happy the look of the gray water lapping on the bit of beach near the window made me feel when I stood there. Insidious Spirit of Beauty—you lurk everywhere! I rode over to Bedford[4] in search of my missing chairs & camp stools, and when I came back met my old luck of finding two letters at once from Stoddard. There is a lovely roar of wind, the night is big with it.

24th.
A gale of wind. Two letters. A little staring at the sea, and about money some perplexity. Father told me this evening that Sam's tombstone was put up in our burying place. The poor fellow is lying in his unnamed grave in Stockton, So much is done not for him, but for the eyes of respectability. [5]

25
Spying inside and outside of myself for the fashion of my novel. With me now much that comes to pass is sacred to the future of——. My boy makes me love him so, and his exactions are so annoying and so winning that isolation seems impossible.

26
At night it may be seen that I write up my journal. Lorry has been ill today.

27
Hanging pictures & a day of reckoning. My boy remembers to play today. Altol caught three trout. A letter from my Dick. A visit from Father. A visit from female relations—who did not look about them.

28th.
I have been happy under this sky and before this sea. Happiness then is atmospheric. I have read "The Toilers of the Sea."[6] It is a Greek poem in French.

1st May
Happy perhaps because a cloud was to wrap me—in sickness. I fancy I'll write this journal for Dick to read if he will.

2d

Every civilized man when he falls sick has some woman at hand to nurse him, but many civilized women, one for instance, myself, have no one to care for them. No woman comes to aid and tend me. I am shattered with my ill turn.

May 4th.

Altol rounds off the epidemic which has attacked us all. "Pottered" but did not "dawdle" once the last four boxes of books opened today, they made me gay. So much good reading in so much good solitude. I can understand in reading "Faith Unwins Love" why Wilson considers it a model novel & can well understand thereby how he can never thoroughly enter into what I write.[7] The lovely, pathetic, simple even tenor of human feeling suit[s] his temperament.

May 6th.

I watched the road for Dick this morning with a gay longing expectation and, he did not come. But he is coming in the morning. I walked out and picked the first flowers today of the year, the faint pretty "slat anemone[.]" Made little changes here and there for Dick's eye, which said eye wont observe, how could it when he hasn't been here?

May 6th.

43 to day. Dick brought me a picture, an autumn landscape and Wilson sent me a delicate pair of amethyst earrings, with a dear note. Dick likes the house and me. I have discovered to day how much more people in the country think of religion and speculate on Hereafter than we city people—Why? as Julia Mills would ask. Of all the on dits that Dick brought me, the one that proves the last infirmity of an ignoble mind, is that of Bayard Taylor's writing Godkin in reference to the review of his novel in The Nation.[8]

May 8th.

I am painfully lonesome for Dick is gone—"we parted at the gates of Ispahan"[9] that is, at the Bedford depot at 20 mins to 5 pm, over a drink of whisky from his flask and a depot mug. The room here, does not seem the same—his coming and going have changed its tone, and I have got to fight myself back into the old channel. I don't say half I feel.

May 10th.

The summer was round for an hour or two at midday, I took Lorry to the beach and we threw stones in the water. I killed one or two small vermillion spiders, the companions of a larger black spider very swift in its gait. I went out for flowers, and found the blue scentless violet, growing almost under the dead sea weed in the old ship yard. Found in sandy spots the vivid yellow "five finger" "cinque foil" I suppose. Read the cook book considerably. Finished Miss Maryatt's bright book "Woman against Woman."[10] Thinking I am thinking about my novel.

May 13.

My fourth Sunday here. All peaceful though disturbed by shadows, flying across the scene—or death ripples rolling over the calm surface. I picked this morning a delightful bunch of the white sweet scented violet in the old boggy field below the house— nothing could be more exquisite than the delicate things growing as they do in tufts of moss, wet and green. A bunch of violets often reminds me of Eugene Sue's Matilda.[11] She found by her bedside, each morning so long as her lover played the farce of love, a basket of Parma violets. The sea looked awfully full to night, the tide being very high—"It runneth here, it runneth there." crowding round all the points, pressing into every pier, and every wave hissing on its own account. I have reread "Tom Cringle's Log"[12] a capital old novel—unpretendingly and truly nautical. This book must have given birth to the whole school of adventurous nautical fiction.

May 15

I spent yesterday in Plymouth—walked over the bones of the pilgrims, and caught a cold. To day a ray of electricity in the shape of a Telegram from Wilson—telling me that his appointment is promised him. I have no leisure—made cake in the morning and filled up the new book shelves in the afternoon.

May 16th
Finished "Agnes," Mrs. Oliphant's novel.[13] It is full of nature and art too.

May 18th.
The 'May Storm'—days & nights of rain or mist. Have broken the ground of my novel, And have also by some unknown means broken my back.

It would be worth the trouble if I could do so—to make a picture, in words, of my situation. It struck me just now, as I laid down a volume of Wordsworth and looked about the room. I shall never be *happier* than I am now. What makes me so? Because I am alone with *my own power!* It is the scene outside & the scene within. The soft shaded lamps, the fine pictures, the pretty furniture, the warm window curtains, my desk, its knick knacks which suit me—*my novel begun*—the pile of books on the green sofa, Keats, Byron, Wordsworth. My darling boy asleep overhead. The faithful Altol in his chamber. And outside, *close* to me, the gray misty sea, around me the cold moaning wind.—All this for Dick.

20th
"What the moon says" tonight shining through the old cherry trees, which are shedding their white blossoms. The toil of the wind is over, and it is once more serene—a blue sea & orange sky. The Sunday is the dullish day here—I have to *pull* it through with all the do nothing devices I can think of, but I am continually saying to myself that I shall never be any happier than I am now. I am either happy without happiness, or I have happiness without being happy. Droning on my first chapter with misgivings and faith & a tormented conscience.

21st May
Bills, bills. Preaching and practicing economy all the time, and asking Dick all the time for money. Still I had a lovely walk on the

beach tonight, the moon waning with me, & a vessel down the
harbor coming to meet me. The violet purple bank of cloud was
in the west. Two hams came from New York today.

25 May

The first few hours after Dick goes away are such a wretched
blank. He came with Wilson on Tuesday. Violets still blow. Boston
looked lovely by the green common when I was there on Wednesday. My visit though was stupid. We did visit Cambridge, and the
dinner at West Can "did" us—I felt cold, poor, & shabby with it.
More might be said.

29th.

My first visitor has come & gone Abbey Torrey. The moon
dazed her with delight. I watched it too last night, the [sea?] rolled
under it delightfully. There's too much chaos here for me to be
laborious with the pen, It is too pleasant a life here—I love to loiter
over all that pertains to my domestic affairs, parlor & kitchen. I
am reading Wordsworth. It seems remarkable to me to find in him
the germs of the mannerisms of Byron & Tennyson. but I think I
do find them. Wordsworth is a teacher, as many painters and
musicians are—able exponents of art, & poor artists. I got a letter
today from Caroline Chesebro—Something in that woman moves
my deepest feelings ignorantly.[14]

June 1st

Went on Lorry's first woodland walk—he said the "fields were
handsome"—Altol found the nest of a thrush, the first I ever
saw—four chocolate covered birds in it. The cinnamon colored
square tailed parents, handsome creatures, kept in the neighborhood while we looked into the nest, crying and distressed. I saw
from the first the "Lady's Slipper" growing—the pink, veined
bulbous flower protruded from the dead leaves and twigs of the
underbrush—found also, the dwarf Solomon's Seal, and several
varieties of flowers. The grasses are just beginning to bloom. The
air is indescribably delicious. I have had a good fire all day in my
dear parlor—I feel dull, illish, and sad, homesick for Stod.

June 4th

Emerson is not original, but makes the originality of others appear in his pages[.]

June 6

Read George Sand's "Simon";[15] her ease makes my despair. "My days go on[.]" Tonight, when every soul but Lorry & myself had gone to the "gift concert" and the dusk was deepening, it seemed to me that the walls of an invisible, fearful Destiny were slowly closing round, typified by the cold gray sea. In me was a central calm. Horrible horrible existence which for the present is serene, but which realizes death.

I am never so physically conscious as when I am composing. I feel the action of the organs, especially the *wrong* action. All the tissue complains to the brain, which must work and give as little heed as possible.

June 10th.

We had a 4th-sh dinner today roasted chickens and the gold champagne. Capt. Hughes was with us. The ice-bergs dont melt, there is no summer in the air, though the grass is beautiful, and the flowers are coming out fast. Father said there was a frost on the night of the 7th which killed his pumpkin vines.

17 June

Seven days gone. & no writing, I think to night I must do all my work over, having begun with a lack of motive. Have had several distractions, one of them is the moth miller, they flit about the house, and give me visions of destroyed valuables. Have had company, Gen Van Buren & Mr Cole, that has kept me stirring. Also made a sheet & sewing is now a wretched distraction. The beetles fly about greatly o'nights, the full blooded summer is here. I like this place.

How often I think of Willy. how different my memory-love is, from the love I feel for Lorry. That fine, sacred vanished soul, had he not the best of my heart, and has he not it eternally?

19-June
    Dear Stoddard.

21 June-
    Until now I have not recognized the beauty of the fields. At present they all strike me wonderfully, being a mass of white, yellow & blue on a green ground—the daisy, "bull's eye," "pissabed" "white heed" and I know not by what other name, the beautiful blue eyed grass & butter cups compose the colors, but no description can equal them. The old fashioned rose, the Mayrake or primrose, now in bloom is dying out, the old bushes round this house are greatly eaten by "camperpillers" as Lorry calls them, I love them dearly and hate to see them so imperfect. I have been out of doors because of my disquiet. I have a heart ache because Stoddard cannot be here, because he is alone, because he has an everlasting struggle to keep *me*. It is grim and lonesome since the house was emptied day before yesterday.

25 June
    The night is a splendid time here. Dull & unhappy as I may have been through the day, I feel a change at night—when the door is bolted, and the family are abed. My papers are like life then. The shaded lamp with its strong light, is agreeable[;] the room looks beautiful too, I always have flowers in it. I perceive their scent. There are beautiful white roses on my desk now[.]

July 6th.
    Stoddard went home yesterday after spending several sick days with me. My novel lags, and so do I. The woods and flowers are fresh still. Mrs. Bleecker and Altol are playing cards this morning. Wilson is abed. The flies worry me, and the work of something for dinner.

July 9th
    One of the sunsets we dont read of[:] purple drifts all round the horizon, and then a crimson fire suffusing the west. The sea copy-

ing it. Wilson went to NY today, the *spirit* of the house has gone. A note from Eugene Benson which annoyed me a little.[16] I found in the woods this afternoon clinging to a stalk a large pea green moth, brought it home in my handkerchief gave it chloroform & then pinned it to the curtain—this evening it stirred & I gave it some more. Got a beautiful bunch of the round leaf winter green flowers—they grow on the stalk like lilies of the valley, and the perfume is the same. Yes, I am conscious that I want some thing more than the "glory in the grass[.]" the beauty I perceive is but akin to the beauty I long for.

July 24
    Gaps I see here. Everything resolves with the bare struggle with life, wherever I am. I find no more repose, no less wear in one way than another. Lately I have been aware of being on the strain. My cares tug on me and so do my sensations. This is a large moonlight evening[.] Wilson, Altol & Virginia have gone out to sail. Kate is up at the village, & Lorry is in his bed wide awake. I am desirous of seeing Stoddard in a quiet dual way. And I have had a dreadful panic, which rose from a dream, concerning him. I thought I had lost him—and I was dropped in the awful void, life would be without him.

July 26—
    In this moon I walked up the road by Gallon's,[17] just as I did one moonlight night when Willy was there asleep. How my heart ached as I stopped before the bedroom window. *He* lying behind me in his grave, those tears which only form under the lids came through my eyes, and I saw when I thought of my boys, that I love Willy the best, I shall have no more love in this world like it. To day I went to ride with Virginia, Altol & Wilson and we gathered fresh immortelles. I filled the glass from which Willy last drank with a fresh bunch.

Aug. 6th
    Stoddard is writing a review of "Land at Last" for the Albion. I am in my writing den also—with my uphill novel on hand. I have

lately read "Gilbert Rugge," "Madam F'ontenoy" and "Miss F'orrester," also "Miss Majoribanks."[18]

From this to August 21st
 Something worse than a Blank

Sept—
 Not that there has been another blank—but living puts down a journal so. I am afraid to write what *implicates* people. Virginia left today. Last night Wilson telegraphed me from Washington that he had got his appointment[.]

Sept 4th. Dog Days
 The highest problem of every art is, by means of appearances, to produce the illusion of a loftier reality. That is however a false effort which, in giving reality to the appearance, goes so far as to leave in it nothing but the common every day actual. Goethe.[19]

Sept 5th.
 The clock is striking four—it is a grey calm afternoon inclined to mist. I have been sitting at the open window, and the cool, soft air brings me lethargy. The crows cawing in the woods, the crickets in the grass, a voice occasionally sounding in the distance add to the pleasantness of the moment. As I noticed the change in the beach grass, through which the tide washes, that it has already put on its sere and yellow look, I thought how I had failed to write out the power that has passed and repassed in my life since I came here. The points which have most claimed my active interest are unmentioned. A journal suits meditation, not action. Yesterday, I was thinking all day, how fully and strongly I was living. how much better I felt with the better prospects in Wilson's future—that there were some things worth the having, &c—yet no journalizing thought came to me.

Sept 27th

Now I am alone with Lorry. No one lives with me besides. But for my frets, I should like it, as it is I am ready to go to the city and be unhappy as I know I shall be. The clumps of brake along the old gray stone walls, are beautiful, so delicate in form & rich in color—red-brown, cold-brown—yellow-brown. The grass still fresh and green, covered with the bright autumn leaves looks cheery, delightful. So far, it is lovely like summer, but a different loveliness. The sun is so yellow and still now, his light drawn farther, on the shadows have more power.

Oct. 7.
Sunday.

I'll leave this ineffectual record behind me, and look at it next year, or will another do it for me, Stoddard perhaps. I am going away Tuesday, and I am melancholy. Lovely old house—lovely new Nature!

NOTES

1. A story for which Stoddard received ten dollars published in the *New York Leader,* 22 February 1862.

2. Elizabeth Stoddard's third (and only surviving) child, Lorimer (b. 1863). Later in this journal Elizabeth compares her love for him with her love for her first son, Willy (1855–61). A second child, born deformed, died in early infancy (1859).

3. Elizabeth Stoddard's younger brother (1835–69), the Alton of "Collected by a Valetudinarian."

4. New Bedford, Massachusetts, near Mattapoisett.

5. The allusion is probably to Elizabeth Stoddard's younger brother Samuel (1829–65).

6. Novel by Victor Hugo (1866), set in the Guernsey Islands.

7. *Faith Unwin's Ordeal* (1865), popular novel by the British writer Georgiana Marion Craik (May) (1831–95), mentioned also in "Collected by a Valetudinarian" (p. 297). Wilson was Elizabeth Stoddard's favorite brother (1831–69), despite her awareness that he didn't care for her fiction. *Faith Unwin's Ordeal* is a domestic novel in which the "low-bred" Australian-born heroine struggles to retain the affections of her genteel English husband despite her mother-in-law's disapproval and his jealous reaction to her attentions to his cousins, toward whom she is strongly attracted but whom she dutifully dismisses in the end. The melodramatic plot, and the protagonist's ultimate decision to define herself in terms of her husband's expectations would have appealed to Wilson but displeased Elizabeth.

8. Edwin Lawrence Godkin (1831–1902), editor of *The Nation,* had reviewed slightingly *The Story of Kennett* (1866), by Bayard Taylor (1825–78), of whom the Stoddards were personally fond yet resentful on account of his success and critical on account of what they perceived to be his opportunism. The review appeared in *The Nation* 2 (1866): 501. Julia Mills is the go-between between Dora Spenlow and David Copperfield in Charles Dickens' novel (1849–50). "On dits"-pieces of gossip"(Fr.).

9. See page 308, n. 15.

10. An 1865 novel by British writer Florence Marryat (Lean) (1838–99).

11. The title character of Eugène Sue's novel *Mathilde* (1841).

12. See p. 308, n. 16.

13. An 1866 novel by the British writer Margaret Oliphant (1828–97), a number of whose works Elizabeth Stoddard read.

14. Caroline Chesebrough (1825–73), prolific and successful writer of woman's fiction, toward whose work Stoddard felt strongly ambivalent, as indicated in her 3 August 1856 *Alta* column (p. 325).

15. An 1836 novel by the French feminist writer (1804–76), whom Stoddard greatly admired, as seen in her several *Alta* references.

16. Benson (1839–1908) was an American painter, literary journalist, and friend of the Stoddards. He once praised Elizabeth as a potential *frondeur,* or slinger of truths at the entrenched literary establishment.

17. James Gallon (d. 1870) was Richard Stoddard's stepfather, a sailor and stevedore whom Richard's mother married in the early 1830s. The Gallons moved to Mattapoisett in the early 1860s.

18. *Land at Last* (1866) was a novel by British author Edmund H. Yates (1831–94) that Richard Stoddard was preparing to review for the New York weekly *Albion.* As her own reading, Elizabeth lists four recent popular British novels: *Gilbert Rugge* (1866) by Henry Jackson (1831–79); *Madame Fontenoy* (1864) by Margaret Roberts (1833–1919); *Miss Forrester* (1865) by Annie Edwards (d. 1896); and *Miss Marjoribanks* (1866) by Margaret Oliphant. All had been reprinted in America within the year.

19. See p. 308, n. 19.

Emendations

Listed below are all editorial changes made in Stoddard's texts. With one exception (see p. 335.30) we have limited ourselves to correction of what appear to be obvious printer's errors and to corrections of mechanical errors by Stoddard that seemed necessary in order to avoid unintelligibility or an excessive number of distracting "*sic*" 's. The emended version of the text is indicated following page and line number; the uncorrected version is given in parentheses.

The Morgesons

3.3 prevailed (yrevailed)
20.33 lost the (lot thse)
24.19 established (establisher)
25.31 fit of shyness (fit or shyness)
39.32 "you would like?" (you would like?)
52.22 "that my (that my)
59.4 generosity, (generosity.)
67.17 me. (me.")
86.35 defy (defy.)
94.26 "Good-by, Alice" ("Good-by," Alice.)
97.40 I ("I)
104.3 that (hat)
104.34 midnight. (midnight)
111.39 Business (Business,)
114.11 supervision?" (supervision?')
117.3 Morgeson's mills?" (Morgeson'smills?")
129.6 next (nex)
130.19 Rosville." (Rosville?")
139.33 son, (son.)
142.30 habits? (habits.)
146.17 look out." (look out.)
162.27 courtway. (courtway)
163.20 must (mast)
177.15 "And ('And)
184.1 me (we)
184.20 Ben. (Ben)
189.6 I spoke ("I spoke)
189.14 plum, (plum.)
189.27 nucleus (nucelus)
191.10 name." (name.)
208.20 I'll stay ("I'll stay)
210.6 because (bacause)
221.11 "Are you (Are you)
226.9 and (amd)
229.35 matter? (matter?")
229.35 I guessed (I guess)
230.25 now (how)
248.40 I made ("I made)
249.45 answer" (answer?")
251.38 While I ("While, I)
251.39 Sphinx," she (Sphinx" ;she)

"Collected by a Valetudinarian"

286.6 said, (said)
299.14 strangers. (strangers')
305.38 way, (way.)

Early Journalism: The *Daily Alta California* Column

313.10 furors. (furors On)
314.15 are (a e)
319.8 resistless (resistle s)
319.13 disposi[tion] (disposi-)
320.28 teeth (teeh)
325.22 you (y-)

Manuscripts

335.26 Heights[;] that (Heights that)
335.30 "creed of life and letters" ('creed . . . letters'; here and throughout this entire section quotation marks setting off a phrase are used in place of the inverted commas which EBS always uses.)
336.9 to his (tohis)
336.21 to you (toyou)
337.7 can't (c'ant)
337.10 to me (tome)
337.25 terrific[.] I (terrific I)
338.24 to my (tomy)
340.31 Stoddard[;] if (Stoddard if)
341.11 poverty, "Every (poverty. "Every)
341.26 Thaxter's (Thaxter)
341.30 criticism[.] Look (criticism Look)
342.19 soon, but (soon but)
342.20 to you (toyou)
343.2 to me (tome)
343.18 to be (tobe)
343.22 charity, unrelenting (charity unrelenting); unselfishness, (unselfishness)
343.31 worth[y] (worth)
343.32 to him (tohim)
344.14 to have (tohave)
344.18 you[r] (you)
344.22 should [have] felt (should

felt)
344.26 fortunate [as] they (fortunate they)
344.31 management [that is] so (management so)
345.2 goes[.] We (goes We)
345.17 Valenciennes[.] Are (Valenciennes Are)
345.20 one [of] us (one us)
345.26 to me (tome)
348.26 boxes, ornaments (boxes ornaments)
348.30 newly[;] when (newly, when)
348.35 either[.] (either)
349.29 I'll (Ill)
350.3 women, one (women one)
350.14 suit[s] (suit)
350.19 anemone[.]" (anemone")
350.21 hasn't (ha'snt)
351.20 exquisite (exquiste)
352.2 new book (newbook)
353.3 New York (NewYork)
354.3 pages[.] (pages)
354.6 on[.] (on)
354.9 round, typified (round typified)
354.27 company, Gen (company Gen)
355.8 & butter (&butter)
355.18 & unhappy (&unhappy)
355.21 agreeable[;] the room (agreeable the room)
355.23 now[.] (now)
355.31 of[:] purple (of purple)
356.9 grass[.]" (grass")
356.16 evening[.] Wilson (evening Wilson); & Virginia (&Virginia)
356.29 & Wilson (&Wilson)
357.1 Rugge," (Rugge,); F'orrester," (F'orrester,)
357.9 appointment[.] (appointment)
357.30 to me (tome)
358.13 I'll (Ill)